continued . . .

My Seduction

"A well-crafted, engaging read."　　　*—Publishers Weekly*

"A fabulous love story . . . wicked, tender, playful, and sumptuous. Too wonderful to resist."　　　—Lisa Kleypas

My Pleasure

"This is why people read romance . . . an exceptionally good read."　　　—All About Romance

Bridal Favors

"A scrumptious literary treat . . . wonderfully engaging characters, a superbly crafted plot, and prose rich in wit and humor."　　　*—Booklist*

"Never predictable, always refreshing, wonderfully touching, deeply emotional, Ms. Brockway's books never fail to satisfy. Connie Brockway is simply one of the best."　　　—All About Romance

The Bridal Season

"Characters, setting, and plot are all handled with perfect aplomb by Brockway, who displays a true gift for humor. Witty and wonderful."　　　*—Booklist*

"If it's smart, sexy, and impossible to put down, it's a book by Connie Brockway."　　　—Christina Dodd

The McClairen's Isle Series

The Ravishing One

"Skullduggery, bitter English-Scottish hatreds, and harrowing cat-and-mouse pursuits fill the ebb and flow of this eighteenth-century romance."　　　*—Publishers Weekly*

HOT DISH

Connie Brockway

A SIGNET BOOK

SIGNET
Published by New American Library, a division of
Penguin Group (USA) Inc., 375 Hudson Street,
New York, New York 10014, USA
Penguin Group (Canada), 90 Eglinton Avenue East, Suite 700, Toronto,
Ontario M4P 2Y3, Canada (a division of Pearson Penguin Canada Inc.)
Penguin Books Ltd., 80 Strand, London WC2R 0RL, England
Penguin Ireland, 25 St. Stephen's Green, Dublin 2,
Ireland (a division of Penguin Books Ltd.)
Penguin Group (Australia), 250 Camberwell Road, Camberwell, Victoria 3124,
Australia (a division of Pearson Australia Group Pty. Ltd.)
Penguin Books India Pvt. Ltd., 11 Community Centre, Panchsheel Park,
New Delhi - 110 017, India
Penguin Group (NZ), cnr Airborne and Rosedale Roads, Albany,
Auckland 1310, New Zealand (a division of Pearson New Zealand Ltd.)
Penguin Books (South Africa) (Pty.) Ltd., 24 Sturdee Avenue,
Rosebank, Johannesburg 2196, South Africa

Penguin Books Ltd., Registered Offices:
80 Strand, London WC2R 0RL, England

First published by Signet, an imprint of New American Library,
a division of Penguin Group (USA) Inc.

First Printing, November 2006
10 9 8 7 6 5 4 3 2 1

This one is for you, Doodah.

With all my love, Mom.

ACKNOWLEDGMENTS

The decision to strike out in a new direction is always fraught with excitement and trepidation. So many people helped me make this book happen in so many different ways. Doris Egan, Bob Howard, Jay Halvorson, Kent-Erik Halvorson, and Kyle Mairose lent me their expertise in making sure the devil stayed out of my details, and I most gratefully thank them. The following people were always there to offer encouragement, direction, and most importantly, their unswerving confidence in me and my craft. Thank you, Damaris Rowland, who as my agent for more than a decade has always made me feel like a star and encouraged me to follow one. Thank you to my editor, Claire Zion, who provided a desperately needed lantern when the way got murky and I could barely feel the road beneath my feet let alone see it. Thank you to the Squawkers (Liz Bevarly, Christina Dodd, Eloisa James, Lisa Kleypas, and Terri Medeiros); a finer, more talented group of friends would be unimaginably hard to find—a more generous one, impossible! And finally, thank you, David, best friend, unflinching critic (a few flinches now and again would be appreciated), most trusted adviser, and wittiest companion. You put every hero, real or imagined, in the shade, and I love you.

Prologue

Present day
Blue Lake Casino, Blue Lake Reservation, Minnesota
Fifteen miles northeast of Fawn Creek, Minnesota

I hate this town.

Jenn Lind dragged her gaze away from the crowd held back from the poker table by a velvet rope and peered through her wraparound sunglasses down at the cards lying on the green baize table. She spat out a strand from the black polyester wig that kept finding its way into her mouth.

"Your bid, Ms. Uri," the dealer said. When she'd given the dealer her pseudonym it had seemed appropriate.

"Yeah. I know." She notched back the corners of the two cards, squinting at them again in the futile hope she'd been mistaken. She hadn't. She sighed. *Crap. Now what am I going to do?*

Jenn lowered her head further, using the black plastic curtain of hair—it had begun life that morning as a witch's wig in Pamida's Dollar Bargain Bin—as a shield.

"Miss Uri?" the dealer prompted again.

"I'm thinking." He could prompt until he went hoarse. There was no time limit on making up your mind. And she had some serious contemplation to do.

How the hell had she come to be sitting in a poker tournament across the table from Ken Holmberg, a middle-aged, small-town potentate sporting a MOSQUITO: THE MINNESOTA STATE BIRD cap, with a hundred thousand dollar cash prize for first place and the fate of a town, and one she wasn't all that fond of to begin with, riding on the outcome? She wasn't a gambler.

Oh, yeah, Before the Fall, before gambling had led to the collapse of the family dynasty, she'd played poker. Her whole family had. It had been the Hallesby family's recreation of choice and damn good at it they'd been. And Jenn, as early as age eight, had been something of a prodigy. But after the family's leisure pursuit had led to the demise of the family's leisure lifestyle, she'd seen poker for what it was: a fool's game. One's dad losing the family fortune on the turn of a card could bring about such epiphanies and Jenn was no fool.

So what was she doing here?

She scoured her memory for some past misstep that would have turned the Powers That Be against her and found nothing. All she had done was accept an invitation to be the Grand Marshal of Fawn Creek's sesquicentennial. Nothing even the most vengeful Greek god would have gotten pissy about. But then, this was Minnesota and its Nordic gods were a whole lot more particular about what constituted a yank of the old celestial wang.

How had everything gone so wrong? She'd come to town with no other plan than to lead their Snow Pack Parade perched atop an ATV beside that damn butter head. . . .

That damn butter head.

Oh, yeah.

That's where it had all gone wrong.

Chapter One

". . . and *that* is how dairy products changed my life," finished seventeen-year-old Miss Fawn Creek, Jennifer Hallesby. Behind her, Duddie Olson's prizewinning 4-H milk cow, Portia, also representing Fawn Creek, mooed approvingly.

"Thank you, Miss Hallesby," the emcee said. "Miss Delano?"

Jenn bobbed a little curtsy and was rewarded when the Minnesota Dairy Farmers' Federation's only female judge winked and mouthed the words, *"Very nice."*

Jenn step-glided her way back to her plastic lawn chair among the other Buttercup finalists, no easy feat while navigating the minefield of mementos left by the nine blue-ribbon cows now stationed behind their respective princesses.

Please let my bangs stay up, she offered heavenward as she took her seat and smoothed out her pink satin skirt. Though she'd sprayed the magnificent prow of bangs three times and the Hippodrome was relatively cool, it *was* August and it *was* humid. Maybe she should have gelled it, too.

She looked up into the stands as Miss Delano launched into her prepared speech, the last portion of the competition. Only five of the cavernous Hippodrome's thirty-six tiers were filled, mostly with finalists' family and friends, but also with die-hard pageant enthusiasts and a few hundred marginally interested fairgoers who'd wandered in seeking relief from the noontime heat. Here and there clusters of people in like-colored T-shirts frantically waved banners emblazoned with the names of proud hometowns.

Fawn Creek was not represented.

What a crappy thing. *Someone* should be here. She was representing their town, wasn't she? You'd think they would at least show up to hear Fawn Creek's name called out if she won. She couldn't figure them out.

But then, she'd been confused ever since her parents had appeared in her walk-in closet almost two years ago as she'd sorted through clothes for the Poor People—little suspecting that within a few minutes she would be revealed as one of them.

"There's no pleasant way of saying this, Jenn," her father had announced. "We've been living on credit for years and the business has filed for bankruptcy."

"Huh?"

"Compounding the situation, while we were in Vegas, your mother and I got to thinking 'in for a penny, in for a pound,' and my luck was running really hot—honey, I had a straight flush!—so we went for it. All of it."

What was he talking about?

"It was a crap shoot. Unfortunately, well, the bottom line is that we lost everything."

Crap, she recalled thinking, she supposed this meant she and Tess would be flying coach rather than first-class to Cozumel next winter vacation.

"Everything except your grandfather's hunting camp in Minnesota," her father had gone on. "So we'll be leaving Raleigh and moving there at the end of the month."

She'd just looked at him then, because his words had ceased to make any sense. His mouth moved. Sounds came out. He looked serious. Then why couldn't she figure out what he meant? It had sounded like her father thought they should move to Minnesota. Which was ridiculous. Minnesota was cold. And there was snow. And it was cold.

"That'll never work," she'd finally said. "I have a white convertible."

How could they have forgotten? They'd given her a white BMW convertible for her Sweet Sixteenth birthday. It had only been a couple weeks ago. "You can't drive a white convertible in Minnesota."

"Had a white convertible, Jenny," her mother said. "I'm afraid we're all going to have to make some sacrifices for a while. But it's just temporary, dear. Just for the summer."

That had been twenty months ago. A summer had since come and gone and the second was disappearing as she sat half listening to Miss Delano attempt to convince the judges that Dairy Was Her Life.

Movement halfway up the tiers of seats caught Jenn's eye. She smiled. So she wasn't completely abandoned, after all.

An unlikely duo sat together, the younger one waving a red bandanna: Jenn's fellow student and fellow outsider, Heidi Olmsted, more comfortable with animals than people and more manly than any guy in town, and little, gray-haired Hilda Soderberg, not an outsider at all, but undisputed Ruler of the Lutheran church's basement kitchen, from whom Jenn had covertly acquired every bit of knowledge she owned about Scandinavian cooking. Not that Jenn had started from base zero. She'd always loved cooking. . . .

"Ladies and gentlemen!" Miss Delano had taken her seat and the emcee was tapping on the microphone. Jenn straightened. "Just a few minutes now and we'll announce our winner."

Please. Please, please, please.

With the scholarship that came with the Buttercup crown, Jenna could afford the out-of-state tuition to Chapel Hill and rejoin her friends from Raleigh there. All of her friends except for Tess, because Tess had died six months ago, just after she'd returned from the winter break vacation Jenn was supposed to have gone on, too.

Jenn's decision not to go hadn't only been because her parents couldn't really afford to send her—Tess's parents had made it clear that once Jenn landed they'd pick up the tab for everything else—but because she'd discovered a wiser way to use the money earmarked for the plane fare: she'd used it to enter regional pageants and to buy her first sequin and satin gown. It had seemed like the most practical decision at the time but Tess had been furious. Jenn had called Tess long distance to explain that ten days on the beach was a small price to pay for four years at Chapel Hill but Tess hadn't listened. She'd refused to take the call. And Jenn, angry her friend could be so shortsighted when it was her future they were talking about, had reacted by not calling again.

Six weeks later Tess was dead, killed in a traffic accident. And Jenn had never gotten a chance to explain.

Jenn shoved the thought away, focusing on the future because it hurt too much to do anything else. If she won this pageant, that future would mean not only that she could return eventually to her remaining friends next year but it could also make her last one at Fawn Creek High School bearable. As Buttercup Queen, she was bound to get invited to some of the things she heard the other kids talking about in Monday morning study hall. A party or two, a shopping trip to "the cities"? Hell, at this point, she'd be happy to be invited to join the debate team.

Okay, she might have been partly responsible for her lack of a social life. She hadn't made any huge effort to "blend." She hadn't really seen the need; she was only passing through. And then, after Tess had died, she'd just been too angry to care what the hell anyone thought of her. But lately, the last few months or so . . . well . . . she missed having friends.

She missed late-night phone calls that lasted hours; swapping jeans and shoes until no one knew who the original owners were anymore; silly, ardent feuds about stupid things; and impromptu puppy piles in front of the television set. She missed Tess—

And she missed *boys*! She hadn't had a date in over a year. She missed their posturing, their crude jokes, their bravado, their flirting. She missed openmouthed kissing and steamy car windows and yearning looks behind the current girlfriend's back.

She missed movies, and malls, and beach parties and being someone and a part of some group. She missed not having to be careful about what she said, or how she sounded, not having to be vigilant about not appearing too urban or too Southern.

It was like some evil magician had snuck into her house one night and disappeared her whole life and she had woken up here, in Minnesota, among strangers. But she'd found a way out of here . . . a way back . . . a *way*. . . .

"Okay, then!" the emcee announced. "We're ready to

announce the first annual Queen Buttercup. But first, I think
we should assure all nine of our Buttercup Princesses that in
our eyes they are all queens, eh? So let's hear it for the Buttercup Princesses!"

The crowd applauded, and banners waved.

"And you all know, don't you, that throughout the week
all the Buttercup Princesses, not just the Queen, are being
carved in butter over at the Emporium Building?"

Again the crowd applauded.

Okay, she knew it was lame, but she was sort of excited
about the Butter Head thing. How many seventeen-year-old
girls got their heads carved out of a hundred-pound block of
butter to be displayed in front of thousands of people? And
if she *won* the Buttercup Crown—*please, oh please*—then
they would put that head in a specially designed, all-glass,
refrigerated unit at the entrance. *Her* smiling butter face
would be the first thing the public saw upon entering the
fairgrounds, with a voice-over—*her* voice—saying, "The
Minnesota Dairy Federation welcomes you to the Minnesota
State Fair!" Which was totally cool.

"So go have a look-see, okay?" the emcee said. "Great.
Now the moment you've been waiting for!"

Beneath her nosegay of artificial buttercups, Jenn crossed
her fingers.

"The second runner-up is . . . Miss Thief River Falls,
Tiffany Gilderchrist!"

Tiffany bolted out of her chair and jump-skipped toward
the lady judge, who received her with a kiss on the cheek.

"First runner-up is . . . Miss Young America, Karen
Wexler!"

Oh, God, Jenn thought, her heart pounding, she was
going to win! She'd caught a glimpse of the deportment tally
sheet and she'd won that—no surprise, five years of cotillion

had to be good for something, didn't it?—and the lady judge had winked at her and that had to mean something, right?

"And here she is, ladies and gentlemen . . ."

The fat pink cabbage rose decorating Jenn's décolletage was quivering violently. She was losing sensation in her lips. *Smile. Please, God! Smile.*

"Our 1984 Queen Buttercup is Miss Fa—huh?" One of the judges was tugging at the emcee's jacket, hissing something up at him.

There was no other princess from a town that began with an "f." *Fawn* Creek. He'd been about to say *Fawn Creek*!

She tucked her feet under her chair, preparing to rise. It was all going to be worth it. Her future was going to get right back on track, starting right now. *This one's for you, Tess.*

"Ah . . . hold on a sec." The emcee held his hand over the mike.

A man in plaid short sleeves had appeared out of nowhere and was leaning over the judges' shoulders, talking excitedly. The lady judge scribbled something on a sheet of paper and handed it to the emcee, who looked at it, blinked, and uncovered the mike.

"Ladies and gentlemen, it is my pleasure to announce the Minnesota Dairy Farmer Federation's first ever Buttercup Queen . . .

". . . Miss Trenton Mills, *Kimberly Dawn Ringwald*!"

Jenn froze halfway to her feet as Kimberly Dawn erupted from her chair, squealing with delight. The lady judge stomped over, stuck the rhinestone crown on Kimberly Dawn's head, and shoved an enormous bouquet of silk buttercups into her arms.

The crowd went wild. The princesses exploded out of their seats, bouncing and crying as they swarmed Kimberly

Dawn, who was whooping into the mike the emcee had thrust in her face. Somehow, Jenn made it to her feet and managed a few face-saving hops.

The emcee had been about to say, "Fawn Creek," she knew he had!

"Would you like to say a few—"

Kimberly Dawn grabbed the microphone from the emcee, and sobbed, "Thank you! This is so cool! Thank you! I don't believe this!"

Neither did Jenn.

Chapter Two

Dismissed, the princesses fell into line and trudged across the arena toward the tunnel leading from the Hippodrome. At the door, the line broke as a sea of jubilant Trenton Mills-ians engulfed Kimberly Dawn and swept her away while smaller, and somewhat less jubilant, groups carried off their own princesses, leaving Jenn alone inside the passage.

What had just happened?

She'd been a second away from being Miss Buttercup and then, a tug on a polyester sleeve, a whisper to some guy with a farmer's tan, and poof! Gone. And with it all the things she'd worked for: validation for all the hours spent in the Lutheran church's basement kitchen learning the art—and yes, it was an art!—of Scandinavian cooking; the money for Chapel Hill; maybe even some sort of social life this year.

"You never did stand a snowball's chance," a familiar voice broke through her reverie.

Two female figures, separated in age by nearly half a century, chugged purposefully toward her. Together, they composed the sum total of Jenn's Fawn Creek social life.

The smaller, Mrs. Soderberg, sported an orange Budweiser visor holding aloft a puff of puce-colored curls above a phlegmatic pink countenance. Jenn had spent her happiest—no, "happiest" indicated that there was a "happy" to feel "ier" about. There hadn't—she'd spent her most content moments in Good Shepherd's basement kitchen, watching Mrs. Soderberg mix the batter for *julbrod*, or trying to divine the arcane calculations by which the old Swedish lady determined exactly how many juniper berries to float atop her corned venison, and being silently watched in turn as she attempted to duplicate those recipes.

There was something comforting in Mrs. Soderberg's silence, her silent condemnation and silent approval being more or less interchangeable. It was reliable and uniform inexpressiveness in a world gone mad.

Her companion, Heidi Olmsted, wore a ubiquitous uniform of overalls and a brightly colored T-shirt beneath, her brown hair hauled back from her square face into a short ponytail. Jenn and Heidi's friendship was as unlikely as it was inevitable. Heidi, wry, self-effacing, and agonizingly private, had the dubious distinction of being Fawn Creek High's other perennial outsider. But where Jenn's status was the result of circumstances, Heidi's was the consequence of nature.

"But then I wouldn't have given you a snowball's chance of being a finalist to begin with, so you should be satisfied with getting that far, I think," old Mrs. Soderberg finished upon making it to Jenn's side.

"What do you mean?" Jenn asked.

"Just observin', is all. Best get goin', then," Mrs. Soderberg said. "Gotta find Neddie before he does somet'in' stupid."

Neddie was Mrs. Soderberg's grandson, a souvenir of her daughter Missy's summer visit to Florida years earlier. Missy

had long since flown the coop, leaving her mother to raise
Neddie alone. Maybe that was why Mrs. Soderberg had
been a little more accepting of outsiders: she had practice
accepting the unacceptable—at least by Fawn Creek standards. Although she wasn't exactly a friend of Jenn's, she
had taken a detached interest in her cooking abilities.

"No. Please!" Jenn grabbed the old woman's wrist and
won a "look" from Mrs. Soderberg.

Minnesotans didn't touch one another in public unless
they were getting married and even then it was looked upon
as being a little gratuitous, a handshake being considered adequate to express most heightened emotions.

Jenn let go, and with the alacrity of a cat loosed from a
Have-a-Heart cage, Mrs. Soderberg scooted off.

"Why was she so sure I wouldn't win?" Jenn asked
Heidi, who was looking longingly after Mrs. Soderberg's
disappearing figure. Like most of the state's natives, Heidi
resisted "unpleasantness," and from the way her broad face
was contorting, Jenn suspected Heidi anticipated this conversation was going to more than qualify.

"Well, not that it's any of my business," Heidi ventured,
looking pained, "but I saw Carol Ekkelstahl talking to that
guy in the plaid shirt while they were announcing the run-
ners up."

Jenn waited. Heidi waited.

"So?" Jenna prompted.

"So? Wasn't it her kid Karin that you beat out for Miss
Fawn Creek?"

"Huh? You don't think Mrs. Ekkelstahl . . ." Too many
days spent with no one for company except the pack of dogs
the Olmsteds kept had taken their toll on poor Heidi. "Listen, even if Mrs. Ekkelstahl did want me out of the pageant,

how much influence would she have with the Federation judges?"

Heidi shrugged. "I'm just saying, is all. And there's no 'even' about her wanting you out."

"Why would Mrs. Ekkelstahl have it in for me?" Jenn asked as confused as she was startled.

"Because, Jenn," Heidi said in the careful tones of one addressing the mentally challenged, "you came to town and took what she thought was little Karin's. That Miss Fawn Creek title."

"That's the dumbest thing I ever heard."

Heidi let out the same deep sigh she had when Jenn asked her if the ice stayed on the lakes all summer. "You gotta remember that Fawn Creek is a small town, Jenn."

No shit! Jenn wanted to say.

"People in small towns are sure outsiders, 'specially people from the city, all think that they're better than them. And it doesn't help that deep down, most small-town people think so, too."

"I don't get it."

Heidi's dour face filled with exasperation. "Look, Jenn. Most of the kids around here don't have rich parents and they don't have much to look forward to unless you play hockey and can get a scholarship to the university. Especially girls.

"One of the things girls"—she caught Jenn's questioning glance—"most girls, look forward to is thinking that someday they might maybe be Miss Fawn Creek. And their moms probably dream about it even more. Then you show up, an outsider from the city, and not even a Minnesota city, with your *Seventeen* magazine wardrobe and the sort of polish no one else around here has and before you can say, 'Jack Pine Savage,' you get yourself named Miss Fawn Creek."

"That doesn't make any sense," Jenn said. "If everyone thought a girl from Fawn Creek should have won, why'd the judges choose me? I wasn't holding a gun to anyone's head."

"The judges were guys," Heidi said flatly. "Guys see things different. Ken Holmberg? I'm betting he took one look at you and figured you stood a whole lot better chance of being crowned Queen Buttercup than Karin Ekkelstahl, and if you got the title, the Federation might hold its regional conference in Fawn Creek."

Right. *She* was Fawn Creek's ticket to the Dairy Big Time. "If you thought all this, why didn't you *say* something?"

Heidi shrugged. "Wasn't my business."

"So why are you telling me now?"

"You asked. And you're just not too bright when it comes to people, Jenn, and I didn't think you'd figure it out by yourself. At least, you're not too smart about small-town people—or maybe it's small-town society. You don't get it . . ." She trailed off thoughtfully. When she wasn't playing with dogs, Heidi considered herself something of a budding sociologist.

"So I told you." Her face lit with one of those abrupt and transforming smiles common to native Minnesotans. It wasn't pleasantness that engendered that smile, Jenn had learned. It was a reflex. It was one of the reasons, Jenn was sure, the whole "Minnesota nice" illusion had evolved—"Smile and keep 'em guessing."

"So then, I guess I'll be off to watch the K-9 unit," Heidi said. "You want to come, too?"

"No. I can't," Jenn said.

"Okay, then. We'll be seeing you later, I'm sure," Heidi said cheerfully and took off, leaving Jenna alone in the nearly empty building.

Jenn walked slowly, her uncomfortable thoughts swinging between undeserved guilt and righteous anger. Even if what Heidi had said was true, it wasn't like Jenn had known she was committing some social crime. Besides, even the kindest critic would have to admit that none of the other contenders for Miss Fawn Creek would have made it as far as Jenn had.

Outside, the sudden sun dazzled her eyes and the air smothered her like a sweat-soaked sauna towel. Noise bombarded her. She stopped in front of a human river of twenty thousand jostling, munching, slurping, sweating, stinking visitors to *Minnesota's Great Get-Together.* People hollered and vendors shouted while kids yelped with delight and wailed in frustration, the racket fed by rock music blasting from the radio station booths scattered along avenues as over it all roared the amplified sound of screams siphoned from the midway rides.

"Jenn! Sweetheart!" Like Glinda in *The Wizard of Oz,* Jenn's mother seemed to float not so much out from the crowd, as above it. Even here, Nina Hallesby managed to look wealthy and feminine, from the tortoiseshell sunglasses perched atop her auburn hair to the discreet gold knots winking in her ears. "I was so proud of you."

"You were?" Jenn regarded Nina doubtfully. Other than expressing first disbelief ("You want to enter a Butter Pageant?") and then fake enthusiasm ("I'm sure you'll make a wonderful Butterball Queen!" To which she'd had to respond, "That's Buttercup, Mom. Butter*CUP*!"), her mother had never said much about Jenn's Run for the Buttercups. "But I lost."

"I know." Nina patted Jenn's shoulder. "I saw."

Jenn was surprised. She hadn't realized her mom had even been there. It didn't really seem like Nina's thing. In

Raleigh, Nina had been more likely to be holding Monte Carlo Casino Charity Nights (gambling being her favorite and most successful fund-raising endeavor) to finance the new lacrosse field than sitting in the auditorium watching the seventh-grade play. Jenn's parents had once been high rollers, taking over the penthouse at the Bellagio, front row seats at Caesar's Palace. Now they lived in a broken-down old hunting lodge and tried to convince themselves they were all about living the Simple, Healthy Life.

"I'm sure the decision to crown that Mill person was strictly political, but while I'm sorry you lost, it's not the end of the world."

No, Jenn thought, that had ended when they'd yanked her out of school, stealing her away from one last year with her best friend, and hijacking her into the middle of this . . . this Jack London wet dream.

"Don't look so glum," her mother said. "How many times have I told you that our current situation is only temporary? Your father is just taking some time off before jumping back into things—"

"He's taken over a year off," Jenn exclaimed, as startled by her uncharacteristic outburst as Nina looked. But now that the flow of words had started, she couldn't stop them. "And while he's taking time off, my life is falling apart! I won't be able to stand it up there another year with the loons. I can't! I have to get out of there before I go nuts."

Nina regarded Jenn with a wounded expression. "I thought you liked the Lodge."

"I did!" she said. "I liked the Little Pathfinders Wilderness Camp you sent me to when I was nine, too. But I don't want to live there, either."

"Now, Jenn, I know it seems right now that living in Fawn Creek is the worst thing that could ever happen to you," her mother said, "but someday you will look back and realize that 'you cannot reach the dawn save by the path of the night.' "

Jenn stared. "Where do you *get* this stuff?"

"It was on a Kahlil Gibran poster I had in college," her mom answered serenely.

This was pointless. "Where's Dad?"

"He's at something called Machinery Hill, looking at tractors."

Was she kidding?

"I told him we'd meet him at the Poultry Emporium as soon as you were done with this pageant thing." Her mother's expression brightened. "They have these adorable chickens there that look like little Russian army officers. You know, with those tall furry hats?"

Again, Jenn could only stare.

"It says in the program they'll announce the winner at noon. I wonder if they'll have a little crown for it." She giggled and then, catching Jenn's expression, *tched.* "Oh, Jenn, I was kidding. What happened to your sense of humor? Come on. It'll be fun. Let's go, shall we?"

"I'm not done with 'the pageant thing,' " Jenn said. "I have to have my head carved out of butter and then go appear on some local television show."

"A butter head?" Nina giggled again until she realized Jenn wasn't joking. She abruptly sobered. "Oh. Well. Then we'll see you afterward at the car, shall we? Bye!"

She gave a quick wave and stepped off the curb, her face lighting up. It dawned on Jenn that her mom *liked* the state fair. And her dad was at *Machinery Hill*? Looking at *tractors*? Holy crap. Her parents really had gone off the deep end.

Well, that was sad and everything if it was true, but the

bottom line was that her parents had had their shot. Jenn wanted her shot, too. And she'd been that close to getting it. . . .

Across the street, she spotted Ken Holmberg, one of Fawn Creek's councilmen, pumping the hand of some old Swede (she knew he was a Swede because as a Swede, and thus not being the sort to leave anything to conjecture, he was wearing a T-shirt that said: DON'T KISS ME. I'M SWEDISH).

Though he couldn't have been much more than thirty-five, Ken looked older, like a gnome out of a kid's Scandinavian fairy tale book: short, stocky, the middle of his flat face adorned by an improbably upturned nose, his pink scalp peeking through a neat little oiled comb-over of brown hair. Not only had Ken been one of the judges for the Miss Fawn Creek pageant, but as one of the biggest employers of the town—he owned a hockey stick manufacturing plant—he'd been instrumental in convincing the Fawn Creek council to sponsor her bid for Buttercupdom. Not because he liked her—he didn't—but because . . . Well, maybe Heidi wasn't so off base where Ken was concerned. But she was way off base with her Carol Ekkelstahl conspiracy theory.

Sure, Minnesotans were a tight-knit group, but they also prided themselves on their virtue. Especially simple, uncomplicated virtues like honesty and integrity, things you could paint black and white. Now, if you were talking about exceeding the daily fish possession limits or illegally tiling a field, that was a different matter. But some things just weren't done. Small-town pageant fixing being primary among them.

Jenn picked up her pink satin skirt and waded through the crowds across the street to tap Ken on the shoulder. He turned around, a politician's beam stamped on his face.

Upon seeing her, his smile vanished. "Jenn, I can't tell you how disappointed I am."

"Me, too, Mr. Holmberg," Jenn agreed earnestly. "That's why I was wondering . . . Do you think . . . That is . . ." *Spit it out!* "I think it might be a good idea to ask for a recount of the judges' score cards just to make sure, you know . . . to see who won. I . . . I mean—"

"There was no mistake, Jenn. You lost," Ken said tersely. "And if I was you, I'd be thankful you weren't publicly disqualified."

"I don't understand."

"Oh, fer crying out loud, Jenn"—he clicked his tongue— *"you don't live on a dairy farm."*

"Dairy farm?"

"It says right there in the application you filled out, right there in black and white, that the competition was open to women seventeen to twenty-one whose families lived on, operated, or were otherwise substantially associated with working dairy farms."

"But . . . my parents rent out their pasture to a dairy farmer," she said, utterly confused. "That counts, doesn't it?"

"No," he answered slowly, looking at her closely, as though he couldn't believe she could be so dim-witted. "It don't."

"But I thought . . . I didn't know!" she said. "I'm not from a farm. I'm from a city! There were cows in that pasture all the time. I swear it. Why doesn't that qualify as 'substantially associated?' I don't get it!"

"No, you sure don't," he said. "Maybe you shoulda asked someone."

Who? Who in that entire town could she go to for advice? Even Heidi's input had come too late to do anything but hurt. She stared at Ken, dumbfounded and near to tears. She shouldn't have applied. She shouldn't have run for the title. She should have known. She should have found out.

She couldn't be more of an outsider had she been born on another planet.

And now he was telling her she'd lost because she didn't wade through cow manure on her way to the school bus? And someone had actually seen it as their Christian duty to rat her out?

"Luckily"—Ken leaned forward to emphasize his point—"luckily, the judges got wind of it before the media found out. We might just've ducked ourselves one helluva scandal."

Her future was on the line and he was worried about a scandal? "Revealed *where*? In *The Cow Quarterly*?"

Ken snapped back, his pink scalp turning scarlet. "You don't take any of this seriously. You don't take us seriously. Maybe it's best you didn't win. We wouldn't want the Minnesota Dairy Farmers' Federation's very first competition tainted by fraud and . . . and mockery!"

Her lips started to tremble and she bit them.

"Fer chrissakes, Jenn," Ken said, irritated. Minnesotans were always irritated at displays of emotion. The whole "nice" trick was an illusion to keep outsiders off balance. "Don't cry. You're not the only one disappointed. I thought you were a shoo-in. You look like a young Inger Stevens and I swear my great-grandpa Olson would climb out of his grave for a taste of your lefse."

Her lefse. Perfect griddled circles of the thinnest, tenderest, buff-colored potato goodness known to man. "I must have used forty pounds of potatoes getting that recipe right," she whispered. While the other candidates had relied on beauty queen standards like baton twirling and aria singing for the talent portion of the competition, Jenn had laid out an authentic, table-groaning smorgasbord. The plump lady judge had actually teared up at the sight.

"No one is saying you can't cook," Ken said impatiently. "But the bottom line is this, Jenn: you lied. You aren't who you said you were. *What* you said you were."

No. She wasn't. She wasn't Inger Stevens and she wasn't Grandma Olson. She wasn't even Scandinavian. She'd learned most of her cooking skills from Tina, their Jamaican housekeeper. The rest she'd purloined from a bunch of old Swedes cooking for Lutheran weddings, anniversaries and funerals. She hadn't been born in Fawn Creek, and her mom hadn't spent the last ten years promising her that if she did well in school and stayed off the chocolate she might someday grow up to be Miss Fawn Creek. No, her mom had told her different stories with different happy endings and none of them had come true either!

What difference did that make? She was still the best-qualified Buttercup Queen in the whole *damn* state and she'd given up so much, too much, to get here only to be betrayed by a bunch of holier-than-thou small-town snobs. The unfairness of it boiled up and erupted.

"Here!" She snatched the rhinestone tiara off her head and thrust it in Ken's chest. "You can have your Miss Fawn Creek crown. I don't want it!"

He didn't take it. "Well, you got it. A deal is a deal. You signed on the dotted line saying you'd represent Fawn Creek for the next year."

They couldn't hold her to that. She was leaving! Okay, maybe she wasn't going to Chapel Hill, but she was going *somewhere* and it wasn't back to Fawn Creek. "What about the 'scandal?'"

"There's no rules about Miss Fawn Creek living on a farm. Only the Buttercup Queen."

"Well . . . well . . . what if I just won't do it?" she demanded, desperation creeping into her voice.

"In that case, I'm real afraid we'll have to sue your folks for everything the town spent sponsoring you. Your folks got money to fight a law suit, Jenn?" he asked. "That pretty pink dress you're wearing cost four hundred dollars.

"Look," he went on in the manner of a man who had decided against all provocation to be reasonable, "we already have your schedule for the year. There's Vern's Farm Implements the first Saturday of every other month. And we got you signed up for two SuperSmart Food Store grand openings, and you'll be pulling the bingo balls at the regional dairyman's convention in Karfart, Wisconsin. That's not that much. Just weekend stuff. I don't expect there's much for a city kid like you to do up there most weekends anyway."

Except she'd have to be there during all those weekends. It was enough to keep her in Minnesota. She knew when she was beaten. She had no idea if Ken could sue her parents or not. It didn't matter; she couldn't take the chance.

She gazed dully at him, the fifty-two weeks ahead rolling out like an endless row of corn into a perpetually distant horizon. No scholarship. No Chapel Hill. No mild February breezes, no bougainvillea, no clambakes. No friends. Instead, a year of servitude to Fawn Creek and the Minnesota Dairy Farmers, being bused from tiny town to tinier town extolling the virtues of butter and udders.

She'd wasted the last six months for nothing. She'd dieted. She'd learned everything there was about dairy production. She'd haunted the Lutheran church basement like a freak. She'd given up trips back to Raleigh to go to regional contests. She'd backed out of her last opportunity to spend a vacation with Tess—

"There. I knew you'd see sense," Ken said. He started to turn.

"Wait!"

He stopped, looking around at her with renewed annoyance.

"I have to know. *Who* told the judges I didn't live on a farm?"

He vacillated a second before reaching into his jacket's inner pocket and withdrawing a folded piece of paper. He handed it to her and walked away. She read:

> Dear Judges,
>   As president of the Fawn Creek High, I, Karin Ekkelstahl, along with the other elected officials, regret to inform you that one of the contestants under consideration—

Heidi had been right, after all. Jenn had been narced out by the Fawn Creek Student Council but it might as well have been the whole damn high school.

Man, she hated that town.

But not nearly as much, she thought, as they hated her.

Chapter Three

Steve Jaax, whose sculptures would one day be represented in eight separate Fortune 500 companies' art collections, was on the lam and he liked it. Had he not been on the lam he would not now be leaning against the peeling exterior of one of the Minnesota State Fair's most popular venues, the Beer Stube, watching carnies load people into the sky ride's caged buckets to be sent flying along a cable high above the fairgrounds.

Steve liked that, too, since he was sort of flying himself. On the sticky surface of the table in front of him sat his fifth—sixth?—Leinenkugel's, which he was nursing with profound care since he didn't have the cash for a sixth— seventh? His cup was half empty. Or, he thought philosophically, half full. Either way, there was barely enough left in his plastic cup to tide him over until his date with destiny— destiny being a hundred-pound block of frozen butter.

So, deciding atypically to exercise a little moderation, Steve amused himself by walking a small, shiny key across the backs of his knuckles, impressing himself with his dexterity. The key he liked, too, even though it filled him with a pleasant sort of melancholy. A man had died for that key. . . . Well, not strictly speaking but a man he had known (though only for a few months) and liked (as much as one can like someone you've only spent ten hours with) had died somewhere (where was unimportant) sometime after sending him that key.

As he fiddled with the key, he looked around at his fellow man with a woozy affection completely uncomplicated by any feelings of commonality. He not only liked them—he *loved* them, all of them: the clutch of gum-smacking teenage girls shrink-wrapped into their jeans; the tattooed giant feeding curly fries to a petulant-looking toddler with the wariness of a marine biologist offering chum to a shark; the preppy-looking guy in a yellow Lacoste shirt who had just lifted a wallet from the back pocket of a fat woman screeching at her equally fat spouse to get her some cheese curds; and especially the young chick in a pink ball gown with an immense bang curling out and over her forehead like a cresting tsunami on a Japanese woodcut.

She was trying to convince the guy dispensing beer that she was twenty-one and had left her ID at home in her . . . what? Glass slipper?

Steve snorted and the key fell. He lunged after it. By the time he fished it out of the dirt at his feet, the toddler had begun screaming and the girl was forgotten.

He righted himself. He wasn't sure yet exactly what he was going to do with the key but he definitely had to do something with it and fast because without a doubt his days on the lam were numbered. The key, and the note accompanying it, had caught up with him at his rented PO box a couple days ago after following him around the country for the last six weeks. The contents of the note had been brief:

Done the deed. Your statue is safe and tucked away in—sit down, dude, 'cause you're gonna fall over laughing—a mausoleum crypt. All you got to do to get her back is stick this key in the lock. Check this out. I bought the vault under your wife's name. Not Fabulousa, the one on her passport. She don't know anything about it! Thought you'd appreciate that.

Course, if you ever lose the key you're gonna have to prove to the cemetery guys that you're her in order to get a new one, so don't lose the key.

Don't bother trying to get hold of me for a while cause I'm going to be out of touch. Which you might think of doing, too, dickhead. If this letter can find you, no one else is going to have any problemo. Including the guys she's hired to find you and that statue.

Stay cool.

A second letter postdated a few days after the package, had shown up today. It had been even briefer.

Don't know who you are but we found your name and this address in Tim Greer's wallet and thought you might want to know that Tim's dead. His appendix burst. His funeral's over.

The note hadn't been signed. Poor ole Timmy. Best thief he'd ever befriended. And that bit using Fabulousa's real name for the crypt? Sweet.

He hoped Tim had had a chance to spend the money he'd paid him to rob Fabulousa's brownstone. He hoped he'd been coming from a great meal, great sex, a great drunk, or all three when the Grim Reaper had caught up with him.

He decided he loved Dead Tim, and even though he recognized he was getting a little maudlin, he didn't care. Because thanks to Dead Tim, whom he loved, there was at least one piece of him Fabulousa was not going to get her little, taloned fists around, no matter what the judges overseeing their divorce said. You can't award property no longer in your possession, can you?

Every single art critic in New York agreed that *Muse in the House* was Steve Jaax's seminal work. Some had even declared it "the vanguard of neorealistic sculpture in America." No divorce court judge—who was *not* coincidentally also banging his ex—was going to give his vanguard to that soulless bitch just because she'd posed for it. He'd rather cut off his arm and give it to her. . . . Okay, maybe his left arm but it was still an arm.

Which led back to the question of what to do with the key because while Steve didn't think the NYPD would waste their time chasing after a sculptor who had jumped bail, if Fabulousa had hired private investigators to find him, find him they would. Fabulousa would hire only the best. And after the settlement she'd gotten out of him, she could damn well afford to.

"Hey, mister, buy us a beer and you can keep the extra."

Steve looked up into the faces of three nervous, acne-riddled pubescent males whose names he would never know, those being Eric Erickson, Jimmy Turvold, and Ned Soderberg.

"Piss off," he said kindly.

"Come on, man," said the stocky redhead. "Don't you want a free beer?"

Well, yes. As a matter of fact, he did. "How old are you boys?" Steve asked.

"Fo—seventeen."

Maybe thirteen. "Right. Why don't you guys go home and raid your old man's liquor cabinet?"

"Jaax! Jaax, you better not be drunk!"

Steve looked up into the scowling face of a neckless, balding man broiling in a navy blue polyester sports jacket two sizes too small. The kids slunk away. "Hi, Carl."

"Are you drunk?"

"Nope."

"You are. Damn it. I told the committee this was a mistake," Carl muttered. "You show up with an art magazine no one's ever heard of with an article in it about a sculptor named Steve Jaax and say you're him and Ruth Dalquist thinks a famous artist wants to carve our butter. We shoulda done like the Dairy Association does and gotten a volunteer to carve this stuff, but no, we gotta do better than the Dairy Association. And does Ruth ever think to ask *why* a New York sculptor is willing to carve butter at the Minnesota State Fair for a couple hundred bucks a day? Nope. But I do. And I don't like any of the answers I come up with."

"You came up with answers?" Steve asked, interested. A man with answers in a world full of questions. He might love Carl, too. "Cool. Let's hear 'em."

Carl held up his left fist. His stubby index finger shot up. "One, you've hit the bottle and are on the downward slide."

"Plausible," Steve agreed, nodding encouragingly.

"Two"—Carl's middle finger shot up, joining the first one—"you aren't Steve Jaax at all. You just look like Steve Jaax—that picture in that article is pretty fuzzy—and figure since this is just a state fair you can produce any old piece of crap and we won't know the difference. Well, let me tell you, mister, we will."

"You take your butter seriously," Steve said seriously.

"Damn straight," Carl said. "Now, frankly, I don't give a damn who you are as long as you deliver. But if those butter heads don't look like those girls, you're not getting a red penny and I will sue your ass—after I beat the crap out of you."

At this, Steve felt a long dormant flicker of pride raise its teensy head and take umbrage at having his artistic integrity questioned. He started to draw himself up but then remembered he was being paid to carve *butter*. Relieved, since every fight he'd ever been in had ended with him saying, "Ow," or worse, he relaxed back in his chair.

"Any other reasons why you think a guy like me would take a crap job like this?" he asked curiously.

"Yeah." Carl's hand dropped. "You're trying to put as much distance between you and whatever's behind you as possible. In which case, I still don't care as long as what you're running from doesn't catch up with you here."

"Impressive."

Carl settled his fists on well-padded hips. "You want to tell me which one it is?"

Steve saw no reason not to tell him. At least, most of it. "I'm broke. My soon-to-be-ex-wife is trying to bleed me dry in the divorce. I wanted to get out of New York City. I like state fairs. The gig is short. I'm qualified. And, gee, it sounded like fun."

At this last, unmitigated bit of bullcrap, even the stolid Carl had to smile.

"Okay," he snorted. "Get off your ass and get some coffee in you. The first girl is gonna be in the freezer in twenty minutes waiting for you to do her."

A girl waiting for him to do her in the freezer, Steve thought, pushing to his feet. The world was full of mystery and wonder.

Chapter Four

12:35 p.m.
Fifteen feet away

Walter "Dunk" Dunkovich, who would someday soon share a prison cell with Steve Jaax, gave a quick once-over to the guy in the baggy chinos who the kids had been trolling for beer. He could have told those poor punks they'd been wasting their time. The guy was busted. But he had other plans for them.

He adjusted the collar of his marigold yellow Lacoste shirt—look the role, fill the dole—and hailed the trio, "Hey, guys! Come here."

They looked around and saw a regular guy waiting for his college pals to show or maybe his girlfriend to get back from the john. They shrugged and shambled over.

"What's up?" Ned asked suspiciously.

"Saw you with that dude over there. No joy, eh?" He didn't wait for an answer. "Wasn't so long ago I was where you guys are now."

"Oh, yeah?" the skinny kid asked. "You lived in a pissy little town where everyone thought they were better than you?"

"Sure." Dunk smirked back. "Got out, though. Someday

you will, too." *Probably not.* "Tell you what. Hand over the twenty and I'll get your beer for you."

He held out his hand, and without a second's hesitation, the skinny kid slapped the twenty in it, saying, "Thanks, buddy."

"Look," Dunk said. "I don't want to get into any trouble, so why don't you guys disappear? Meet me over on the other side of the sky ride in five, 'kay?"

"Sure. Cool."

The kids headed around the cement engine house and Dunk pocketed the money, sauntering away in the opposite direction to disappear into the crowd, thinking that not only was a sucker born every minute but sometimes they came in litters.

Chapter Five

"I want to see the Butter Head! You said I could see the Butter Head! You *promised*!"

A bang shook the freezer as a fat little cheek smashed into the Plexiglas window like a bug hurtling into the windshield of a VW. The cheek stuck, glued there by equal parts sweat, syrup, and sunscreen. Above it, a kid's single visible eye rotated in its socket like a gecko's, coming to rest on the hundred-pound, head-shaped block of butter inside. A grubby hand crept up the Plexiglas, leaving a sticky smear next to other sticky smears relating the countless journeys of dozens of gooey noses and sticky fingers.

"Butter head," the kid crooned.

Jenn, perched disconsolately atop the model's stool inside, eyed the unappetizing specimen and shrank even lower within the embrace of her Eddie Bauer parka.

The eye found her. "Hey! *That* ain't the queen! You ain't the queen! You're *no one*!"

Even this snot-faced little brat had her pegged. The tears she'd held in check for the last two hours seeped into her eyes.

"Where's the queen? I don't wanta see *her*! I don't want to see you! *You're* no queen!"

A hand appeared out of nowhere and snatched the creature away. Too late. Augmented by three beers and nose-diving blood sugar levels (the result of two bags of Tom Thumb doughnuts), what was left of Jenn's defenses shattered. She buried her face in the puffy sleeves of her parka and sobbed.

"Hey!" said the sculptor, some young guy named Steve.

Jenn lifted her wet face. Steve had electric blue eyes, like a young Paul Newman, dark wild hair, and a really nice body, and he wasn't so much older than her that his interest—hitherto uncommunicated—would be icky, and she didn't care at all. She lowered her head back down.

"Hey, princess. What's the deal? Are you sick?" He sounded rattled.

She lifted her head again and found that he'd come around the side of the butter block and was standing over her, the grapefruit spoon he'd been using to carve in his hand. He was really good-looking in an Irish-barroom sort of way and she still didn't care.

She didn't care that her nose was running and her eyes were puffy and her lips were wobbly. She didn't care that her mascara was running and the bang she'd spent ten minutes lacquering into a big, glamorous pouf was flat. She didn't care that the cute artist thought she was a case or that the people outside the freezer looked really uncomfortable.

Because, like that gecko-eyed kid had said, she was no one.

She wasn't the queen; she wasn't even the "real" Miss Fawn Creek. She was a pretender. An also-ran who had elbowed her way past her far worthier competition for nothing. All she'd managed to win was the town's resentment and her schoolmates' enmity. Well, they'd shown her all right.

A fresh wave of sobs shook her.

"You want to quit? Come back later? I can do another girl first."

Come back? Once she left the state fair today, she wasn't ever coming back. "No. I'll be fine in a minute."

Outside the freezer, some guy shouted, "Whatda ya say to her, asshole?"

"Nothing!" Steve shouted back. Tentatively, he patted her on the shoulder. Like you would a dog of suspect temperament.

"Come on, kid, snap out of it before that guy out there decides to beat the crap out of me, will ya?"

"I'm . . . I'm trying!" But not too hard. It felt too good to cry. She wasn't crying anymore just because of the gecko-eyed kid, or the Buttercup crown, or the student council, or even the last fifteen months. She was crying because she suddenly realized how alone she was. And that it wasn't going to stop. And neither were her tears. Maybe ever.

"Crap." Steve had squatted down in front of her and was trying to peer up at her face between her hands. "What's there to cry about? You're a princess, aren't you? A pretty princess."

She'd been wrong. *That* stopped her tears.

She spread her fingers apart and stared down at his face. He looked a little like a hound dog, but not nearly as sincere. My God, she realized in horror, he was patronizing her.

"And you have a real pretty pink dress"—he nodded— "and a crown and a—"

"Stop that."

He rocked back on his heels. "What? What'd I do?"

"You're being a condescending jerk—that's what. You're

acting like . . . like I'm crying because I wasn't crowned the stupid Buttercup Queen."

He stood up, clearly a little hurt that his stab at playing sympathetic adult to her pathetic teenager had been rebuffed. "Why are you crying then?"

"Because I wasn't crowned the stupid Buttercup Queen!" She burst into a fresh wave of tears.

He threw up his hands in exasperation.

"But it's not that simple!"

He crossed his arms over his chest. Her lower lip trembled.

He sighed, yanked an unused pallet over toward her, and sat down at her feet.

"Okay, kid," he said, "why don't you just settle down and tell me about it?"

"You don't really want to hear," she said. But she wanted to tell him.

He'd lost that phony, wide-eyed sincerity. He didn't look especially sympathetic but he did look interested. "Yeah, I do. Let's face it. I can't carve you if your face is buried in your sleeve, so out with it. What's with the waterworks?"

Outside the refrigerated unit, the spectators had grown bored and drifted away. Jaax didn't seem to notice or, if he did, to care. He really was listening to her.

"It's not like it's a big tragedy or anything." *Except to me.* "It's just . . . well, I sort of thought maybe . . . no—" She broke off angrily. "I was supposed to be the Buttercup Queen. The emcee guy had actually said 'Miss Fa' and there's no other princess from any place that begins with an 'f,' but at the last second, they stopped him because someone showed up with a petition the whole freaking Fawn Creek student council signed that said I'd lied on my application and so I couldn't be Queen Buttercup. They disqualified me right on the spot."

Steve looked impressed. "Wow. That's cold. But, man, if you were going to lie on your application, you had to know there were risks."

"No!" she protested. "I don't *take* risks. I don't gamble. *Ever.* I thought I was telling the truth. I didn't understand. It wasn't my fault."

She knew how she sounded and sure enough the interest had faded from Steve's bright blue eyes.

"Okay," he said. "They're assholes and you were screwed. At least you can sleep the sleep of the pure and virtuous while they will be haunted by . . . Hold the phone. Are you blushing? You are blushing. Why? You can sleep the sleep of the pure and virtuous, can't you?"

She mumbled.

He stood up. "Nah-uh. You did something. What? Come on, kid, you can tell me. I am the champion of Been There, Done That, Wish I Hadn't."

"It's stupid."

"It usually is," he said. "Unburden yourself. You'll feel better."

She looked into his somber, earnest, homely-handsome face and . . . she did.

She told him about her parents losing everything on a gamble, being uprooted and moving from urban splendor to rural insignificance, her loneliness, her parents' weird complaisance and how she was sure it was simply a brave front, her subsequent determination not to add to their financial burden, the brainstorm that had visited her when she'd heard about this Buttercup scholarship, how she'd worked her way up through the regional pageant qualifiers to the final round and the final chapter today, what Mrs. Soderberg had said about why the rest of the students hated her (okay, Mrs. Soderberg hadn't used the word "hate" but it had been implied), and her betrayal by Fawn Creek High.

She told him everything.

Except about Tess. Because that was private. Too private to tell strangers.

He sat hunkered on the pallet at her feet the whole time, his gaze never leaving her face. No one had ever listened to her like that before.

When she ran out of steam and trailed off, he stood up and slapped at his pant legs.

"I better get to work," he said.

She regarded him blankly. "That's it? I spill my guts and all you have to say is that you have to 'get to work?' "

He shrugged. "You've stopped crying and I see some really promising directions I could go with your face and—"

"You haven't been listening at all, have you?" she demanded, shocked and hurt. "You've just been studying my face."

"No!" he denied. "Well, yes. I've been studying your face, too. I can't help it. It's just reflex, like a teenage boy with a *Penthouse* gets—" He broke off as he realized what he'd been about to say. "It's involuntary."

She gave him an unfriendly, unblinking stare.

"Look," he said, angling back around to the front of the butter head, "I'm just gonna go around here and listen while I work. I'm totally on autopilot. Now you were saying how you really felt you deserved this thing." He smiled. "Why?"

It was an obvious sop but she didn't care. His had been the most sympathetic ear she'd had in fifteen months. And he could have told her to either shut up or get lost but he hadn't.

"Yeah. Well," she said, "the thing is. I would have made

a kick-ass Butter Queen. I knew my shit, Steve. I mean, I *knew* my shit."

She was surprised to hear herself using language like this, especially in front of a stranger. "All that Suzie Home-maker stuff they want the Butter Queen to be able to do? I can do it! *All* of it. I've won five ribbons here in the junior baking and canning division. Two firsts, a second, and two thirds.

"Now that's great if the Pillsbury Doughboy ever wants to get cozy," she continued, "and since I am doomed—and I do not think that I overstate my case here, Steve. I mean *doomed*—to live in Fawn Creek for another three hundred and sixty-five days, he's probably as close as I'll get to a guy without back hair. You know what I mean?"

She leaned forward. "Lumberjacks. Or Sons of Lumber-jacks."

She expelled a heavy sigh, her gaze falling to the freezer floor and the little curls of yellow butter scattered over it.

"So what are you going to do next?"

Jenn looked up. He really had been listening, after all.

"I don't have a choice. I have Miss Fawn Creek obliga-tions, so I can't even apply for an early admission to some school. I'm stuck through my senior year."

"Gee, that sounds like fun." He ducked down and disap-peared behind the sculpture.

"No." It wouldn't be fun. It would be hell being trapped with no way out in the same school with the kids who'd de-railed her would-be freedom train. "I'll die."

"Probably not," his disembodied voice said. "If you re-ally want to get out, you'll find a way. Look at me. I was married to a vampire and yet managed to escape. I was just this far"—a hand rose above the butter head, forefinger and thumb illustrating a half inch space—"from becoming one of the undead myself."

"A vampire? Like in she sucked your blood?" she asked only half sarcastically. He did come from New York City. . . .

"There are more important things than blood, kiddo. There's your confidence. When you sculpt for a living, you got three things that you gotta have: the ability to see things other people can't see, the talent to translate that vision into something other people can see, and the absolute faith that you have both.

"She sucked all three things out of me. And then, because that wasn't enough, she went after the only good thing that ever came out of our relationship." He tilted sideways and met her eyes for a second before disappearing behind the butter again. "My statue. The statue she posed for."

"That's rough," she conceded. "Is that why you're here carving butter heads?"

"Sorta." He stood up, rummaged in the fishing tackle box he used as a tool kit, and came up with a flashlight. He flicked it on and focused the beam on the butter head. "The thing I'm trying to get to is this: things happen for a reason. It's the nature of things. You've just got to figure them out."

"Easy enough to say."

"Nothing easy about it, Jenn," he said, still working away, but now at an accelerated pace. "Look. If Fabulousa hadn't been so extraordinarily evil, I'd probably have still been married to her and still spending my nights puking my guts out behind the bars in the Village."

Fabulousa must be his wife.

"And if Fabulousa hadn't slept with that judge and tried to screw me not only out of every penny of money I've ever earned but, on top of that, frame me for the robbery of my own sculpture to get me thrown into jail, I wouldn't have ended up in Minnesota and I wouldn't be sculpting this butter and I wouldn't . . ." He trailed off, his mouth dropping open a little as he switched off the flashlight.

He frowned, blinked, and turned the flashlight back on. "Holy shit," he whispered.

"What? What?" she demanded, and started to slide off the stool to see what had him riveted.

"No!" His arm shot up and he pointed at her. "Stay right where you are!"

She froze. Steve stared at her as though seeing her for the first time. His gaze fell on the butter head, jerked back to her, fell, rose, back, forth, quicker, quicker—

"What is it?" she whispered.

"Freeze!"

"Wha ith it?" she demanded through stiff lips.

"Do *not* move a muscle. Hold it right there. One minute. One . . . more . . . minute . . ." He was in the midst of a whittling frenzy, slashing off gobs of butter and flinging them toward the white plastic bucket at his feet.

"Look at this." He shoved the flashlight against the butter head's ear and turned it on.

It looked like a yellow bug light shaped like an ear.

"Yeah?"

" 'Yeah?' " he echoed. "You bet your ass, 'yeah.' "

He began working fervently, muttering all the while.

"So that's your big advice?" Jenna asked, reluctant to let the former conversation go. " 'Things happen for a reason. Figure it out?' " Her mom and Kahlil Gibran could have done better.

"No," he said and abruptly stopped working. He came to the side of the butter head and set his hands on his hips.

"Here's my suggestion. You got robbed of a crown? Find a different crown to win. Then flaunt it."

He'd gone off the deep end. "I'm done with all this stuff. No more pageants for me," Jenn said.

"Who said anything about pageants?" he said, returning to the front of the butter head. "This is about *kingdoms*, not tiaras. No one ever got handed a crown worth having. The real question is always what are you willing to do to get what you want?"

"Huh?"

"Sacrifices, baby. Everything you go after demands a sacrifice. Either from you or someone else."

"Bull."

"You sacrificed the other town beauties' hopes to win this Buttercup crown, didn't you?"

"I didn't know I was doing that!" she protested.

"Maybe not. But you should ask yourself this: would you do it again knowing now what you claim you didn't know then? Would you have jettisoned a few milkmaids' dreams for your ambition?"

Would she? She didn't know. It seemed like a random question. She *hadn't* known. And she didn't like what-if games. They were too dangerous, like opening Pandora's box. *What if* her parents had gone to Palm Springs instead of Las Vegas? *What if* her grandfather had owned a lodge in the Catskills instead of Minnesota? *What if* she'd gone with Tess on winter break . . . ?

A sudden commotion outside drew Jenn's attention to the far right side of the crowd gathered around the freezer. A huge guy in a leather biker's vest had started pushing his way through the crowd.

"It needs to be etched," Steve was muttering, "and something with lights. Maybe . . ."

Jenn wasn't listening anymore. She was too busy watching the biker. He wasn't pushing now. He was shoving, bowling through the crowds of bystanders, his expression fierce.

"Geez," she said uncomfortably. "Where the hell does he think he's going?"

Halfway through the crowd now, the biker raised his huge paw and pointed straight at the freezer window. *"You are mine, bitch!"*

Jenn's jaw dropped; her eyes popped wide. She'd heard about weirdoes like this, men fixated on beauty queens or movie stars. The biker thrust an old lady and her corn dog out of his way, his steel-toed boots punching the ground, the chains on his hip bouncing.

"Oh . . . my . . . God." Jenn jumped off the stool. "Steve!"

She looked around for a savior only to see Steve look up, spy the biker, and instead of doing something like barricading them in the freezer, go back to attacking the butter head with renewed fervor. He gouged a hole in the butter head with his grapefruit spoon again.

She wasn't about to wait around and see why. She headed for the freezer door, but before she reached it, the door slammed inward and the biker burst into the tiny booth. His mouth spread in a wide, evil grin. Outside the cubicle, someone shouted and someone else screamed.

"Your ass is mine!"

"Holy shit," Jenn whispered, her mind filled with images of becoming this guy's Butter Head Bride right in front of all these people.

She scrambled for the corner, snagging a sculpting knife on her way, and wheeled around.

The biker guy ignored her.

All his attention was fixed on Steve, who was still fiddling with the butter head—filling in the hole?

Poor Steve, he'd lost it. He looked way too nonchalant for someone whose ass purportedly belonged to a two-hundred-fifty-pound guy in black leather. Her own heart was galloping and the hand holding the sculpting knife out in front of her was shaking uncontrollably. Outside the freezer, people were yelling and pointing.

"Bounty hunter?" Steve asked, finally turning around.

"Yeah."

Bounty hunter?

The biker reached behind his back and pulled out a set of manacles. "The bounty hunter who got here ahead of the cops and you'll witness that, won't ya, Toots?"

He glanced at Jenn, who was trying to disappear down into the neck opening of her parka as the biker grabbed Steve's forearm and snapped the manacles closed on his wrist. *"Won't ya, Toots?"*

"Ah, yeah. Yes, sir . . ."

"Good. And here's Minnesota's finest now. Right on cue," the biker said as a confused-looking cop ducked through the door, his hand on the butt of his gun.

"Officer, I've made a citizen's arrest of this man, Steve Jaax, for jumping bail and fleeing the great state of—" The biker frowned.

"New York," Steve provided helpfully.

"Whatever," said the bounty hunter and pushed him into the waiting arms of Minnesota's finest.

"What the hell is going on here?" Ken Holmberg appeared at the door, took one look at Jenn, and squeezed into the booth with the rest of them. A lump of gratitude swelled in Jenn's throat. Maybe Ken wasn't so bad, after all.

"What do you think you're doing, Jenn?" he scolded. "You were due over at the KMSP building fifteen minutes ago."

"But the police . . ."

"Officer, do you need this young lady to stay here?" Ken demanded. "She's supposed to be on the set of *Good Neighbors* right now."

"Really?" The officer looked impressed. "You better go, then. If I need her later, I guess I know where to find you, huh, Miss—"

"This is Miss Fawn Creek, Jennifer Hallesby," Ken supplied. He grabbed her upper arms and started pushing her toward the door. In doing so, his foot caught the dais, setting the butter sculpture teetering ominously.

"Watch it, man!" Steve yelped. "That's art!"

"Oh gosh." Ken half turned. "Sorry. You bet . . ." He trailed off.

Behind Jenn, everyone fell silent. Still hanging in Ken's grip, Jenn craned her neck around to see what everyone was looking at and so, for the first time, got a full-on view of the sculpture.

At first glance, the sculpted face was pretty enough. The smile was winning, the features symmetrical and pleasant. But when you really looked at it, you saw something else. Something vulnerable, something defeated. Even the prow of bangs springing from the forehead looked forlorn.

And then it hit her: *This was it. This was all she had to show for all her months of effort.* She'd traded the few weeks she could have been with Tess for a butter head.

"It's . . . radiant," the bounty hunter whispered.

"Exquisite," one of the cops opined.

Radiant? Exquisite? The word choices coming from two

traditionally tough-type guys caused Jenn to look at the butter head again. She couldn't see it, though. All she saw was a waste of time. The face of a loser.

Well, not anymore. Not ever again.

Chapter Six

The room seemed surprisingly crowded for a press conference introducing an unknown lifestyle maven to the jaded New York media until you took into account who had done the inviting: megaconservative, ubercontroversial multibillionaire Dwight D. Davies Junior. Dwight was an intolerant man, the list of things of which he disapproved including, but not limited to, smoking, drinking, gambling, swearing, illicit-drug use, and any kind of sex—unless it was between a married (and definitely heterosexual) couple. He openly admitted that making up for the excesses of his youth had led to his zeal for reforming decadent American society, leading some wags to speculate that at one time old Dwight must have been one helluva guy to party with.

As a businessman, Dwight was notorious for his pharisaical policies. He'd been known to come in, after taking over multinational corporations, and decimate entire upper managements simply on the basis of "inspired intuition," a practice that made both political parties leery of accepting his donations. All of which made him daily fodder for every newspaper cartoonist and editorial writer in the country.

Dwight didn't care. He had a whole lotta work to do before he died. Mostly reforming things. And (some said not coincidentally) making a whole lotta money doing it. Lately, he'd turned his attention to reforming America's television-viewing habits.

A year ago he'd proclaimed his mandate to eradicate America's love affair with sex, drugs, and violence. He'd bought himself a successful cable network and renamed it American Media Services to accentuate his view that he provided the public a service, not just an entertainment. Then he hired a slew of like-minded men—or at least men who said they were like-minded and who could not be proven to be otherwise through an intense background check—and rebuilt it.

It should have been a joke, but old Dwight wasn't stupid (quite the reverse). He was just a dogmatist. When he did something, he did it right. Whether through sophistry or luck—and those who knew him best weren't saying— Dwight had tapped into a huge reservoir of baby boomers wanting to rekindle their *Leave It to Beaver* days, Gen Xers looking for a little moral substance to pad their financial portfolios, and young Americans worried about being blown up.

Last month, Dwight had begun unveiling the lineup for the spring launch of his new, "values-oriented" programming, and today, AMS was introducing Jenn Lind, the star of Dwight's pet project, a biweekly lifestyle magazine entitled *Comforts of Home* (debuting concurrently with a monthly magazine and iPod cast of the same name). Dwight had personally supervised the vetting process that had brought Jenn Lind from the Midwest, where she'd been enjoying an impressively robust popularity based on a week-day morning show, regular contributions to women's magazines, and guest appearances on several of the Food Network's most popular programs. With a sardonic nod to her home state of Minnesota, the media had already dubbed her "Martha 'Nice.'"

So yes, the level of interest rose when AMS's president, Ron Patella, trim, diminutive, and dapper, appeared from a side door and approached the podium.

"Good afternoon and thank you for coming," he said. "You all have your bios and other material? Good. Then you already know you're in for a treat."

He gestured with an open palm toward the door. "It is with great pleasure that I introduce Jenn Lind, the star of *Comforts of Home*."

He clapped as a tall blond woman in a powder blue sweater dress walked without hesitation or haste to his side and shook his hand. Ron had to look up. Pens started scribbling.

Jenna Lind was a good-looking woman, a quarter past young but holding well, her soft cashmere dress flowing over a curvier figure than other television personalities allowed themselves. Her honey-colored hair was pulled back in an old-fashioned French twist, à la Tippi Hedren in *The Birds,* which accentuated her high cheekbones and clear gray-blue eyes.

With the modest dress, the pastel colors and the upswept hair, there was definitely a late fifties vibe going on. But then, just when the reporters were ready to tack "vintage" on Jenna Lind, she stepped out from behind the podium and revealed a pair of tawny Christian Louboutin stilettos on the end of a rather spectacular set of gams. She shifted and the little satin tassels set at the back of the ankle strap shimmied.

"Hello," she said, detaching the wireless microphone from its holder and approaching the reporters as Ron melted back among the AMS executives. She had just a hint of an accent, something round and soft. Like oatmeal with maple syrup. Nourishing and sweet. More reporters started jotting notes.

"First," Jenn said, "let me say how delighted I am to be here and how happy I am that you've made room in your busy schedules to come down and visit with me."

Visit with her? Who was she kidding? They were here because of Dwight Davies. And yet there wasn't a trace of guile in her expression. "I'm sure you have some questions, so by all means, let's get started, shall we?"

An old tabby renowned for making talking heads cry cleared her throat. "You're being touted as the next Martha Stewart. I assume you don't want to be another clone. So what makes you different?"

"I don't crochet."

A ripple of surprised laughter ran through the group. The subtle reminder of Martha's prison record was unexpected, cute, and a little wicked. Dwight might not have approved.

Jenn smiled. She had a wonderful smile. It belonged to the ultimate girl next door—well, maybe not. She was a little old for the girl next door, but in this era of aging baby boomers, she might be something better. For women, the best friend next door I never had time for, and for men, the mature second wife who understands that aching joints sometimes sideline even the most sexually active mature male.

"Okay," the old tabby said, clearly not as amused as her associates. "You're squeaky clean, duly noted. Considering who your boss is, you'd have to be, wouldn't you? But there is a glut of lifestyle shows on the networks and cable today.

What are you bringing to the mix that makes you worth watching?"

The playful smile turned thoughtful. "I'm not going to try and make a room over for one hundred dollars or turn tuna cans into napkin rings. I'm interested in comfortable, stylish, and affordable living. Sometimes that takes more than fifteen minutes with a glue gun."

The door in the back of the room suddenly swung wide open and the man himself, Dwight Davies, entered. Every reporter in the room grew instantly alert. This was what they'd come for.

Dwight was a big man, barrel chested and long legged, all six foot three of him covered in an expensive hand-tailored dark navy suit. He had a big, balding head and a set of peculiarly delicate features squished into his big, blocky face. Right now those features were serene, but his little eyes whiplashed around the room. He held up his hands—they were big, too, the fingers sausagelike, a thick band of diamond-encrusted gold around his pinkie.

"Go ahead with what you were saying, Jenn. Sorry to interrupt." His voice was not big; it was a tenor in a bass body.

A very young woman in Manhattan's ubiquitous "Take Me Serious" black suit decided to be noticed and piped up. "But most of us don't have the time to donate ten hours to a project. At least here in New York."

"Now," Jenn said with a soft smile, "you have no idea how hectic life can be on the tundra." A couple people chuckled. The young reporter blushed. "It's true some of my projects take time. For those unable to devote a day or a weekend, I design the projects to be spread out over the course of a week or even a month."

"Excuse me." Dwight Davies moved to Jenn's side. "I'm sorry to break in but I just want to clarify that Miss Lind will keep in mind the resources and skill sets of her audience, and her projects will reflect her consideration. Right, Jenn?"

"Of course, Mr. Davies," she said, smiling at him like they were old friends meeting at a cocktail party. "I am always mindful of my audience."

"Isn't she a peach, folks?" Dwight said, slinging a long arm around her and giving her a friendly hug. "You can take some pictures now."

Cameras appeared out of nowhere, the sound of snapshots being taken filling the air like rifle reports at a shooting range for precisely forty-five seconds. "That's enough. I just wanted to come and tell you a little about Ms. Lind and why I handpicked her to be the central figure in AMS's daytime programming. Ms. Lind comes from Minnesota, where she's enjoying her eighth straight year as the Midwest's most popular media personality. The viewership for her show has risen 480 percent since she took over the spot. She's going to be big, folks. Bigger than big. You might say I'm betting the bank on it." He checked the Rolex strapped to his broad, hairy wrist. "I got time for one question, so make it a good one. You in the first row." He pointed at a ready-looking guy.

"Mr. Davies, you're spending a lot of money launching your network and you've tagged an unknown to be the star. Isn't that a gamble?"

Dwight gave the man a flat look of contempt. "I don't gamble. And you shouldn't either. None of you. Gambling is for fools and wastrels, and I am neither. Jenn Lind is a bona fide lady who will make all of us at AMS proud." Then he gave Jenn another little squeeze and, having bestowed his official blessing, left.

A few reporters checked their watches. Three minutes.

Jenn turned back to the group. "I can see I'm going to

have to get him a 'Minneapple' mug," she said, brokering a few polite laughs.

"You clearly love Minnesota. Is there anything Minnesotans do poorly?" someone asked.

"Well," she said, "Minnesotans are not known for public displays of affection. Not that they aren't passionate. For example, I knew an old Swedish couple that went out to dinner for their fiftieth anniversary. He looked across the table at her and saw in her eyes the pretty young girl he wed, and in her smile the tender mother with whom he raised four kids, and in the gentle lines on her face the grandmother who so generously shared her wisdom. And he thought of all the years of companionship and joy they had shared, and how very, very much he loved her. So much, in fact, that he almost told her."

A riff of light laughter arose from the group.

"Miss Lind, it says in the material here that you got your start at age seventeen when you stepped in to pinch-hit for a local morning show hostess. Would you expand on that?"

"Certainly," she said. "I, along with the other finalists in a local pageant, was scheduled to appear on *Good Neighbors,* a program being broadcast live from the Minnesota State Fair. When we arrived on the set, we saw the star of the show, Sharon Siverston, being taken away in an ambulance. She'd had an accident in the previous segment at the Baby Barnyard Petting Zoo."

"What was that?"

"A calf bit her," she said with a small sigh, as if calves biting people were a common but unfortunate occurrence in Minnesota. "Her next spot was a cooking one and the producers were trying to decide how to fill the sudden eight-minute gap. I had just won a blue ribbon for baking, so I volunteered to do the segment.

"Shortly afterward, I was asked to do a regular spot. When Sharon stepped down a few years later (the poor dear's nose never did look quite the same)"—here she paused and, by God, she really *did* look saddened—"they asked me to replace her and there I have been ever since."

"You were Miss Fawn Creek?" a voice from the back abruptly asked.

She looked around to find the speaker. "Yes."

"Your hometown must be very proud of you."

"I hope so."

"Do you ever get back there?"

"Oh, yes. As I always say, I'm very fond of the Fawn." Her press release credited her upbringing in Fawn Creek as the inspiration for many of the "heritage" recipes used on her show. "My folks still live there. So, yes, I get back quite often."

God, you had to love a gracious, mature woman who called her parents "folks" and did so without a hint of self-consciousness.

"If you were Miss Fawn Creek 1984, then you were also the model for the butter sculpture Steve Jaax cites as being the turning point in his career. Am I right?"

At this, a buzz arose. A couple reporters who'd been eyeing the door stopped. This was unexpected. Apparently by Jenn Lind, too. And that was interesting.

She blinked and, using the armrests on her chair, lifted herself up so she could better see the questioner. "Excuse me?"

"Dan Piccatto, contributing arts editor for *Vanity Fair.*" This awoke a fresh surge of murmurs. What was an arts editor doing here? Especially an old silverback like Dan, who usually only covered highbrow art news. "Are you the model for Jaax's *Butter Epiphany*?"

Someone guffawed. Steve Jaax, arguably one of the most celebrated sculptors of the twenty-first century, pinpointed the origins of his signature works to a few weeks in the summer of 1984, a period he fondly, and without any consideration for veracity, referred to as his "outlaw period."

Over the years, the story had gained almost mythical stature. Jaax, so it went, was running from the law (and his then wife, the internationally famous fashion model Fabulousa) when he'd taken a gig at the Minnesota State Fair carving the busts of winning dairy princesses out of frozen butter. While working on a hundred-pound block, he had been visited by a vision, seeing in the way light shone through the semitranslucent butterfat the basis for the fiber-optic-and-resin pieces that would become his trademark.

Though a few detractors claimed Jaax had become as celebrated for his celebrity as his art, it didn't matter. Jaax was still big news. The reporters started scribbling away.

"Are you?"

"Yes, I . . . I am." She adjusted an earring. "I haven't thought about that . . . it . . . in years. To be honest, I hadn't realized anyone even knew about it."

"But that's why I'm here," Piccatto replied, clearly surprised, "because of the butter sculpture."

Jenn Lind's perfectly arched brows lifted.

"My office received a fax this morning from the AMS publicity department saying that you were going to be grand marshal of the Fawn Creek sesquicentennial this December."

This definitely caught her off guard. "Well, I—"

"There was a bullet on the bottom saying that you would be appearing alongside the butter sculpture of you created at the Minnesota State Fair by Steven Jaax." Piccatto held up a piece of paper.

Jenn's face abruptly cleared. "Then the sculpture must be

a facsimile. The original was melted down and used at the Lutheran Brotherhood Corn Feed the weekend the fair ended. All of the princesses donated their sculptures to the event. It was well covered by the local media. I'm sorry but I—"

"No," Piccatto insisted. "I called the town. They swear it's the original. Apparently your parents had it in a freezer in a"—he shuffled through some papers—"barn all these years."

"Really?" She seemed a little discomposed. "Still, whoever sent out that press release may have gotten it wrong. It may be the same source that has me accepting Fawn Creek's flattering invitation to be their grand marshal, which, I must tell you, I have regretfully declined due to my current obligations to AMS—"

"Excuse me!" Vice President and Programming Director Dan Belker, who'd been standing along the wall with the other coterie of AMS officials, beaming like a proud grandfather, bustled over to Jenn's side. He raised a hand. "This is all my fault, I'm afraid. A representative from Fawn Creek contacted me late yesterday with information regarding the amazing discovery of Mr. Jaax's butter sculpture," he explained. "The conversation got around to how they'd invited Jenn to be their grand marshal. I wasn't surprised to hear that she'd declined because of the shooting schedule for *Comforts of Home*. Jenn has a great work ethic."

He patted her shoulder approvingly. "But I got to thinking about it, and well, I called Mr. Davies and after a quick chat we agreed. You just don't turn down an honor like that. So I called the town back, and knowing how she feels about Fawn Creek and how happy this would make her, I accepted on her behalf.

"I haven't had a chance to tell her yet." He nodded at

Jenn, who was regarding him with a wide-eyed stare, frozen between amazement and . . . something else. Probably delight. Probably.

An abrupt, odd, but transforming smile suddenly covered her face. "Well, then, thank you, Mr. Belker. I can't tell you what this means to me. Thank you."

She rose to her feet. "So! I'm thinking this is as good a place as any to wrap this up, eh, friends? So thank you for coming. It's been my pleasure."

Chapter Seven

1:50 p.m.
Park Plaza Hotel hallway

"You laid on the Minnesota accent a little thick there at the end," Jenn's agent, Natalie Fishman, said as Jenn finished shaking the last reporter's hand and escaped into the hall beyond the conference room. "I was afraid you were going to break out the 'Sure, you betcha's.'"

"Not to worry, my small, cynical friend," Jenn said lightly.

Only a nudge over five feet and just poking into her third decade, with her stick-straight black hair chopped off at her jaw and her thin, flat figure, Nat looked uncannily like an Edward Gorey character. One of the scary children.

"And 'Fond of the Fawn?'" Nat said, falling into step beside Jenn as they headed to the other side of the hotel, where the AMS executives were waiting. "How do you sleep at night?"

"Rocked to sleep by the sound of all those thousand-dollar bills crinkling inside my mattress," Jenn said cheerfully. It had been a slam-dunk performance.

Nat made a disgusted sound that turned into a chuckle. "You don't even like Fawn Creek."

"So what?" Jenn asked. "It's an arranged marriage. Think of Fawn Creek and me sort of like Charles and Diana. I'm the queen they never wanted, and believe me, they are definitely not who I saw spending the rest of my life with. But there you are. We're locked in a mutually beneficial relationship and both of us—" She broke off, frowning. "Can you be a 'both' with a town?"

Nat shrugged. Jenn shrugged. She went on. "All of us would be idiots to mess with it. They pretend they like me. I pretend I like them."

"I'm glad there's no children involved," Nat said dryly.

"Hey," Jenn said lightly, her mood rising with each step. "It works. Especially—again like Chuck and Di—since we don't have to live together. Which is something we need to discuss with Certain People who have overstepped their boundaries."

She'd worked hard for this. She'd worked her ass off— she gave a metaphorical glance to said ass and amended— half her ass off. She was poised at the brink of national stardom and she felt terrific.

Dan Belker's unexpected preemptive strike was the only blemish in the otherwise bright, sunny place that had become Jenn's life. Her contract with AMS would assure her of the success she'd been pursuing for twenty years. Their people had come through on every single promise they'd made and the contracts had been signed. Her future looked secure.

All she needed to do was back out on Dan's doubtless well-intentioned acceptance of Fawn Creek's grand marshal gig.

"Let's just remember the sweet voices of those thousand-dollar bills in your mattress when we're talking to those

Certain People, shall we? I'd hate to see your beauty rest disrupted."

The advice was unnecessary. Jenn wasn't going to do anything to rock the Good Ship AMS. "Since when am I a diva?"

"It's not your fault. It's your fate," Nat said, unconvinced. "No one can make as much money as you're going to make and not become a diva. And it's already begun."

The idea was unexpectedly appealing. Jenny Hallesby: Diva. Yup. She liked it. She looked down at her miniature agent. "Enlighten me as to when you saw the first signs."

"Your little Hissy-That-Wasn't when that chickie got huffy about New Yorkers not having time to do some of the stuff on the show? It was almost a Hissy-That-Was. Probably would have been if old Dwight hadn't arrived."

Jenn waved her hand in the air as if dispelling gnats. "Nah. I was just playing with her."

"You were not."

That was the problem with mixing friendships and work. Nat knew her too well. The criticism had rubbed. But it wouldn't have rubbed so raw if it hadn't already been a sore spot. Even in Minneapolis, the guys from the head office had been pushing a litany of faster, cheaper, and easier.

"Just remember, Jenn, AMS wants everything you demonstrate on the show doable within the average American woman's time limits, personal capability, and financial means. Emphasis on *simple*."

They'd reached the office where the boys from AMS waited to debrief her. "Well, hell, we'll make phones out of empty soup cans and call it a goddamn day then, shall we?"

"Only you can screw this up, Jenn."

Nat was right. "I'll be good."

She plastered her "Madonna of the Milk Cows" smile in

place, opened the door, and sailed through, Nat drifting behind like a little black tugboat.

The gang was all there: small and exquisite Ron Patella, seated in a huge wingback chair sipping tea; crusty old Dan Belker; and the vice president of current programming, the scrumptious, ambitious, and young Bob Reynolds. There was something unsettling about Bob, something besides his movie-star good looks. He looked like an overfriendly puppy.

"That was wonderful, Jenn," Ron said, putting down his cup and applauding lightly. "You did a fabulous job. And wasn't it terrific of Mr. Davies to show up to support you?"

"Absolutely." And may he hitherto absent himself from her life and her career, she offered heavenward.

"Everyone in that room left with a crush on you. Brava!"

"Thank you."

"Here, have a seat. Can I get you something? No? Fine." Dan came forward to take her arm and lead her to the sofa. Nat headed for the buffet table out by the window. And Bob Reynolds.

Dan waited until she'd been seated and then sat down next to her. "You didn't know the butter sculpture by Jaax was still around, did you? You were surprised, weren't you?"

That was the understatement of the year. The idea that the butter head lived and apparently had been living all these years in her parents' barn was sort of creepy, with a kind of "Telltale Heart" vibe to it. Mom had some 'splainin' to do.

"Boy, I'll say!" she enthused just to keep old Dan company in his delight. And now the segue . . . "You really did take me by surprise. As did the announcement I would be going to—"

"I knew it!" Dan broke in, chuckling and rubbing his

hands together. "I knew you didn't know. Wait. It gets better. You'll get a kick out of this, Jenn: *The Guinness Book of World Records* is interested in seeing it. And you," he hurriedly added. "Together. It seems it might be the oldest surviving intact butter sculpture in existence.

"And *Ripley's Believe It or Not* might want to do a fluff piece, too."

Great. Instead of the Queen of Lifestyles, she was going to be known as the Methuselah of Butter Sculptures. As amazing as this was apparently going to be to Dan, she didn't want to be in the World Record Book as being the oldest anything. And they shouldn't want her to, either.

But now was no time to deflate that particular balloon. Not in front of Dan's subordinates.

She should answer. She just had to focus, envision herself as a rock, a serene Nordic rock in a calm body of water. Abruptly the rock turned into a yellow monolith.

"That's wonderful, Dan" was all she managed instead of the single word that sprang immediately to mind. But that wouldn't have been *Jenn Lind–like*. She couldn't remember the last time she'd used that word. Probably the last time she was in Fawn Creek, where nobody paid any attention to her or expected anything from her, anyway.

Except they were paying her attention, the sneaky bastards. Going behind her back to get her to play master of ceremonies at their sesquicentennial. Good try, but no way. Fawn Creek was not going to screw this up for her.

Granted, she had done some stupid things in high school trying to get out of her Miss Fawn Creek obligations but most reasonable people wouldn't care about a seventeen-year-old kid "acting out." In fact, the people who'd done her background check hadn't even bothered with her teenage years aside from looking into the state court records. But if

Dwight Davies found out about her little stunt at the high school homecoming dance the fall of her senior year, he was just the man to magnify that minor sin into a felony offense. One worth firing her over.

Now she was on the cusp of real celebrity, national recognition, lasting success, and she was not going to blow it. No mistakes this time. No misunderstood instructions in an application. No would-be friends secretly salivating for her comeuppance. She had this particular crown bought and stamped SOLD.

"—so you can see, the whole thing will work out beautifully." Bob Reynolds had pattered over to where she sat and was regarding her eagerly. If he had a tail, he'd have been wagging it. She still wasn't sure she'd pet him, though. She suspected he had big teeth. "Right, Ms. Lind?"

She'd only been half attending. No matter. It was time to put the whammy on their Fawn Creek Fantasy.

"I'm sorry but I can't ask AMS to rearrange their entire shooting schedule around a selfish whim to see my face on the front of the *Fawn Creek Crier*. I can't. I wouldn't feel right about it."

"Besides," Nat said, hopping off her window perch and coming to stand next to Handsome Bob, "Jenn told me it's a weeklong commitment, not just one afternoon sitting in some snowmobile at the head of a parade."

Good old Nat.

"It's an ATV, actually," Bob said.

"Whatever. The point is, it's a week and my client is not going to waste her precious vacation time on it."

Oh! Good one, Jenn thought appreciatively, even though it had been literally years since she'd actually used vacation time for a vacation.

"And I'm sure you could put that week to better use than

paying her to sit up there in the middle of nowhere judging curling contests or whatever she'd be doing." She reached across Bob, plucked a croissant from the buffet table, and smiled up the front of his Brooks Brothers white shirt. He blushed.

Leave it to Nat to get a thing done.

"Of course." Dan frowned. "But as I said, we intend this to be a combination work-pleasure trip for Jenn. Mostly pleasure for her, mostly work for us."

Is that what he'd said? Jenn had better start paying closer attention.

"Please." Bob turned away from Nat, facing the room in general to make his case. Nat pouted. "There's an unprecedented opportunity here for us to get some footage of you in your hometown to use for the credits. What could be more picturesque than you all bundled up in a fur jacket—*faux* fur—strolling through your quaint little town? It's part of the Jenn Lind mystique, the charm, the country's fascination with all things rural. I love this idea. I really do and I want you to love it, too. Especially you, Ms. Lind."

He looked like he might crawl into her lap and lick her face if she said yes.

This was not going as she'd planned.

"It does sound great," she said. "But there's no reason to send a crew all the way up to Fawn Creek for footage of snow. There are some terrific locations in Minneapolis or St. Paul. Say, by Minnehaha Falls or along the river. I assure you, it snows all over Minnesota."

"But it's not *hometown* snow," Ron Patella suddenly piped up from where he still sat enthroned in the wingback.

"I'm not sure I understand the point," she said carefully. "I don't believe anyone would think AMS was trying to pull a fast one by showing Minneapolis snow rather than Fawn Creek snow."

"Yes, but, well"—Bob's smooth cheeks were pinking up again—"Mr. Davies is a real stickler about veracity."

They had to be kidding. She looked at each of the three men. They weren't kidding.

"You're kidding," Nat said around a mouthful of croissant.

"Mr. Davies is a . . . a little bit of a fanatic on the topic of honesty," gray-haired Dan stepped up to bat.

Mr. Davies was a lot fanatic about a lot of things, Jenn thought.

"Right now," Dan said, "this network is his pet project, and you're a big part of that. He's convinced—*we're* convinced—that the public is starved for wholesome role models. Like you."

"Now I know you were married pretty young and it didn't last too long—" Dan said apologetically.

"I was twenty-three," Jenn jumped in confidently. "The marriage lasted eighteen months."

There was no way her short-lived marriage could be construed as anything but an unfortunate mistake. On both sides. When . . . Tim—geez, she was always forgetting his name!—and she had realized that she was not going to be a perfect hostess for his burgeoning consulting career and she'd gotten a look at his fantastically high-risk, and criminally irresponsible, portfolio, they'd both backed gingerly toward the door. Neither of them held a grudge. Tim had actually kissed her as they'd left the mediator's office. With maybe a little more relief than was flattering, but still . . .

"The divorce was amicable," she continued. "In case you or Mr. Davies is worried, let me assure you no one is going to show up one day with a bunch of nude negatives from my days as an aspiring actress."

"Of course not," Ron said, crossing one perfectly creased slack leg over the other. "We do a background check, you know. But bear in mind that Mr. Davies hates being lied to. You recall a few years back when it turned out one of the hostesses for some kids' decorating show had been an occasional stripper while she was at college?"

Nat nodded. "She was fired, poor kid."

"Mr. Davies thought she got off too easy."

Everyone fell into a moment of silence—time Jenn spent wondering just what beyond firing Dwight Davies had contemplated.

"So"—Dan Belker clapped his hands together, signaling the end of their impromptu mourning—"it's settled. Jenn will head to her hometown at the end of the month, and we'll send a crew up for a couple days to shoot some footage."

"Great! You couldn't stage the potential photo opportunities this thing'll generate," Bob said, rubbing his hands together. "All those adoring faces surrounding her, folks cheering her, wishing her well, proud to call her one of their own . . . It'll be a Norman Rockwell print come to life— only with better-looking people." He looked at Jenn. "*Are* the people in your town good-looking?"

Jenn was caught off guard by the unexpected turn of the conversation, mostly the fantasy about Fawn Creekians adoring her, and didn't have time to frame a politic reply. "No."

Bob laughed. "Of course, they are! All Minnesotans are good-looking. Tall, blond Nordic types with fresh faces and strong bodies."

He caught Dan's surprised stare. "It was in the demographics profile."

"Not these people," Jenn burst out. *Jesus!* If they expected people to be milling around her with homemade signs and banners . . . Her stomach started making knots. "I'm sorry. That sounds so awful. Of course, I love them all dearly, but in order to be fair to . . . to AMS, I have to tell you, a few years ago the American Medical Association used the whole town for their obesity focus group." Which was true.

Bob stopped laughing and regarded her blankly. "Oh?"

"Don't worry," Dan said confidently. "Even if we only get footage of a bunch of uglies, we always have pine trees and kids skating and church steeples to fall back on."

"And snow," Bob agreed. "Don't forget the white stuff. If this all works out like I think it's goin' to, we might wanta do a Christmas special up there. In fact, instead of just footage for the credits, we should seriously consider doing a spot right there during the festival or whatever it is."

From the e-mail the mayor of Fawn Creek had sent her, Jenn knew they were expecting about seven thousand people for the fishing tournament alone. That meant that as well as dozens with the unwitting power to end her career, seven thousand more simply to ignore her. Her head was swimming. She stared helplessly at Nat.

"I'm afraid you'll be disappointed," Nat said, correctly interpreting the desperation in Jenn's eyes. "It's really a bland little town. More Home Depot than Norman Rockwell."

"Ha-ha!" Dan laughed and turned to Bob. "That reminds me. Have you gotten hold of the artist? Is that a done deal?"

Artist? What artist? What were they talking about now?

"Jaax? Not yet," Bob answered. "I've sent his manager some letters but haven't had much luck getting a response, so this afternoon I'm going to a charity auction that he's attending. I'll approach him there and see if I can get him to commit."

Bob caught her flabbergasted expression. "Mr. Jaax has been invited to be co-marshal."

They were trying to get Steve Jaax to go to Fawn Creek, Minnesota? She started to laugh, then caught herself as she realized no one else was joining her. They didn't seriously expect an artist of his caliber to co-marshal a tiny town's celebration, particularly as it wasn't even his small town, did they?

"Do you really think he's right for the show, Dan?" Ron asked, sounding a bit worried. "He has a reputation as being a foulmouthed SOB."

Steve Jaax. The memory of him was even more of an ice shock than that of the butter head. Charisma, sex appeal, and absolute conviction about all things—that was what she remembered. And the "electric glide in blue" eyes. He'd never go for it.

Dan, who'd leaned over the coffee table and begun shoving papers back into their folder in preparation for leaving, paused. "He's not so bad. I've heard him talk about his sculpture and he can be nearly poetic. Just don't ask him about his first ex-wife, that supermodel. Besides, we can edit."

"Will he accept?" Ron prodded.

"Frankly, I don't see how he can refuse. Not after all the years he's spent talking about that damn"—Dan caught Jenn's eye—"darn butter sculpture. And I don't see how we cannot take advantage of the potential publicity his appearance with Jenn and her likeness will generate. We've already put some feelers out regarding a spot on the *Today* show, and like I said, the *Ripley's* people are interested."

He turned to Jenn. "Do you realize that your butter head may be the oldest butter sculpture around?"

"Yes," said Jenn, "I think you mentioned that."

Jenn waited until she and Nat were alone on the elevator to break down. "This is going to be a disaster!"

Nat regarded Jenn unsympathetically. "So? You have to go to Fawn Creek for a week or so. Buy long underwear. You'll survive. Besides, Steve Jaax is yummy in a been-there-done-too-much-of-that sort of way. Pal around with him. You'll get through it."

"Like he'll really show," Jenn muttered. She grabbed Nat's arm. "You don't get it, Nat. AMS expects me to get a hero's welcome in Fawn Creek so they can tape it. I'm lucky if more than one person says hi to me when I'm in town."

"You're exaggerating," Nat said flatly. "You've become a diva and you're exaggerating."

"No!" Jenn protested. "Remember when I did that book on Scandinavian farm interiors and you talked me into doing a signing at the Pamida store up there? Do you remember how many books I signed? *Three.* And my mother bought all of them."

Nat's unsympathetic demeanor relaxed. She patted Jenn's hand, which was still clinging to her arm. "Jenn. Honey. You are the Midwest Martha. At every appearance, you bring in hundreds of fans. I've seen it for myself. You know I'm right."

"Not there." Jenn shivered.

"Look. You told me yourself that your little town is expecting around seven thousand tourists to show up for this sesquicentennial, right?"

Jenn nodded cautiously.

"So then you're golden," Nat exclaimed, "because those

seven thousand aren't Fawn Creekers, are they? They're all people from your end of the state. Your viewers. The same people who come out in droves to see you when you appear at the Mall of America or some store opening. Right? Right."

Jenn was feeling better. She'd stopped hyperventilating.

"They'll love you and their love will swallow up any lack of love from the Fawn Creekites. How many people live there?"

"Twenty-eight hundred."

"Exactly. A pittance. So just keep cool, and if the AMS crew shows up before the crowds, stay out of their sight. Tell them you're sick or something and can't shoot any film until all those loving strangers are in town."

Okay. That made sense. People *did* love her. She was popular. She *was* bound to have some fans among seven thousand people. God, she loved Nat. She threw her arms around her agent and hugged her but, because Nat was so small, mostly Jenn smothered her head in her bosom.

"Yeah, yeah," Nat said, struggling free and whisking her black hair out of her face. "We're a cute couple. Now get off me. So. Anything else?"

Jenn shook her head. She felt loads better.

"Excellent. Go forth and have a great time." Nat hesitated, scowled, and glanced up at Jenn. "Ah. You don't . . . want me to . . . ah . . . go with you, do you?"

The offer did not come willingly from Natalie's lips, and it was almost too much to resist. The thought of little Gorey creature Nat facing down the sisterhood of the Lutheran church basement kitchen . . . Delicious. But just because she'd made the offer in the first place, especially when Jenn knew how she felt about anything remotely rural, Jenn couldn't even bring herself to tease her.

Nat didn't deserve that. Nor, come to think of it, did the sisterhood of the Lutheran church basement kitchen.

"Thanks, Nat, but no," Jenn said. "Why have you marooned up there in the middle of nowhere for no good reason?"

There was no mistaking the relief on Natalie's face. But she never had been in any danger. No one went to Fawn Creek if Jenn could help it. Nope. The fewer people on whose respect she depended saw her in action in her "hometown," the better.

Up there, Jenn Lind didn't exist. Up there, she was still just Jenn Hallesby.

Chapter Eight

4:00 p.m.
Soho, New York

"The final piece in lot forty-five donated by Fabulousa is this aluminum statue *Medusa Migraine* by the renowned American artist Steven Jaax."

The crowd seated on the upholstered Louis the Fifteenth armchair reproductions responded with a smattering of light applause.

"The bidding shall begin at fifty thousand."

No one twitched.

"Fifty thousand." The auctioneer scanned the audience, his expression of superior confidence thinning. Someone blew their nose. "May I have— Fifty, ma'am! Very good. May I have sixty?"

"Who bid?" Steve Jaax, seated in the middle back, asked out of the side of his mouth. His hair was uncombed and his eyes a little bloodshot but at least he'd tucked his white dress shirt into the jeans and donned a charcoal gray mohair jacket. The jacket had cost a fortune; the jeans he'd found after a party in his studio.

Beside him, Verie Meuwissen of VM Galleries and sole dealer of the works of Steven Jaax leaned forward, his Gucci belt dissecting his well-padded tummy. He pushed his rim-less glasses up on his nose, peered, and straightened. "Button Lipscomb."

"Shit. Why does she want it?"

"She's bought a place in Miami. I've heard she's decorating the cabana."

"Shit," Steve repeated.

"I have fifty—sixty. Thank you. Do I hear sixty-five?"

"Where do you hear this stuff?" Steve asked.

"It's my job, dear boy."

"I thought selling art was your job, not interior decorating."

"A thin line, you know."

Unfortunately, Steve did know. He'd been a lot happier when he didn't, when he'd simply worked in his studio until he couldn't hold the tools any longer, emerged for a burger and a few hours of convivial company, and disappeared back inside again.

Nowadays, he only went to his studio when he had a show pending. The rest of his days were spent in Manhattan or Paris or London or Prague, crawling from party to party. Not that Steve didn't like celebrity. He loved it. It just was a hard balancing act and one he sometimes, late at night, when one is prone to self-doubts, wasn't entirely sure he'd gotten the hang of.

He didn't like thinking about it; he wouldn't think about it. He might come to some unfortunate conclusions. Like he was full of bullshit.

He stood up. "Let's get a drink," he said and headed for the bar at the back of the room. Once there, he ordered a vodka gimlet. "What do you want, Verie?"

"Campari and lime."

The bartender began sorting through bottles as Steve morosely regarded the proceedings. Things had pretty much come to a halt. The auctioneer was standing behind his podium with his arms crossed over his tuxedo-clad chest, glaring at the audience.

Steve felt a little stupid rising to the bait Fabulousa dangled by auctioning off the works of his that the judge had awarded her in their divorce. Of all his ex-wives, Fabulousa was the only one he still felt passionate about, as in passionately disliked her. It was a knee-jerk reaction exacerbated by the fact that she had so completely taken him to the cleaners. He hadn't seen her in two decades and he should have just kept it that way, but knowing that she was here, selling his history like secondhand ties and that Button Lipscomb was going to buy his statue and use it as a hat rack—ouch!

He touched his jaw. Damn, he was grinding his teeth.

"You knew people with more money than taste would be here trying to pick up a deal. It was bound to hurt," Verie said, correctly interpreting Steve's hangdog expression. "I really don't know why you insisted we come in the first place."

"I didn't insist you come. I didn't even invite you. You just showed up." Steve leaned against the bar.

"And a bloody good thing, too. I am here to protect my interests. Why is it exactly that you are here, Steven?"

"To say good-bye to my children," Steve said, his sorrow growing more pronounced. "I haven't seen any of them in twenty years and now God knows where they'll end up. Button Lipscomb's cabana or some Soho restaurant's john, I suppose. I had to come."

Verie collected Steve's cocktail and handed it to him. "You don't own them. Why this sudden emotional attachment? They aren't even your best work."

But they had been *hard* work. It didn't matter that they

lacked the polish (glibness) or spontaneity (carelessness) of his current work. They represented the honest (desperate) exploration (shots in the dark) of a hungry (literally hungry) young artist who was just coming into his full talent (brainstorm). Talent. He really had had talent. He'd poured himself into those pieces.

He accepted the gimlet and downed a quarter of it. "Would you put your dog to sleep without saying goodbye?"

"Now there's a rather off-putting comment."

"I don't expect you to understand."

"Sixty-five? Sixty-five. Very good!" the auctioneer said approvingly.

"Who was that?" Steve asked without turning around. "Look."

"Why should I be the one peering and peeking about like some ridiculous Peter Sellers character?" Verie complained. "You look."

"It wouldn't be good for my image. Someone might think I care who buys it. Once it's out of the studio it's supposed to be dead to me. I was quoted in the *Wall Street Journal* as saying that. You look."

"That is a lot of unmitigated bullshit."

"True," Steve agreed without the least bit of defensiveness. At least he still knew bullshit from truth. Most of the time. He thought. "But collectors eat bullshit for lunch. You've been quoted in the *New Yorker* as saying that."

"Yes, yes." Verie gave up the argument. "Fine. And I have no idea who the bidder is. Some studly young blond fellow. Odd, I thought I knew all the serious Jaax collectors."

"Maybe he's a new collector?"

Verie's flat-eyed glance said it all. Young collectors weren't able to afford original Jaax's. Mostly Steve's work was bought to fill out collections, or for investment purposes, or as a tax write-off.

Steve tossed back the rest of the gimlet and led the way back to their seats. He flopped down in his chair, his legs stretched out, his thumbs tucked into the pockets of his jeans and his chin resting comfortably on his chest as he gazed ahead through half-closed eyes.

Verie, glad to have sidestepped the uncomfortable direction the conversation had been taking, sat down more sedately. Steve Jaax still sold well. So did the scribbles Pablo Picasso made on cocktail napkins. It didn't mean that the intrinsic value was there. Just the celebrity. And, God love him, Steve Jaax was a celebrity. His earlier works were transcendent. His current works were . . . cocktail napkins. Familiar, immediately identifiable as a Jaax, and rank with celebrity.

"Seventy. I have seventy thousand."

"It's that little Asian man," Verie whispered before Steve asked. "The one with all the toy train stores."

"Thank God," Steve muttered, eyes still closed. "Button would stick a plate in *Medusa*'s hand and use her as a canapé server."

"Seventy-five. Thank you, ma'am."

"Oops," Verie said.

"Button?"

"Um-hum."

Steve's eyes popped open. "Damn. I like that piece."

"No, Steve." Verie caught Steve's hand, returning it to the armrest and patting it comfortingly. "You mustn't."

"Do I hear eighty? The bid is seventy-five. Seventy-five, going once . . ."

"Why not?" Steve asked.

Verie glanced down their row at a well-known collector

and the society columnist sitting next to him. Both were staring at Steve. Verie nodded, beamed, and shrugged with just a trace of bemused tolerance, suggesting that though handling a mercurial and temperamental personality like Jaax's was a full-time and often thankless job, it was one he nonetheless did willingly, a mere handmaiden to the Muse, Erata.

"Foremost," he whispered at Steve through a toothy smile, "because this is a *charity* auction of prominent artists' works, and it would not look good for you to be the only prominent artist here bidding on his own pieces—"

"Wouldn't it look good if I bought *Medusa* for some ungodly amount of money?" Steve asked. "I think it would. I think I would look like a damn saint, buying my own stuff for charity."

"Which brings us to the second reason you cannot bid," Verie said softly. "You haven't got that kind of money."

Steve pondered this. Damn, but Verie was right. He didn't have that sort of money. At least not without selling off some of his own collection, which he was not going to do. Ever. "That's because she took it all."

"There have been other wives upon whom you have settled money," Verie corrected calmly. "It was not all Fabulousa. It was not any of your wives either singly or in combination. You have had a great deal of money. You have spent a great deal of money. And enjoyed the process very much in doing so, I might add."

Well, he had a point there. He really did. At least no one could accuse Steve Jaax of being one of those god-awful gloomy sons of bitches who wallowed in artistic anguish.

"Sold! For seventy-five thousand dollars. Thank you, ma'am!" the auctioneer announced.

"I'm sorry, Steve," Verie said sincerely.

Steve nodded dolefully. "Thank you."

"We'll be taking a short recess. Fifteen minutes. Thank you."

Steve got to his feet, his interest in the auction over, and began picking his way over the still-seated people in their row. Verie followed suit, smiling weakly at the woman upon whose Prada-encased toe he trod, wiggling his way past a corpulent sheik who was buying everything selling for less than ten thousand dollars, and surreptitiously slipping his card in Button Lipscomb's handbag as he edged past her.

"You know, this is the only time that I have actually ever been glad *Muse in the House* was stolen," Verie said. "At least it won't end up gracing Button Lipscomb's cabana."

Abruptly, Steve grinned, his good humor completely restored. He hadn't given a thought to *Muse in the House* for a while now. The only satisfaction he'd derived from his divorce from Fabulousa was knowing that the one sculpture she wanted the most was the one she couldn't have. At least, that was one part of his past that wasn't for sale. And, presumably, never would be.

The *Muse in the House* theft had joined the ranks of art mythology along with the Chagall theft and the Nazis' Art Train. Steve rather liked it that way. He liked even more knowing exactly where *Muse* was even though he could never touch it because he no longer had the key to the vault that contained it. He did have some regrets, however; he wished he could display it in his studio and have the pleasure of telling Fabulousa as much.

He'd thought about how to recover *Muse.* He couldn't ask Fabulousa to get it for him. He'd considered hiring people to break in but not only did that feel a little, well, *wrong*, but the cemetery where the Muse was hidden was one of the most well guarded in the country, and he couldn't afford a thief of that caliber (the Timmys of the world only came along once in a blue moon). Nope. Steve had come to the conclusion that the only way in was the key, and God alone knew where the only key to the crypt was.

The last he'd known of it, it had been encased in a one-hundred-pound block of butter and was being shipped off to a Lutheran Brotherhood corn-on-the-cob feed held in some Minnesota field. The story had been carried on the local news more than twenty years ago. He'd watched the broadcast in his cell in St. Paul, Minnesota, where he'd been awaiting extradition to New York.

Nope, for all intents and purposes, the *Muse* was lost to him.

But at least, he thought with another grin, it was lost to Fabulousa, too.

Chapter Nine

4:25 p.m.

The blond guy who'd been bidding for *Medusa* ambushed Steve three feet from the door. "Mr. Jaax? This is a real pleasure. Let me introduce myself. Bob Reynolds."

He stuck out his hand, and Steve, a sucker for good manners and not adverse to making nice with someone who'd been about to drop sixty-five thousand on a piece of crap—now that it was cabana fodder, it had been relegated to the realms of "crap"—took it. "Hi, Bob."

"I'm sure you don't recognize the name. Heck. You probably get a hundred letters a week, but I'm the guy who's been hounding you about going to Minnesota to act as grand marshal in that little town's sesquicentennial."

Oddly enough, this was actually ringing a bell. Something to do with a parade and snow and— Oh, yeah!

"Verie," Steve said, as his agent, having finished licking some society columnist's fingers, sidled up, "this is Bob. Bob, Verie. Bob wants me to go to Minnesota and sit on a snowmobile—"

"An ATV, actually." Bob smiled at Steve's blank look. "All-terrain vehicle."

Steve nodded sanguinely. "An ATV at the head of a parade. In December."

Verie, bless him, knew his part. Which was to make Steve look gracious. "That sounds very nice. Why don't you drop us a line with all the particulars?"

"I have!" Bob said and blushed. "I mean, the town has. I'm here representing AMS. American Media Services? We're interested in doing a segment up there and your inclusion would frankly just *make* the piece."

Steve could practically see Verie's pointy little ears twitch. Even Steve, who was arguably one of the least political creatures around, knew about AMS and its owner, Dwight Davies.

So did Verie. "Really? I would imagine Mr. Davies would be more interested in the taxidermist's arts than that of someone like Mr. Jaax."

Oh, yeah. Dwight Davies was a known homophobe. Point for Verie.

"But perhaps with the expansion of his empire, Mr. Davies has decided to begin a corporate collection?" Point having been scored, Verie decided to play nice and dropped the offensive. Corporate collections were meat and potatoes to Verie Meuwissen.

Handsome Bob, who didn't look the least homophobic but did look horribly embarrassed, eagerly grabbed the lifeline. "Oh, yes! Yes. Of course. I was bidding on behalf of . . . ah . . . Mr. Davies. And as future investors in Mr. Jaax's works"—he let that comment linger a second—"we at AMS are, of course, very excited about the promotional possibilities of having him attend Fawn Creek's sesquicentennial." He chuckled.

"They have those for towns?" Steve asked.

"Oh, yes. They're very popular."

Steve's knowledge of small towns, medium towns, hell, anything less than a city, was severely limited despite his propensity, when in his cups, to expound upon his youthful adventures in the Great American Heartland.

"Cool," said Steve.

"Then you'll come?"

"No."

"Steve! Dear boy!" exclaimed Verie, grabbing his forearm and half spinning him away. "A moment please!"

Verie dragged him a few feet away, smoothed his jacket sleeve, and rumbled in a dramatically sotto voce voice, "One oughtn't piss off the representative of a major media mogul. Besides, a nice feature on some AMS show might just be the thing to jump-start your career."

"Maybe putting a show together would help that," Steve suggested, but without too much rancor. Verie and he had done very well over the years. It wasn't Verie's fault Steve was feeling a little itchy lately.

"Listen, Verie. I understand and I appreciate the promo potential here, but lately, I really just want to . . . well . . . work. You know? And I think I oughta do just that while the feeling lasts."

Verie's face fell. "Steve—"

"Really."

With a deep sigh, Verie turned to face Bob, who was hovering eagerly in the background trying not to look like he was eavesdropping.

"Tell you what, dear boy," Verie told him. "Send along the information and we'll see if we can possibly fit it in to Mr. Jaax's schedule. But I must in all fairness inform you, it doesn't seem likely. He's preparing for a show."

"I understand." Bob nodded eagerly. "But we'd make all

the arrangements and make sure everything went as smoothly as possible for you. Mr. Davies could send his private jet."

"I don't like to fly," Steve said, smiling politely. As far as he was concerned, the conversation was over. His gaze drifted over the top of Bob's head and stopped dead.

She emerged from the crowd at the door, stomping toward them with her signature runway walk, an oddly sexy jackhammer jolt of foot and heel and hip. *Fabulousa.*

And she looked, Steve was forced to admit, fabulous. Her hair was still a straight glossy waterfall of tar, her hip bones still jutted like architecture through a peach-colored silk slip, and her skin was still the exultant dead white of an alabaster doll—or an underfed vampire.

Steve looked at Verie. His agent had seen her, too. Steve looked at Fabulousa. Her face had lit with feline pleasure. Steve looked at Bob; he was babbling happily on about making travel arrangements—and then he wasn't.

With a graceful thrust of her hand—Fabulousa had always been much stronger than she looked—the onetime supermodel straight-armed Bob to the side and planted herself directly in front of Steve. Sitting comfortably atop four-inch matchstick heels she was eye level.

He was amazed he didn't feel more of a reaction: hands clenching, skin crawling, at least a gag reflex. But he had nuthin'. Huh.

"Steve." Her full lower lip—and as much as Steve wanted to believe it had been collagen enhanced, he knew it to be completely natural—curved into the sullen-sexy semblance of a smile. "Dar-link boy."

Steve's eyes widened. "You picked that up from Verie!"

Fabulousa drew back. Frowned. "What? What is you are talking aboot?"

Her accent, Steve noted, had grown notably thicker with

the years. But he wasn't sure it was identifiable as East European anymore. It was weird. Oddly familiar . . . Wait a minute. . . . He almost had it. . . .

" 'Darling boy,' " Steve said slowly, trying to suss it out. "You never used that expression before you met Verie. Verie, you old dog"—he turned and waggled a finger under Verie's nose—"you didn't tell me you'd become an NYC pop culture icon."

Fabulousa's brilliant green eyes narrowed to kohl-rimmed slits. "You are having a leetle joke. Still, I am pleased to see you. Is good of you to come after so long—"

He had it! "Boris Badenov."

Verie blinked at him.

"You know," he said, "from the *Rocky and Bullwinkle Show*?"

"Oh, yeah!" Bob chimed in from where he was disentangling himself from the Louis XV chair Fabulousa had tipped him into. "Boris and Natasha, the Russian spies."

Verie, raised without the delights of a Rocky and Bullwinkle childhood, scowled and turned to Fabulousa, who, for similar reasons, was also scowling at Bob and Steve, who were smiling at each other in sympathetic accord.

"You look well, Fabulousa," Verie said, stiffly polite.

It was an understatement. She looked spectacular, as leggy and buff and mean as she had when she'd prowled the pages of *Esquire* and *W* and *Vogue* twenty years ago.

"Sank you," she purred. "And you, too. You"—she pinned Steve with a smoldering look—"are appearing . . . not unhealthy."

The silence drew out a little longer than was comfortable. For her.

"I gave up drinking and smoking," Steve finally announced, as though he'd just recalled this fact. He nodded. "Years ago."

Verie stared. He ignored him, sticking his hands in his pockets and rocking back and forth. An expression of unwilling admiration flickered across Fabulousa's generally inexpressive face. She coughed it away.

"Really?" She flicked a satiny panel of black hair back with her hand, seeking to recoup her momentary lapse into approval with cold indifference.

But it was too late. She'd already been impressed, and Steve, ever quick to pick up on the subtleties, knew it. That he was lying through his teeth would never have occurred to her, and he knew that, too. Not that Fabulousa would have ever realized this. A major problem in their marriage—aside from money, goals, friends, jealousy, work, fidelity, and money—had been his imagination and Fabulousa's utter lack of one.

"Well, zen, everything they say about the healthy lifestyle must be true. You look much better than last time I saw you."

"You mean in your boyfriend the judge's quarters twenty years ago?" Okay, now he felt an old familiar surge of anger.

"Was it so long ago?" She tapped a perfectly manicured nail against his chest and pouted. "Naughty boy to remind me of my age. But yes, I believe it is."

He refused to look down at the nail that had begun innocently enough by tapping but was quickly becoming a spirited stabbing.

"Yeah. Well. I wasn't myself that day." Steve shrugged. "I feel better now. I sleep better."

"Really? Yet they say a guilty conscience kept one awake," Fabulousa purred. "Thieves, for example, must have a terrible time sleeping. How glad I am that you seem to be the exception that proves the rule."

He turned to Bob, who was looking confused again. "My former wife, the former supermodel Fabulousa, is implying that I oughtn't to sleep well because she thinks I stole the statue she was holding hostage in her house. It was my seminal work."

Fabulousa turned a five-hundred-watt smile on Bob. "This is why he tries to run away to Minnesota. Tries and fails."

Steve continued providing his interpretative services. "It is beyond my former wife's ability to conceive of anyone escaping her clutches. You will note that I did not say 'beyond her ability to conceive of anyone *wanting* to escape her.' This is because even my former wife, even in that deluded state of self-adoration in which she exists, can't quite ignore the fact that many people"—he paused, tipped his head, and mused a second—"in fact, most people, want to escape her. Few, however, do.

"I did, though. For a few short weeks and"—he smiled at Fabulousa, who was wavering uncertainly between flying into a rage and laughing derisively—"and it was there, away from . . . well . . . her, that I was finally able to find myself, rediscover my talent, and see the new direction my art would take."

"The Butter Head?" Bob whispered.

Steve smiled approvingly. So the kid really was an art lover. "Yes. The Butter Head."

"I thought it was lard," Fabulousa said.

"No"—Steve swung around—"that would be your—"

"Steve has been asked to return to Minnesota!" Verie broke in. "To be grand marshal of a parade."

"Actually," Bob said, "it's as co-grand marshal."

He wasn't the main attraction? Well, that hurt.

"Excuse me," Verie huffed. "If you think Mr. Jaax is sharing the limelight with—"

"With *The Butter Head.*"

Whatever words any of the trio had been about to say faded away in a moment of unorchestrated wonder.

"The Butter Head," Steve repeated, staring at Bob. He wouldn't, he couldn't, joke about something like that, could he? The butter head, the key, the *Muse* . . . the last point in the Big Game.

"But they said . . . they said it had been melted down and used for corn on the cob."

"I know! I know!" Bob couldn't have looked any more like a golden retriever if he grew a tail and wagged it. He bounced up and down on the balls of his feet. "Jenn's mom saved it."

"Who is Jenn?" Fabulousa demanded.

"Jenn Lind," Bob said. "The model for the butter head. You might have heard of her?"

The three of them glanced at one another before shaking their heads in unison.

Bob looked a little offended. "That's okay." Clearly not. "She's like the Next Big Thing on cable."

Fabulousa laughed. "Cable? Are you selling your work on the QVC now, Steve?"

Verie's breath caught, even Bob paled, but Steve didn't care. The Butter Head. If he got the key inside it, he could retrieve the *Muse*. It had been stolen before the judge had divided their property. He could get it adjudged his and, even more important, not hers.

Verie was watching him, paralyzed in morbid fascination.

Fabulousa continued. "But you must go, darling boy! Just t'ink of the promotional possibilities! The Next Big Thing and the Last Big Thing. There is a certain . . . how is zis? Poetry? No. *Symmetry*. You always did love symmetry."

Her words had no meaning. He couldn't even hear her. All he could hear was her imagined shriek sometime in the near future when he would send her the cell phone picture of him holding *Muse in the House*. He turned to Bob. "Just tell me where and when, and I'll be there, Bob."

Bob's eyes popped wide. "Really?"

"I wouldn't miss it for the world." He shifted his gaze to Fabulousa, who was shivering with either silent laughter or fury at being ignored. It was hard to tell with Fabulousa. "Well, it's been great seeing you again after all these years, Fabulousa. Just great. What you're doing here for charity . . ." He waved his hand at the room which had begun filling back up. "Special. Really special."

Verie knew a cue when he heard it.

"Look, the Ackermans! They've been pestering me for months to introduce you." He pointed vaguely into the corner of the room, grabbed Steve's arm, and pulled him away, the ploy allowing Steve to shrug regretfully as he was forced into the arms of his adoring fans, muttering under his breath, "God, I hate that woman."

"I know," Verie said sympathetically.

He smiled. "But I love Minnesota."

Chapter Ten

"Well, now, you know," began Ken Holmberg, leaning back in his chair and knitting his fingers together over his little round belly, "I spoke to the Rapella people this afternoon, and they're pretty sure they're going to donate one of those new clamshell ice houses for the winner of the fishing contest."

Paul LeDuc, newly elected mayor of Fawn Creek, tipped back in his office chair. In actuality, he'd spoken to the Rapella people last week to secure their donation. Ken was blowing smoke and they both knew it. But Ken was one of those guys who had to lift his leg on every idea another guy had and take ownership of it, and because he was the biggest deal in Fawn Creek, people let him.

"Why, that's real good news, Ken." He guessed he probably shouldn't have gushed by adding "real." He knew better than to overdo the applause but sometimes he still made the outsider's mistake of using an adjective when none would do.

He'd have to watch his step if he wanted the continued support of the rest of the city council, and in Fawn Creek, town council and Ken Holmberg, owner of Minnesota Hockey Stix, were synonymous. The primary reasons Paul had been voted into office were because he was originally from Canada, and thus had a similar accent, and that he'd once played right wing for the Minnesota North Stars and thus had Ken's blessing. His most effective campaign promise had been that if elected he'd play in the men's senior league.

He'd yet to prove himself either on the ice or off. But he would. Ken and he had been the force behind the sesquicentennial, which they were going to use to introduce the rest of the state to the golden opportunities awaiting them here for investment, retirement, and recreation. Fawn Creek was at a crossroads—either people would have to commit themselves to pulling this town from the brink of extinction, or they would have to pull up stakes and let it fade into footnotedom. And among those leaving would be Ken and his hockey stick company.

Ken had been holding on for some time now, ever since the plant expansion he'd thought would bring new prosperity to his little company had failed to produce the anticipated profits. Rumors, coming direct through Paul's wife, Dottie, who was best friends with one of the officers' wives over at the bank, were that the company's pension wasn't fully funded, the money earmarked for the pension having been used to finance the expansion. It was only a rumor, but it was a rumor that had that pension around ninety thousand dollars shy of what it ought to have had. And while ninety thousand dollars didn't exactly put Minnesota Hockey Stix in dire straits, any further disappointments or financial troubles and Paul could see Ken saying, "To hell with it."

And that, everyone understood, would be the beginning of the end. With fifty-three full-time employees Minnesota Hockey Stix was the town's largest employer. If it went, the domino effect would just lay this town to waste.

Paul would hate that to happen. With a mere ten years of residency under his belt, Paul might still be a newcomer, but he loved this damn little town with the ardor that only a convert can bring. People took care of one another here. They had one another's backs. No one living in a city—of which Paul was secretly an alumnus—could ever really understand how important that was. Why, hell, where else would the mayor hire a bunch of stoned slackers? Because in small towns, you looked after one another.

"This Jaax guy is really coming all the way out from New York?" Ken asked.

"Absolutely." Another long hard look from Ken. The only thing a Minnesotan was sure of was death and . . . well, death.

"Everything is going"—Paul checked himself—"pretty good. Only thing I'm concerned about is that I haven't heard from Jenn Lind. You know she said no to us originally. I hope she don't change her mind again."

"Don't worry about Jenny," Ken said stolidly. "She loves this town. She owes this town. And she knows it. Comes back all the time to get away from whatever it is people like that want to get away from. She's probably out to her folks' place right now."

"The Lodge, right?" It was either one of the most exclusive B and Bs in the Midwest or the most unsuccessful, because Paul had never met anyone who'd ever stayed there.

"That's the place."

"Well, that makes me feel some better, then, Ken." In Minnesota there were no absolutes. One lived squarely in the center of the emotional spectrum, being some better and some worse, but never edging too far out in either direction.

"Good." They sat, staring off at a forty-five-degree angle from each other while Paul tried to think of some polite way to get rid of Ken. By Paul's estimate, in about ten minutes, Ken would start blowing hard about the great hockey career he never had because he was too busy building a financial empire. Paul was not in the mood.

"I got an idea," he said when inspiration finally dawned. "Let's drive up to the lake and check out that ice."

"It's okay by me," Ken said. "But why'dya want to?"

"Well, Butter Sinykin broke through by the spring there last year, didn't he?"

"So?" Ken's tone suggested Butter had gotten no better than he deserved. "That was April and Butter was hauling rip rock with his tractor. It's December and we're just gonna have a buncha folks sitting around on overturned pails, is all."

"Well, you can't be too careful." No phrase in the entire lexicon of secret code words known as Minnesotan was more calculated to draw a favorable response from a native than this, because, without a doubt, a guy could not be too careful.

Without another word, Ken shoved himself to his feet, following Paul out of the city hall into the parking lot, where Paul's GM half ton waited, the black umbilicus connecting its block heater to the electric socket lying on the ground like a frozen snake.

Paul waited while Ken climbed into the cab and looked around. It had started to snow again, and though night had fallen, the light reflecting off the new snow had turned the sky above to pewter. Around the overhead arc lights, the snow flakes swirled like gnats around a bug zapper, thick and anxious, while on the edge of the parking lot, the windbreak of pines whispered. Fawn Creek, which honesty compelled a guy to admit it wasn't all that comely most of the year, looked downright picturesque tonight—and more snow was promised.

Better than pretty, this year's unprecedented snowfall after three brown winters meant that the sound of snowmobiles, too long dormant, would once more be roaring through the winter landscape, bringing a smile to the face of every tourist-based operator in town. As well as bringing back the snowmobilers, the snow meant that the muzzle-loader deer season was bound to be a success, and that meant that this Sunday, when the sesquicentennial got under way with the opening fishing tournament, there would be Polaroids of trophy-sized bucks pinned to every corkboard in every diner and supermarket in town.

And if the tourists didn't want to snowmobile or hunt, there was the casino twenty miles to the north. They were holding their first annual all-amateur, dusk-to-dawn poker tournament this weekend, and that looked like it was going to be a big deal, too. The winner of the tournament was going to get a cash prize, aside from the pot, of one hundred thousand dollars.

Best of all, no catastrophes had hit the country all week and hopefully none would because that meant that coming into the holiday season as it was, the network reporters would be cruising the AP briefs for human interest stories, and with both Jenn Lind and this sculptor coming to town, Fawn Creek had one tasty story. Why, the NBC affiliate in

Minneapolis was doing a piece on them for the five o'clock news tonight.

"You going to get in or what?" Ken's muffled voice came from inside the truck.

Paul smiled. "You bet."

Chapter Eleven

5:20 p.m.
The Ramsey County Adult Detention Facility
Plymouth, Minnesota

The Ramsey County Adult Detention Facility had a crappy lounge with a crappier television watched by the crappiest bunch of sad-ass losers "Dunk" Dunkovich had ever had the misfortune to see. And Dunk, slouched in a leatherette armchair, had seen a lot.

They all stared up at the TV watching the local news, afraid that their panicked faces were going to be plastered across the metropolitan viewing area, revealing them as losers. Like it was a secret.

"Though not unexpected, few in key management positions are expected to retain their positions after Davies takes possession of the company," the news anchor guy was saying.

"I believe it. Davies is a complete prick," a forty-something guy with a Florida tan and a fifty-dollar haircut said. He claimed to be a consultant from Chicago here on a long-term project and that he got lonely and went to bars. Evidently, he got lonely a lot. Because this was his third DWI.

"How would you know?" another guy asked.

"I did a thing for his company a few years back. Had to report to old Dwight himself. He fired me the first time we met and all because I swore in front of his secretary. Shit"— he sneered—"all I said was 'shit.' The guy is a sanctimonious, tight-assed dog turd."

"And when we come back, a related story. A small town gets some big-name visitors."

Dunk's fellow detainees went back to babbling among themselves. Most were in for DWIs, a couple for failing to comply with restraining orders, and some, like Dunk, for violating the terms of their parole. Losers to a man.

Except for Dunk. He caught sight of his reflection in the darkened window overlooking the parking lot and smoothed back his hair. By God, he still had that "look," like he was the top salesman for some high-tech business, or maybe a junior college teacher. This latest trip to the workhouse was just bad luck. He'd be out of here in another fifteen hours and back in the game.

But what game? Grifting? Gaffing some Lotto tickets? Scamming high school hotties at the malls by signing them up for his "model agency?"

Small change. His looks weren't going to last forever. He was fifty years old and getting older and he didn't have a pension and lately that had started bothering him. He needed something big. Something to fund the Dunk Dunkovich Retirement Plan. What he needed was an IRA—

"—ALREADY KNOW THAT LOCAL CELEBRITY JENN LIND WILL BE STARRING IN THE NATIONALLY SYNDICATED COMFORTS OF HOME."

Someone had cranked the volume way up on the television. A ratty-looking kid popped up out of his seat and readjusted the volume on the set while the anchor guy flashed more teeth than a shark.

"Jenn launched her career at the Minnesota State Fair twenty-two years ago as a finalist in the Minnesota Dairy Farmer Federation's Buttercup pageant."

A dated yearbook picture of a good-looking blonde, who'd probably been the wet dream of every football player in her school, smiled down from the screen.

"Though the pageant is no longer held, recently the hundred-pound block of butter that had been carved into her likeness was discovered in her parents' barn. Evidently, Mom Hallesby had kept it in a freezer all these years."

An old photograph of a yellowish sculpture bearing a distinct resemblance to Jenn Lind appeared on the screen. Something about it sparked a memory. Dunk pushed himself higher up in his chair.

"Hey, Dunkovich, lean back! I can't see through you, man!"

"Shut up," Dunk muttered.

"The Guinness Book of World Records people are trying to determine if this is, in fact, the oldest surviving butter sculpture in existence," the anchor guy's disembodied voice informed them. *"But it's not its age that is attracting attention in New York. It's the man who chiseled it, internationally celebrated sculptor Steven Jaax, who's causing the stir. Jaax has agreed to appear with Miss Lind this weekend as co–grand marshal of Fawn Creek's sesquicentennial parade right alongside his butter sculpture!"*

The camera cut to a lean, affable-looking guy with unkempt salt-and-pepper hair. A crowd of reporters were shoving microphones in his face. Steve Jaax? Yeah. That was his name. Dunk leaned closer. The guy didn't look all that different from when he'd shared a cell with Dunk a couple decades ago.

"*Mr. Jaax, your last piece sold for nearly four hundred thousand dollars.*"

Dunk's jaw dropped.

"*What price would you put on the butter sculpture?*" The reporter was making a joke. Jaax didn't look like he got it. He gave an elaborate shrug.

"*I'm guessing it wouldn't come out too well in an actual appraisal. It's butter and it's old butter, so it's gotta have deteriorated, you know?*" he said. "*It has loads of sentimental value for the people who've kept it all these years. And Ms. Lind would probably say it's priceless because it is a bust of her. And, well, the mayor of Fawn Creek thinks a lot of it. He's named it co-grand marshal of the town's sesquicentennial. So who knows what someone might pay for it for the right reasons?*"

The reporter was nodding in a dazed fashion. Jaax, Dunk thought, was prone to oversharing.

"*You must have been pretty surprised to hear of its existence,*" the reporter said.

"*Man, I have never been more surprised in my life, not even when I found out my ex-wife, the ex-supermodel Fabulousa, was bi,*" Jaax said. "*Well, that wasn't really that big of a surprise, so I was actually more surprised about the butter head because I'd read that it had been melted down for pancakes or something. I was devastated.*"

He hadn't been devastated; he'd laughed his ass off. Dunk should know; he'd been watching the newscast carrying the story right alongside him. Jaax had been his cellmate.

It hadn't taken much prompting to get Jaax to tell Dunk the whole story and why not? The butter head and the key buried in it were gone, lost forever on a rural field trampled over by ten thousand people gorging themselves on corn on the cob. Jaax had spilled about his ex, the "seminal piece" he'd had stolen from her, the crypt, the key, and the fact that the only person besides his ex-wife who could get to the statue without using the key was dead. Then he'd laughed.

At the time Dunk had been skeptical about whether Jaax was as hot shit as he seemed to think he was. Well, Dunk thought, looking at the swarm of reporters, apparently Jaax hadn't underestimated himself. If the statue in that mausoleum vault was half as "important" as Jaax had claimed, it would be worth a pretty penny by now.

"Mr. Jaax," a reporter was saying, *"you have been quoted many times as saying that this butter sculpture was responsible for the renaissance of your career and gave you the inspiration for your resin-and-fiber optic pieces. You must be excited to see it again."*

Jaax grinned like a rat in a room full of cheese. *"Man, you have no idea."*

Dunk grinned, too.

Because he knew just what Jaax meant.

Chapter Twelve

"Look, Ned, the city isn't paying you to park that plow in Duddie's lot here and spend the afternoon drinking beer with your buddies."

Ned Soderberg, innocently sitting at the bar enjoying a beer with Eric Erickson and Jimmy Turvold, spun around at the sound of the mayor's voice. Paul LeDuc stood just inside the door to Portia's Tavern, dripping melting snow from his bomber cap ear wings onto the lapels of his black wool dress coat.

Now that Paul was mayor, he dressed like some TV lawyer, Ned thought, eyeing him sourly. How the hell had LeDuc gotten to be mayor, anyways? He wasn't an American and he wasn't all that great a hockey player, neither, and let's just say some folks weren't too thrilled they'd been sold *that* particular two-teated sow.

"Did you hear me, Ned?"

"Yup, Paul. I sure did." Ned nodded soberly, sliding off the bar stool and standing to attention. Apparently, old Paul had been driving by, seen the plows in the parking lot, and

decided it was his civic duty to spend a few minutes ream-
ing him and Jimmy Turvold a couple new ones. Asshole.

Hell, a guy couldn't be sure of getting a little peace and
quiet anywhere in this stupid town anymore. It wasn't like
he was gettin' paid squat for driving that plow, neither. He'd
like to see that Paul manhandle a two-ton plow down an icy
highway for eleven bucks an hour.

"Well, then, get your ass out there, Neddie. And that goes
for you, too, Jimmy." Paul's gaze shot to where Turv was
trying unsuccessfully to fade into the shadows. Eric, the
only one of them currently not employed by the city of Fawn
Creek, slurped his beer contentedly.

"And I want the sidewalk in front of the city hall shoveled
and salted before the offices open in the morning. Got that?"
Paul said.

"You bet, Mayor!" Ned snapped smartly, making a show
of zipping up his insulated coveralls. It was a tight fit and
the zipper protested the climb up and over Ned's impressive
keg gut.

Turv, too, hopped off his stool, squatted down, and began
snapping closed the metal buckles on his Snowpacs. He
looked up, smiling winningly. "Been at it all day, Mayor," he
puffed. "Since before sunrise. Just warming up is all. Saw
Ned driving down the southbound and—"

"I don't care, Turv," Paul broke in. "Just get back to work.
Both of you. Weatherman's calling for another four inches
by midnight." The door opened and a swirl of fresh snow
buffeted in against his exit.

"Stupid chinook," Turv muttered, climbing back up on
his stool.

"I'd like to tell LeDuc where to get off," Ned said, jerking the zipper on his coveralls down to his waist. Not that
he would act on the urge. Since his grandma had started

demanding payment for room and board, and his other income venues had been literally plowed under, he needed this
job. He wouldn't put it past the old biddy to kick him out if
he was late with the rent, neither. Hilda Soderberg was a
heartless woman. He woulda been glad to vacate, too. Maybe
move in with Eric, except . . . well, heartless she was but she
was also a damn good cook.

"Hey, Dudster, 'nother beer here, dear." Ned picked up
his Leinie's bottle and wiggled it suggestively at Duddie
who was polishing glasses on the other side of the bar and
staring at the television set suspended in the corner of the
room. Duddie probably hadn't even noticed the mayor and
his pal had been here. Duddie loved his television.

"Let's see the money, honey," Duddie said without bothering to look around.

There was no money and old Duds didn't extend credit.
Not since the well had gone dry. The dope well.

For the entire summer, Ned and Jimmy and Eric had
babysat a quarter acre of dope, hauling water by hand from
the Lake (a few yards from where they'd cleverly sown their
crop), carefully pruning each little plant, staking their little
stems, and making sure they were well-camouflaged from
the highway by a thick wall of tall weeds and grass. They'd
been only a few weeks from harvest when he and Turv had
gotten calls from the mayor telling them to drive the grader
and the front-end loader out to the Lake.

Ned had thought LeDuc was going to show them which
ditches to mow.

Instead, they got there to find LeDuc and the whole damn
city council waiting for them wearing stupid plastic construction site helmets, which they'd worn the whole shitty
day as they personally supervised the clearing of a new
parking area for the reams of tourists they were sure their

shitty sesquicentennial ice fishing tournament was going to bring in.

Ned took his last swig of beer, recalling the expression on Turv's face. He'd thought old Turv was going to die of a broken heart. He'd seen the tears tracking muddy courses down his sunburned cheeks when their vehicles had passed. He hadn't tried to hide his own tears, neither. There was no shame in it. The only shame was that all that excellent dope had been lost on account of some damn birthday party a bunch of assholes were throwing for a dead town, fer chrissakes!

And Eric and Turv and him? All their initiative, which even Ned conceded was little and rare enough not to be squandered nor taken for granted, gone in the span of one afternoon. Plowed under. Scraped clean.

Damn. He needed a beer.

He leaned back on his stool and reached around Turv, jabbing Eric in the shoulder. "Float me a couple bucks?"

"I'm broke," Eric said, curling his fingers around his own bottle and sliding it closer. Ned regarded him suspiciously. Eric had worked over at the Lodge yesterday and Mrs. Hallesby always paid as she went.

"I had to buy gas," Eric said defensively, reading Ned's mind.

"I'm tapped, too," Turv said before Ned could ask. "Wish we had some dope. Beer is expensive."

"Hey, look," Duddie announced to no one in particular. "They're talking about Fawn Creek. There's Jenny Hallesby."

"Lind. She's Jenn Lind, now, Duddie." Ned sneered. It always galled him that Duddie Olson, who had about as much personality as that old pet cow of his, should own a bar while he didn't. "She changed her name, oh, about a million years ago so she'd sound like she really comes from here."

Ned glanced up at the television just as Jenn's face disappeared and was replaced by a girl reporter drooling over some guy and babbling about how he'd revolutionized modern American art. Hell. It was that fruitcake artist they were shipping in from New York. Okay, maybe he didn't look like a fruitcake, but who could tell?

Ned swiveled his stool all the way around and settled his elbows on the sticky bar behind him. "Well, now, about this little dearth of dope problem," he said, liking the sound of the phrase. He'd heard it on an MTV reality show. "You can thank our asshole mayor for that, can't you?

"After all, he's the one made us grade over an entire damn field of the stuff for his sasquatchtennial." He yanked a fisted hand, thumb extended, toward the television set behind him.

"It's *sesquicentennial*," Duddie supplied helpfully.

"Yeah, fine, Duddie. The point is that while we work our asses off, for which we get paid crap and no thanks whatsoever, that guy up there on TV whittles butter and the whole goddamn state goes ape."

"I don't think—" Duddie began.

Ned cut him off. He'd had enough of Duddie's commentary. "And *Jenn Lind*? What's her big talent? Telling people how to fold their laundry!" The pure unfairness of it made him choke. "Why'd anyone want to fold laundry, anyways?"

"She cooks, too," Turv mused, sipping his beer.

"Who gives a fart? I cook. No one gives me a couple hundred thousand a year to do it. And sure as *hell* no one has asked me to lead their stupid parade. This town sucks."

"It does," Turv agreed. Eric nodded.

"Where would they be without me?" Ned asked, warming to his subject. "I'm the guy that keeps the Pamida lot clear so that the minute it hits the stores, they can all rush out and buy the latest Jenn Lind DVD telling them how to wipe their butts! I'm a whole helluva lot more important to this town than some laundry folder or a butter-sculpting fruit-cake from New York."

"Me, too," Turv said, his eyes riveted blissfully on some inner vision of himself heroically leading the assault on Pamida's snow-choked parking lot from the comfort of the front-end loader's CozyKab.

Turv's vision didn't bear comment. *Ned* was the head plower.

"I bet he wears an earring," Ned muttered, catching Eric's eye. "That sculptor."

"I wear an earring, Ned," Eric said reproachfully.

"Yeah, but you aren't near fifty. You're still a young man." Sort of. "Prime of life." If you were a tortoise. "This Jaax dude is an old geez."

Eric frowned, not entirely buying it. "Well, they haven't asked me to lead the parade either and I'm mosquito-control officer for the whole town. Can anyone here think what this place would be like if I didn't pellet the sloughs with Bug-B-Gone?"

Like that was as hard as using a plow. "Yeah, but that's only part-time."

"It's seasonal work. So's plowing."

"I mow the ditches, too. But whatever. Point I'm trying to make is that we get paid crap. We get treated like crap. They forced us to plow under an entire year's profit margin while they stood by and watched and *no one even paid us over-time.*"

"You have to work twenty hours in a week to make over-time," Duddie said.

"Who asked you, Duddie?" Ned spun around. "Don't you have a toilet bowl to scrub out or something?"

Instead of answering, Duddie bent down under the bar and rose with an iron rod in his hand. Humming, he pushed it through the levers of the three spigots that delivered beer —so no one could help himself—locked it in place, and headed for the john.

"What a dickhead," Eric said, hopeful until the last click that Duddie would leave the spigots unguarded.

"No. We're the dickheads," Ned said sourly. "We're staring at five months of winter here, boys, with no dope, no money, and no credit."

Above the bar, a dated image of Jenn Lind's head sculpted in butter reappeared on the television screen. She really had been hot. Even as butter.

"*—your last piece sold for nearly four hundred thousand dollars. What price would you put on the butter sculpture?*" the television guy was saying.

"*I'm guessing it wouldn't come out too well in an actual appraisal. It's butter and it's old butter, so it's gotta have deteriorated, you know?*" the artist said. "*But it has loads of sentimental value for the people who've kept it all these years. And Ms. Lind would probably say it's priceless because it is a bust of her. And, well, the mayor of Fawn Creek thinks a lot of it. He's named it co–grand marshal of the town's sesquicentennial. So who knows what someone might pay for it for the right reasons?*"

"Doesn't that just suck?" Turv grumbled. "No one'll pay us overtime but the mayor gets all goosey about some stupid butter head just because this Jaax guy whittled it."

An idea jumped out of the backwater of Ned's brain and flopped on the floor of his imagination like a landed northern on a dock. He slammed his palm down on the bar, making Eric's empty beer bottle jump.

"This town owes us. That damn mayor owes us. Well, I

say we get what's owed us and give the finger to the town while we do it! What d'ya say?"

Eric and Jimmy looked at each other. In unison, they shrugged. "Yeah, sure, Ned. You bet."

Chapter Thirteen

It was a beautiful night in the north woods. A soft snow had begun to fall and what could have been a monotonous silence was broken by the cheery vroom of a snowmobile.

Dunk was in a good mood. For once, the locals hadn't been full of crap. The snowmobile was easy to drive, the heated seat did keep his ass toasty, the heated handles did keep his fingers warm, the helmet did keep the snow off his face, and the trail he was following did lead straight across a big flat lake toward a tree-covered shore marked by some sort of windmill or something. The guy at the gas station hadn't been too clear on what it was, only on the fact that Dunk would know it when he saw it—and again, Dunk smiled at the wonder of it all—he had!

Another quarter mile, take the first turn right off the main path as soon as he left the lake, up a steep bank, then two hundred yards to the Hallesby barn, and hello, IRA. Or maybe a Keogh? He would probably be in a higher tax bracket by the time he started withdrawing, in which case it made sense to pay the taxes upfront. Then again, he was starting from a position of nothing here, and cash flow was important.

He was still weighing the advantages of the various financial instruments at his future disposal and climbing the trail up into the trees when the headlights of two snowmobiles appeared ahead of him, their beams aimed toward a structure tilting drunkenly in the dark. The Hallesby barn.

Which meant the snowmobilers were the Hallesbys—the current, but soon to be dispossessed, owners of the butter head. You might have guessed that old geezers in a nowhere town like this would get their yucks chasing around on snowmobiles in the dead of night. He eased way back on the throttle and considered his options.

He wasn't worried. He could always claim that he'd followed the wrong trail, gotten lost, and was seeking help. But hell, if he waited long enough, they'd just take off on their own. So he pulled off the trail and stopped, idling the engine. Then he switched off the headlights and pushed the visor up on his helmet and waited, the engine purring comfortably between his thighs. With the snow growing thicker, it was hard to see, but Dunk considered that all to the good; this way the Hallesbys couldn't see him either.

He could make out two figures heading into the barn, preceded by the weak beam of a flashlight. Someone else waited on one of the snowmobiles. A north woods threesome? He chuckled. Then his chuckles faded. If that *was* the case, they could be in there a while.

Dunk pulled off his chopper mitten, unzipped his snowmobile suit—also rented—and fumbled for a cigarette. Finding one, he cupped his hands around his Zippo light, sucked in a lungful of smoke, and peered through the peppering snow toward the barn. Visibility was going to hell. He could barely make out—bingo! There they were. The pair had reappeared sans flashlight, hunched over and lugging something between them.

He pitched the cigarette into the snow. He had a bad feeling. *Calm down,* he told himself. *Why would the Hallesbys take their own butter head on a joy ride in the middle of the night?* They wouldn't. Whatever they were carrying probably wasn't the butter head at all, but a salt lick, or a hay bale, or some other rube crap.

The pair hoisted whatever it was onto the back of the waiting driver's snowmobile and strapped it on. Dunk's bad feeling grew worse. He zipped up his snowmobile suit and shoved the snowmobile into gear, standing up in the seat to get a better look.

The duo finished their task, got on the empty snowmobile, and was now easing around so that the arc of their headlight would eventually sweep across the back of the other snowmobile and reveal— Holy Mother!

A huge, bilious face leered through the snow at him!

Dunk jerked back, releasing the snowmobile's throttle. The engine died. The face disappeared.

Face? That had been the butter head!

"Thieves!" Dunk shouted, slapping the visor down on his helmet and torquing the gas throttle. The snowmobile roared to life and bucked forward. For a second, he thought he was going to get dumped, but he hung on, hauling himself back onto the seat.

Crap! Who besides him and Jaax knew about the key buried in the butter head? Obviously someone. There was no other reason in the world anyone would steal that . . . thing.

Luckily, the trio ahead didn't realize he was following them, or if they did, they didn't realize he was not just following them but was after them, because they were diddling along and Dunk was drawing close fast. He charged up the slope, catching about three feet of air at the top before slamming back down on the trail with a bone-jarring thud and shooting forward. Bastards! Thieving bastards!

As he chased them, the butter head tipped and lurched in and out of his headlight beam, smiling maniacally at him through the thick pelter of swirling snow, like an unholy reject from the Magic Kingdom.

Behind the visor, he ground his teeth. It was not getting away from him. No way. A Jaax statue like the one in that crypt was worth a hundred fifty thousand dollars. That was what his pal who knew a guy who sold black-market art had said. Maybe more.

The gap between them closed to thirty yards . . . twenty . . . ten. The driver of the butter-head mobile casually raised his arm and waved him ahead. Dunk pushed his machine right up on his ass. The guy turned his helmeted head. Ahead of them the second snowmobile with its two passengers slowed.

Dunk rammed the visor up on his helmet. At once, the snow blinded him. He squinted and opened his mouth, shouting above the engine noise, "Pull over, asshole!"

The driver lifted a gloved hand and gave him the finger. Then, like the damn thing had afterburners or something, the snowmobile—along with the butter head—leapt ahead in a roar of power and exhaust fumes. The other snowmobile followed suit, speeding off and leaving Dunk far behind, cursing at the guy who'd rented him the broken-down piece of shit he straddled.

No. No way! He wasn't giving up!

Far ahead, he could see where the trail curved back down onto the lake. He could cut through the woods and down the slope, beating them to the shore. Then he would ram that son of a bitch! He didn't give a rat's ass if the butter head broke in a dozen pieces, as long as one of those pieces held a certain key.

He jerked the handles around, heading down the steep slope, crashing through the underbrush, the skis under the machine slipping and catching, then bouncing up and over. He leaned forward and clung fast, tearing down the bank toward the lake.

Piece of cake, he thought.

The snowmobile hit a hummock and took flight.

So did Dunk.

Chapter Fourteen

9:30 a.m.
December 8, Friday
Fawn Creek, Minnesota

"I've only been here a half an hour and I've already gotten a seventy-five-dollar traffic ticket for parking on a snow emergency route during a snow emergency. I am telling you, Nat, I am standing on Main Street looking around right now and I count three—no, four—people on it. How do they come up with the balls to declare a snow emergency in a town of less than three thousand people?"

Jenn held her new cell phone away from her ear and wondered if she could make the camera function function. A bank of teeny buttons etched in glowing neon blue symbols, like the eldritch ciphers on Frodo's ring, gleamed up at her. She decided she couldn't.

"So," she continued, returning the cell phone to her ear, "I move the rental car to the Food Faire parking lot, and as soon as I walk away, some jerk driving the city snowplow goes by and walls me in behind a three-foot pile of solid ice. Now I'm stuck waiting for the owner of the Food Faire to plow open the parking lot entrance."

"Tell me how cold you are," her agent and business

manager ignored her tale of vehicular woe and demanded with way too much glee. "Is it under zero? Does flesh really freeze in under thirty seconds?"

"Sure. Why do you think so many Scandinavian women have beautiful skin? Minnesota's answer to Botox." Before Nat could frame a reply, Jenn's voice dropped all disingenuousness. "No, none of my flesh is currently freezing. Mostly, because I dress appropriately. I have on a coat, a scarf, mittens. My feet are a little cold because my real boots are at my parents' place, but other than that, I'm fine. Sorry to disappoint."

"Are you kidding? I want you healthy, babe. I got a vested interest in your nose staying on your face," Nat said. "So if you're not going to regale me with stories of people freezing various pieces off, tell me what cool present you are going to bring me."

"Nothing," Jenn warned. "I left my checkbook at home, and all I have is an ATM card with a two-hundred-dollar daily limit on it, so once I pay the traffic ticket, I'll be strapped."

"You know if you would be an American and use plastic for purchases, you could get me something really nice," Nat said. "At least get a debit card with a higher cash advance."

It was a standard Nat comment and Jenn gave her the standard Jenn reply. "First, if you can't pay cash for it, you don't need it, and second, I don't need a bigger cash advance." She glanced longingly behind her at Smelka's Café. It wasn't the coffee she was longing for. It was Greta Smelka's kringle: a soft, flaky pastry, yellow with butter, studded with toasted almonds, glistening with a thick gooey layer of glaze. She looked down at her thighs and vacillated. "Should I lose some weight?"

In reply, Natalie's disembodied voice crackled, split, and fused together into incomprehensible syllables.

"What'd you say?" Jenn shook her cell phone, hoping to improve reception. She supposed she should count herself lucky she could make any contact with the outside world at all, even sporadically. "Natalie! What did you say?"

Across the street, a middle-aged man stomping the snow out of the treads in his boots outside of Hank's Hardware gave her a "hard look." Jenn knew that look. It was meant to undermine your confidence and make you feel guilty. Looks just like that had followed her around town her entire senior year after her ill-fated but highly flamboyant attempt to get divested of the Fawn Creek crown.

"Nat, are you there? I can barely hear you! Try again—"

Something came out of nowhere and jabbed Jenn from behind with the force of a striking cobra.

"Ouch!" Jenn jumped sideways, almost losing her footing.

She turned. No one was there. Her gaze dropped.

A tiny and ancient woman, in a heavy blue cloth coat and with an improbably bright red ski cap pulled down around her crinkled little face, peered up at Jenn from behind thick, gold-rimmed bifocals, her bony index finger occupying the space between them. Her unblinking eyes were the watery blue of old rinse water.

She looked like a garden troll.

Jenn didn't recognize her . . . or maybe she did. It was hard to say.

The old bird looked harmless enough. Still, it wasn't a hypothesis Jenn wanted to test. Just because a Scandinavian was tiny and antique didn't mean she wasn't dangerous. Witness her shoulder. She was going to have a bruise from that jab.

"Hold on there a minute, Natalie," Jenn said and lowered the phone. She regarded the old lady suspiciously. "Yeah?"

"Excuse me. You're Jenny Hallesby, aren't you?"

"Yeah," Jenn admitted slowly.

"That's what I thought. I'm sure you don't remember an old lady like me but I'm Hilda Soderberg. I was president of the lady's circle over to Good Shepherd when you were in high school. You used to hang around the basement kitchen on funeral days. Always t'ought that was kinda odd but you were an odd girl. Good cook, though."

Mrs. Soderberg? Her Mrs. Soderberg? The woman from whom she'd surreptitiously gleaned so many recipes? Recipes and tips she brought to thousands of viewers in the Midwest and would soon bring to millions more? Mrs. Soderberg, the Lefse Queen?

True, the old gal had never seemed to like her all that much but that hadn't stopped her from teaching Jenn how to cook. The last time they'd spoken had been Jenn's senior year of high school when Mrs. Soderberg had bitched her out for using a Brill-o pad on the Lutheran church's best krumkake iron after the traditional Christmas cookie baking extravaganza. Jenn hadn't seen her around town in years.

"Why, of course, I remember you, Mrs. Soderberg! How could I forget you?"

Mrs. Soderberg beamed, exposing a brilliant set of fake choppers. She was smaller than Jenn recalled. And older. Which was pretty impressive as she'd been old by any standards twenty years ago. Bless her withered little limbs.

"I didn't mean to bother you when you were on your phone," Mrs. Soderberg said.

"Oh, no. Don't apologize," Jenn said. "Wow. You were, like, my guru."

"Well," the little old lady said, coy and cute as an antique Kewpie doll, "I don't know that I know exactly what that means . . ."

"Can I do something for you?"

"You could if you wanted to," Mrs. Soderberg purred.

Jenn smiled. "What's that?"

"You can stop telling everyone those awful recipes you make on your show are the real t'ing!"

The physical jab hadn't been nearly so powerful. Jenn's head snapped back like she'd been struck. She'd been caught completely off guard. She should have known better. It wouldn't matter if one day the rest of the world fell at Jenn's feet. Even if that day ever came, Fawn Creek would still find fault with her. They always had.

"Swedish pancakes in ten minutes. Bah! *Stekare.*"

Jenn had a vague recollection that *stekare* meant something like "idiot" or maybe "imbecile." Mrs. Soderberg's hand rose, her index finger seeming to telescope away from her knuckles like—

"Ow!"

The troll had stabbed Jenn in the breastbone!

"Real Swedish pancakes take at least three days in a cool room to sponge proper and thin real good." *Jab.*

"OW!"

"That's what makes 'em smooth. Not some *enfaldig* electric blender."

Jenn thought she knew the translation for that word, too. She backed away, Mrs. Soderberg stalking her step for step, until Jenn banged into the snow-covered bus bench behind her. She rubbed her breastbone, eyeing the shrunken little troll resentfully.

"Well, that's great if you happen to have three days to wait, but most people don't," Jenn said, hoping Hilda here didn't miss the implication that people who *did* have three days to waste making perfect pancakes had a little too much time on their hands.

"If you go to the trouble of doing something—" The Finger came flying back up. Instinctively, Jenn caught the old biddy's wrist. Ha! Foiled!

"Ya might wanta do it *right*." The Other Finger came out of nowhere, delivering a round-house stab right to the sternum.

"*Damn* it."

"Nasty girl," Mrs. Soderberg muttered darkly and started to turn.

Jenn relaxed. The old termagant swiveled. Jenn jumped back, hit the bench with the back of her legs, and fell heavily, landing squarely on her ass in the center of the bench. The Finger hovered above her, poised like a rapier in the hand of a master fencer.

"I t'ought you woulda known better," Mrs. Soderberg declared. "Always t'ought you had more sense than a lot of them silly girls but I s'pose I shoulda known you'd come to dealin' in nonsense what with all them stunts you pulled in high school after you lost that pageant. Sour grapes was all them stunts was—that's what I always said. But *this* is just plain wrong."

Jenn barely heard her. Her eyes were fixed on the Finger.

"Now. You understand what I am saying about effort?"

"Yeah, yeah! I understand!" Jenn said.

"Good. There's no shortcuts fer quality." The troll

swung around and trudged off, the tassel on the back of her ski cap swinging jauntily.

"Your yulekage wasn't as good as Flo Larson's," Jenn muttered, rubbing her poor breast bone. She remembered the cell phone she still held and brought it to her ear. "Natalie?"

"Well, that took long enough," Nat's voice boomed, suddenly crystal clear.

"Sorry about that," Jenn said, watching with a mixture of unwilling admiration and unreality as Mrs. Soderberg made it to the end of the street and, of all things, clambered arthritically atop the shiny black Polaris snowmobile parked there, something big and lumpy strapped to the back in a monster burlap bag. Probably potatoes for lefse. Enough lefse to feed every damn celebrant who showed up for the sesquicentennial. With a few deft movements, Mrs. Soderberg fired the snowmobile up and glided smoothly out onto the poorly plowed road, her tassel flying.

"What?" Nat squeaked from the phone.

"I hate this town." Jenn stood up, brushing the snow from her butt and noting the size of the ass imprint in the snow on the bench. Nope. No kringle.

"Do you ever get tired of saying that?"

Jenn pondered. "Everyone has a raison d'être, Natalie. Tess had her D'Uberville. Felix the Cat had the Master Cylinder. It is our enemies who define us."

"Great, and you see yourself as having been defined by some poor dying little town. That's pathetic."

"I notice you're not here, doling out Mother Teresa–sized piles of compassion and encouragement—to either the town or me."

"I got stuff to do. Deals to make. You're not my only client, you know."

"Ha. You would have been here if my hometown had been Charlottetown. Or Santa Barbara."

"Damn straight. But it's not. Look, Jenn, if you really want some moral support—"

"That's sweet. But no," Jenn said, hurriedly cutting off Natalie's offer. She didn't need Nat witnessing any Mrs. Soderbergesque run-ins. Nat's poor little ticker wouldn't be able to handle it. You can only laugh so hard.

"I was going to suggest you get a dog," Natalie said. "Look. Call me if you need me. I got another call coming in, and you're just whining, anyway."

"Gee, thanks. Your support means so— Nat? Natalie!" The signal was gone.

Jenn clicked the phone shut, looked around, and found herself peering over the dingy café curtains that covered the lower half of Smelka's front window into the café. The five booths lining the wall were empty; the only occupants were two men sitting at the lunch counter. From the size of the hands cupping their coffee mugs, Jenn guessed they were farmers. Friends, too, she surmised from the fact that though they sat one stool apart and faced straight ahead, their lips were moving.

Small-town men avoided making eye contact during a casual conversation. Jenn had decided long ago that there was some sort of canine component to this, a convention that held eye contact to be unnecessarily aggressive. Besides, it was better to stare at nothing when you chatted. That way no one could be accused of "looking funny" when they heard something stupid.

Jenn could almost hear the kringle calling her name, but she resisted. She considered what to do next. Experience told her it would do no good to call the Food Faire owner up and try to hurry him along in plowing the parking lot entrance clear. So she brushed the snow off the bench and sat down to wait, looking around for changes since her last visit four months ago.

Nothing much.

Fawn Creek didn't look like an anachronism. The storefronts, at least those belonging to businesses still operating, didn't look any more like throwbacks to dime-store days than their suburban counterparts. The gas stations sold Lotto tickets, Food Faire did a steady business in prewashed bags of Dole salad (though heads of iceberg heads still sold best), and the lone video store boasted all the latest DVD releases.

True, a dusty Brylcreme poster still lurked in the back of Haarstad Drug's display window, and no one in a long succession of owners of Myerson's Department Store had ever replaced its pointy-breasted mannequins with their Jackie-O hairstyles with newer models, but these were small things. The men didn't *all* sport Elmer Fudd hats and none of the pickup trucks in town—and there were lots of pickup trucks in town—had gun racks tacked up in the back window. Sure, the few women on the street looked like they'd sewn seams up the sides of their favorite down comforters and poked their heads through the tops, but haute couture was hard to find in any arctic climate, especially during arctic periods. Even the women lawyers in Minneapolis, the fashionable young ones who still dreamed of warm and successful futures in L.A., wore down coats when they were forced to emerge onto the streets rather than take one of the ubiquitous skyway tubes that linked the entire downtown district in a construct bizarrely reminiscent of a giant gerbil city.

Not that there were any skyways in Fawn Creek. Hell,

there wasn't even a crosswalk. Nope. Fawn Creek was an anachronism because there was no reason for it to exist.

It should have died along with the family-farm dynasties and timber barons who had once fought over it. No dairy, no farming, no lumber, no soft industries were interested in investing here, and certainly no manufacturers had considered putting in a plant. The only place doing a profitable business was Ken Holmberg's hockey stick–making plant, and just how profitable was open to speculation. Yup, Fawn Creek was a town with a terminal case of obsolescence going through a cruelly protracted demise. Only the fact that it was the county seat, and thus law, justice, and the Medicare central, kept it from a quick and clean expiration.

That and, unaccountably, the fact that the people who'd stayed here had dug in and refused to leave.

Jenn could understand a guy wanting to stay. Especially a professional guy like Ken Holmberg. Fawn Creek was a middle-age, middle-class, professional guy's wet dream: huntin', fishin', drinkin', and if you were a "townie," twice-a-month dinner parties where you'd surreptitiously goose your best pal's wife before taking turns shooting squirrels from the back deck with the rest of the boys—a "sport" at which Ken held the title.

But what was here for any woman with two brain cells to rub together? Nothing. Yet Jenn couldn't condemn every woman in Fawn Creek as an idiot. Far from it. Which left only one reason for them to stay: fear.

They were afraid to leave, frozen by their apprehension of the unknown, unexplored world beyond.

Jenn could empathize. Fear, she understood. Fear of failure, fear that somehow everything she'd worked for could be snatched away, and fear that if she didn't make it big this time there would be no second chances. Because with every achievement, every penny accumulated, every success she notched on her belt, she came closer to the guarantee that no one could ever just walk in one day and—poof!—take what she had away.

The AMS gig was going to be that guarantee.

Okay, she might be a little ragged around the edges lately but who wouldn't be? For twenty years she'd worked eighteen-hour days, researched everyone with whom she'd come into contact (because Jenn did not take chances when it came to knowing what to expect and from what corner it would come), smiled and smiled some more, forgone any semblance of a home life (except for that brief foray into wedded bliss: nice guy, good in bed, a risk taker), and kept her eyes on the prize.

But, Lord, didn't she look forward to the day she could just . . . relax?

Not yet. She led a public life, one open to scrutiny anywhere, anytime. You wouldn't spot Jenn Lind wearing baggy sweats and a T-shirt. Jenn Lind's face would never be photographed naked and splotchy. No mike was going to pick up Jenn Lind muttering an unkind comment. She kept a smile like a vice cop kept his gun, unholstered and ready to be used to take down the enemy: suspicious media, an uncertain audience, a jaded critic.

And, yeah, it was tiring. Even exhausting. So what?

"Relax when you're dead," she muttered, stretching her legs out and idly noting the worn spot in the corduroy.

A trace of disquiet rose at the sight of this blemish on the Jenn Lind facade. Then she remembered where she was: Fawn Creek, where no one had any expectations of her, where old ladies tried poking holes in her sternum, where no one cared what she was because they *knew* who she was. No one but Jenn Hallesby. Certainly not the construct known as Jenn Lind. She could fool the rest of the world but she couldn't fool Fawn Creek. Not a one of them. So that hole in her corduroys? It didn't matter. Not here.

She spread her arms out along the back of the bench, tilted her head back against the brick wall . . .

And relaxed.

Chapter Fifteen

10:05 a.m.
Same place

A black Mercedes town car swerved on to Main Street, as out of place in Fawn Creek as a shark in a goldfish bowl. And like a shark, the black beauty fishtailed as it came, reeling violently from side to side as though hunting in the shoals of the snowbanks for some tasty Pontiac or Chevy to crash into.

As Jenn watched, the driver hit the brakes and the back end slammed into the snowbank on the other side of the street. It shuddered to a stop and the driver's door swung open. A guy got out, went around to the front, and climbed awkwardly over the snow onto the sidewalk in front of the hardware store, his back to her.

He was not from around here.

First, because rather than boots he wore beat-up deck shoes, and second, because he wore nothing more up top than a gray leather jacket unzipped and open, exposing a white shirt beneath. Oddly enough, in a land where everything was white—food, skin, attitudes—the one thing no self-respecting native would be caught dead in was a white shirt. Plaid, yes. Or a nice faded chambray if you were the "sensitive" type. And soft polar fleece pullovers had gained a staunch following in recent years, especially in a color that resembled dead grass, dead marsh, or something dead floating in dead marsh or dead grass. But the most telling confirmation of this guy's out-of-town status was that he was looking around and smiling like he'd just arrived in the Emerald City.

That would be the Olive Drab City, tin man, Jenn thought.

He hailed the same guy who'd given her the hard look and who was now leaving the hardware store. The stranger gestured animatedly, "animated gesturing" adding to the list of "tells" proclaiming his tourist status.

Fawn Creek males always dug their hands in their back pockets when forced to have a street-side conversation, never using the front pockets because, well, a guy didn't wanta accidentally bump into something in his pocket that he shouldn't. Sure enough, the Fawn Creekian rucked up his jacket and stuck his hands, palms out, in his back pockets.

The stranger should just carry a sign, Jenn thought with a small smile. *I Am Steve Jaax and I Am Not From Here.*

And it was Steve Jaax. There was no one else it could be. People from AMS, like the camera crew or production-value folk, would be traveling en masse. And there was no reason for anyone else to be here until the sesquicentennial started. Plus, there was just something about his posture, the way he moved, that awoke a sense of familiarity.

He turned as he spoke, so she finally got a good look at his face. It was unmistakably Steve Jaax's face.

She was impressed. The years hadn't been too hard on him. Oh, he still looked like an Irishman who got into bar fights, but he still looked capable of winning some of them, too. Wide shoulders, flat stomach, sinewy. His face hadn't fared quite as resiliently as his body. Mostly it looked like he'd weathered a lot. Pouches hung beneath the sad-dog eyes, and his skin looked brown. The dark, rumpled curls that had been a big part of his youthful black Irish good looks had been cropped and stuck out at noncoiffed angles. And it wasn't so dark anymore. Even from a distance.

The guy he was talking to jerked his head in Jenn's direction and Jaax looked around at her. A huge smile broke over his face, and her pulse skipped forward, reminding her of the hours she'd spent in a freezer with him. *Charisma.* Even from twenty yards and through twenty years, she could tell that hadn't changed.

He waved and scrambled over the snowbank, heading across the street toward her.

She wasn't sure she wanted him coming over to her. Here she was, resting easy, happily pondering her future retirement, and now he was going to come over and she was going to have to slip on the old Jenn Lind mask, which, while not precisely *un*comfortable, was definitely not as comfortable as what she was wearing now, which was nothing— Oh, to hell with it.

This was Fawn Creek. No cameras were rolling. Jaax would just have to take her as he found her. At least until the film crews arrived this weekend.

"Hi!" he called out, slipping his way toward her and climbing over the mound of snow on her side of the street. "Jenn, right? Hi."

"Hi."

He leaned over, hands on his knees, face only a few feet from hers—definitely way inside her Personal Comfort Zone—and studied her. She let him lean. He had remarkably bright blue eyes. She hadn't forgotten them, either. They sparkled like gemstones. Blue cubic zirconium. Probably contacts.

"Wow," he said. "You look exactly like I thought you'd look. The way your skin molds over your cheeks, the lips, the jawline . . . everything. Just like I thought you would age." He straightened.

"Age."

He shrugged. "Yeah. You know. Ripen. Mature. Grow older—"

"Yeah, yeah. I got it."

He frowned. "Except for the hair. I would have thought you'd let it go natural by now."

"It is natural."

His smile became a grin. "Sure."

An occasional partial foil did not constitute a dye job. She decided maybe he wasn't so charismatic after all. "Why are you here so early?"

"You know who I am?" His eyes widened in wonderment. "You remember me?"

This did make her smile. "Don't be coy."

The disingenuous expression disappeared, replaced by unrepentant pleasure at having been caught. "Okay," he said.

"You didn't answer my question."

He shrugged again. "I needed a break. A vacation. You know."

She didn't. Not since her honeymoon in 1997. It had been Jamaica. Or maybe that had been Cozumel? She'd had to work double time to get all her *Good Neighbors* segments taped for airing while she was away, and as a result, she'd slept the entire plane ride to wherever it was they'd gone and then, except for all the newlywed sex, most of the two days that composed the rest of her honeymoon. She remembered a beach outside the window, though . . . didn't she? Yeah, there'd definitely been a beach.

"And you thought Fawn Creek would be a good place to take it?" she asked doubtfully.

"Sure." He looked genuinely surprised by the question. "I loved my days in Minnesota. You don't know what a good thing you got here. No cell phones—"

"I hate to ruin the rural bliss thing, but cells are supposed to work here. Please note my use of the word 'supposed.'"

"Really? Damn."

"You can always hope yours fails."

"I don't have one."

"Then why—"

"Hi!" Steve chirruped brightly, looking past her.

Jenn turned her head. The pair of guys who'd been lunching in Smelka's had emerged from the diner.

They took one look at Steve grinning with maniacal goodwill in their direction, assumed he could not possibly be grinning at them, and spun about to look for whoever it was who warranted that sort of suspicious friendliness. When they discovered no one behind them, they turned back around in confusion.

Almost in unison, they realized that Steve was smiling at them. They blinked, took a halting step toward him, stuttered to a stop, looked at each other, looked at Steve, and by God, a few facial muscles on each seamed and leathery face twitched into something half resembling a smile. But before they could catch each other at it, they ducked their heads and hurried by.

"Shy." Steve spoke matter-of-factly. "I get that sometimes. They probably never thought they'd meet someone like me."

"Someone like you?"

"Yeah. You know. An internationally celebrated artist." He didn't look the least self-conscious. Not a whit of modesty clouded his absurdly blue eyes. "I'm practically an American icon."

Okay. She hated to pop the dirigible that was the Steve Jaax ego—"Mr. Jaax, let me do you a favor."

He tilted his head and for a second looked so much like her former neighbor's bloodhound when asked if he wanted a treat that she forgot what she'd been about to say. She'd always liked that dog.

"Call me Steve," he said encouragingly, that confident, winning smile still in place. So confident and guileless, that she was beginning to feel like a heel for the scrap of schaudenfreude she'd been experiencing just by thinking about telling him the facts of Fawn Creek celebrity. Oh, well.

"This isn't New York. Or London. Or Paris. This is Minnesota. *Northern* Minnesota. I don't know what you're expecting but I can pretty well guarantee you're not going to get it. Not here." She waited to see if any of this was sinking in. He was listening intently, again like the neighbor's dog when she used to give it really specific commands. Commands it didn't understand. "People up here don't do celebrity."

"Geez, Jenn." He glanced away, his expression distinctly embarrassed. "Look, I certainly am not up here looking for a little local hookup. I would never use my name—"

Heat exploded up her throat and into her cheeks. "That is not what I meant!"

"Oh?"

"I said people here don't do *celebrity*, not don't do *celebrities*!" Her tone was withering.

"Oh?" He puzzled over the distinction. The discomfort faded from his face. Connection made. "I see."

Not that he seemed embarrassed by his comment. Nah-uh. Instead, he simply drew his brows together in an expression Jenn immediately identified as "This is fascinating! Please. Tell me more," because it was exactly the same as an expression she used when speaking to Dwight Davies.

"Look," she said, and her voice was testy, "I'm only trying to keep you from making a fool out of yourself by expecting the people here to fawn all over you. I've been in and out of this town for twenty-three years now and no one has ever even asked me for my—"

"Can I have your autograph?" a breathless young voice gushed, as a herd of teenage girls, identifiable as such by the spray-paint fit of their jeans under the pink puffy baffles of their ski jackets, rushed past Jenn and surrounded Jaax. "You are Steve Jaax, right?"

"Yes," Steve said, smiling politely. "I am."

No. Not possible. Why would these little cupcakes give a rat's patootie about Steve Jaax? They wouldn't. They'd been watching the media hype from the cities and got caught up in it—that was all. But, a small hurt voice inside her whimpered, she'd been hyped, too. . . .

"Now you girls just let Mr. Jaax get settled before you start pestering him for autographs. And why aren't you girls in school, anyway?"

Jenn looked around. Ken Holmberg chugged down the street toward them, his portly body snugged into a black cashmere coat, ruddy face all smiles, the tip of his well-oiled comb-over flickering in the wind. At the sound of his voice, the girls broke and scattered like a covey of quail, dispersing down the side streets and along the sidewalks to regroup later.

"Mr. Jaax? It's a pleasure to meet you again." Ken stuck out his hand and shook Steve's. "Ken Holmberg. I was councilman of Fawn Creek back in eighty-four. Still am. As well as owner of the Minnesota Hockey Stix Company," he added importantly.

"Catchy name." Steve nodded.

"I was the guy in the freezer with you just after you finished the sculpture of Jenny—oh, hey, Jenn! Didn't see you there—when they, well, when they—"

"Arrested me," Jaax finished for him. "Oh, yeah. I remember. I was acquitted, you know. She couldn't prove anything. And I had an alibi."

Ken looked a little nonplussed by the turn of the conversation. "I didn't. But that's great."

"Yeah." Jaax nodded some more. "So . . . ah . . . where is it? My butter head."

The world had gone along quite nicely for twenty years without the butter head's presence, Jenn thought. It was too bad it couldn't just continue that way, but if it couldn't, Ken and even Steve sure as hell weren't going to appropriate it. "That would be my *parents'* butter head," she said.

Both men ignored her.

"Well, that's a good question, now, Steve," Ken was saying in his best "big dog" voice. "And I wish t'hell I could answer it for you. But the truth is, I can't. Someone busted into the Hallesbys' barn night before last and stole it. They were on snowmobiles."

"What?" Jenn asked.

"What?" Steve echoed even louder.

Ken's head dipped up and down, like a glum bobble-head doll. "Yup. We even got a witness. Some tourist was out on one of the trails that night and saw the thieves while they were at it. He took out after 'em cross-country, stupid bastard, but ended up going airborne over the Lake. Got himself busted up pretty good in the bargain. He's over t'the hospital in a body cast."

"But you're looking for it, right?" Jaax asked. "You have the cops looking for these thieves, right?"

"They don't have cops here," Jenn supplied helpfully. "They have a sheriff." Einer Hahn, on whom Jenn had once had a tiny crush in high school.

"Sheriff then!" Jaax looked a little wild-eyed. "The sheriff is searching for these guys, right? You've talked to this tourist, right? And you're investigating—"

Ken went from troubled bearer of bad news to compassionate comforter in a heartbeat. And they said Minnesotans lacked dramatic range. "We only have a sheriff and a deputy sheriff here, Mr. Jaax, and they're busy fellas already, what with the celebration and all. But you rest assured they're looking into it, all right."

"They're all off on the muzzle-loader opener, aren't they?" Jenn asked with sudden inspiration. They were deer hunting and Ken was covering. God! Fawn Creek could run amuck with aliens, and if it happened during December, no one would even report it lest it interfere with the muzzle-loader opener.

Ken gave her a sullen glance. "Maybe."

"What? What's a muzzle?" Steve asked.

"Nothing to do with nothing, Mr. Jaax," Ken said. "More'n likely this is just some prank. Teenagers. You know how they can be, Jenn." He speared her with a look. Point taken.

"Yeah," she agreed. She wasn't too worried he'd rat her out. Over the years, they'd developed a symbiotic relationship. Ken supported the myth that she was a hometown girl, and every now and then she said he made nice hockey sticks. At least his sticks were nice, which is more than she could say for him. Her parents called him "Babbitt of the Bog." He was a not so secret misogynist who masqueraded as

a paternal figure of goodwill. None of his employees, Jenn
knew, were women.

But he probably *was* right. Why would anyone steal a
butter head except as a joke? "Kids."

"You're not going to assume that, are you?" Jaax sounded
incredulous. "I mean, someone was robbed. This woman's"—
he gestured at Jenn—"this poor woman's elderly parents
have been violated! That's a felony offense."

"No one had a weapon, Mr. Jaax."

"That anyone *saw.* What about this tourist guy? Maybe
he knows something that could lead you to the criminals."

"He's a stranger in town, Mr. Jaax. Came up for that
poker tournament at the casino. Besides, it was dark and
there were flurries and everyone was wearing helmets. I
know this is a disappointment to you." Ken's gaze bounced
off Steve to Jenn. "Both of you. But it's bound to show up
sooner or later."

Steve's shoulders lifted and fell in a deep sigh.

"Look, Mr. Jaax," Ken said, "I hope this doesn't affect
your plans, but if you want to forget the whole thing and go
back to New York, I guess I'd understand."

"What about me?" Jenn asked. "Can I skedaddle, too,
Ken? Because without a butter head . . ."

"Ha-ha," Ken said, his eyes never leaving Steve. "Well,
Mr. Jaax, can I convince you it's still worth your while to
stay?"

Jaax stared at him. "Are you kidding? I'm not leaving.
I . . . I promised I'd be your grand marshal"—a quick glance
at Jenn—"co-marshal, and that's what I plan to do. If you
still want me . . . ?"

"Of course, we do! Dang right!" Ken pumped Jaax's
hand.

Steve smiled, withdrew his hand, hunched his shoulders, and shivered. "Geez, it's cold. What is it, thirty below?"

"Twenty above," Jenn said.

"Let me go get my hat," he said, taking off for the Mercedes tipped up on the opposite curb.

" 'Bout time you used your celebrity to bring a little attention to your hometown," Ken finally muttered, smiling, his eyes on Steve, who was struggling up the snow mound.

Jenn stared at him, sure she must have misheard him because Ken had neither a sense of humor nor irony, and in order for him to call Fawn Creek her hometown, you'd have to have one or the other. Or sarcasm. That must have been it; he was being sarcastic.

"It's not my hometown, and you and I both know it," she said through her teeth, smiling pleasantly at Steve, who was digging around in a duffel bag without much success.

Ken glanced at her, looking startled. "Okay. Maybe not. But your media pals don't know that, and I think we'd just as soon keep it that way, eh?"

We'd? He meant her. She was the one with a career built on a shaky foundation. Great, she'd been here an hour, and she was already getting veiled threats from the town Babbitt.

She didn't dignify his comment with an answer, waiting while Steve recrossed the street. He was bare-headed. He looked sheepish. "I didn't think of a hat. I know, stupid."

Ken clapped him on the shoulder, his snub nose bright red with the cold. "That's okay, Mr. Jaax. We got plenty of hats here," he said. "In the meantime, why don't you let me drive you over to the Valu-Inn?"

Steve, whose gaze kept shooting around the streets like

he expected to spy the thief trying to sneak the stolen sculpture past them under his coat, did a double-take.

"The motel? I'm not staying there. It was booked up. I'm staying at some place called—" He dug into his jacket pocket until he found a scrap of paper. He held it at arm's length and squinted. "The Lodge."

Chapter Sixteen

A soft, cool hand brushed his forehead and Dunk swam up out of a happy pool of morphine, eyes rolling back in his head. "Mommy?"

The light touch disappeared and Dunk opened his eyes to a moon-faced female floating a foot above him, a no-nonsense expression on her face as she tugged at the pillow behind his head.

Definitely not Mommy.

He'd been drifting in and out of consciousness more frequently today—they must have been cutting back on his drugs—and every time he'd been "in," she'd been in the room nursing about.

"So you're awake, then." It sounded as much like an accusation as a statement. Adroitly, she slipped the pillow further beneath his shoulders and added another behind his head. Then she smoothed the bedsheet over the body cast that wrapped him from his hips to his shoulders. "How are you feeling?"

"Awful," he mumbled.

"Well. You look better." She stood back. "Some."

"I'm not." He wanted to dive back into that nice pool of semiconsciousness, buoyed on a cushion of morphine.

"You broke a couple ribs and cracked your pelvis. You're just lucky that Polaris didn't land on your head."

"Polaris . . ." A memory floated sluggishly out of his clouded mind: snowflakes, trees, and the machine beneath him suddenly taking flight over a silvery lake far, far below as far, far ahead of him the butter head—*the butter head*! Those bastards had stolen his butter head!

He jolted upright. *"DAMN, THAT HURTS!"*

The nurse pushed him flat. "Yeah, I betcha it does. Poppin' up like that. Lie still." She began sponging off the sweat popping out over his forehead.

"The butter sculpture," he gasped. "Where is it?"

Her mouth pursed up. "Fool thing's gone. Least I haven't heard anything about anyone finding it."

He whimpered. He couldn't help himself. He had to get his hands on that butter head before Jaax did. As soon as Jaax dug the key out of it, all Dunk's newly hatched hopes for financial security vanished.

"Now, then, I gotta say how it was real decent of you to try and stop those good-for-nothings from stealing that sculpture." A tiny ember of . . . something warmed her brown eyes. "Not sure it was worth getting all busted up for, but it's the principle of a thing that counts, I always say, and you got principles."

First he'd ever heard of it.

"But you can't let some fool butter head sculpture upset you. You need to rest."

She thought he was some sort of *hero*, Dunk realized in amazement. Well, this was new. Maybe useful. At least he was thinking clearly now, pain having a tendency to focus his thoughts.

"You can imagine," he said, gazing up at her with somber eyes, "that I'd hate to think I ended up here all busted up for nothing. I'd really like to see that the—butter head, you say it is?—butter head gets returned to its rightful owners."

She regarded him approvingly.

"Principles being principles," he added. "You'll let me know if you hear something, won't you? It would make me feel better."

"You bet, Mr. Dunkovich." She gave a curt nod. "Now I expect you'd like to call your family? We didn't find any emergency number in your wallet, so we couldn't notify anyone. But if you don't feel up to making the call, I can do it for you."

He liked her accent. It was all soft and round and comfortable. Like her ass in those baby blue drawstring pants . . . Geezus, he must be higher than he realized because not only had the pain disappeared—well, not disappeared, exactly; it was there, just cruising beneath the radar—but because as a rule he liked his women younger, thinner, and a whole lot more exciting than this solid-looking woman with her inexpressive face and Clairol brown hair showing a bit of gray at the roots. She had really nice skin, though. Peaches and cream.

"I don't have any family," he said.

"Oh." The corners of her mouth twitched once before going dormant again. "Can I get you anyt'ing else, then?"

"Nah." He had some hard thinking to do.

"How 'bout a sponge bath?"

"Maybe later."

"Should I turn on the television maybe?"

"Sure."

She found the universal remote on the tray next to his bed and clicked on the TV set suspended on the wall opposite him. "What do you like?"

"Whatever." His thoughts had started moving again. How the hell was he going to get that damn sculpture before Jaax showed up in town? He had to be coming any day. How was he going to get that damn sculpture at all, come to think of it?

Even if he could figure out who'd taken it, what could he do about it? He wasn't even mobile. He needed an accomplice.

He glanced at the nurse still fussing around the room. No way. Not Miss "Principles are Principles."

As Dunk watched, she suddenly looked up at the television set. Dunk followed her gaze to where Jenn Lind's Midwest Madonna face glowed with warmth and decency from the picture tube.

"—Minnesota's quintessential hostess, Jenn Lind, is taking some well-deserved time off before moving to New York to begin her duties as hostess of *Comforts of Home*. She'll be helping her hometown of Fawn Creek celebrate their sesquicentennial by acting as their grand marshal. Now *that's* 'Minnesota Nice.' "

His ministering angel snorted. It wasn't a little snort, either, and her face wore a "tell me another" expression.

"What's up?" he asked.

"Nuthin'."

"No, really. Why'd you sound like that?"

"I just laugh every time someone holds Jenn Hallesby up as this ideal woman."

"You know her?" Hm. A little small-town rivalry?

She nodded, still looking a little smug, a great deal superior, and far too close-lipped. "We were in the same senior class in high school."

Dunk would have pegged Jenn Lind as being at least five years younger than his nurse. "She's not the ideal woman?" he asked, only mildly engaged. What did little Jenny do, a few members of the football team? Big deal.

"Depends on your definition of ideal," she said, then added tellingly, "or woman."

Now *this* sounded interesting.

"Huh. Well, well, well," he said, recalling what the guy in the Ramsey Workhouse had said about Jenn's soon-to-be employer, Dwight Davies, and his absolute brand of morality. There might be something useful here.

"Not that I'd say anything bad about her. She was just a kid. We were all just kids." She blushed.

His nurse had clearly convinced herself that whatever bit of dirt she had on Jenn Lind couldn't be used for malicious purposes. And from that blush, it looked like maybe because Jenn had something on her, too. But then, who didn't like to gossip a little—especially about celebrities? Especially about celebrities you actually knew. Gave a girl a little cachet.

He gave her his best confiding smile. "Interesting, isn't it? There's what the general public thinks it knows, what the media are sure they know, and then there's what people who really know know." He shook his head. "And when it all comes down to it, most of the things we are so worried about other people finding out don't make any difference to anyone anyway."

"Well," she said gruffly, " 'course, it don't matter to me. But not everyone's so open-minded."

More intriguing by the minute. "You know, maybe I'll have that sponge bath after all, Miss—" He gave her his best insurance salesman smile. "Heck. I don't even know your name."

"Ekkelstahl," she said. "Karin Ekkelstahl."

Chapter Seventeen

10:40 a.m.
Back on Main Street
Fawn Creek, Minnesota

"Thanks for the ride," Steve said, tossing his battered duffel bag into the back seat of her Subaru. The Food Faire owner had arrived a short while ago and pushed open a passage through the snow blocking the parking lot entrance, releasing her car from captivity.

"No problem. Climb in," she said. His face was ruddy with cold, and though he hadn't complained, his feet in those cloth shoes must have been aching with cold. Jenn, slipping in behind the steering wheel, turned the engine over and flipped on the floor heaters full blast.

Since Steve's rental car's axle had been whacked out of alignment when he'd driven it over the curb and consequently he was without a ride, it only made sense that she should offer him one, especially since they had the same destination. Besides, she wanted to see his face when he got an eyeful of "Minnesota's most unique and historic north woods bed-and-breakfast experience." Even odds she'd end up driving him the twenty miles to the reservation hotel and she didn't want to make that drive at night.

She was feeling a lot more kindhearted toward the world in general since finding out the butter head was gone. At least now she wouldn't have to listen to people comparing Old Current Jenn with Young Butter Head Jenn. Besides, she was honest enough with herself to admit that she'd been crushing on Steve Jaax for twenty-some years and she wanted to see if time had diminished his charms. So far, nope.

Steve got in and at once slipped his feet out of his deck shoes and wiggled his stocking-covered toes in the blast of warm air. He beamed at her. "Look at that snow. There's got to be a couple feet out there, right? And that guy . . . Ken? He said we're expecting some 'weather', like that meant something dire, and when I asked him about it, he admitted more snow was being predicted and that we might even end up being cut off from civilization. Which is completely cool. This is so wilderness. You must love it here."

Her head snapped around to see if he was kidding. He wasn't. He was staring out at the streets like a kid looking at the Christmas display windows on Madison Avenue.

She'd replayed the hours in the State Fair Dairy Federation freezer so many times in her head, it had never occurred to her that something so important to her could be insignificant to someone else. Which was what ego was all about, she supposed. But those hours had been a turning point not only in her life but in Steve Jaax's life, too. Or so he'd claimed. It was part of the Jaax-verse—the Descent into Post-Fabulousa Hell and the Return with the Butter Prize.

"Love it?" she asked. "Were you listening to *anything* I said in that freezer?"

He looked over at her, still all smiles. "You're kidding, right? Of course not."

She felt her jaw loosen at the corners. The crush lost some of its patina.

"Hey, don't look at me like that," he said. "I was in a really bad place, having just come from a worse place. I was possibly a little tanked, and let's be honest here, you were a high school girl complaining about high school. Hey. *That's* gotta be a first."

Her brows lowered in a frown as she pulled out of the Food Faire parking lot and headed down the main street.

"Come on," he continued reasonably. "If you'd been stuck in that freezer with some high school jock whining about how the football coach didn't put him on the A squad, would you have remembered the particulars of the conversation twenty years later?"

It was the reasonable part she disliked the most. That and the fact that even though what he said was insulting, or maybe mortifying, he still managed to be inexplicably charming saying it. He was so artless. He wasn't condemning her whining. He was simply stating a fact.

At the same time, she didn't doubt for a second that if she'd trumped the false modesty of his earlier remark, "You remember me!" by pretending she hadn't, he would have been shocked. Not that she hadn't remembered him, but that she would have lied about it. Because he simply wouldn't have believed *she* could have forgotten him. After all, who could forget having met Steve Jaax? It didn't matter that he would have been right. It was still irritating.

"Well," she said, trying to sound as casual as him, "I told you that I didn't like this town and this town didn't like me. So, no, I don't love it here."

"Oh, yeah. The Great Buttercup Betrayal. See?" he said, clearly pleased with himself. "I do remember some things."

"Wow. I'm flattered." He made it sound silly. It hadn't

been silly. It had hurt and they had betrayed her and it had taken a long time to get over it. Like, maybe, never.

"Look, Jenn—I can call you Jenn, right?—look, Jenn, I had my thing going on. I thought I was about to fall off the end of the world and never be heard from again. Creative-wise, I felt done. But then you started talking and I finally started really looking at you. Seeing you. You took my breath away."

Okay, this was more like it.

"But not in any creepy pedophile sort of way," he explained. "You were just a kid."

She thought Jaax might have protested too much. She hadn't been that much of a kid. And she definitely had been good-looking, and from the few and far between society bits about Jaax's love life that landed in Flyover Land, he appeared to like young women. Stunning young women.

But then she looked at his face and realized that self-delusion was one character flaw he didn't own. He hadn't been attracted to her like that.

"Anyway, I started to get into it, really into it," he said, "for the first time in a couple years. I was trying to figure out some way to visually articulate who you were at that second, that instant, and there was the butter and the light coming in on it and I saw it. Not only your face but a whole body of work, form borrowed from dusk, movement revealed through a quixotic combination of light absorbed and refracted."

His voice had gone deep and vibrant and Jenn remembered what Bob Reynolds had said about Jaax being damn near poetic when it came to his art. Bob was right. Little goose bumps were lifting on her skin—

"So," he said, abruptly coming out of tortured artist mode

and slapping his thigh, "you say you don't love the town. How come?"

The abrupt transition made her head spin.

"It seems like a real nice town," he said. "The people have been friendly and accommodating. Everyone has a smile. So what's your problem?"

Problem? She had a problem? Fine, she'd lay it out straight. "It's an incestuous little burg, like a lot of little isolated towns. Gossipy, with a chip as big as Lake Superior on its collective shoulder, smug, morally superior, adulterous. . . ."

She glanced over at him. He was frowning at her in perplexity.

"I hate to point this out, but for someone who's supposed to be the Next Big Thing in Charming Lifestyle Hostesses, you're kinda light on the 'charm,' aren't you?" he asked.

"I'm a lot more charming when I'm not up here. This town tends to bring out the worst in me," she said, perversely pleased he'd called her the Next Big Thing. If Steve Jaax had heard of her, her little star must really be on the rise. "Besides, you asked. I'm just telling you the truth. Small towns pretty much suck."

"So why do you hate this town?"

He still wasn't listening. She'd just explained. And she didn't *hate* Fawn Creek. . . . Oh, sure, she said as much to Nat all the time but that was just reflex. Her feelings toward Fawn Creek were perhaps a little bitter from the experience of having lived here, but for the most part impartial and objective. Fawn Creek had its good points, foremost being they understood a good thing when they had it, and second most, they knew when to be uncommunicative. Of course, that was as much a matter of genetics as discretion. . . .

"It's not like I have a personal relationship with this town, Steve. I never did. Another point you might not recall from the conversation in the freezer is that I only lived here a couple years. As soon as I could, I bolted. But in the public's mind, Fawn Creek is my hometown, and since that fits in a lot better with my image as Martha of the Midwest and it lends Fawn Creek a little reflected glory, we both go with it. But we both know the truth."

"And that is?" he asked curiously. Jenn had to admit, Steve knew how to listen.

"I'm not one of them."

"So if you're not one of them and they don't think of you as one of them, why are you their grand marshal?"

"You're being coy again."

"No," he denied. "I'm not."

"Okay. For their part, whether or not I'm a native daughter, I draw crowds. So they're willing to go along with the charade, hoping that the crowds include some entrepreneur looking to invest in a dying town a hundred miles from nowhere.

"For my part, it's called making my new bosses happy. I have a new show coming out on a new network and the people that decide things there decided this would be good for my image.

"You must've heard of Dwight Davies and his new cable network, American Media Services? That's who I work for and, yeah, I know," she said, catching his eye as they came up to the stop sign that marked the literal edge of town. "He's not the most tolerant man in the world but—"

"I'd quit," Steve said. "I wouldn't work for him. A few years ago, he fired an entire department in a company he purchased because the women had posed nude for a calendar, even though the proceeds were donated to breast cancer research."

She'd been about to pull away from the stop sign but instead she rotated in her seat. "That's not true."

"Yes, it is."

"How do you know?"

"I hear things. I'm connected." He pointed out the front of the car. "Shouldn't we get going? I mean we're just stopped here."

"So what? It's not like we're causing a traffic jam. And if Davies had done that, he'd be sued a thousand times over," she protested.

"He's an asshole, not an idiot. There's ways around these things," he said. "Davies is the worst kind of bigot, the kind that masks his bigotry under a mantle of concern. He's the kind who convinces people that it's their duty not to tolerate the things he dislikes for the good of their children, their neighborhood, their community, or their country."

He was right. Davies was exactly that sort of bigot but she couldn't see him firing a bunch of women who'd flashed their breasts in the name of cancer research. "Well, I don't believe it. About the calendar," she said, aware she sounded touchy.

"No one looks at the devil while they're sitting at his dining table." He didn't so much say this as intone it.

"What's that supposed to mean?"

"I made it up. Just now. Good, huh?"

A stripped-down tan Dodge pickup traveling toward them from the opposite direction slowed as it passed. The middle-aged woman behind the wheel cranked down her window. "Okay, then?" she called out.

It was Leona Unger. Jenn opened her own window and the cold air rushed in. "Fine, Mrs. Unger, thanks."

"That Jenny Hallesby? Up early, eh? Say hi to your folks for—say." Leona Unger's head, well insulated by what Jenn suspected was one of her son's fur caps, poked out the window. "Is that Steve Jaax there next to you? Well! This is a pleasure, Mr. Jaax. A real pleasure."

Steve leaned forward over Jenn's lap, ducking his head down so he could see Mrs. Unger. "Thank you. Likewise, Miss—"

"Leona Unger." She was blushing like a schoolgirl and Steve had all but crawled over Jenn in order to suck up a little more adoration.

Jenn stuck an elbow in his chest. "Down, boy."

"I saw your picture in the *Crier,*" Leona was saying. "So I went online and Googled your work. It was somet'ink. I t'ink I like *Lantern Dance* best, though."

"Really?" Steve asked, settling in to the conversation like it was going to last. It wasn't. "Why is that?"

Leona's face screwed up in thought. Fawn Creekians did not give social answers when questioned. "Way it moves and expands out, like an osprey opening its wings—sorta disturbing you, ya know?" He nodded. "And the way you used—oops."

Thank God, another car had shown up and slid to a halt behind Mrs. Unger. In the summer, Mrs. Unger would have waved the Ford around her and no one would have thought twice about it. But the banks of snow pushed up by the plow made it impossible to move around her. "Best go," Mrs. Unger said. "Nice to meet you, Mr. Jaax. Real pleasure. We don't get celebrities up here."

Steve met Jenn's cold look and gingerly eased back into his own seat as Leona took off. "I'm sure she meant 'artists.' "

"No, she didn't."

"You married?" His question came out of nowhere.

"Nope."

"Ever been?"

"Once." She provided the classic answers to the questions no one was ever rude enough to ask. "It didn't last too long. We were young, and it didn't take."

"Bull," Steve announced calmly. "Someone screwed it up. Whose fault was it?"

"No one's."

"Bull."

She glanced at him. He looked perfectly composed, absolutely confident. "There has to be a fault?"

"Always," he said. "For example, I've been married three times. The last two times the breakups were completely my fault."

"That's a lot of divorces, Steve. You don't look too torn up about them." But then, she hadn't been torn up either. Maybe she and Steve shared a similar inability for lasting romantic love. Not that her love life had ever been all that romantic. Sex had been nice, though.

She missed sex.

She'd decided soon after her divorce that serious romantic entanglements only complicated her ability to focus on her goals, and hookups, as well as being personally unappealing, could be anathema for a career like hers, one based on a wholesome image.

Oh, she dated. Once or twice per guy but nothing serious. Not "sex serious." Consequently, her sex life had never been what you'd call "great," more like "barely adequate." Then, when Dwight Davies's people had started looking at her a few years ago, she'd cut herself off completely.

Still, she really did miss sex, even though she knew it wasn't safe in more ways than she could count.

"I'm not," Steve was saying. "If I was going to be torn up about it, I wouldn't have screwed it up, would I?"

"Is everything simple in your world?" That would be nice.

"Things are simple in everyone's world, Jenn. People complicate them to make themselves feel better. I was a dick. My wives divorced me. They were right to divorce me. *I* would have divorced me."

"Did you know you were going to be a dick when you got married?" she asked, curious in spite of herself.

"No!" He looked offended.

"But you guessed," she said slyly.

"Maybe."

"So why did you get married?"

"I wanted kids. A home." His eyes were straight ahead and his bloodhoundy face looked melancholy but with a familiar sadness, like he'd gotten used to it a long time ago. Like a chronic cough or arthritis.

"Do you have any kids?" she asked gently.

"No." He smiled without looking at her, eyes straight ahead. "I said I wanted a home with kids, not to make a bunch of broken homes with kids. How 'bout you? Any little princesses around?"

"No."

"Never found Mr. Right Genes?"

"Never found the time. Never even had the time to think about when would be a good time." Then she added softly, "Now I suppose the time's passed."

How could that have happened? How could she be forty and still feel like she was just starting out, that there was so much more to be done, accomplished, tied up, before she turned her attention to other matters?

She couldn't remember a time she hadn't put things on the back burner and focused on the future and making sure it was secure before she started populating it with things like a dog and a garden and writing that book on Scandinavian cookery and learning how to relax. And thinking about kids.

"You could still get knocked up."

"Not me. I'm too careful." And too celibate. Not that she was going to tell him that. This little Subaru Confession episode was only going so far. "You could knock someone up," she suggested.

"Not me. I'm too careful, too."

It was a glib answer and she shot him a quick glance. Could he be celibate, too? Nah. He was Steve Jaax, fer chrissakes. The sperm banks would probably pay him tons for the results of ten minutes with a *Maxim* magazine.

Chapter Eighteen

They drove in companionable silence, Steve distracting himself from worrying about his butter head by peering out of the window at the view. He'd considered asking Jenn for a little more reassurance—she had a calm, dispassionate way of stating things that made them seem not only probable but inevitable—but the fact that she'd corrected his unintended, but in no way untrue, comment about the sculpture being "his" made him think this might not be wise.

He didn't want to set off any warning bells.

So, instead, he focused on the scenery. It was great. Who would have guessed white could present so many aspects, so many colors and forms and dimension? Hard, knife sharp, and crystalline, bruised and sullen, pebbled and crunchy, feather soft and ethereal. Salt shakered, cloud whipped, clotted and stretched, thin and dense. And that was just the snow!

His breath had fogged up the window and he scrubbed it away with his sleeve. He wasn't going to miss any of it. It gave him ideas. And ideas, as any artist pushing fifty will tell you, are nothing to sneeze at.

At least, he hoped that was what they'd say.

A dearth of ideas wasn't exactly the sort of thing you chatted about over a bottle of beer. It might lead to unpleasant speculation about, say, burnout. And over-the-hillness. And ends of roads.

He snapped his thoughts back from their current direction and focused on the trip rather than the destination. He was an expert at that.

The road carved through patches of trees and open ground, following a gentle kiddies-ride roller-coaster path until they turned into some kind of pine forest. Whatever type of pine tree they were Steve wanted one. Or at least to find where they might grow in New York.

They stood crowded together, dark empresses frozen by the Medusa face of the Northern Lights, their branches entangled, their heads caught close together in whispers overhead, a carpet of darkness at their feet, mauve-skinned with beryl needles. God, that was poetic.

He should tell Jenn.

He looked over at her. He thought maybe she was humming. Her head was subtly, but definitely, moving from side to side in time to some inner tune. He wondered what sort of music she listened to. She looked too perfect to like flamenco guitar—his current favorite music. Flamenco lovers were inevitably messy people and there wasn't a hair out of place on that smoothly groomed head.

She had on some sort of faux-fur coat, from under which peeked the hems of light brown corduroys and from beneath these the pointy tips of black Italian cowboy boots. Oversized lilac-framed sunglasses covered her eyes and she'd covered her honey-colored hair with a sable-colored silk scarf, à la Audrey Hepburn. Her skin was smooth and ivory like thick vellum. She looked expensive, sexy, and out of place. But she also looked warm. In a bunch of ways. He liked her. And he could tell that she liked him, too.

But she didn't want anything from him and she didn't think he wanted anything from her, either. Which was not his usual experience. Women generally thought he was sort of a lech.

He wasn't.

He liked her hands, too. Because they weren't encased in leather like the rest of her outfit suggested they ought to be. She wore mittens. Goofy white-and-red mittens knit in some sort of Scandinavian design with hearts and stylized deer. They were unexpected. What else about Ms. Lind here would surprise and delight him? He suspected a lot. She might be a lot like the view: not so much cold as bracing, challenging, something you could experience only if you were willing to risk some discomfort.

"Could you ever get tired of a view like this?" he said, deciding to draw her out.

"Yup," she answered without a glance. "Give it five months."

"Ah, come on." He gestured outside the car. "Just look at it. The snow, the sky, the trees, the— My God! Look! A wolf!"

He reached across her, pointing out her window at the huge gray wolf standing by the roadside. It was big and brawny-looking, ticked in gray and black, its enormous head lowered between its shoulder blades, its big ears flickering back and forth like bug antennae.

Jenn glanced casually out the window, did a double-take, and slammed on the brakes. "Geez!"

She must have a camera somewhere, thought Steve, as she half dove over the backseat and began rummaging around. He hoped so. Verie would not believe this.

Only a few feet away, the wolf's head dipped even lower. Its lips curled back. The huge plumed tail began a slow, measured wag, as if to say, "Okay, baby. Bring it on."

"Crap," she muttered.

"Forget it," Steve said, besotted by the beast. "But can we stay until—"

Jenn kicked open her door and tramped toward the wolf.

"Christ!" Steve yelped, eyeing Jenn's open door. "Get back here!"

In answer, she grabbed the wolf by the scruff of the neck with one hand, opened the back passenger door with the other, and shoved it into the backseat of the car.

"Shit!" Steve scrambled off his seat and twisted around, knees on the floor, back jammed against the dashboard. He groped for his door handle, eyes on the big canine face peering back at him from between the front bucket seats.

"Stay!" Jenn commanded.

"Forget it!"

"Not you. The dog. Stay, you big baby!" She slammed the back door shut.

Dog? Steve stared at the great fur face. The huge jaws opened and a pink party-favor tongue rolled out, lolling happily. Tentatively, Steve slid back onto his seat, half turning to keep an eye on the thing. If it was a dog, it was the biggest damn dog he'd ever seen.

The driver door opened, Jenn got in, and the creature went ape shit, jumping up and down on the backseat, wiggling and whimpering and nipping at the back of Jenn's head in an ecstasy of delight. Jenn's reaction to this excess of canine affection was to snatch off her mittens and start whacking at the wolf—dog's—head with them, alternately cursing and giggling.

"What's it doing?"

"Not it. He. He's an idiot. You saw him out there. He was trying to act butch because he was afraid. But now that he's realized he knows me, he's lost it. The fool!" She swatted the monster dog again. Not that he seemed to take offense. He suddenly turned his face and gave Steve's a happy swipe with its—his—tongue.

"He knows you? You know him?"

"I wouldn't grab a malamute I didn't know, Steve," she said reproachfully. "That would be stupid. This is one of Heidi Olmsted's sled dogs, Bruno," she said, shifting the car into gear. "Heidi is one of the most successful dog sledders in the country."

The dog abruptly stopped dancing, curled up, and dropped down atop Steve's duffel bag. "Are we going to bring him back to her?"

"Nope," she answered. "Heidi probably isn't even there. I'll leave a message on her answering machine and she can come and get him later. Besides, we're almost there."

"Home?"

"No. The Lodge."

Chapter Nineteen

True to Jenn's word, as soon as they'd churned through the snow up a steep hill, they came into view of one of the oddest constructions Steve had ever seen. Jenn got out of the car and opened the back door. Bruno hopped out and looked around. Steve followed suit. A little wind nickered down the collar of his jacket and the snow beneath his feet squeaked. Verie had been right: a leather coat was not going to be adequate for a Minnesota winter. Steve noted these things absently, his gaze riveted on the building in front of him.

The description of the Lodge on the outdated B and Bs of Northern Minnesota Web site had said it was "an authentic rustic hunting lodge made of hand-hewn logs." The words had conjured images of Bing Crosby in Vermont singing "White Christmas" in front of a square, cozy cabin made of cinnamon-colored logs, its fieldstone chimney puffing little commas of smoke into the sky behind him as he crooned.

It was not cozy. It was not square. There were logs.

The Lodge rose two stories high in some places and dipped down to a single level in others. It had angles and cantilevers and none of the materials matched. A dozen windows, of as many varieties and sizes, pockmarked the log surface at random intervals and heights while overhead, at the highest and most central part of the structure, it looked like someone had tacked on a twelve-by-twelve box. A one-person balcony jutted out from it like a ship's prow. Only the twin front doors sported what appeared to be newer paint, a green the color of Astroturf. Fifty yards behind the main structure stood a small, weathered, but completely normal-looking barn.

Steve took one long look and let out a low whistle of appreciation.

"What is it?" he breathed.

"The Lodge," Jenn said, hands on hips and head tipped back, peering through the lenses of her dark glasses as if she were inspecting it for structural damage, which she might well have been doing. Because the next thing she said was "If I were you, I wouldn't let them stick me in the tower room. Probably not too safe. Nice view, though."

"I want it."

"No, you don't," she replied. "Even if the floor holds and you don't crash through, there are bats up there."

Bats? He shared a studio with rats. "I want it. I don't care."

She smiled at him. Bruno padded up behind him and gave his dangling hand a nudge with his massive snout. Without thinking, Steve reached down and scratched, eliciting a moan of pleasure from the dog.

"Hey, Miss Hallesby." A skinny man in his early thirties wearing a quilted jacket and earmuffs plodded toward them from the direction of the barn. "I emptied out a place in the barn for you to park your car."

"Thanks, Eric," Jenn said. "This is Eric Erickson, Steve. He keeps the place glued together. This is Steve Jaax."

The man nodded, ignored the hand Steve stuck out, and said, "Sure thing. So, then . . . bye," before quickly walking off.

"Sometimes people react with shyness," Steve explained to Jenn and then went back to studying the edifice before him. "Where did it come from? Who built it? Why did they build it?"

Jenn had returned to looking the place over, too. "It was my great-grandfather's hideaway, boys' club, hunting camp. My mom inherited it," she said laconically. "After the Fall, this is all they had left. So here we came and there they stay."

She caught his sideways glance. "They've been trying to find a way out of here ever since. And do not look at me like that. I have offered, begged, and tried everything I could think of to get them to let me help them. The only thing those two have in greater abundance than bad business sense is pride."

"I didn't look at you any way."

"Humph. Anyway, they've tried raising free-range chickens, which all turned into pets, fancy herb gardening, my mom even had a little cottage industry in food miracles—not to be confused with miracle food. Food with religious images imprinted on them? She had this great French toast Madonna. . . ." She trailed off a little wistfully. "Until the folks on eBay realized that the same miracle was appearing on other auction sites. The latest brainstorm is a golf course."

"That sounds feasible." He had no idea whether it did or not but it seemed a likely thing to say. Apparently, it wasn't feasible because Jenn gave him a sardonic look.

"Anyway," she continued, "what you're seeing here is yet another scuttled plan. About ten years ago my mom decided to register it as a B and B. Until they actually experienced guests. They keep reregistering it, though, mostly for tax purposes.

"I don't think anyone's actually stayed here for . . . I can't think when. I wonder if my dad knows you've reserved a room. I bet not. Man, he's going to be mad. He hates company."

She waved him forward. "Come on. I'll give you the two-buck tour."

"Please."

He fell into step behind her as she led the way to the front door. The knob turned but the door stuck. She gave him a "told ya so" smile.

"I bet Eric painted the door shut. When I said he kept things glued together, I meant it literally. We always use the side entrance but . . ." She didn't finish, instead ramming her shoulder into it. The door popped inward and Bruno darted in, followed by Jenn and Steve.

They entered into a two-story great room, the exposed rafters overhead hung with pairs of antique skis and ancient snowshoes. A set of stairs on their right led to a second floor, disappearing through an archway at the top. On the left-hand side, another archway led to some sun-filled interior he couldn't quite make out. Years of light streaming in from the mismatched banks of windows had faded the pegged yellow pine floor and chinked log walls to a honey-colored patina.

Someone had hung the walls with literally hundreds of antlers, not in pairs, but single examples, ones each mounted in the center of little ornately carved plaques.

Jenn, catching the direction of his gaze, smiled. "My dad doesn't hunt but he likes the idea of big antlers displayed on the wall, so he collects the ones the bucks drop each winter and does that. It's either a hobby or a joke. I'm still not sure which."

"I think I like your dad."

Had that been the sum of the experience, Steve would have accounted himself charmed. But it wasn't. Rather than the Hudson Bay blankets, braided rugs, and early-American chairs that traditionally belonged in a place like this, someone had furnished it with two big, cream-colored sectional couches piled with blue suede pillows, an enormous glass-and-chrome coffee table, and a low-backed Italian chair of Wedgwood blue leather. On the opposite corners of both sofas, Japanese paper lamps stood suspended on the end of gracefully arcing curves of teak. The entire suite sat on a huge white shag carpet. Well, off-white.

The whole tableau could have been lifted from the pages of *Architectural Digest* circa 1978.

He wasn't charmed; he was besotted.

He turned to Jenn. She was shrugging out of her coat; her eyes were dancing.

"Green Acres," he whispered.

"That's just what I've always thought!" she exclaimed in surprised delight, unwrapping the scarf from around her head.

Bruno slipped past them and made directly for the nearest sofa. He took a graceful leap, landing squarely in the middle of a cushion, turned three times, and dropped.

"Jenn?" An old man in baggy brown pants and a flannel shirt appeared in the archway to their left, sporting a pair of reading glasses atop a head of magnificent silver hair and holding a folded newspaper. Even though he was clearly in his late seventies, his resemblance to Jenn was unmistakable. "What the hell are you doing out here, Jenn, and how'd you get in? I thought Eric had painted that damn door shut last—" He spied Steve. "Who's that? Who're you?"

He had an odd accent, the slow drawl of the South mixed with round Minnesota vowels.

"This is Steve Jaax, Dad. The artist? Steve, my dad, Casmir Hallesby, aka Cash."

"Hi." Steve stepped forward and shook Casmir's hand. "I gotta say, I love what you've done with the place."

Cash shot a questioning glance at Jenn.

"He's being funny," she said.

"No, I'm not. Your daughter thinks I'm mocking her, but I'm not. This is wonderful." He smiled. "Can I have the room with the balcony?"

"Huh? What're you talking about? What's this guy talking about, Jenn?"

"He's staying here. Mom booked him a room."

"That's ridiculous. We don't take in strangers. We stopped that nonsense years ago."

"Not according to your accountant."

Her father gave her an irritated look. "That's just for tax purposes. Everyone knows we don't really board people out here."

"Mom thinks you do. She's the one who took his reservation."

"You're enjoying this, aren't you, Jenn?" Cash asked.

"A little."

"Well, the answer is no. Take him back to town and dump him at the Valu-Inn. Fred'll wet himself with joy to get him."

"They're booked. Full up. For the entire ten days of the celebration," Jenn explained, employing that fascinating conversational shorthand Steve suspected was common to northern Minnesota. "You have to let him stay. There's nowhere else for him to go."

Steve had remained dutifully mute during this exchange, doing his damnedest to appear to be unproblematic. "Look," he said now, using his most conciliatory tone, "if it's a matter of paying a little more . . ."

This won a quick but newly interested look from Cash. "Just how famous are you?" he suddenly asked. "And no bullshit."

"Real famous."

Cash looked at Jenn. She nodded.

Cash's eyes narrowed. "Okay. A hundred twenty a night."

"That's—" Jenn started.

"Deal," Steve said before she could protest. "Can I have the room with the balcony?"

"Well, I think it would be okay—"

"No," Jenn said firmly. "You want to kill a living legend? Your insurance premiums would skyrocket. Where is Mom?"

"She's out with the chickens." He spotted the lump of fur on the couch. "Is that one of Heidi's mutts?"

"Chickens?" Steve asked, interested.

Jenn spared him a glance. Another quality unique to Jenn. Most people paid attention to Steve even when, by his own admission, he didn't warrant it. She seemed to have no problem ignoring him. "Yeah. My mom raises fancy fowl—"

"Fancy Fowl? Please, can I see—"

"It's Bruno, Dad." Having answered Steve's question, she returned her attention to her father. "He was on the side of the highway about two miles back, so we brought him along."

Cash's expression softened. "Poor old boy. Heidi retired him from the line this year and he's not taking it too well. He keeps getting out and taking off after them."

"Ah!" Jenn said. "Poor guy."

"Why? Why's he a 'poor guy?' What's a line?" Steve demanded, fascinated.

"He was one of Heidi's lead sled dogs," Jenn explained.

"Sovereign of the Sled, if you will. But he's getting old, so Heidi retired him. Only old Bruno here thinks of it as being dethroned."

Steve regarded the fur lump. He was snoring again. "What was he planning on doing once he found the sled?"

"Beating the shit out of whoever took his place as lead dog," Cash said.

"Sounds reasonable," Steve said, looking with new favor on the huge creature.

"Dangerous," Jenn said flatly. "He's too old. He'd only get hurt."

"Old? How old is he?"

"Six."

One of the models Steve used had occasionally brought to the studio her chihuahua, carefully wrapped in a pink blanket and tucked in a basket. She knew all about dogs and she liked to talk. One of the things Steve recalled her saying was that the human-to-dog-year ratio was something like seven to one, which meant that Bruno was . . . "Hell, that's not old! He's only like forty-two in human years. He's just hitting his stride."

Jenn regarded him sympathetically. He wasn't sure he didn't find that a little demoralizing.

"I agree with you, Mr. Jaax. But try telling Heidi Olmsted anything about dogs." Cash regarded him approvingly. It seemed that he'd proven himself worthy of Cash Hallesby either by agreeing to pay an inflated room rate or by coming to the defense of middle-aged sled dogs.

"Well, he was right, after all. You are here, Jenn." A woman came through the archway, carrying a cordless phone nestled against her shoulder.

Except for a white feather clinging coyly to her carefully coiffed temple, Jenn's mom would have fit in any group of society matrons haunting the couture shops on Fifth Avenue in New York City. Her straight, rail-thin body displayed her perfectly tailored and perfectly timeless clothing like a mannequin.

"Mom, this is Steve Jaax, the—"

"Artist," finished Mrs. Hallesby, sailing forward with her hand outstretched. He took it, bowing slightly. "Of course, I know who this is. I'm Nina Hallesby. It's lovely to meet you, Mr. Jaax." She had no accent whatsoever, but the evenly modulated voice of a news anchor. "Welcome to"—her elegant hand fluttered in a circle above her head like a conjurer's—"the Lodge. We've been expecting you."

"We?" Cash muttered.

"Your room is ready, of course. But before I show you, why don't we all have a nice hot cup of chamomile tea, shall we?" She swept by him, heading for the couch, where she nabbed the sleeping dog by the scruff of the neck and dragged him off with an ease that belied her slight frame, for a second reminding Steve forcibly of Jenn. "There."

Nina snapped her fingers at Bruno, who was blinking, having been rudely awakened. "Come on, Bruno. We'll get you something to eat, too. Shall we adjourn to the conservatory?"

"Most people call it a kitchen," Jenn whispered from behind Steve.

Nina didn't wait for an answer but sailed through the arch, Cash at her side. Steve fell into step behind her, Jenn following.

"Of course, we're really only summer people," Nina said.

"In spite of the fact that it's winter," Jenn said in a voice pitched for Steve's ears alone.

It was like having a voice-over only he could hear, or a devil on his shoulder, or a disembodied narrator. Jenn sounded amused and a little, well, *sad*. And why that was, Steve couldn't begin to guess.

"I'm afraid we enjoy our little haven in the north woods so much we haven't been able to bring ourselves to leave it for some time now," Nina was saying.

"Like twenty-four years."

The kitchen wasn't as fantastical as the great room. The table was a simple, round oak pedestal variety and the chairs were all traditional ladder-backs.

"Please, have a seat wherever you like and I'll just—"

She stopped, suddenly remembering the phone buried against her shoulder. She thrust it toward Jenn. "I don't know who this is, Jenn, but he knew you were here before I did. He's been calling all morning, insisting he has to speak to you and that he cannot possibly leave a number where you could return his call. Then about ten minutes ago, he called insisting that you'd arrived."

Jenn took the phone and held it to her ear. "Yes?"

Pause.

"Yes, this is she."

Pause.

"I'm listening."

A longer pause.

"Forget it." She took the phone from her ear, depressed the OFF button, and handed the phone back to her mother.

"Who was it?" Cash asked.

"I don't know. Some guy," Jenn said. "He claimed he has the butter sculpture and said he wanted a thousand dollars to return it."

Steve felt his heart stop in his chest. He opened his mouth but no words came out at first. "He wanted . . ." was all he managed after a few seconds.

She turned to him, head nodding empathetically. "I

know." She sounded completely taken aback. "Can you believe it? A thousand dollars for—"

Abruptly the phone rang in her hand. She pushed a button and raised it to her ear.

"Hello? Oh. Well, that makes all the difference." Another pause. Steve reached for the phone but she lifted a finger, waggling it in the manner of one saying, "I have it covered," while she nodded at whatever was being said to her from the other end.

"Forget it," she said. "I know what I said but I was being sarcastic. Really. Yes, that means no."

By the time Steve realized what she meant to do, she'd already hung up.

"You didn't—"

"Of course not," she said. "He wanted five hundred dollars this time."

"Is that who that was?" Nina exclaimed. "He called here yesterday and asked for five hundred from your father and me."

"You said no?" Steve's voice came out as a whisper.

"Of course, we did." Nina sniffed. "Hallesbys don't submit to blackmail."

"But it . . . it's worth—" He trailed off. He didn't know what it was worth.

"Not much, I'm afraid," Cash said. "Nina had it appraised some time back and, well, the guy said its only value is as an oddity."

"But . . . Picasso's cocktail napkins sell."

"Yeah," Cash said gently. "But you can frame those. You're not Picasso—sorry—and you're not dead. The bottom line on the butter head, Steve, is you can't frame it, you can't exhibit it, and eventually it's going to degrade to the

point where it's unrecognizable. It's not all that pretty now."
He gave Jenn an apologetic glance. "Sorry, honey."

"I don't care," Jenn said. She really looked like she didn't
care, too. "I like the idea of it being a *Picture of Dorian Gray*
sorta thing. 'The Butter Head of Jenn Lind.' And as my sins
grow darker and my soul more corrupt, the butter head—"

"That's nice, Jenn," Nina interrupted. "Don't worry, Mr.
Jaax." She patted his hand consolingly. "Whoever it is will
likely realize they've targeted the wrong people and just
abandon it somewhere. I mean, who in Fawn Creek would
pay five hundred dollars for a block of dehydrating butter?"

Chapter Twenty

"What she say?" Ned demanded.

"Exactly what she said before," Turv said, tossing the cell phone to Ned. "Forget it."

"Well, shit." Ned raked a hand over his scalp, displacing his thinning red hair. He paced back and forth between the broken-down Crestliner occupying one of the car stalls in the detached unheated garage and the butter head perched atop the backseat of the snowmobile in the other. He gave the butter head a sour look.

He'd unwrapped it a while ago just to see if it had survived its ride the other night without any damage. As far as he could tell, it was the same, but if he didn't know better, he would say the thing had somehow shifted on the seat it occupied. Of course, that couldn't be because Ned hadn't been out on the snowmobile since they'd stolen the butter head.

"Throw a blanket or something over that thing. It's giving me the willies," he told Eric, who'd perched himself atop the freezer chest on the side of the garage.

Eric had hot-footed it over to Ned's house—technically,

his grandma's house—as soon as he'd seen Jenn Hallesby arrive at the Hallesbys'. Eric had almost made the call to Jenn himself, right from the Hallesbys' barn, but at the last moment had decided it would be too risky since Mrs. Hallesby might answer the phone and recognize his voice.

"Does this thing look different to you today than it did last night?" Eric said, hopping off the chest and approaching the butter head.

"You mean like it's . . . moved?" Ned asked.

"Nah. The face . . . it's . . . Look at it."

Ned and Turv studied the sculpture. Ned started to shake his head but then changed his mind. He scratched his chin, glanced at the light streaming in through the garage windows landing square on the butter head's face, looked at the butter head, and swore. "Shit! The damn thing is melting. Her bangs are about to drop and her lips are sliding off! Shit!

"Don't just sit there. Help me move the snowmobile into the shade," he yelled at Eric. Together they managed to push the snowmobile and its cargo out of the direct sunlight.

"Think it makes any difference?" Turv asked from the broken-down sofa he hadn't bothered to vacate during the crisis. He popped a handful of sunflower seeds into his mouth.

"No," Ned said, not at all certain. "No one's gonna be close enough to see it real good until after we get the money, anyway. But just in case . . . You took woodworking in junior high, Turv. Get your ass over here and fix her up."

Instead of kicking and fussing, like Ned had expected him to do, Turv popped up off the couch and headed toward the butter head, unfolding the deer knife he kept in his back pocket as he came. "Cool."

"Seems like this ransom idea isn't turning out to be as good a deal as you thought it was going to be," Eric said, watching as Turv squatted down in front of the butter head. "No one but you seems to think this thing is worth squat."

"We just haven't found the right buyer, is all," Ned answered. "Think we should try that Jaax guy? The guy who made it?"

"Nah," Eric said after a thought-filled pause. "You heard him on television. He said the only value it has is a sentimental one for the Hallesbys. I always thought Mrs. Hallesby was sort of tenderhearted, what with those chickens of hers and all. Guess not." He parked his chin dolefully on his chest, looking distinctly disappointed in Mrs. Hallesby.

"What the hell are you doing, Turv?" Ned, for a second distracted by the fact that Eric was talking and actually making sense, looked around to find Turv bent at a ninety-degree angle, eyeballing the butter head from near floor level.

"I'm studying it."

"Well, get to work," Ned snapped. "We gotta think, you guys. If the Hallesbys don't want it and Jenn Lind don't want it, there's gotta be *someone* who does."

"Who'd want a crappy-looking hunk of rancid butter?" Eric, the master of the obvious if ever there was one, asked.

The three of them considered this quizzer for a few minutes until Turv, who'd risen and begun poking at the butter head face with the flat of his knife, said, "Well, it was the mayor that got all goosey when he found out Mrs. Hallesby had the head, and it was the mayor who talked her into loaning it to the town for their parade."

"Yeah," Ned said slowly. "So, then, maybe the mayor'd pay something to get it back. Even that Jaax guy mentioned how Paul was all excited about making it some sort of marshal. On TV, remember?"

Turv, squinting at the butter head with one eye closed, had made a rather graceful slice across the forehead, his tongue parked in the corner of his mouth. He didn't appear to hear Ned.

"Someone should call the mayor and find out," Eric said around a mouthful of seeds.

A few minutes later Eric, having gotten the mayor's cell phone number from the city clerk by telling her he was Ken Holmberg's plant manager, punched in the appropriate numbers and waited. On the fourth ring, Paul LeDuc answered, "Eh?"

Eric, nominated to do the call since he had the least face time with LeDuc, stuck a handkerchief over the receiver and piped in a falsetto, "Is this the mayor?"

"Put it on speaker phone!" Ned hissed. Eric pressed a button.

There was silence on the other end.

"Mayy-oor?" Eric sang.

"Oh fer chrissakes, Dot." LeDuc's voice dropped to a low, embarrassed whisper. "I told you not to make these kinda calls when I'm working. I'm the mayor—"

Eric blushed and abruptly changed keys, dropping about three octaves. "This isn't Dot."

"Eh?"

"This is one of the guys who has the butter sculpture."

"Yeah?" LeDuc didn't sound too desperate but then all those damn Chinooks were cool customers. "So where is it, then?"

"We'll tell you for a thousand dollars."

"You guys are nuts." He hung up.

Chapter Twenty-one

12:00 p.m.
Oxlip County Hospital

At Dunk's insistence, and with much reluctance, the mayor had called Sheriff Einer Hahn down from his tree stand to investigate the robbery of the Hallesbys' butter sculpture. Einer, a muscular guy with a shaved head, still sporting camouflage-paint stripes on his cheeks, had been standing at the foot of Dunk's hospital bed "interviewing" him when the mayor's cell phone chimed.

The mayor stepped away from the bed, muttered into the phone, and a half a minute later came back looking real pissed. He made another call, listened a few seconds, and then made a sound of annoyance.

"Wouldn't ya know it? Blocked ID." He crammed the cell back in his coat pocket.

"Who was it?" the sheriff—and who the hell named their kid Einer?—asked.

"That," the mayor said, "was one of our thieves. The little shit had the balls to tell me they wanted a thousand bucks to give the butter head back."

"But you said no!" Dunk said, appalled. These idiots were going to lose him that butter head yet.

"Of course he said no," the sheriff said, looking disappointed with Dunk. "I don't know about you, sir, but I was in the military. Desert Storm. A man never gives in to terrorist demands."

Dunk regarded him blankly. "This isn't a terrorist. It's some guy who kidnapped a hundred pounds of butter."

"Same thing."

From the pugnacious set to the sheriff's jaw, Dunk realized he meant it. "Is Mr. Jaax here?" he asked suddenly. God, he hoped not. "Has he arrived yet?"

The sheriff and the mayor traded quick unreadable glances. "You bet, Mr. Dunkovich," the mayor said. "And he seems like a real nice guy. I'm pretty sure he'd be happy to stop by and thank you for your efforts on behalf of . . . of his head."

Shit. They thought he was some sort of celebrity stalker. The last thing in the world he wanted was Steve Jaax laying eyes on him. Steve Jaax struck him as someone quick on the uptake. If Jaax recognized him, he'd realize in a minute what his old cellmate was doing in town, particularly as that old cellmate just happened to show up the same time as the butter head where Steve had hidden a key to a literal fortune, and about which he'd blabbed to said cellmate, resurfaced.

"No!" he said and then, seeing their curious looks, added, "I don't want Mr. Jaax to see me like this. I . . . I'd rather wait until I could stand up to shake his hand." He was going to make himself vomit.

"Sure thing," the mayor said.

Damn it. With Jaax in town and looking for his sculpture—which of course he would be—Dunk would have to think fast and work faster. The only thing Dunk had going for him was that Jaax didn't realize that he had competition for finding it. He'd probably be doing just what the sheriff suggested to Dunk that he do, relaxing and waiting for it to show up all on its own. Which meant Dunk couldn't relax and wait. He had to act and act quickly.

"Damn!" he muttered under his breath.

"Are you upsetting our patient, Einer?" Nurse Ekkelstahl, ever vigilant for any ripple in her patients' smooth course of recovery, charged through the door, arms akimbo. She'd changed from the no-frills blue scrubs of yesterday to scrubs with little yellow baby ducks waddling all over the mint green expanse of her bosom. It was perversely sexy.

"No. The jerks what stole the butter head are upsetting me," the mayor announced. The sheriff had flipped open his spiral notebook and was scratching things down in it. Dunk suspected he was doodling.

It was time to let a cooler head prevail. It was perhaps a little surprising it was going to have to be his. Scrapping together every bit of gravitas he could muster, Dunk said, "You know, if you were to tell these guys that you would pay their thousand dollars, you could get your team to set a trap for them."

"That'd be great if we had a team. We have Einer here"— the mayor nodded at the deer hunter—"and a deputy, who's on vacation until tomorrow when we'll start to see some of those seven thousand people showing up for the start of the sesquicentennial. So he'll be busy with traffic duty. So there's not going to be any trap setting."

Einer nodded his concurrence with the mayor. "No way, buddy."

"You have to do *something*."

"You yourself pointed out, Mr. Dunkovich, it isn't like anyone's in danger here," the mayor said. "We'll find it eventually. Probably some deer hunter'll stumble over it on his way to his stand. Or whoever has it will decide it isn't worth the trouble it already cost him and just dump it back at the Hallesbys'. Guy on the phone didn't sound like a bad sort, just not too bright."

"But—"

"Look." The sheriff had obviously decided they were due for a man-to-man. "Mr. Dankwitch."

"Dunkovich."

"Yeah, that's what I said. Dunkovich. I understand you got a stake in this butter sculpture being recovered. Shit, I'd feel the same way if I found out I'd gotten busted up chasing something, even if it was nothing but a whittled-up block of butter. But the fact is, we don't have the time or the manpower to devote to the recovery of a butter head. Now, then"—he made a show of snapping the spiral notebook closed but not before Dunk caught a glimpse of the inside pages; he had been doodling—"there's a ten-point buck out there somewhere with my name on it, and I got two days to find him before seven thousand tourists turn this town into a traffic nightmare. That doesn't mean I'm not going to look for it. I'll ask around. Leave word at the gas stations, over to Smelka's, and such. This is a small town, Mr. Dunkovich. Someone's gonna say something somewhere and I'll hear it. In the meantime, you just get well, okay?"

Paul nodded gravely in concurrence and reached down to give Dunk's exposed big toe a friendly tweak.

"Listen," he said. "For all you knew, those thieves coulda been making off with a priceless artifact. Just because it was butter doesn't make you any less heroic in anyone's eyes."

"It's an original Jaax sculpture," Dunk said. "Doesn't that mean something to you guys?"

The mayor shook his head. "You said it best. It's butter. If it had been worth something, the Hallesbys woulda sold it long ago. Those folks could sure use the cash." His handsome face crumpled with compassion. "Now you take it easy, okay?"

With that, the mayor headed out, followed closely by the sheriff.

Dunk watched him go, thinking hard. "Karin," he finally said, "does this town have a Kinkos or something like it?"

"Well, the *Fawn Creek Crier* does some of that sort of stuff. Copies and xeroxes and rents out computer time. Why?"

If those two clowns weren't going to do anything to help him get that key, he'd have to do it himself.

"Could you get me the local phone book? I have a couple calls I need to make."

Chapter Twenty-two

12:00 p.m.
The Lodge

"Can't you redial?" Steve asked for the third time.

"No," Jenn replied patiently. "I cannot. The call was blocked. You cannot redial a blocked number."

"There's got to be a way around it," he insisted. "I really wanted to see her again."

What was it with him and that sculpture? Jenn wondered, eyeing him. His attachment to a thing he had spent four hours carving twenty years ago bordered on peculiar. She gave a mental shrug. Maybe he'd forgotten to bring along his meds.

"Don't worry, Steve." Her father and Steve had quickly progressed to first-name basis. "It'll turn up. Without anyone having to pay a penny."

For whatever reason, Cash seemed to have taken to Steve. As had Bruno. Of course, Bruno's adulation was a little easier to explain, seeing how Steve kept tearing off chunks of the oatmeal-raisin cookies her mother had put on the table and was surreptitiously feeding them to the dog under the table. Jenn hadn't seen Steve slip her dad any cookies; ergo the attraction was something of a mystery.

"If they call back, tell them you'll give them whatever they're asking for," Steve said. "I'll pay."

"Now, then, no good has ever come of giving in to a blackmailer's demands," her father advised in the tones of one who has a vast expertise dealing with blackmailers.

"It's wrong," her mom said, pushing the plate of cookies toward Steve.

He picked one up and took a bite. He lowered his hand—with cookie—to his lap. "I'm not particularly interested in the moral aspects of the situation," he admitted sadly. "I just want my butter head back."

Jenn couldn't keep quiet any longer. "You know, you keep saying 'my butter head' like it was, well, yours."

He regarded her earnestly. "Yes?"

"Well, it's not yours."

"Jennifer Lynne Hallesby!" her mother breathed.

"Really, Jenny," her father protested. "Steve's our guest—"

From "dump him at the Valu-Inn" to "Steve's our guest!" in less than two hours. The man must exude some sort of charisma pheromone.

"No, please," Steve said, raising his hand—sans cookie—and lowering his eyes modestly. Beneath the table, Bruno smacked his lips. "Jenny's right, Nina, Cash."

Jenny?

"I have been acting possessive about something that doesn't belong to me. Except . . . well . . . an artist always feels he owns his creation to some degree."

"Bull," Jenn said. "I read an article in the *Wall Street Journal* where you were quoted as saying that once the art was out of your studio, it was dead to you."

Steve didn't look the least bit disconcerted. "Yes, I know. But that was just press. It sounded lofty. Artists always say things that sound lofty. Don't you, occasionally, in the course of polishing your public persona, say things just for an effect?"

Her mother turned an assessing eye on her. Busted.

That wasn't fair. Jenn expected her mother to be sympathetic at least. It wasn't as if her parents didn't pad their own lives with a few pleasant untruths like "we're biding our time while we sort out our options" and "we'll be moving out of here as soon as our plans come together." They'd been "biding" and "planning" for twenty-four years and were no closer now to leaving Fawn Creek than they'd ever been.

Jenn had tried a dozen times in as many ways to provide them a way out. She'd attempted to give them money and tried to convince them to let her make them a loan. She'd even offered to make investments for them via her broker, hoping that the return would be enough to set them free even if she had to provide it herself. They wouldn't accept any help, in any manner.

Every time Jenn walked into the Lodge, she felt like she was walking into the home of political exiles bravely putting up a front that had become nearly farcical. But the worst part was that over the years, with every offer she made and every refusal given, a wall had grown between them. Any real conversations about what they could do to leave and how she could help had ended long ago. Nowadays, they played stock parts: her pretending that any day they were going to call the movers, them pretending they had the company on speed dial in anticipation of their emancipation.

There was no question they'd been plucky in the face of their exile, but part of Jenn could not help asking at what point plucky simply became pathetic.

No one wanted to think of her parents as pathetic. Just

allowing the word to slip into her thoughts made Jenn feel awful.

"Of course, she has," her father said, dragging Jenn back from unpleasant musings. "But that's just part of being a celebrity, saying what you think people want to hear. No one's happier than when they've had confirmed what they already think. Even if it's not true."

"Exactly," Steve agreed. "Which is why I am sure you understand when I tell you that, to some degree and at some level, I will always feel that the butter sculpture is mine. Please, don't think anything of it when I call it 'my butter head.' I mean . . . in my heart."

He touched his hand to chest, dividing his most charming smile between her mother and father. They smiled back. It was a moment.

"That's really touching," Jenn said. She had no intention of letting him get away with such outrageous pap. "But if you paid for the sculpture's ransom, wouldn't you feel like you were entitled to a little more than ownership in here?" She folded her hands over her heart and batted her eyelashes.

"Well," Steve said, "sure."

"Ha! Just as I thought!"

"I wasn't trying to put anything over on anyone."

"I'll believe that when—"

"Have another cookie, Steve," her mother interjected. "They're my own recipe. I'm quite a different brand of cook from my daughter, I'm afraid," she said with an apologetic glance at Jenn that somehow managed to be more superior than apologetic. "I'm a health- and heart-conscious cook. Those cookies are made from sprouted grains, bran flours, and natural vegetable sugars."

Steve accepted the cookie a little slowly but without flinching. Served him right.

"Now," Nina continued in the voice that had ruled the boards of at least half a dozen Raleigh nonprofits back in the day, "should it prove necessary, we will discuss the ownership of the butter head upon its return. For the moment, the butter head, wherever it is, is ours."

"Yeah," Jenn said slowly, taking the opportunity to address a subject that had been bothering her since she'd first heard the thing still . . . lived, for want of a better word. "And why is that?"

"Why is what?" her mother asked.

"As I recall, I told the guy from the Lutheran Brotherhood to melt that thing right along with the other butter princess heads. By the way"—she glanced at Steve—"the person they got to carve the other princesses was terrible."

Steve received this info with a gratified nod. She turned back to her mother. "So how'd it end up in your barn?"

"I went over to see it before they took it off. I didn't intend to do anything but look at it and"—she lifted a hand from the table; it was thinner than Jenn remembered—"well, once I saw it, saw *you,* Jenny, how could I let them melt it?"

"You knew it was a Jaax. Even back then," Steve said understandingly.

"What? Oh. Certainly." What was it about Steve Jaax that made people willing to protect his enormous ego? Because obviously her mom hadn't had a clue who Steve Jaax was twenty some years ago.

"Here." Her mom unceremoniously handed him another cookie, her attention on Jenn. "I knew you didn't like it. I mean, I knew it had bad associations for you—"

"My butter head had bad associations for you?" Steve

broke in, the cookie frozen halfway to Bruno's open maw. He sounded hurt.

"Anyway, dear," her mother said, "I never told you. I suppose I should have."

"That's okay," Jenn said. "I was just curious."

At least the butter head hadn't arisen from the depths of some murky cornfield drainage ditch in the middle of the night on the anniversary of its melting.

"How did Paul LeDuc find out about it?" Jenn asked.

"It was Eric Erickson." Cash took over the story. "The handyman. Mows the grass, plows, that sort of thing."

"Yeah. I know him, Dad."

"He was cleaning out the barn this summer," Cash said, "and found the freezer. I'm sure he was hoping there was some beer in it. Anyway he opened it. Says he screamed when he saw her staring up at him—we'd nested her on the back of her head—"

"Can we not call it a her?" Jenn asked. "It's creepy."

"I always think of my pieces in terms of gender," Steve said.

"That's creepy," Jenn told him, though not unkindly.

"Anyway," her father went on, his tone suggesting he didn't like having a good story interrupted, "Eric found it and he told some of the people in town and they remembered you posed for it and someone told the mayor and he contacted us. After contacting the *Guinness Book of Records* people and *Ripley's Believe It or Not.* Do you realize that there is a good chance that this is the oldest surviving intact—"

"Yes," Jenn cut him off at the pass. "I know. It's old. Very, very old."

The phone rang and Jenn, closest to it, reached back and picked up the receiver. "Hello?"

"We'll let you have the butter head for two hundred dollars," a sullen voice announced without preamble.

"One hundred bucks and not a penny more," she answered calmly.

The conversation around the table stopped dead.

"Aw, that's not fair!" the male voice on the other end sputtered. "That barely covers the cost of the gas. And what about the danger we put ourselves in? That freak on the snowmobile tried to run Tu—" He cut himself off. "Tried to run us off the trail! Oughtn't we get compensated something for that?"

"Your choice, your problem," she clipped out. "Look, you guys, if you have a brain between you, you'll take the hundred I'm offering and count yourself lucky I don't call the cops."

"Shit," muttered the guy. "Hold on. I gotta talk to my posse."

He covered the mouthpiece and Jenn covered hers. "It's the thieves. They're talking it over."

"If he insists on two, give it to him!" Steve said.

"Look, the banks aren't open weekends," she explained patiently. "All I have on me is a hundred and twenty. Do you have the rest?"

"I have MasterCard." Apparently not.

"Cool," Jenn said dryly. "Do you think he'll charge us the in-state tax?"

"Sarcasm duly noted," Steve said with a lift of one brow. "Mom? Dad?"

"Probably," Cash answered but he didn't sound too sure.

"Okay. We'll take a hundred," the guy on the other end of the phone announced. "But you're being a real bitch." He waited, as though expecting her to apologize.

"Well?" she finally said.

"Well, what?"

"Where do you want me to bring the money? Where are we going to make the exchange?" She looked at Steve and rolled her eyes.

"Oh. Wait a minute." He covered his end again.

"Are you going to call Einer?" Cash whispered and then added for Steve's sake, "Einer's the sheriff."

"I dunno," Jenn replied, one ear attuned for any voice coming from the cordless. "Think I should?"

"I wouldn't," Steve said. "The sheriff would set a trap and that might scare off the thieves—"

"I doubt it," Nina put in her two cents. "I think he's hunting this weekend and he'd be real unhappy if he missed a trophy buck for a butter sculpture."

"How do you know he's hunting?" Jenn asked. She was always fascinated how her parents managed to know so much of what happened in Fawn Creek.

"HEY! HAL-LO!" A voice boomed from her hand. She uncovered the receiver and held it to her ear.

"Yeah?"

"Sorry to interrupt you and everything." The guy was clearly in a peeve. "But we got a ransom drop to organize here. Now you know where the old Storybook Land is?"

"Sure." Her family had visited Storybook Land on family vacation to the Lodge when she was a kid, when two weeks of "roughing it" had seemed romantic. The theme park, never much of a success, was long since defunct, just a bunch of tipped-over cement statues in an overgrown woods north of town.

"Bring the money there. Tonight at seven. Leave it in Sleeping Beauty's Castle."

"And where will my head be?"

"You'll see it on your way out."

"And why should I trust you?"

Her question proved a poser. There was a long silence during which the guy on the other end didn't even bother to confer with his "posse." Evidently he didn't have much confidence in their ability to come up with an answer.

"You'll just have to is all," he finally snapped out, "if you wanta see the butter head again."

Chapter Twenty-three

"It's settled. I'm going to go out to Storybook Land, drop off a hundred bucks, and load up the butter head," Jenn said, standing up from the table.

Her hair had begun escaping from the perfect little knot at the nape of her neck and though he was more concerned with what she said than how she looked, Steve could not help but think she was one of those women who looked as good a little unkempt as well-polished. Maybe even better. "Can I borrow the pickup, Dad?"

"Sure," Cash said. "But you'll have to gas it up."

"That's okay. I'll take Steve's MasterCard," she said with a teasing smile.

"Sure."

"Don't worry, Steve," she said, correctly interpreting the lines between his brows. "I promise I won't tell the sheriff— which is against all my best instincts because all we are doing is encouraging these idiots to steal—but I can see by your faces that I am in the minority here and so will let it go."

They all looked at her with approval.

"As soon as I get it, I'll call the mayor and he can contact the *Guinness Book of World Records*. The parade will have its mascot, Steve will see his Beloved again, Mom can thereafter continue doing with it whatever she was doing with it, and all will be right with the world."

"Thank you." Steve supposed he ought to be feeling more excited about this, but the promise that the key to his long-lost statue was slowly working its way back within his reach made him feel odd and he wasn't certain why. He definitely wanted that key. He definitely wanted to see the butter head again. So what the hell was going on?

He probably needed to eat something.

Something hearty and homegrown, packed with vitamins and earth-friendly goodness. Something the good people of Minnesota ate daily and for which he would spend forty dollars a plate in Manhattan. A Nina Hallesby specialty. She had to be a good cook, right? What with Jenny being some sort of food icon or something. The cookie had been an anomaly.

"Am I having dinner here or should I go back into town?" he asked.

Nina's face bloomed. "Why I would be happy to make you dinner, Steve."

Jenn's face froze, and then she was moving toward the doors. "I better unpack and change, and then I should call Heidi in case she's worried about Bruno, so why don't I see you all at dinner?"

As soon as she'd left, Steve stood up, showering Bruno's head with a lapful of cookie crumbs. Happily, Bruno didn't share Steve's complaints about the cookies; he began eagerly polishing the floor with his big pink tongue.

"Can I have the tower room?" Steve figured his chances of getting that room rose tenfold as soon as Jenn, who he suspected often cast herself in the role of the Voice of Reason, left.

Nina shook her head. "It's not safe."

"Now that might be overstating things, Nina," Cash said. "I don't think it's likely to fall through the ceiling or anything." He didn't look too certain. "But Jenn had a point. If something happened to you, our insurance premiums would be impossible to cover."

"I'll sign a waiver." Steve really wanted to stay in the tower. "Can I at least look?"

"Ah, what the hell? Come on," Cash capitulated. He pushed himself up from his chair and led the way toward a hall at the back of the kitchen. Nina stayed behind, but Bruno didn't. He trotted behind Steve, his feet making a nice, little castanet sound against the floorboards.

In the hall, Cash rolled back a pocket door, exposing a set of stairs so steep they could more appropriately be called a ladder. He motioned Steve forward. "After you. Just go right past the doors on the first and second floor, and when you can't go any further, push on the ceiling. It's a trapdoor."

"A trapdoor? That's so Disney. I love it." Steve headed up, Bruno climbing after him. "Can he come up?"

"I wouldn't let him," Cash said. "Oh, he'll make it up okay, but if the stairs are too steep for him to come down, you're going to have to take care of him up there for the rest of his life. Malamutes leave crap piles the size of small dogs."

Steve looked down at Bruno's head. It wasn't far to look. It was next to his hip. Bruno smiled. "How much do you think he weighs?"

"At least a hundred and fifty."

"I can do that." Steve nodded. He probably could do that.

He started climbing again. "And after we're done here, can I see the Fancy Fowl? And the barn thing?"

"You're not a regular kinda guy, are you?" Cash asked.

Steve, halfway up the first flight of stairs, looked over his shoulder. "Everyone experiments a little in college, Cash."

"That's not what I meant. I meant you're not . . . Forget it. That's the trapdoor above you. Just give it a good push."

It was heavier than Steve would have imagined. After a few unsuccessful "pushes," he gave up and braced his shoulders against the floor, pistoning up from his legs, all too aware of two sets of eyes—one masculine and one masculine canine—regarding him with a faint air of disappointment.

Finally, the trapdoor broke free of whatever held it and popped open, flopping backward and bouncing against the floor. Steve looked down, wiggling his fingers invitingly as he gave the universal sign for "you can applaud now." Bruno shot past him on the stairs and Cash, who had been peeling a fingernail as he waited on the landing below, started up.

Steve climbed into the tower room, with Cash close behind. Bruno was already standing at one of the windows, front paws on the sill, ears alert as he surveyed the land below. The dog had paws the size of salad plates.

The room was notable for the number of windows it contained, so many windows in fact that finding wall space to put the head of the brass bed against had proved impossible. Instead, it stood at an angle in the corner, flanked on either side by end tables. A single narrow chest of drawers crowded another bit of wall to the right of the door that led out to the small, prowlike balcony. Two serviceable-looking rocking chairs sat parallel to each other five feet apart, both facing out of their respective windows at the view below, their backs turned to the rest of the room, a low table set with a pair of binoculars between them.

And then Steve's gaze strayed out the window and stopped.

Jenn was right. The view was breathtaking. He could see—well, not that far, because there were heavy banks of clouds hanging low in the sky, and the snow falling from them had obliterated the horizon, but he bet on a clear day you could see to Canada. Whichever direction that was. Beneath, the pine forest spread out in all directions, even surrounding the huge silvery disk of the lake. A couple snowmobiles chased each other across its surface like cars on a kid's wind-up race track, following a graphite-colored track. Other than that, there was no evidence of another human being.

There was no one out there.

The sudden appreciation of their isolation hit Steve like a brick to the head.

"There's nothing to do here, is there?" he asked Cash.

"We have satellite. And there's Netflix."

"I mean out there." Steve pointed at the nothing outside.

"Of course, there is," Cash huffed. "There's snowmobiling and fishing and cross-country skiing, and when I get hold of the right investors, there'll be one helluva golf course."

"That's not what I meant. The people who live here. Not the vacationers. There's nothing new for them to try. No new restaurants, no theaters, no bars, no dance clubs, no new galleries, no new shops, no new exhibits. There's nothing new to draw them out of their houses or their yards."

"You have that right," Cash agreed. He didn't sound too put-out about it and Steve wondered if Jenn had ever noticed how content her father was in his exile. The old guy was walking gingerly along the perimeter of the room in increasingly tight concentric circles, testing the floorboards as he went.

Cash had to be pushing eighty. When Steve was eighty, he'd be content not to be drooling, and yet old Cash had made it up those stairs with no more panting than Steve had done.

"People raised on the plains never seem to like it much up here," Cash was saying. "The way the trees close in on the roads and fill in all the empty places makes them feel claustrophobic."

Steve's gaze drifted back out the window, a little uneasy, a little fascinated. It was like watching a horror film. You knew it was going to scare you but you watched anyway.

"I'd like to buy the butter head." The words just popped out before Steve had a chance to consider them. A flight-or-fight instinct, he supposed. Secure the butter head and run.

Cash had found a suspect board near where Bruno stood and was rocking back and forth on it experimentally, one hand carefully clinging to the window jamb. He didn't answer.

"Whatever you feel is a fair price. Hell, fair price or not, I'll pay it."

"Now, then, don't go jumping the gun there." Cash might have started life as a mover and shaker of industry, but it was pretty clear whatever he'd begun life as he was going to end it as a Son of the Nord Star. His accent might be a conglomeration of north and south, but the word choice and the rhythms said Minnesota. "If I was you, I'd wait and take a look at what you're so eager to buy. Besides, I'm not sure Nina would sell."

"No matter what I paid? Why not?"

"Hm." Cash whipped a grease pencil out of his corduroy pocket, leaned down, and marked a big, thick X on the suspect floorboard. He straightened. "You know how moms keep the things their kids make—handmade cards, and macaroni art and programs from school plays and that kind of thing?"

They did?

"Well, Nina didn't do much of that when Jenny was little. She was busy with other stuff. Charity work. Playing hostess for the company. We entertained a lot. Traveled even more. You know?"

"What does that have to do with the butter head?"

"I've lived here too long," Cash said with a short, mind-clearing shake of his head. "I forget there's a front door to every conversation. Nina doesn't have anything from Jenny's girlhood except that butter head."

Steve waited, listening carefully for some clue as to how he was going to talk Nina into giving up the butter head.

"She was really proud Jenny won the Miss Fawn Creek pageant," Cash went on. "It wasn't just because she thought her daughter was beautiful. Most moms think that. It was because Jenny had set her mind on a goal and she went after it tooth and nail. We were both proud of her, trying to fit in and at the same time pay her own way through college. She never did fit in much here," he said in a thoughtful voice. He looked up. "Anyway, that butter head is one of the only things Nina has from Jenny's girlhood."

"But Jenny didn't make the butter head," Steve protested. *"I did."*

"Yes. But we didn't have any senior pictures taken of Jenny. She wouldn't hear of it. So the butter head is as close to it as we've got."

"Look, it's not like you can hang it on the living room wall," Steve said, confident such a reasonable argument would win over Cash. "What do you do, go out in the barn and visit it once a week?"

"Of course not," Cash said.

"When was the last time you saw it?"

"'Bout four years ago."

"Then it shouldn't make any difference to you if I own it. I'll have a hologram made of it and send it to you." He was flummoxed. Cash didn't appear any closer to giving up the butter head than he had ten minutes ago.

"Nina has every clipping covering Jenny's pageants in an album. Not that she's weird about it or anything. I mean, she doesn't sit up at night, fondling the pages and dabbing at her eyes," Cash said a little defensively, enough of a Minnesotan to consider sentimentality a no-no.

"Okay." For a minute, Steve considered telling Cash exactly why he wanted the butter head but if Nina Hallesby was sentimental about it, he doubted telling Cash his plans to open it up would convince him to part with it. He'd do better playing the roles of Artist and Creator. Besides, just because he wanted to lop off the back of its head didn't mean he didn't really want to see it first. But if it really meant something to Nina . . .

Damn, he hated moral conundrums.

"Anyway"—Cash discovered another floorboard, swooped down on it with the elan of Zorro marking an evildoer, and X'ed it—"I don't know if Nina would sell it but you can always ask.

"There." Cash had finished checking off the floorboard and was looking around the rest of the room with a critical eye. "Whatcha think?"

Steve considered. "It's cold up here."

"Yup," Cash said equitably. "And not likely to get much warmer. The place wasn't exactly built to code. Whatever heat does get up here is jerry-rigged. I'd give you a space heater but the same goes for the wiring and you'd probably burn the whole place down."

"Can I have an extra blanket?" Steve asked.

"Sure. Or"—he considered Steve critically—"you *could* take one of the bedrooms on the second floor. You can get to them by a regular staircase, they're a lot warmer, and they have a more cozy feeling, having drapes and less windows and more furniture."

"No! I gotta stay here," he said earnestly. "Please."

"Okay. But you'll have to make up some sort of waiver clearly acknowledging that I told you not to step on the floorboards with the X's and you understood the dangers and you agreed not to bring a space heater up here and that if you die your estate will not sue us."

"Agreed."

"And if Bruno goes through the floorboards, you have to tell Heidi."

Steve looked at Bruno in delight. "He's staying with me?"

"Unless Heidi comes and gets him. He sure as hell isn't staying with me. I already got a bed partner. And Jenny's not a dog-in-bed type, you know." He looked a little saddened by this, as if his daughter was denying herself one of life's pleasures. Steve, who'd never slept with a dog in his bed, either, was more than willing to believe this.

"I'll write something up before dinner," he said.

Chapter Twenty-four

"You know," Steve said, "I'm sorry I forgot to tell you this, but I'm allergic to mushrooms."

Nina's Fiberlicious Risotto was the dietary equivalent of a high colonic, a grayish heap of grains more uncooked than cooked, with sharp bits and scratchy pieces floating on top of it in a watery, flavorless broth. The only ingredient he was certain about was a leathery piece of mushroom. Thus, his sudden allergy.

The Hallesbys, Steve decided, must have had cast-iron stomachs. Jenn was dutifully paring away at her mound while Cash, after one look at his plate, had donned the expression of a man determined, and pitched in, forking food slowly and methodically into his mouth.

"Oh! Oh, dear," Nina now exclaimed in alarm. "Are you going to be all right?"

Across the table, Jenn, unconcernedly dabbing at her mouth with her napkin, set it down and asked, "Are you going into anaphylactic shock?"

Nina's alarm became outright agitation. "Should we call the ambulance?"

Jenn pushed back her chair. "I'll get Uncle Phillip's beesting kit—"

"No!" God, no. Steve hated needles. "No, that won't be necessary. It's not that kind of allergic reaction. I just break out. Hives. Itchy. Not dangerous."

"Oh, dear," Nina said. "We have calamine lotion. Jenny, find the calamine—"

"There's no need." Steve caught Jenny's arm as she popped up to do her mother's bidding with suspect alacrity. He caught a glimpse of her turned face. She was trying hard not to laugh. "I don't think I had enough to cause a reaction."

With a look of disappointment, Jenn sat back down. He wouldn't have recognized her as the sophisticated, well-groomed woman of this morning. She'd exchanged her corduroys for a pair of jeans and her silk blouse for a raspberry-colored waffle-knit long-john top. Her hair hung in soft waves just below her jaw, framing a face scrubbed clean of makeup. Her skin wasn't perfection. There were laugh lines at the corners of her gray-blue eyes and just the very first hint of loosening along that strong jawline. A few freckles dusting the tops of her cheeks. Her nose was just a little asymmetrical and a tiny scar marked the bottom of her chin.

He thought she looked great. Demeter after her first run-in with Hades: forceful, female, ripe but ripening still.

She'd probably kill him if she knew what he was thinking.

In his experience, women, especially women who made a living out of celebrity, hated being ripe. Which was too bad. He liked mature women. And it didn't have anything to do with their vast wells of experience, wisdom, or endurance. He simply thought succulent was sexier than green.

"Well, I can't let you go hungry," Nina was saying. "I'll

just scoot back in the kitchen and fix you something else. It won't take but a few minutes."

"Mom," Jenn said tentatively, "I could—"

Nina stood up and pressed a hand on Jenn's shoulder. "No, Jenny. This is my kitchen and here health takes precedence over taste. Besides, as you educate your palate, you'll discover that the taste of all those fats and sugars and red meats becomes less appealing. Don't they, dear?" She directed this last question to Cash, who just kept eating.

Nina smiled at them as if her point had been made. "Now, then, how about a nice preserved-fish omelet? I preserved the fish myself. It'll take fifteen minutes."

Steve was by no one's account, including his own, a fussy eater but there were some things instinct alone convinced him to avoid. Like Bruno under the table, whom he'd been trying unsuccessfully to entice into licking the rest of the risotto off his fork.

"That is so sweet of you, Nina," Steve said. "But I'm afraid the mushrooms upset my stomach a little. So I'll just sit here and keep you company, if I may?"

"You're sure?" Nina said doubtfully, reseating herself.

"Absolutely."

Cash, who'd been eating his way through his risotto with a singleness of purpose that precluded paying attention to anything else, including Steve's allergies, finished his last mouthful and set his fork down. He looked up and beamed. "Why's everyone popping up and down like jack-in-the-boxes?" he asked.

"No reason, Dad," Jenn said.

"Oh? Okay. Then let's have another glass of wine." He held up the bottle. "Jenny?"

"Please." She held out her glass and Steve followed suit.

The shortcomings of the food were made up for by the Hallesbys' wine cellar.

"I should go online tonight and restock the wine cellar. The Buck Rub closed," Cash told Jenn.

"I'm not surprised," she answered. "I'm just amazed he lasted as long as he did, the way he gouged on prices."

"And the Tinker Hut has closed, too. But just for the winter."

"The Christiansens bought a place in Naples, didn't they?" Jenn asked. "Dub always said he was going to."

For someone "disconnected" from the town, Jenn certainly knew a lot about what was going on.

"How long do you think you'll be staying, Jenny?" Nina asked.

"Eleven days."

"Ten hours, thirty-two minutes . . ." Cash muttered. He steeled a glance at his daughter. "Have you set your alarm yet?"

"Dad, don't be like that. I have lots of things to do with the new show and wrapping things up in Minneapolis. It's crazy."

"Your father just likes your company," Nina said. " 'Love knows not its depth 'til the hour of separation.' "

Steve looked at Nina, interested, waiting for someone to comment on her quote. No one did. "Kahlil Gibran," she finally said.

Jenn and Cash continued looking at each other without expression. There was something going on. All Steve's instincts were quivering and he had good instincts. His own parents had died when he was a kid, and afterward he'd been sheltered, if not raised, by a maiden great-aunt. She'd been too old to do much "raising." She'd love him, though, vaguely, inattentively, but with unstinting approval. Thus, not having had too much interaction with families, Steve was a little reticent to trust his instincts regarding them, but still . . .

"I have to get back to the apartment," Jenn finally said in careful tones. "I haven't packed anything and I'm expecting the Realtor to have found me a new place by the end of the month."

Cash shook his head. "How can you live somewhere you haven't ever seen?"

"Because I pay a very reputable firm to make sure that it meets a very strict set of criteria—that's how."

"But what about the 'feel' of a place?" Cash protested. "The ambience. What if it isn't right? Not homey?"

Huh. "Home," Steve realized, was a word he'd never heard Jenn use. "Place," "apartment," "house," but never "home."

"It's a place to sleep and do some work. If I spend as much time in my new place as I have in the old, it won't amount to that much. Don't look so worried. People hire people to find them places all the time." She looked at Steve for support. "I bet you had a residence finder, didn't you, Steve?"

"I sleep in my studio," he said. "Never really saw the point in having a bunch of rooms I'd never use anyway."

"See?" Jenn said triumphantly. And why was she triumphant? Because he knew as little about "homes" as she did? What a pair they made.

"Are you really sure this is what you want?" Nina asked suddenly.

"What?" Jenn asked.

"This new job of yours. It sounds like a lot of pressure."

"It will be," Jenn conceded easily. "But who cares? I'll be one of the most widely viewed lifestyle authorities on television."

"That's what you are, a 'lifestyle authority?' " Nina asked softly.

Whatever the target of Nina's subtext, she'd obviously scored a direct hit because a red stain spread up Jenn's throat. "It's what the public seems to think I am," she said stiffly. "It's what they pay me for."

"You're not doing something just to say you made it to the top of the heap, are you?" Cash asked. "You have choices, you know. It's important to take the time to figure out not only what you're doing but why you're doing it."

There wasn't any anger in Jenn's expression anymore; the stiffness had dissolved. She looked frustrated, sad, a little embarrassed. Her father wore the same expression. Steve wondered if either of them realized that their disapproval and disappointment were mirror images of the other's.

"Your father is proud of you, dear," Nina, playing peacekeeper, was saying. "He's just concerned about some of the things he hears about this Dwight Davies."

"He's a prick," Steve said. The Hallesbys traded knowing glances. So they thought so, too. "He is," he said gravely. Then, seeing the dagger strike in Jenn's glance, he added, "But sometimes you have to work for pricks."

Cash mulled this over for a second. "Jenny had such—"

"Oops! Look at the time!" Jenn cut off whatever he'd been about to say, making a show of sticking her wrist watch over the table. "And it was snowing earlier. If I want to make it to Storybook Land by seven, I'd better get going."

Steve stood up, too. "Let's go."

"You don't have to go," Jenn said. "It's dark out and I won't be gone long. You'll only be bored."

"I think I should." There was no way he was leaving the procurement of his butter head to a woman who clearly didn't care whether she came back with it or not. "These

men are kidnappers. There's no telling what they're capable
of. I won't feel right sitting back here while you're out there
alone, facing God knows what sort of danger."

"Steve," Jenn said, "they stole a *butter head*. It was
hardly a violent crime."

"Yeah," he allowed, thinking quickly, "but still."

"Still nothing," Jenn said. "I appreciate the sentiment but
these guys are clowns, not hardened criminals. Fer chrissakes, I talked them down to one hundred dollars! If you'd
have let me, I'd have probably gotten them to return the
thing gratis. So just stay here and keep Bruno company and
I'll be back in a jiff."

She was right. Steve had the uneasy feeling that Jenn was
often right. But he'd already come up with another excuse to
accompany her. "I have to go with you because what if they
leave it on the ground? Do you think you'll be able to manhandle a hundred-pound block of butter into the bed of a
pickup by yourself?"

He had her. He could see by the way her eyes went sort
of squinty and assessing. "And you could?" she asked
doubtfully.

"Yeah."

"He did bring Bruno down three flights of stairs in a fire-
man's carry," Cash affirmed. And would need about a bottle
of Motrin to get out of bed tomorrow morning, but Steve
wasn't about to admit that now.

"Okay," she said. "You can come along if you want to,
but I wasn't going to drop the butter head off at the city
dump, in case that's what you were worried about."

Only one day, and already she knew him better than most
of the people in his life.

Chapter Twenty-five

6:15 p.m.
Stop 'n' Go gas station
Fawn Creek, Minnesota

"I'm guessing you didn't learn to cook at your mother's knee," Steve said as they stood under the arc lights at the Stop 'n' Go gas station.

It had begun snowing in earnest, the flakes no longer falling but sweeping across them laterally. Steve didn't have to stand out here in the Sorel boots he'd borrowed from her dad, his collar pulled up around his ears, hands deep in the pockets of his leather coat, but he did. The man had an insatiable curiosity about things, people, and places. It was probably why he was so good at what he did, curiosity coupled with his ability to render what he learned in three dimensions.

"How'd ya guess?" Jenn said, ramming the nozzle into the tank and feeding Steve's credit card into the self-serve machine.

"How is it that you're, well, this renowned home-style cooking cook and she cooks like"—he paused, searching for a diplomatic term—"that?"

Jenn locked the lever in place and reached over the side

of the trunk into the bed, grabbing the old brush kept there. She began brushing off the front window.

"I dunno," she admitted. "She never cooked at all when I was growing up. She started after we moved here. I'd be tempted to say it's penance but I really think she likes cooking that stuff and I know she believes it's what keeps her and my dad in the pink. And, God knows, they are in the pink."

She moved to the driver's-side window. "If it's her food that's keeping them healthy, they'll live forever."

"But at what price?" he muttered under his breath.

She laughed. "Similar words have occasionally been bandied around the house by both my father and me. Out of her hearing, of course. I'm not going to take that away from her. She has little enough to feel good about."

"Yeah." He hesitated, the snow collecting in his hair and turning the spikes into improbable curls. Graphite-colored curls. Kinda sexy. "You know, I'm not too sure about this whole 'my poor miserable parents' thing you got working here, Jenn. They don't seem all that unhappy to me."

"Yeah, well," she said, "they've made the best of the situation. I don't deny it. But come on. Back in Raleigh they were . . . like rock stars . . . like . . ." She searched around for a comparison and found one. "They were like you are in New York. Everyone knew them. They were *the* people to have at any fund-raiser or any sort of event or dinner party. In a way, I think that's what's kept them here for so long. They never could accept the idea of rebuilding slowly. This golf course my dad is talking about? Just another pipe dream where they recoup the past with interest added. But it's not going to happen."

Steve was unconvinced. "People generally do what they want to do. I think your parents want to be here."

The idea was ludicrous. Preposterous. Her parents had no more of an abiding affection for Fawn Creek than she did.

"If people have a choice, they do what they want," Jenn said. "But mostly people do what's easiest to do. And it's easiest for my parents to make plans that'll never work. Better that than to see things as they really are, give up, and die."

"Wow. Remind me not to call you when I'm feeling low."

"I'm just being honest," she said, hurt at his suggestion that her objectivity was depressing.

"Maybe your parents make all these plans because it's fun to think about and that's as much as it needs to be," he suggested. "You know, sometimes, as you close in on a goal you've held on to for a long time, it doesn't look that important anymore. And you wonder if you've wasted your time, not to mention the energy."

He looked distinctly uncomfortable and she wondered what goal he'd been pursuing that he'd begun to doubt was worth the effort.

"Maybe the trick is to keep changing the plan. Adapting them to current demands," he said, still wearing that painfully contemplative expression.

"Now that"—she waggled her snow brush at him—"is defeatism. I would suspect anyone who suddenly changed their plans of doing so because they'd realized they weren't going to succeed and were trying to save face."

The side of his mouth curled up in a lightly mocking manner. "But not you."

"Nope. I haven't veered off course or taken my eye off the prize. Not once," she said, waiting for the pride to fill her voice and surprised when it didn't. "I've been making my way slowly but inexorably toward my goal for twenty years."

"Sorta like a glacier?"

Once more, he'd made her laugh. "The Minnesota ice pack. That's me."

"I gotta give you credit," he said, stomping his feet. "I don't know anyone else who's worked so long for a dream."

Dream? The word brought her up short, surprised the hell out of her. Being a success wasn't a dream; it was a *goal*. She wasn't exactly sure what the difference was, but she knew there was one and she knew which one she'd been pursuing and it hadn't been a *dream*. She opened her mouth to protest but wasn't sure what to say. She was saved from having to say anything by a young male voice suddenly hailing her from the gas station's door.

"Ms. Lind, you oughtn't be standing out here pumping gas!" A skinny kid in an insulated jacket came slipping out of the gas station, a sheath of pink Xerox paper in one hand and a staple gun in the other. It was Ken Holmberg's grandson if she wasn't mistaken. Bill? Will?

"That's okay. I'm almost done." Nice kid. "Go back! You don't even have a hat on!"

"I don't have a hat on," Steve said pointedly.

Will? Bill? Ignored her. "I'm real sorry. I was in the back looking for the staple gun. . . . Say! Are you Steve Jaax?" he said, sliding to a stop near the gas pump.

"Why, yes, I am," Steve said, donning his Modest Star smile.

"Wow! I was just getting ready to come stick these up before the storm hit." He held up one of the Xerox sheets. "Supposed to be a big one. But it's always supposed to be a big one, in't?" he asked in the jaded tone of the true Northerner.

Jenn edged in front of Steve and read the sign:

REWARD!!!
$2500.00 for the return of the butter sculpture
of Jenn Lind by the artist Steven Jaax.
Call 218-888-0008. No questions asked.

"Crap!" Jenn exclaimed. "Who's responsible for this?" *And please, Lord, don't let those buffoons with the butter head get wind of it until after I get the damn thing back.*

Bill? Will? looked taken aback. "I dunno. Some lady came by about an hour ago and asked me to put these up."

Panic had surfaced on Steve's face. "Calm down, Steve," she told him. "The mayor's probably decided it wouldn't look good if his celebrity cha-cha'ed when the town failed to produce his sculpture, so he talked the council into offering a reward."

"Really?" His tone said, *Convince me.*

"Really."

"Mr. Jaax, it's a pleasure to meet you, sir." The boy wiped his hand on his blue mechanic's pants and held it out. Steve took it with a gravity suitable to shaking the hand of some foreign dignitary.

Yes, Jenn allowed. There was something weirdly appealing about Steve's catholic views regarding the equality of all his admirers.

The handshake clearly went to the kid's head because in the space of a few seconds he went from shuffling, gawky grease monkey to ambassador of Fawn Creek. "It's a real honor to have you in our town, Mr. Jaax."

"Thank you, son." Steve looked over the boy's head at her. "What did you say?"

"Nothing."

"You made a noise."

A rude noise, but she wasn't going to fess up in front of

the kid. "Don't think so." She gave the pump a wiggle, hoping the tank was already full and the detector just hadn't noted it yet. No such luck. Okay, she was jealous. Why the hell was she jealous? It wasn't as if Fawn Creek meant anything to her.

"Can I ask you a question?" Bill? Will? asked.

"Shoot." Steve leaned against the side of the car, the snow collecting along his collar's seam, his face sandblasted red by the rising wind, but looking as nonchalant as if he'd been standing beside a Palm Springs pool hobnobbing with the art-collecting set.

"When you made *Titus Wrecked*, was aluminum your original choice of material?"

"No," Steve said, his face pleated into all kinds of earnest lines. "It wasn't. I had originally intended to do that piece in silver, but it proved too brittle to support the upper flights, so I ended up using aluminum instead."

"I knew it!" The boy punched the air with his fist.

Jenn stared at the kid, stupefied. Had the world tilted on its axis? Had someone come in one night and switched the inhabitants of the town with aliens . . . aliens with advanced degrees in American art studies?

"You guessed that?" Steve said. "Good catch, kid. What gave you your clue—"

The gas lever snapped off. "Done!" Jenn chirped cheerfully. "I'm sorry . . . Bill."

"Will."

"Right. Will. I'm sorry but Mr. Jaax and I have an important engagement we have to get to, so if you'll excuse us . . . ?"

"Oh. Sure!" Will stepped back. "Wait until I tell some of my friends I met you, Mr. Jaax. Thanks and, ah, drive safe there, Ms. Hallesby. Wouldn't want to hurt the sesquicentennial's star attraction, now, would we?"

"No. We sure wouldn't. Get in, Steve," she said sweetly. She managed to keep her smile in place as she climbed into the cab and looked out her window at the grinning kid. She lifted a single finger off the steering wheel in the standard Minnesota substitute for a wave, applauding herself for the self-restraint that kept her from making it the middle one, and turned the ignition key with the other hand. As soon as the engine turned over, she stepped on the gas.

"You have a problem with my celebrity, don't you?" Steve said.

"No," she said, eyes on the road. It was a little slick on the curves going north out of town. "Why would I?"

"I don't know. Some people do, though. And every time someone asks me for an autograph—"

" 'Every time?' " she echoed. "Come on. You've gotten asked once."

"Well, they'd ask me if they had paper and pen handy," he said, utterly sincere.

She looked over at him. "Does it ever occur to you that not everyone is in awe of you? That some people might not know who you are, or do know who you are and just not care?"

"No," he said without hesitation. "Although you don't seem to care."

"Does that bother you?" She wasn't about to let him in on the little secret that she did, indeed, care. It would only support the wholly illusionary construction keeping his ego afloat. Except, if it was true, it wasn't illusionary, was it?

"Nope." He meant it, too. Whether a person chose to worship at the Jaax altar or not made pretty much no difference to him. He caught her sidelong glance.

"Look, Jenny, that thing with the kid at the gas station? That's what it's like for me everywhere. People are fascinated by celebrity. They want to get close to it, see what it looks like, if it has a feel, a taste, maybe hope a little of the magic dust will rub off on them. I don't know what they want. I don't even know if they get it." He smiled. "But you already know that from experience. It just doesn't happen to you here."

He was right, she realized.

"Do you ever wonder why?"

She did and she was curious about his thoughts on it, too, but the storm had grown in intensity during the last few minutes. Jenn turned the wipers to high to keep up with the snowfall, the flakes dancing in the headlights like feathers at a pillow fight. So she slowed the truck, leaned over the steering wheel, and concentrated on driving instead.

Ten minutes later, she found the turnoff to Storybook Land.

Chapter Twenty-six

6:30 p.m.
Hilda Soderberg's house

One hundred fucking bucks, Ned thought, jerking up the zipper on his snowmobile suit as he prepared to deliver the stupid butter head to its stupid cheap owner. A hundred split three ways. Not *even* ways, you could bet his granny's *rulle pose* on that, but he still wouldn't end up with more than forty bucks. Shit.

"I'm heading out, Gran," he called toward the kitchenette of the little five-room bungalow.

She pattered out of the kitchen on her scrawny little poly-knit-covered shanks, a huge bowl of some yeasty-smelling goodness cradled in her spindly little arms, beating the batter in a quick circle. "Where are you going in a storm? The Chevy don't have snow tires."

"I'm taking the snowmobile and meeting up with Turv. We're going down to Portia's to see if Duddie needs any help with anything. He's out there a ways alone, you know."

From deep within puckered skin and lines, her eyes narrowed suspiciously. "Are you up to somet'ing rotten, Neddie?"

"No! I'm just gonna have a beer or two and maybe help Duddie shovel a path for Portia, is all."

"Okay. But don't call me when that thing flips over."

"No, ma'am."

"Why're you all fired up to plow Duddie's cow a path? We got a walk right here that needs some work—"

Someone banged on the front door, saving him from the interrogation. Muttering to the sound of his grandmother's warning not to let anyone in to track snow all over her clean front hall, Ned headed to the front door and flung it open.

Paul LeDuc stood in the doorway, his shoulders hunkered up around his ears, a close-fitting cap pulled down over their red tips. He looked cold and miserable. This considerably brightened Ned's mood until it occurred to him that this was not a social visit.

"Hey, Mayor, what's up?"

Paul didn't waste any time. "I don't know where you were going, Neddie, but you're gonna have to cancel your plans."

"What?" he squealed. "Whaddaya mean?"

"I mean when I hired you it was with the understanding that you would be available to plow during snow emergencies. Well, this sure as hell—sorry, Mrs. Soderberg! Didn't see you there. That sure smells good! Sure as heck is a snow emergency and you're plowing."

Shit. "And you just had to come over personally to deliver this message?" he asked, so pissed off he didn't care if he was endangering what little income he had. "You coulda just called."

And he could have come up with some excuse why he couldn't go. It was gonna be a little hard to sell the mayor on a sudden illness when he'd obviously been on his way out.

"I was thinking maybe you'd appreciate a ride seeing how's your car doesn't have snow tires," Paul said.

Did everyone in this damn town know everything about everyone else?

"Besides," Paul went on, "I thought maybe I'd drive along with you a bit since the last time I told you to make sure you cleared Route 442 you forgot where it was."

He was coming with? Shit!

"That's not necessary, Paul—"

"Just for a while," Paul interrupted. "Now get your hat and let's get moving. You can call Turv on my phone and tell him we're on our way to pick him up."

Shit. Just . . . shit.

Chapter Twenty-seven

Jenn turned the truck off the county highway and onto a gravel road, where the snow was collecting in the ruts. The trees crowded close here, no ditches to act as a moat separating the road from the wilderness. The dense canopy of interlocking limbs overhead had kept most of the snow from reaching the ground, but a determined wind had bullied enough through the piney defenses to cover the ground and mound over the windfalls.

They had gone a hundred yards when Jenn cranked the wheel and turned the truck around. "I'll walk the rest of the way. I don't want to bottom out in here and be stuck all night. And do not give me that eager look. You don't want to, either. Winter camping is not fun. Especially without a camp."

"Okay." Steve opened his door.

"You can stay here. Really. It's like two minutes away." She gave his leather jacket and jeans a critical once-over. "And let's face it, honey. You are not dressed for the weather."

He blinked. He couldn't remember the last time a straight

person had called him "honey." And she said it so naturally, so comfortably.

"I'm fine," he said. "Your dad's boots are great and I want to come. I've just never been anywhere like this. I'm loving it."

She shook her head. "Ho-kay."

She got out and led the way along the road. It was quiet. Nothing in any of Steve's previous experiences had owned this same quality of silence. What sound the soft, damp snow didn't absorb was muffled by the pine trees or snickered away on the huffing sighs above them.

"It's like we don't exist," he whispered. "It's like being a ghost."

"With big feet," she whispered back and pointed at the imprint left by the boots Cash had lent him. She reached out and hooked his arm in hers, compelling him to stop. Her face was alive in the light bouncing off the snow, glazing her skin with a bluish patina, blackening her irises. Flakes caught on her ski cap and made epaulets on her shoulders.

He wanted to kiss her.

He didn't move.

"Look if you dare," she said, her voice bubbling with amusement, "and prepare to be freaked." She lifted her mittened hand.

He looked in the direction she'd indicated and broke out into laughter.

A few dozen feet away, a big cement gnome, his paint peeled and faded, tipped drunkenly against the back end of a three-legged fawn. The gnome looked suspiciously like Grumpy and the fawn like Bambi, but each was altered just sufficiently to keep the copyright police away. Still, Steve got the idea. They'd been positioned in such a way that they looked caught in some disreputable act, especially since the wide-eyed Bambi looked more alarmed than innocent.

"Since when were Bambi and Grumpy in the same fairy tale?" he asked.

"Since some local wag with too much time on his hands crept in here about ten years ago and rearranged the statues left behind."

"Who was the local wag?"

"No one knows," she said, starting forward again.

"You're kidding."

"Nope. And believe me, plenty have tried to find out."

"You'd think that in ten years someone would let it slip out," Steve said, fascinated. "I mean, who can keep a secret like that for that long?"

"Ever hear of Olof Ohman and the Kensington stone?" she asked.

He had. He'd seen a special about it on the History Channel. Some farmer late in the last century had purportedly found a stone with inscriptions made by a Swedish exploration party that predated Columbus's journey by several hundred years. Scholars were still arguing over whether it was a hoax or not.

"You think it's fake and that the secret's been kept all these years?" The very idea was awesome.

"Swedes will have their little jokes," she said playfully but without committing. "They still do." She nodded toward Bambi.

"Man, for some guy to change all this round and never breathe a word of it to anyone . . ." he said. "Now that is an artist."

"How'd you figure?"

"He didn't leave his signature. He wanted the work to

stand on its own merits, uncolored by his personality or society's expectation of him."

"Steve," she said, "someone tipped a bunch of cement statues over so they looked like they're fornicating. That's not art."

"It is in a way . . ." He trailed off. "Is that a castle?"

"Yup," Jenn said. Leaving Grumpy and Bambi behind, she followed what at one time would have been a footpath but then broke from it to head straight through the woods toward the turret he'd glimpsed.

"When I was a kid, I thought each of these tableaux were miles apart," she said as they walked. "The deeper we went, the more it seemed like we could get lost like Hansel and Gretel—and don't ask what they're up to. It's not nice. Even when I was eight, I knew it was hokey and the cement figures were bogus, but there was still something about following these twisty paths to see what came next.

"The castle was at the farthest end of the place. By the time we got there, it seemed like we really might be walking through an enchanted forest." She broke off and stepped aside. "There it is."

It was only about one and a half stories high, and a third of the top had eroded away, exposing the structural rebar in the crumbling cement, but someone had taken time with the original. Beneath the crenulated roof, rather than the expected paintings of little windows, real ones had been set in. The entrance on the ground level was to scale, but whatever door had originally hung there had long since left its hinges. In the decades since, roses had been planted beside the little door, and they'd taken over the structure. Now the dead vines rambled up the western side, draping over the ruined top like Donald Trump's comb-over.

"Magic, huh?" Jenn asked.

She didn't sound the least embarrassed at using the word nor did she sound particularly reverent. She said the word as if magic were a given. As if she was used to it, on a first-name basis with it. Maybe it was all the snow swirling softly down from above, or the way the night had leached the color from everything and left behind nothing but sheen. Maybe it was walking abandoned paths to revisit abandoned places, but it was magical.

He lifted his face to the sky, letting the snow blind him, and stuck his tongue out, trying to catch a flake and catching more like forty.

"*Blah!* This snow tastes lousy."

"Oh?" She sounded amused. He looked over at her and discovered that she'd tipped her head far back, too, and was letting the flakes dissolve against her tongue, her eyes narrowed against the snowfall and her arms spread wide to keep her balanced. "You're a snow connoisseur?"

"No. I can't remember the last time I tried to catch snow on my tongue. I thought it would taste different. Like spring-water. You know, pure, innocent, God's tears, that sort of thing? Like when I was a kid."

"You really are a romantic, aren't you, Steve?" She had quit catching snowflakes and squatted down in front of the castle door. "The snow was never pure and innocent, hon. You were."

She wrapped a rubber band around the money she'd brought and leaned forward, her entire arm disappearing inside as she stuck the bills into the castle's interior: half quixotic goddess, half practical businesswoman.

She straightened, her nose wrinkling. "I think others have been using the castle for nefarious purposes. It reeks of dope."

"Now what?" Steve asked. Magic or not, he was starting

to get really cold. He stomped his feet and wished he'd accepted Cash's offer of a hat. "Do we wait around for them to show up and hand over the butter head? Do we leave and come back? What did this guy say?"

"He said we'd see the butter head on the way out."

They looked at each other.

"Have you heard a car or a snowmobile since we got here?" she asked.

"No, but I wasn't listening for them, either. Have you?"

"No." She frowned. "Maybe I got it wrong. Maybe we're supposed to just sit in the truck and wait for him to show up."

"Okay," Steve said. "Let's sit."

They returned to the truck, got in the cab, and sat.

They sat for an hour and a half, watching the snow first veil, then blanket, and finally completely obliterate the truck's windows. They took turns stomping around and brushing it off, just so they'd have enough light in the cab to see each other. Every fifteen minutes or so, Jenn would run the engine to keep the interior of the cab above freezing. Above freezing, Steve discovered, wasn't all that comfortable.

He wrapped his leather jacket as tightly around himself as he could and dug his hands up the sleeves of the opposite arm to keep his hands from going numb. Only his feet were comfortable in his borrowed boots. His ass was like an ice cube.

"Want to share body heat?" he asked her about an hour in. He could imagine what he looked like: red, drippy nose, red ears, blue-black stubble on his cheeks and chin (he hadn't shaved since five this morning). "It's a survival technique. I saw it on the Discovery Channel."

She raised one of those expressive eyebrows. "Even more

surprising than the fact that you watch the Discovery Channel is the information that you own a TV."

"I don't. I was in a hotel room. I spend a lot of time in hotel rooms with the TV when I'm in some city doing a show. I do a lot of shows." He did a lot of hotels. "Don't look all superior. You can learn things from TV. Like conserving body heat to survive arctic temperatures. So do you wanna?"

The look she gave him was answer enough. "We're not in any imminent danger of freezing, Steve. If we want to leave, we can just leave. Do you want to give up and leave?"

Yes. "Do you?"

"I dunno," she said. "Let's give it another fifteen minutes."

By the time the fifteen minutes had elapsed, his mood had gone even further south. The jerks who'd taken his butter head had seen the ransom note in town and opted for the more lucrative offer, and in the meantime they sat here—not sharing body heat—freezing their asses off. He wasn't keen on the idea of giving up the butter head. He wasn't keen on freezing his ass off. He'd leave the decision to her.

"I'm freezing my ass off," he said.

"Me, too." She started the engine and flicked on the wipers, displacing the latest load of snow that had covered the windshield. "I've been thinking. I wouldn't be surprised if these clowns were pulled off the road somewhere waiting for us to leave before coming in to get the cash and dump off the butter head. What with the snow and all, they might have gotten here late. They might be out there watching us right now, wishing we'd leave. So maybe we should."

For a very practical woman, this was an amazingly dumb suggestion. "And once we leave and they drive in and get the money, what's to keep them from keeping the butter head?" he asked.

"Not a thing," she admitted, "except unless they've seen

that flier in town there's no reason for them to keep it. I think they got the message that my offer was a 'one time only.' "

"And if they did see that flier in town?"

"We're screwed. They never were here and aren't going to be here, and we've wasted all this time and your personal BTUs for nothing." She didn't have to sound so nonchalant about it. But then, of everyone involved, she was the least interested in retaking the butter head. And yet, here she was, shivering beside him.

"Ah, don't look so sad, Steve. If they do turn it in for the reward, you'll still end up riding at the head of the parade alongside it. All's well that ends well. Except"—she hesitated just a few seconds—"it would have been nice to save this crappy little town their money."

Chapter Twenty-eight

7:00 p.m.
Same place

Without waiting for Steve to reply, Jenn shifted into gear and started driving, reaching the highway and climbing carefully over the snow onto the road proper. There was a lot more snow than when they'd arrived. A lot. And the driving conditions, which hadn't been good to begin with, had further deteriorated. The highway was nothing but a pale river in the headlights, only the faintest tire tracks giving Jenn a clue as to where the road curved and where it went straight. Under her mittens, the knuckles gripping the steering wheel were white. She glanced at Steve. At least one of them was enjoying the drive.

Steve, who'd admitted earlier that the last time he'd driven a car before this morning had been to a Bangles concert, sat looking around with the expectant pleasure of a six-year-old on a special outing. Every now and then he'd wipe the window with his sleeve and press his nose to the glass and make some exclamation of delight, pointing out first a hummock of snow ("Is that a bobcat?" "No."), then a road reflector that had caught the headlights ("Are those the eyes of a bobcat?" "No."), and finally a big barn cat scooting across the road ("Is—" "No.").

She wished something would come out of the night to grant him a little wish-fulfillment, but except for the big tom, who was presumably motivated by testosterone levels beyond his control, nothing that wasn't similarly affected was going to be out in a storm like this.

They shouldn't be out in a storm like this.

They were in the midst of nearly whiteout conditions, the snow coating the windshield like Christmas tree flocking and obliterating any indications of where the sides of the road ended and the ditches began. Every strong wind gust pushed the truck sideways toward the unseen ditches she fought to keep the vehicle from sliding into. She hunched over the steering wheel, trying to stay in the proximal middle of what she hoped was the road while Steve sat in idiot contentment.

No one else was out on the road, either. Why would they be? Everyone else had too much sense. She thought briefly of calling the state patrol on her cell phone but as she hadn't driven them into the ditch—yet—and she had no doubt that the state patrol were answering plenty of calls from people who had, they'd probably say, "Good luck, then, and drive slow, okay?"

So slow they went. They'd been driving for thirty minutes when the town's sole snow plow roared past them, heading north up the highway in the direction from which they'd just come, a poor call in Jenn's estimation since there weren't that many people living up there. When they finally made the town limits a few minutes later, she realized good judgment might not have been the plow driver's strong suit because the streets he'd "plowed" in town were a mess.

Heavy banks of snow blocked most of the side streets and

a tall ridge divided the center of the main street, making turns across the center line all but impossible. The wind had already reconfigured the snow left behind by the plow, forming huge drifts that swept across the street at the town's only stoplight, effectively barricading access to the southbound road.

Not that there was any traffic moving south. Or north. Or any direction.

Fawn Creek was a ghost town, the only sounds the driving wind and the rattling of the traffic signs at the intersection. Not a single car appeared in any direction, just sheets of snow blown horizontally down the main corridor.

"Crap," Jenn muttered, her head swiveling from side to side as she looked for a passable side street. "We can't try to ram through that. Even if we didn't get stuck, little ways out and the roads south will all be drifted over by now."

"So what's the plan?" Steve asked, looking monumentally unconcerned. He pointed to the dark storefronts. "Can we knock on some doors and beg, 'Help the poor traveler?' "

"We could if anyone lived above the shops but most of the storeowners live on the residential streets."

"Let's go there then."

She squirmed. "I don't want to."

"Huh?"

She was being ridiculous. It didn't matter. "I don't want to ask for help."

His hands flew up in an age-old expression of bafflement. "How come?"

Because she hadn't asked for anything from them since she'd asked them to make her Miss Fawn Creek. Because that had been a debacle. Because she didn't want to owe anyone here anything. Because, damn it, it still hurt. She cared and that was all that mattered.

"I just can't ask."

"You'd rather freeze or take your chances on the road?" he asked, eyeing her uncertainly, as though he expected her to start frothing at the mouth.

She was stubborn and oversensitive. She wasn't an idiot.

"Hell, no," she said. "We're going to break in to one of these stores."

She chose Smelka's because they were right in front of it and because she knew Greta was too damn cheap to ever have installed anything like a security system. Also, Steve hadn't had anything to eat all day except half a cookie and a spoonful of risotto. They parked the truck—actually, they simply got out of the truck and left it where it stood. At once, the wind tore the breath from Jenn's lungs and thrust icy hands down her collar. She squinted into the snow, shielding her eyes against the gritty blasts.

The temperature was dropping, and the wet flakes froze as they fell, turning into pellets. She blinked at Steve, who'd covered his bare ears with his hands and was looking around, again more interested than alarmed. She had to give him credit; he wasn't a whiner.

"Come on!" she called over the wind and jerked his sleeve in the direction of the café. Together, they scrambled over the drift separating them from Smelka's door. Hoping for a little small-town credulity, she pulled on the handle. It didn't open. They just didn't make small towns they way they used to.

She looked the door over, hoping to spot an easy way in. *Crap,* she thought, heading back toward the truck.

"Where are you going?" Steve hollered.

"Back to the truck," she shouted without turning, "to look in the glove compartment for something to pick the lock with—"

Crash!

She spun around. Steve was standing where she'd left him, shaking pieces of glass off his sleeve. The restaurant's door window was missing. "It's open now," he said, carefully reaching in over the rim of broken glass and unlatching the door. He opened it and waited for her to duck inside before following her in.

"I better find something to cover that window," Steve said, flipping on the lights. "We'll probably be here all night."

His naïveté was charming.

"Steve," she said, "there's probably been a half a dozen calls about us to the sheriff's office already. Nothing in a small town goes unnoticed, unreported, or ungossiped about. Not even if it happens in a snowstorm in the dead of night. We'll be here until Einer has finished pulling people out of the ditch, goes back to his office, and finds the answering machine filled to capacity with reports about the break-in at Smelka's."

He gave her the credit of assuming she knew what she was talking about. "How long will that be?"

"Long enough." She peered out the window at the two-story brick storefronts on the other side of the street. She wasn't sure which ones, if any, housed tenants on their top levels anymore. All of them were dark. Of course, that didn't mean anything. You couldn't maintain your dignity with your nose pressed to the window that was backlit. And people in towns like Fawn Creek did a lot of nose pressing.

"Let's leave the overhead lights off, okay? I wouldn't want anyone who saw the lights risking life and limb investigating—that would be our lives and our limbs—and if someone sees us moving around in here, they just might show up with a twelve gauge."

"You're kidding," Steve said, again looking delighted. The whole damn town just seemed to tickle the hell out of him. "That's sweet."

"You are a very odd man," Jenn said. "Kill the lights."

He switched them off.

"And while you're looking for something to cover that broken window, what say I cook up a little something for you to eat?"

In reply, he simply looked at her, the light from the neon sign in the window bathing his face in blissful blue light. If her ex-husband had looked at her with half as much reverence, they might still be married.

"That would be wonderful."

She moved behind the lunch counter, where she did a quick visual inventory before heading for the pair of doors at the end of the grill area. She pulled open the first door and poked her head inside the walk-in, which was more of a root cellar than a refrigerator. Potato sausage, kielbasa, and a string of homemade wieners hung from hooks on the near wall while the shelves at the back held cartons of eggs, gallons of milk and cream, and a couple big blocks of butter. Beneath the shelves, carrots, onions, and potatoes poked out of sawdust-filled bins.

She shut that door and opened the one next to it. It was a pantry stocked with big canisters of flour, sugar, rice, macaroni, and dried beans. Its shelves were lined with rows of canned and boxed goods.

She cracked her knuckles and got to work.

By the time Steve had found some duct tape and covered the broken window with a heavy piece of cardboard, Jenn had a roux bubbling in a saucepan, a pot of macaroni boiling, and had just begun sautéing her quick dice of onions, celery, and carrots in an obscene amount of butter.

"I'm going to see if there's any beer in the fridge," Steve announced, disappearing into the walk-in. He returned a minute later and slid onto the stool on the other side of the counter.

"No beer?" Jenn asked, sticking a couple pieces of bread in the toaster.

"Nope, but look what I found instead."

"That's aquavit," Jenn said, glancing up from the fine mince she was putting on a couple gloves of garlic. The last time she'd had aquavit had been before Fawn Creek's homecoming dance her senior year. It had given her all the courage she'd needed to make a complete ass out of herself. And Heidi.

Man, she'd been hell-bent on forcing Ken Holmberg and the town council to release her from her Miss Fawn Creek obligations. The homecoming dance, less than a month after the state fair debacle, had seemed to be the perfect venue during which to force their hands—and Heidi the perfect excuse for them to divest her of her crown. But you don't force a Scandinavian to do anything. The entire culture apparently existed simply to provide a definition in the dictionary for the words "unflappable" and "stoic." Still, she'd thought the homecoming dance stunt would have done the trick in a staunchly conservative, Lutheran community like this. Nope.

In retrospect, thank God. Because it had been her position as Miss Fawn Creek that had gotten her asked back on *Good Neighbors* a few weeks later. And from there . . . here.

"That stuff'll kill you."

"Yup." He unscrewed the top. "But at least we'll go out warm." He leaned over the counter and hung, head upside down, as he snagged a couple juice glasses and wiggled his way back upright.

He filled them both and pushed hers toward her. "To Fawn Creek," he said, raising his glass.

She snorted, lifted the glass, and clinked. "You're only toasting them because everyone you've seen has doted on you."

"Ain't it great?" he conceded.

She took a swig and added some milk to her roux, whisking rapidly as she poured. "Yeah, if you're you. But I've been coming back and forth to this town for twenty-three years"—she added handfuls of the grated cheese into the mix—"and no one has ever asked for my autograph. And before you point out the obvious, yes, I am a little jealous. Nah. More resentful. You're jealous of something you want. You're resentful of something you think you should have."

She shifted the white sauce off the stove, took another sip of aquavit, and unhooked some potholders from above the stove. Then she swung the pot with the macaroni over the sink and upended it into a colander waiting inside.

"You're a fixture here," Steve said.

She looked over her shoulder at him and started crumbling the toast she'd made into a small pan sizzling with garlic and butter. "I am not. I only come here to visit my parents. I don't even come in to the town proper that often."

"Bull," he said, twirling his juice glass around. "You've known everyone we've seen today. *Everyone.*"

Had she? She dismissed his observation. "Coincidence. We could walk down the street every day for the next week before I saw anyone else I recognized."

She dumped the drained macaroni into a bowl and poured the white sauce over it, folding the golden silky concoction carefully. Then she took another swallow of aquavit.

"But they'd know you," he said.

She took the sizzling vegetable mixture off the stove and

emptied it into the bowl, along with a few sprinkles of pepper and mustard and a grate of fresh nutmeg. "Maybe. But only because everyone in this town knows everything about everyone else. You know that saying about a person's life being an open book? Well, a small town is like a communal blog that everyone reads every day."

She ducked into the refrigerator and emerged with a plate of sliced ham, which she chopped into bits and added to the macaroni. Then she spooned the mixture into a small casserole dish she'd found and buttered. She finished by sprinkling the garlic-butter-soaked toast bits on top and popped it in the oven. Time for another sip of aquavit.

She lifted her glass to her lips. The alcohol had slid down more easily with each sip twenty years ago, too.

"They asked you to be their grand marshal."

He was still on Fawn Creek? She regarded him knowingly. She'd seen it before in urban dwellers, the Jimmy Stewart syndrome: small town equals virtue. Hell, she should have recognized it earlier; she'd built a career on the precept.

"Look, tootsie cake— Whoa! Sorry. That would be the aquavit speaking. Try again." She concentrated. "Look, Steve, you keep saying that like it's a big deal or something. It's not. It seems to me," she continued, enunciating carefully, "that many have been asked to be grand marshal— some of whom aren't even real. Like your . . . my . . . mom's butter head. To be honest," she went on, warming to the subject, "I'm a little surprised you agreed to co-marshal. Not to be rude or anything, but you just don't seem like the type who likes to share the spotlight."

His expression of offended dignity couldn't have been more contrived. God, he was cute.

"The reality check on all this," she went on, "is that the

town council is desperate for anything that might draw some speculators here and one of those things is me. Their last-ditch effort to get noticed. Come visit Fawn Creek, Jenn Lind's hometown. If Chico, the dog-riding monkey, had been born here, they would have named him grand marshal. And he probably would have been a bigger draw."

"What about me?" he asked.

Ah, crap. Now she'd hurt his feelings. Man, his ego was fragile. Sort of like the *Hindenburg,* enormous but vulnerable.

"You?" She tipped the mouth of her glass in his direction, wiggling it invitingly at Steve and withholding her opinion until after he'd poured her another half a juice glass full. "You are media fodder, babe. Steve Jaax, cosmopolitan hipster, roughing it in the northland? Hell, you'll score all the local news shows and that's just the sort of coverage these poor schmucks are depending on."

She tipped open the oven door and peeked inside. The top of the macaroni was bubbling nicely; the golden crumbs needed only a minute more to turn crispy-crunchy good.

"Not that I begrudge the town their every effort. I hope it works. I don't think it stands a chance in hell of doing so."

"How come?"

"There's no seed money here, Steve. Most of the people make less than twenty-five a year. In order to survive, this town needs a bunch of people willing to invest in little cottage industries. And that means someone needs some cash or a reason to invest here. And there is none!

"There's no freeway within ten miles, no industry to attract people—except for Ken's hockey stick plant and"—she glanced right and left and lowered her voice confidingly— "rumor has it that Minnesota Hockey Stix is not as financially stable as it ought to be, despite its recent expansion. If Ken pulls out, there goes another forty or fifty families. The economy of a small town is sort of like a coral reef. The balance is incredibly intricate and delicate. Ten families leave and the ripple effect is felt everywhere from the public school assistance from the state to the amount of gas sold. Fifty families leave and the impact is devastating. It's not just his employees. It's the people who plow his parking lot, the local drivers he uses to ship his products, and the maintenance service he employs, the café where most of the people at the plant eat lunch every day.

"It doesn't help that the casino has siphoned off a lot of what tourism the town had. The snow has been crappy for three years running and that means no snow trade tourists." She took a sip and mused. "There's nothing here but lakes and woods, and in case you haven't tumbled to it, Steve, Minnesota isn't exactly short on lakes."

"Then the town must be happy with what's happening outside," Steve said, pointing out the window at the near whiteout conditions on the street.

"You'd think, wouldn't you?" Jenn said with a little sigh. Fawn Creek just couldn't seem to catch a break. "All this snow is great, *if* it had either shown up earlier or held off a little longer. As it is, it's just going to keep travelers from heading up here for the sesquicentennial."

The whole conversation was depressing her way out of proportion to what this town meant to her. Time to change the subject.

She opened the oven, slid on a mitt, and took out the concoction, setting it in front of Steve. She found silverware and handed him a fork. She spooned a portion onto a plate and slid it in front of Steve. "Dig in but blow on it first or you'll burn your mouth."

He perked right up, shoving his fork under a huge load of

food and impatiently blowing at his fork until she nodded. Then he stuffed the whole forkful into his mouth.

Euphoric revelation transformed his face.

He swallowed, forked up another mouthful, puffed quickly on it, shoved it in, chewed, and swallowed.

"What is this?" he asked through another mouthful of food.

She shrugged.

"No. No, I have to know the name of it," he insisted. "This is . . . I've never had anything like this. Well, like it maybe, but this is . . . this is transcendent."

She understood. She felt that way about good food, too.

"What's it called?" he persevered.

"I dunno. Hotdish?"

"Hotdish," he breathed rapturously.

Chapter Twenty-nine

8:30 p.m.
Smelka's Café

Steve, finishing his first plate of hotdish in record time, heaped his plate full again and began on that. Jenn watched him eat, sipping aquavit, and nodding contentedly. This was what she loved most about cooking: people loving what she made, discovering their inner gluttons, realizing their sybaritic potential. So many people went through life with their palates dulled by convenience and expediency. Steve had an appetite. He enjoyed things, people, food, conversation. He probably really enjoyed sex, too. Not that she'd ever find out. But a woman could wonder, speculate. It had been so long since she'd even speculated, she felt a guilty enjoyment in it.

She wondered if underneath that white shirt, Steve had any muscle tone. He didn't look like the type who belonged to a gym. But he had a nice, flat stomach. Nice broad wrists, too, probably from the sculpting. Strong-looking, tensile.

"This is what you do?" he interrupted her pleasantly lascivious thoughts. "Teach people how to make hotdish?"

If only. She cupped her cheek in her hand and smiled at him. "There's no recipe for hotdish. It's just what you have on hand and how you put it together. It's never the same twice. I couldn't make that again if I tried."

"It's art," he intoned soberly.

"It's food," she corrected, pleased nonetheless by the compliment. Steve might just get it. Whatever "it" was. She wondered if he was a good kisser. He'd taste like aquavit and hotdish. She took another sip.

"Where'd you learn all this?" he asked. "From your grandmother?"

She snorted again and wondered what was up with that. She generally eschewed snorting but this was Fawn Creek. She wasn't trying to impress Steve with her femininity—not because she didn't want to; she just figured it was a moot point—and what the hell? "Hell, no. My grandmother had staff."

"Staff."

"Yup. You know. Maid, cook, housekeeper, gardener. Staff. My parents did, too, once upon a time. That's where I learned a lot of my stuff. From Tina, the housekeeper. She was Jamaican and she could cook anything." She wondered where Tina was now. "I think of everything my mom misses, she misses Tina the most."

"And you? What did you miss?"

A face popped into her head, a square face covered in freckles, surrounded by bright copper curls. Tess. She didn't think about Tess too often anymore. Time had healed that wound, at least. But thinking about Tess now, Jenn felt like there was something undone about her memory. Like Jenn had missed something important, somehow. Like she'd missed the funeral (she hadn't). It was weird. She couldn't think what it would be.

Jenn tipped the rest of the aquavit into her mouth and gave a little involuntary shiver.

"I'm sorry," he said so quietly that she wondered for a second if she'd said something aloud, something revealing. She looked up and found him studying her, appealing and somber and concerned. She didn't want that. If he was concerned, it made her suspicious that there was something to be concerned about and there wasn't. She had everything under control. On autopilot. Best to steer this conversation back to safe—to less uncomfortable territory.

She leaned over the counter. The room rocked a little then steadied. "What are you doing here, Steve? What are you really doing here?"

"I want to see my—your—butter head," he said.

"Nah." She wagged her finger under his nose. "There's more to it than that."

"There is?"

"Yeah, you're looking for something. Something you've lost."

"Jesus!" He blinked. "What else did you learn from that Jamaican housekeeper? Fortune-telling?"

"A killer jerk chicken." She eased back onto her side of the counter, feeling very wise and very, very old. She sighed. Oh, well, if you couldn't be a nymph, you might as well be a kick-ass crone. Her and the Delphi oracle, sistahs.

The thing was, the real thing was, that she *liked* Steve. She liked his honesty, his charm, and the open-faced pleasure he took in almost everything, including his own mythology. She also liked his . . . wrists, a lot, and she suspected a lot of women did and that made her feel a little low because undoubtedly they were all glamorous young women, and a man as famous as Steve would take pleasure in all that young adoration. Ah, hell. Steve would take pleasure in any adulation. "Answer the question."

"I don't know," he said, looking thoroughly guilty. "Inspiration, I suppose. Why?"

"You need my advice," she said, coming to a sudden decision. That in itself should have raised warning flags. She didn't make sudden decisions. Ever. Oh well, one for the books . . . "I've been following your career—"

"You've been following my career?" he interjected, flattered.

"Come on. You're being coy again, right?"

"No!" he denied.

"You're *Steve Jaax*. You're like an art icon. And *you* carved *my* head in butter and then went on to tell the whole world that while you were doing it you rediscovered your talent and found your focus. How could I not follow your career after that?"

She nodded. Her vision swam. No more nodding. "I've seen pictures of everything you've done. I've seen most of it in person. The stuff that's not in private collections, that is."

She waited. He waited. "You're not going to ask me what I thought of them, are you?" she finally said. " 'Cause you're afraid of what I'll say. Me. A nobody. Well," she said because false modesty was something she never could stand, "really someone pretty big but not someone whose opinion you would normally care about."

"I care about everyone's opinion," he said.

Damn. He was telling the truth. "God, that's gotta be rough."

"You have no idea," he whispered.

"Look. Ask me."

"Really?" he said, doubtfully.

"Yeah."

"Okay. Do you like my stuff?"

"The older work is terrific. Your new stuff sucks."

He stared at her for a full five seconds before slamming his palms down on the counter and surging up over it like Swamp Thing. He looked pretty impressive standing above her, snarling. *"You set me up!"*

Hastily, she reached under the shelf and uncovered the domed plate of *semlor* she'd seen on her earlier forays there. She plopped three small, golden, cream-filled buns on a new plate and slid it under his tensed jaw. At once, his jaw untensed. Slowly he melted back into his seat, his scowl replaced by an unwillingly interested expression. Food, the Great Leveler.

"Eat."

She didn't have a clue where she had grown the *cajones* to talk to him like this. She wasn't an art critic. She wasn't even the kind of person who liked giving advice. Okay, that was a lie, but she didn't give advice out about stuff she didn't have any expertise in. Okay, another lie. She'd never given out art advice. Whatever. The whole impulse was bizarre. Maybe it was being here in Fawn Creek where she wasn't so much Jenn Lind as Jenny Hallesby. Maybe it was because he seemed so oddly isolated.

Maybe it was because she was drunk.

He took a small, grudging bite of the bun.

"What do you think?" Now she was being coy. She could tell what he thought from the look on his face.

"Oh . . . Oh!" He took another bite and closed his eyes, the cream filling oozing out the back end of the bun. "What is this?"

"A cream bun." She laughed at the look on his face. He finished the first one and started on the second. "Want some coffee?"

"No," he said, chewing away. Then he paused and cast her an aggrieved look. "You hurt my feelings."

"Look, Steve, art-wise you're coasting. If I can see it, others can. The real question is why your manager or agent or whatever the hell you guys have didn't say anything."

"Because you're wrong?" he suggested around a mouthful of almond cream.

"No, I'm not." She leaned over the counter again. "Steve, you're making money off being you."

There. She'd said it. She drew back and waited for his reaction. He licked the tips of his fingers clean.

"'Course, there's a chance you just don't have anything more to say," she suggested. "Maybe you've reached a place where anything you come up with will be the epitaph for your career. It's been a good career."

"It's still a good career," he said as he reached for another *semlor.*

"Have you ever considered hanging it all up?"

"No."

"Maybe you should," she suggested kindly. "You have to be pushing fifty. Maybe the best isn't yet to come. Maybe the best is all in the rearview mirror. If all any of it means to you anymore is a chance to see your name in *People* magazine . . ." She trailed off. "I mean, I'm not trying to be cruel here or anything but—"

"Man, then I'd hate to hear you when you were." Remarkably, he no longer sounded all that offended. He sounded . . . *flattered*? Whatever Steve Jaax wasn't, he was seriously odd.

"You're tough," he said admiringly.

"On you," she admitted. What had gotten into her? The burn of "make it righteousness" had left, leaving an empty feeling behind. What right did she have to bitch anyone out about pandering to their own celebrity? She was exhibit number one. "I'm a marshmallow when it comes to me."

"Yeah?"

"Yeah. Do you realize I have spent twenty years becoming the consummate Minnesotan in order to escape Minnesota? How's that for irony?"

"So what? You created a persona, an image. Nothing wrong with that."

He was a much nicer man than she was a woman. She still had a crush on him, she realized.

"The thing to keep sight of is that at least you're doing what you love to do, and you're really, really good at it," he said. "You must be to have attracted Dwight Davies's attention. The man's an asshole but he knows quality when he sees it."

"Crass commercialism," she said tonelessly.

"Why would you say that?" For the first time since she'd met him early that morning, he looked annoyed. "You're doing what you love and getting paid a shit load to do it. What more can you ask?"

"Is this what I love?" she mused quietly. "I don't know that it is. I'll bet you always wanted to be an artist or something like it. I bet you had a soldering gun when you were eight or something, right?"

"Yes. So?"

"Well, I never set out to be a lifestyle coach or a cooking maven or felt some inner calling to bring the torch of domestic enlightenment out of the hinterlands to illuminate the chaotic modern world."

His mouth twitched into a smile. "So what did you want to be?"

"I can't remember," she said, a little sadly, a little drunkenly. "Probably a lawyer. Don't all ambitious little suburban girls want to grow up to be lawyers? It doesn't really matter what I wanted. I just know it wasn't this. In fact, I don't think I've ever wanted to be anything. I've just wanted to succeed. And here I am, forty years old, speeding down a highway straight to the Promised Land of Commercial Success. And you know what I see when I look in the rearview mirror?"

"The Ghost of Martha Stewart Past? No? What?"

He was trying to make her laugh but her smile was wan. *"Nothing.* I look in my rearview mirror and the road behind is empty."

She'd often been mistaken for being younger than she was, and now rather than seeing that as a compliment, she felt it as an indictment.

"At forty you should have a history," she whispered, "things cluttering your past. There should be messy relationships, heartbreaks, bittersweet memories, embarrassments, and extravagances. There should be a first home somewhere back there, anniversaries, champagne dinners, a fast car." She looked up and caught his eye. "There should at least be a dog, don't you think? I mean, a *dog*? I love dogs! Why haven't I ever had a *dog*?"

Because her eyes had always been focused forward, nothing deterred her from the goal; nothing interrupted her forward momentum. No detours. No off-ramps. There were to be no bumps in her road, no siree. She'd routed her life carefully, one straight line to the land of security, to that "home" she'd been promising herself since she was sixteen, the one she not only lost but somewhere even lost the memory of because looking behind didn't get you ahead. *That* was how you got an image like hers in the rearview mirror.

She gave him a wry smile. "But all that's gonna change as soon as I conquer this last frontier, national syndication."

"What's going to happen then?"

"I'm gonna get a dog."

"Why don't you get one now?"

"Because I want to know that I can take care of him like he deserves, that I have the time and the right place for him." Because you never knew when the storm might break, when your home might disappear and you might find yourself an exile.

When your friends might die.

Her eyes stung and she blinked rapidly, trying to clear them, and looked down.

Steve was holding her hand. How had that happened? Her own hand tightened in his. He reached across the counter with his free hand and brushed her knuckles lightly. His eyes were incredibly blue. If she leaned over a few feet, just twenty-four inches . . . there'd be something to see in her rearview. She wet her lips.

His gaze sharpened and he stood up, his hand dipping beneath her hair to cup the back of her head. He leaned forward and his mouth touched hers, at first as soft as chamois cloth, questioning and tentative, not the least bit overconfident.

She practically jumped to her feet, grabbing hold of his shirt front and pulling him in closer, kissing him back, a little amazed, a little desperate, and a little embarrassed. She didn't have to be; he reacted well to encouragement.

With a moan, he hooked his arm around her and lifted her up, dragging her over the counter. No, onto the counter. Dishes flew, clattering to the ground and spinning on the floor as he brushed the last of them out of the way and pushed her down onto the Formica, his arm cushioning her back, his mouth sealed against hers.

She cupped his jaw between her palms and kissed him back, hungry—no, starving. He tasted of almond cream and aquavit, heady and sweet, and his tongue swept between her lips and found hers and she sighed with openmouthed pleasure back into his mouth. Her head was swimming, foggy and sparkling at the same time, drunk, drunken, on kisses, on alcohol, who the hell cared as long as she could stay focused on his lips and hands and the way they were traveling over her, molding her hips and her ribs and riding up to her breast? There he hesitated, a little uncertain, a great deal careful. It was incredibly arousing. She wanted it to go on and on, necking like a teenager, hot and flushed and driven.

He made a sound, low, urgent, and she felt herself being shifted and then his knee next to her hip. He was climbing right up onto the counter with her, straddling her. Not so uncertain after all.

Abruptly, he tore his mouth away and pushed himself up and braced his hands on either side of her head. He looked around a little wildly, as out of breath and befuddled as she felt. "Jenny. This is a lunch counter. . . . There's got to be—"

A blue light suddenly painted his face and his white shirt, disappeared, and painted them again. She turned her head and stared dumbly straight into the flashing signal of the sheriff's patrol car.

"Looks like our ride's here," she said.

"Fuck," he answered.

Chapter Thirty

It was after midnight. From inside the town hall's glass vestibule, Ned watched Turv park the front-end loader in the Quonset hut garage, where Ned had parked the plow an hour earlier, and haul the sliding doors shut. Turv trotted across the empty parking lot, flapping his arms and puffing clouds of vapor into the frosty night air. For being half frozen, old Turv looked pretty happy, and after Ned told him what he'd learned, old Turv was going to look happier still.

He opened the door to the vestibule and Turv scooted in.

"Some weather, eh?" he said.

"Got that right," Ned agreed.

Turv peeled off his choppers and rubbed his hands together to get the blood back circulating. "Did she really leave the money in the castle like you told her?"

"Yup. I couldn't get out there until about two hours later than we told her, 'counta the asshole mayor kept driving by to see if I was clearing the highways to his liking. She had the hundred bucks all wrapped up tidy with a rubber binder and stuffed right in the castle."

Ned, feeling that perhaps someone ought to call attention to his honesty in his dealings with his partners, decided that someone would be himself. "You know, a guy coulda just taken the top twenty dollars for himself and no one would have known better."

"If a guy was an asshole," Turv said.

Ned had wasted his breath. Turv couldn't appreciate a subtle moral problem like that.

Turv's prematurely corrugated brow pleated up into a few more ropy lines as he frowned. "Don't suppose you had a chance to pick up the butter head and drop it off then?"

"Nope," Ned said, hugging his surprise to himself just a little longer.

"Crap. I suppose we should just go do it now then." Turv sighed gustily. "I mean, we got no reason to keep the damn thing anymore, do we?"

"Yes," Ned said, "we sure do."

"Why's that, Ned?"

"Because Providence has finally smiled down on us, Turv. Look what Eric found on his way out of town." He held up a pink Xeroxed sheet like the one Eric had phoned him about, a flier he'd found pinned to Pamida's community bulletin board half an hour ago.

Turv stared at the reward flier. "Holy shit," he whispered.

"Indeed, Turv, my friend," Ned said. "Indeed. All we got to do is call this number, claim we found the butter head dumped out in the woods someplace, and collect us twenty-five hundred dollars. And," he added magnanimously because he was in a really fine mood, "by the way, I think you got a real calling there with sculpting, Turvie. That butter head looks better now than when we took her. Kinda like Angelina Jolie."

"Thanks." Another set of wrinkles joined those already on Turv's forehead. "But . . . but what about Jenny Hallesby?"

"What about Jenny Hallesby?" Ned asked, mildly exasperated. "She had her chance. If she hadn't been so damn greedy and paid us the thousand dollars we asked for to begin with, she'd be staring at her butter face right now. Serves her right. Besides, it's not like she couldn't have afforded it. Greedy, greedy, miserly, and greedy." He shook his head over the failings of modern women.

"So, if she's not paying the reward, who is?" Turv asked.

"Don't know," Ned answered, feeling downright chipper. "And I don't much care."

Chapter Thirty-one

7:30 a.m.
The Lodge

The sun, bouncing off all the white snow outside, filled her room like a movie set's lights, waking Jenn up.

She rolled over in the single bed she'd had since they had moved to the Lodge, wondering—and not for the first time—why she wasn't in a larger bed, and looked around for her clothes. They were heaped in the center of the threadbare rug. At least, they weren't hanging on a hook in the Fawn Creek jail, which is exactly where Greta Smelka had wanted her and Steve to be after Einer had called her to tell her about the café's broken window. Even Steve's celebrity hadn't been enough to save them from Greta's wrath. His checkbook, on the other hand, had done the trick. He'd also added more than enough to cover the cost of replacing the dishes that had been broken during their . . . what? Make-out session?

Jenn smiled lazily and stretched. Despite her throbbing temples, she felt pretty damn good. She supposed she ought to feel some little tickle of embarrassment; she didn't. Making out with Steve Jaax on the counter of Smelka's Café sure wasn't something she regretted. Steve was a really good kisser, and besides, she couldn't imagine him being embarrassed about some excellent necking. It would be anti–Steve Jaax. She decided to take a page from the Steve Jaax Handbook of Celebrity Live in the Momentness and enjoy.

She rolled out of bed, relaxed and with a little girlish frisson of anticipation that she found as goofy as it was unusual. She decided to go with that, too. After a quick look to see if any *semlor* had been ground into them during her Encounter on the Counter (there wasn't), she slipped into the jeans she'd worn last night, and a nubby, oversized gray-green sweater. Then she slid her feet into a pair of shearling slippers and headed down the hall to the bathroom.

She emerged ten minutes later with everything brushed and was about to return to her room when she heard voices downstairs. One was unmistakably her father's. The other was a female voice, thick with a north Minnesota accent. Heidi! Her pleasure in the day grew as she trotted down the steps leading into the back of the kitchen.

Against anyone's expectations—including her own—she and Heidi Olmsted had maintained their friendship after high school. What had begun as two outsiders forging a relationship out of loneliness—and what could have been more unlikely than a beauty pageant princess and a dog sled–racing dyke?—had developed into appreciation, admiration, and real affection. Though painfully shy, once she relaxed, Heidi had proven to have a great wry sense of humor, cool-headed reasonableness, and a vastly charitable nature. Jenn wasn't exactly certain what she brought to the relationship; she was just glad Heidi enjoyed her company.

How odd, Jenn thought as she pushed open the kitchen door, that all the people she liked and loved best were here in the place she liked least.

She found her father sitting at the table with the newspaper spread out before him, a cup of coffee steaming by his hand. Next to him sat a stocky, suntanned woman with perpetually chapped lips and curly dark hair shot with gray. Her hands—Heidi had always had strong, elegant hands—were clasped together on the table, her stocking feet hooked around the legs of her chair like she was afraid if she didn't anchor herself in place she might bolt.

"Heidi!" Jenn greeted her. "How you doing, doll?"

"Okay, mostly," Heidi replied, pushing back in her chair but keeping her feet locked. "I got your message. Sorry 'bout takin' so long getting over here. I was throwing up something awful last night."

Heidi sick? That had to be a first. In all the years Jenn had known her, Heidi had only been ill a handful of times, and when she had been, she hadn't broadcast it. People up here considered sickness a gross form of self-indulgence unless . . .

"Yup," Heidi said, meeting Jenn's widening gaze, "I'm preggers."

"Huh?"

"I got artificially inseminated," she explained in typical prosaic Heidi fashion.

The only times Jenn had ever seen Heidi excited about anything was when she'd come in second in the Iditarod and when she'd told Jenn she'd fallen in love with a "goddess from Alaska," a gifted artist and potter named Mercedes. She didn't look all that excited now. But she did look all glowy, now that Jenn examined her more closely, a hard feat to achieve on forty-year-old skin that had weathered months of arctic wind and sun.

"Heidi," she said, at a loss for words, "that's wonderful. When are you due?"

"Same time as all the other bitches whelp, April." Heidi

grinned. She would never be a gorgeous woman. She looked butch and today, beautiful.

Jenn swallowed. Heidi was going to have a baby. Pregnant. At forty years of age.

Jenn had given up the thought of having children. No, that wasn't true. She'd never been at a place in her life that she felt she *could* have children, and lately, the sight of infants and little kids had only brought with it the melancholy of lost opportunities, of potential expired. But maybe the opportunity was still viable, maybe not as promising as an opportunity, but maybe still a chance.

After all, Heidi, who'd never been interested in any infant creature that didn't walk on all four legs, was going to have a baby. Where had Jenn been while all these changes were going on with Heidi? And had any sort of similar transformation ever happened to her? Did new set designs count?

Kind of, she told herself, a little unnerved by the timbre of her thoughts. Of course they did.

Her dad got up. "This is getting a little too odd for me. I always like to think of Heidi as the son I never had. Now she's pregnant."

"Don't worry, Cash," Heidi said, with deadpan seriousness. "I'm not going to start wearing pearls and calling Mercedes 'Ward.' I'm just incubating because Mercedes couldn't."

"The world is a strange and beautiful place." Jenn's father got up and smiled. "You girls chat. I'll go get Bruno."

Jenn took the seat her dad vacated, reaching across the table and securing Heidi's hand. Heidi blushed fiercely, looking embarrassed and touched. "So when did you decide all this?"

"Well, I'm not getting any younger, and Mercedes and I

figured if we've been together this long, the odds are pretty good we'll last through toilet training."

"Heidi, you incurable romantic, you."

"You should hear my poetry," she said.

Jenn let her hand go, sinking back into her seat. "So where are you going to move?" she asked.

"What do you mean?" Heidi, in the midst of dumping a tablespoon of sugar into her coffee, looked up, surprised. "We're not moving. Why would we move?"

"Come on, Heidi. Won't it be hard? Not only on you, but on your kid? A gay couple raising a kid in a small town? I mean, Fawn Creek isn't exactly a bastion of liberal acceptance."

Heidi finished sugaring her coffee and added a quarter cup of heavy cream. Her gaze was pensive as she stared into the cup and stirred, but a small smile tugged at the corners of her mouth. "All true. But this is our small town, Jenn. It's our home."

"You're not concerned?" Jenn asked quietly.

"I'd be stupid not to be," she said. "Yeah, sure, this town has its share of assholes. What town doesn't? But here I have the advantage of knowing the assholes' names. And there are good people, too. You know?"

"Yeah," Jenn said, unable to keep the doubt from her voice.

"Jenn," Heidi said soberly. "Honey, you bolted as soon as you got rid of that Miss Fawn Creek crown. You grabbed your diploma and ran. I didn't. I stayed."

"I know."

"I could have left."

Jenn nodded. Heidi was a prime example of fear tying a smart, gifted woman to a terrible situation.

Heidi, studying her closely, frowned. She made a sound

of exasperation. "I could have left but I didn't. As hard as it is for you to believe, I stayed because I wanted to stay, not because I didn't think I could make it somewhere else." She must have read some of the doubt Jenn tried to mask.

Heidi laid down her spoon. "Jenny, babe, anyone else and I wouldn't bother saying all this because frankly your attitude is a little insulting. But . . . damn, Jenn, you're my best friend, so listen up. I have raced my dogs all over the world and I have lived for months at a time in all sorts of places. I'm not here because of some 'better the devil you know' crap. I'm here because this is my home."

"Gosh," Jenn said uncomfortably, trying to lighten the mood. "If I were you, I would have chosen a better home."

"It's not a matter of choosing as much as accepting," Heidi said, leaning forward, holding Jenn's gaze with hers. "In all the years I've known you, the only place you are relaxed, the only place you're not worried about making an impression, the only place you wear comfortable clothes and no makeup, the only place you swear is here. Why?"

"Because no one cares."

"No," Heidi said. "Because they know you. The real you."

Jenn looked away, unconvinced. She wasn't even sure who the "real" her was. How could anyone else? But she wouldn't hurt Heidi for the world by disagreeing.

For a few seconds, Heidi looked as if she was going to say more, but she finally relaxed back in her chair, her smile resigned. "So, Debbie Stugaard is throwing a baby shower for me."

At the look on Jenn's face, Heidi burst out laughing. "And you're going to be invited and you're sure goin' t'come. Aren't you?"

"Ah . . ."

"*Aren't you?*"

"You bet."

"Now don't laugh, but I'm thinking of wearing a dress," Heidi continued, serenely, "because it'd make Marcia happy and Mercedes bet me a one-hour back massage that I wouldn't have the guts. So I'm thinking one of those stretchy deals like Heidi Klum wore when she was pregnant."

Heidi Olmsted, not only a mother-to-be, and her pregnancy being celebrated by the wife of one of the county's most conservative junior congressmen, but planning on wearing a spandex maternity dress, to boot. Jenn's dad was right; the world was a strange and wonderful place.

A little, unexpected rush of envy rippled through her. "What do you know from Heidi Klum?"

"Mercedes watches *Project Runway*," Heidi said, a little sheepishly. "We all make concessions for love, Jenn."

Yeah? a little voice inside snickered. *Not Jenn Hallesby.* She'd never made any concessions during her brief marriage. God, she'd been young.

"And how are you doing, my friend?" Heidi asked quizzically. Her head tipped to the side. Her gaze was alert, probing.

"Great!" Jenn enthused. "*Good Neighbors* held seventy-three percent of the viewership last year and the market expanded by twelve percent. We scored a Nielsen rating of four point two for the Thanksgiving special."

Heidi's eyes glazed over. "Cool." She wiggled herself straight, leaning over the table and pinning Jenn with her gaze. "But I was talking about you, personally. Not your show. Tell me about this Jaax guy. Mercedes says he was on the vanguard of redefining representational sculpture."

Jenn smiled. She couldn't help it. Whenever Heidi segued seamlessly from her Minnesota dog-musher lexicon to Mercedes's artistic one, it provoked a smile from her.

"Yeah," Jenn said wryly, "he's even more famous than I'd realized. Do you know how many people have recognized him since he got here? Even the kids."

"Oh, that's because the *Fawn Creek Crier* ran a front-page piece on him last week, and Keith Blum, the art teacher at the high school, made all his classes write a paper on him."

Steve would be disappointed that his fame wasn't as universal as he'd assumed. "Let's just keep that to ourselves, shall we?"

Heidi shrugged. "Sure. He sounds like a decent guy. Cash seems to like him and your dad doesn't like most people. So tell me about him."

"There's nothing to tell. I just met him—" She stopped abruptly and blinked. *Yesterday?* Could that be right? She'd only met Steve yesterday? How could that be?

"You met him . . . ?" Heidi prompted.

"Ah . . ." She touched her forehead, distracted. "Yesterday. But I . . . I met him when he did my sculpture. So . . ." So could that account for this feeling of knowing him so much better, so much more deeply than a mere twenty-four hours could ever account for?

Heidi leaned over the table and snapped her fingers a few inches from Jenn's face. "Wake up there, princess. What's gotten into you anyway?"

Jenn was saved from having to answer by the sound of nails clattering on the floor followed by the arrival of Bruno, Jenn's dad, and trailing in last, yawning hugely, Steve. His gaze went straight to her and his grin was spontaneous. Her pulse fluttered in response. All the estrogen in the air must be affecting her.

If he kept smiling at her like that, all open pleasure, she was going to blu— Hell! She *was* blushing. Now she felt ridiculous and Heidi and her dad were staring at her like she'd just sprouted a second head.

"Hi," Steve said and then realized they had guests. He looked down at Heidi, who tipped her chair on its back two legs to get a better look at him. "You're Heidi, right? Hi, Heidi. I would like to buy your dog."

Heidi's startled glance found Jenn. Jenn shrugged.

"I think Bruno would like me to buy him from you, too," Steve continued seriously.

"He could be right," Jenn said, pointing at Bruno.

Like some orphan kid who sees his chance at living in a mansion, Bruno had latched on to Steve with limpetlike tenacity. He sat down on Steve's right foot, looking alertly and attentively up at him.

"Ingrate," Heidi muttered. Bruno didn't spare her a glance.

"I'm Steve Jaax, by the way." Steve reached across the table and shook Heidi's hand, smiling winningly.

"Oh, I know!" Heidi said. "Been reading about you in the *Crier*. My girlfriend is an artist, you know. Say, I was wondering if—"

"Do not ask him for his autograph," Jenn warned her. "As you value my friendship, do not ask him for his autograph."

"Wasn't gonna," Heidi said, trying to look truthful. "What do you want with Bruno, Mr. Jaax?"

"Call me Steve. And I'll be happy to autograph something for your girlfriend. Jenny has a little trouble dealing with my celebrity." He glanced fondly in Jenn's direction. Jenn smiled back.

Jenny? Heidi mouthed mutely.

Steve turned back to Heidi. "And in answer to your question, I want to be Bruno's companion and I want him to be mine."

Companion. The word hit Jenn with unexpected force. It was that damn old Marc Cohen song—that was why. The word "companion" just reeked of pledges and commitments and linking arms and skipping down life's rose-strewn path into the Great Unknown. It didn't help that Heidi had Mercedes, her dad had her mom, and now Steve was going to have Bruno.

Well, at least she had a TV show. Crap.

Steve was gazing down into Bruno's upturned furry face, studying it seriously. "I think he likes me, too. And as I understand it, you've recently retired him from whatever line of work it was he was doing, so he's at liberty to take on a new gig. I would like that to be as my dog."

"You can't have a dog, Steve," Jenn said. He couldn't have a dog. He had no more business having a dog than she did, and she loved dogs. He hadn't even known he liked dogs until yesterday! "Where would you keep him? What would you do with him when you were, say, opening a show in Prague?"

"He would come with," Steve replied reasonably. "I'd have a stipulation that any shows I did out of the country, Bruno would have to be able to come with me. I'd make it work. If you want something, you make it work."

She didn't have an answer to that.

"Well . . ." Heidi said, looking at Cash.

"He's an okay guy." Jenn's dad didn't dole out much higher praise than that.

"Please," Steve said. "I'll send references. I'll sign whatever waiver you'd like saying you can reclaim him if you even suspect for a second that he's not being treated like a doggie prince." He paused to cast a loving look down at his new best bud. The adoring gaze was returned. "Say, do you think he could learn to answer to the name Prince?"

"No!" Heidi and Jenn and Cash said in unison.

"Okay," Steve said, disappointed but resigned. "Please?"

"Well, maybe. Probably. But only if you promise not to rename him."

"Deal." Steve scratched Bruno's head again.

Jenn watched with the return of the odd feeling that she suspected was jealousy. It was jealousy. She was jealous of Bruno. No, no, no. She held imaginary fingers into her ears, mentally stoppering them.

She was in Fawn Creek. Things always seemed a little skewed here. She was probably just nervous about the immense leap forward her career was about to take and feeling a little anxious. She'd always had a clear idea of where she was going; that didn't mean her life lacked . . . richness. And just because she'd made out with Steve didn't mean she was going to start having epiphanies about Her Life. She knew all about Her Life. She knew what drove her (the loss of her childhood home), she knew what she wanted (security), and she knew how she was going to get it (by working her ass off for AMS). Other . . . *things* could wait.

There, having sorted things out in her head, she felt much better.

"Why does Jenn look like that?" Heidi asked Steve, who, looking profoundly pleased with himself, had taken a seat on one side of Heidi while Jenn's father took the seat on her other side. "All dour?"

"She's probably got a hangover, is all," Steve explained kindly. "A little sustenance and she'll be right as—" He started and glanced furtively around.

"Don't worry, Steve. Nina sleeps in. She's a night owl," Cash told him and prepared to rise. "Now who wants toast?"

"I need more than toast," Jenn announced, pushing herself up from the table. Cooking had always been her refuge. "I need food."

The three at the table exchanged furtive and triumphant glances as she opened the refrigerator, where she found eggs, cream, and all sorts of disastrously unhealthy food. She wondered if her mother surreptitiously stocked up on "bad food" whenever Jenn came to town in order to provide Cash with a little culinary time-off for good behavior. Because over the years it had become a pattern for her to rise early and make her father breakfast—even if "breakfast" sometimes took on the flavor of dinner or, more often than that, dessert.

As she started some oatmeal, her dad, knowing she'd be cooking for at least another half an hour, folded his newspaper under his arm, muttered something about "consulting the porcelain oracle," and disappeared.

"—half a bottle of aquavit," Jenn heard Steve ratting her out as she dug out the bowls and whisks she'd need. No matter. She had no secrets from Heidi. She began dicing a hard green apple she'd found in the bottom of the fruit bin.

"You'd think she'd know better," Heidi replied. "No wonder you look all pruned up, Jenn. You remember last time you got drunk on aquavit? You wouldn't like that happenin' again, now, would ya? Not with the AMS people showing up this morning."

"They're here?" Jenn looked up from the egg whites she'd been beating. They were a day earlier than she'd expected. And not particularly welcome. She wasn't sure she was ready to saddle up as Jenn Lind just yet.

"What did she do last time she was drink on aquavit?" Steve asked, unfazed by news of the media's arrival.

"Nothing," Jenn answered before Heidi could.

"Oh, come on," Steve cajoled. "Tell me."

"It was a long time ago," Jenn said, folding her egg whites into the oatmeal. "I was in high school and I was way drunk and I embarrassed poor Heidi, for which I am still sorry."

"I've managed to live through the ignominy," Heidi said dryly.

"What did you do?" Steve asked. "Out her?"

Heidi gave him a look. "I think by my senior year most folks had a pretty good idea I wasn't interested in guys." She looked at Jenn and shook her head. "Nah. Jenn had another agenda, getting kicked off her Miss Fawn Creek throne. The only reason she got so drunk is that she was trying to build up her courage."

Heidi laughed and Jenn felt her mouth quirk in response. When she thought about it now, twenty-two years later, it was hard to imagine anyone not laughing at how dramatic and single-minded she'd been. In retrospect, she wondered how many of the town council had gone home and wet themselves laughing at her grim-faced determination to hurl herself beyond the pale.

Steve cupped his chin in his hand and was watching Jenn with the same focus she remembered he'd shown in the freezer two decades before. It still had the same impact on her, too; she felt like she was the only woman on the planet. How could certain men do that? "Yeah?" he prompted.

"I'd been accepted at the University of Minnesota for the spring," she explained as she whisked together some cinnamon, maple syrup, and ginger, "but I had these contractual obligations with the town that would keep me here through the whole year. But I thought if I could just get them to dump me, I was home free."

She poured a little more vanilla into the pot along with the oatmeal and apples and stuck it in the oven. "So that fall, when homecoming rolled around, and everyone had dates and I didn't and Heidi didn't—"

"For obvious reasons," Heidi inserted.

"I asked Heidi to be my date."

"*That's* the big secret?" He sounded colossally disappointed.

"Not exactly," Heidi said.

"I snuck in early and stuffed the ballot box with our names for homecoming king and queen."

"How . . . *Carrie,*" Steve said, still unimpressed.

"Yeah. I thought so at the time, too. Don't look like that. There was no blood involved. I wore my Miss Fawn Creek ball gown and tiara, and Heidi wore . . ."

"Overalls," Heidi said.

"Overalls. And before we went, we drank a third of a bottle of aquavit."

"You must have been flying," Steve said.

"Stratosphere," Jenn agreed. "Of course, as soon as they started tallying the ballots, they realized someone was cheating and decided not to announce any homecoming court at all, so I grabbed Heidi's hand and hauled her up onto the stage and right there in front of everyone, including most of the city council who were there as chaperones, I dipped her and gave her a big, old wet one."

Heidi nodded. "No frenching, though."

For a second Steve just looked at Jenn. Then he began to smile, then grin, and then he laughed. Heidi started chuckling like an idiot and, damn, Jenn did, too.

"That's cold, Jenn," he said. "You coulda at least slipped her a little tongue."

"Who wanted her tongue?" Heidi said, mock indignant. "She's not my type."

"Did it work?" Steve asked, watching Jenn stick a tray of almonds in the oven to toast.

"Nope," she replied. "The school newspaper ran a picture of us—but the teachers confiscated most of them. Still, you'd think a little moral outrage would have been appropriate. All that happened was my parents had to go talk to the principal."

"Lucky for Jenny," Heidi said. "You know the show she was on at the state fair?"

He nodded. Liar.

"They asked her to be on the show again about a week after homecoming. And the rest is history. Poor Jenny has been miserably maintaining the secret of her true sexual orientation ever since."

"Brokeback Mountain Biscuit," Jenn agreed somberly.

"Really?" Steve asked.

"No."

His gullibility was cute. He'd even shaved before he'd come down, she realized in surprise. It didn't improve matters greatly. He was still disheveled, disreputable, with a face like a funnel cake, craggy and brown and yummy. She liked well-groomed, successful manager types, she reminded herself. Guys who used after-shave. She just knew that Steve had never owned a bottle of after-shave in his life. But he'd smelled good anyway, she remembered. Like Life Buoy or Dial, something sharp and clean, and his scalp had been warm while his hair had been cool and silky beneath her fingers. Down, girl.

She took the almonds out of the oven along with the porridge, carefully ladled the porridge into bowls, sprinkled the almonds over the tops, and set the bowls in front of Heidi and Steve. Steve looked up at Jenn with the eyes of a child on Christmas morning.

"Didn't anyone ever feed you?" she asked.

"Not like this," he answered reverently. He looked like

any second he might stand up and start kissing her. That must have been why she still stood there over him like an idiot. . . .

The phone rang and Jenn snapped it up so it wouldn't wake her mother. "Hello. Hallesbys'."

"Hello," a male voice said. "Is Jenn Lind there?"

She couldn't contain the sigh that rose at his words. *Jenn Lind*, not Hallesby. No one in Fawn Creek called her Jenn Lind. Which meant it was either a reporter or one of the filming crew. Which meant it was time to get back to work.

"This is Jenn Lind. To whom am I speaking, please?" It was strange that the Jenn mask didn't fall quite as comfortably back into place this morning. But then, she'd never actually had to play the Jenn Lind role in Fawn Creek before.

"Oh, Miss Lind! My name is Walt Dunkovich." The guy paused, like maybe she should recognize the name.

"Oh, hello, Mr. Dunkovich," she enthused. Damn it! She racked her brain. Had that been the name of the filming crew's director? Or was he from some newsmagazine? Or *ET*?

"Hi." He made a gratified sound. "Say, I was wondering if you maybe could do me a little favor. You see, I'm like your biggest fan."

Okay, not the director. And the likelihood of him being a reporter also dipped to near zero. But a *guy* was her biggest fan? Not a straight guy.

"I was wondering if . . . well, it would mean the world to me if I could meet you personally."

And how the hell had he gotten this number? "I'm sorry, Mr. Dunkovich. I wish I could but I am so overbooked right now and my schedule just doesn't allow—"

"Please," he broke in. "I mean, I would've chased after those thieves no matter whose butter sculpture was being stolen— I didn't even know it was your folks that were being robbed, but when I found out that Jenn Lind was these Hallesbys' daughter, well, I was tickled, just tickled, that I could be of service."

Oh Christ. It was that guy. The guy who'd driven Emil Oberg's Polaris off the lake overhang and crashed it while chasing after the butter head. Poor idiot.

"Normally, I'd be happy to stand in line with your other fans, but the fact of the matter is, I'm a little indisposed, if you know what I mean." His weak chuckle turned into a weak cough. "But if it would be too much trouble, I certainly understand . . ."

"Oh, Mr. Dunkovich, I'm sorry. I misheard the name. Of course, I'd be delighted to visit you. You're in the hospital, right? Just say when."

"Today works for me," he chirped. "This morning works best of all."

"How about this afternoon?" She glanced at the clock.

"I sure would appreciate it if you could come this morning. I might have to have more surgery this afternoon. . . ." His voice trailed off.

"Absolutely. The roads are pretty bad, so it'll take a while but I'll be there as soon as I can."

"That's swell, Miss Lind! I'm in room 323. Bye!"

He hung up and Jenn pushed herself to her feet. "I gotta go see the guy who drove off the lake overlook. The one who was chasing after the butter thieves."

Heidi and Steve looked up from their bowls of porridge at her with polite indifference. Then their heads dipped once more to the task at hand. Steve made a nummy sound. "Hm."

"Save some for Dad, okay?" she said, heading out of the kitchen to get dressed. She wasn't sure they heard her.

Chapter Thirty-two

8:55 a.m.
Oxlip County Hospital
Room 323

Dunk was a little disappointed.

He'd seen half a dozen broadcast pieces about her over the last few weeks, read the *Twin City* magazine spread on her, and even caught a rerun of her show this morning, and frankly, he'd have thought Jenn Lind in person would be more Hollywood.

This woman looked like a successful real estate agent: creased slacks and tailored jacket, crisp shirt and smooth hair. Handsome? Okay, yeah. A babe? No. She wasn't nearly as curvy she looked on television. She didn't own a third of Karin Ekkelstahl's up-top bounty.

And that famous Jenn Lind approachability? Gone missing. She looked a little suspicious, a little impatient, and irritated, though she was trying to mask it beneath a bright, facile smile. Dunk had been in Minnesota long enough to recognize *that* ploy. All for which Dunk was glad. Because Karin Ekkelstahl's mothering had begun to awake his long-dormant conscience and he much preferred to let sleeping consciences lie.

If it came down to it, he wouldn't have much trouble blackmailing this woman. And it wasn't like she couldn't afford it.

And Dunk needed to get this little transaction done before the yahoos who'd stolen the butter head realized that Steve Jaax would be willing to pay a lot more than twenty-five hundred dollars for its return. Dunk had no doubt that the guy who'd called this morning to say he'd "found" the sculpture and needed the reward "in cash" and preferred to have the exchange of "reward and butter head handled anonymously" was one of the assholes responsible for his present condition. He'd tried reassuring the guy in order to convince him to show up in person with the butter head—at which point he intended to have that sheriff jail his and his buddies' sorry asses—but the guy had proven too wary.

Damn, Dunk thought irritably as a fresh itch erupted under his body cast, he really would have liked to nail those guys.

"Mr. Dunkovich?" Jenn Lind's voice drew him back from vengeful thoughts. She was standing at the foot of his bed. "Was there anything in particular you wanted me to autograph for you, Mr. Dunkovich?"

"I dunno." He pushed himself higher on his pillows, looking around and finally pointing at the tray beside his bed and the menu he was supposed to mark off for his lunch. "How about that?"

She leaned over, signing her name across the dessert options with a flourish, and straightened. "There. Allow me to thank you once more for trying to stop the thieves, Mr. Dunkovich. I'm sorry it ended badly for you."

"Yeah. About that," he said, feeling his way. He hadn't been a con man and a grifter all his life for nothing. A huge part of conning people was figuring them out, finding their tender spots and exploiting them to his advantage. "I feel really strongly about getting that sculpture back."

"Please, don't worry about it."

"But I do," he insisted. "I can't let it go. I just can't. I even put up a twenty-five-hundred-dollar reward for its return."

That stopped her. "That was you?"

"Yeah."

"But . . . why?"

Time to go to work in earnest. "That doesn't really matter. What does matter is that, well, some guys who say they have it have already contacted me and they want that twenty-five hundred dollars to bring it here."

She continued looking at him, waiting for him to get to the point.

"Unfortunately," he sighed, "the sad truth is, Miss Lind, that I don't have twenty-five hundred dollars, and I don't think these guys are going to return the sculpture out of a sense of civic duty, if you know what I mean. In fact, I strongly suspect these are the original thieves."

"Those assholes!"

Her tone of betrayal was a little out of proportion to the comment, like she'd been the one these guys had screwed over. *Well, lady,* Dunk thought, *you're not the one lying here under half an inch of plaster.* Still, all Dunk said was "Exactly."

"You should call the sheriff," she said tightly.

"Well," Dunk said, "I was thinking more that you might want to put up the money."

She couldn't have looked more amazed than if he'd thrown his pillow at her. "Ah . . . no."

"Yes."

Her eyes popped wider. She took a step toward his bed,

not away. A fighter, then, someone who confronted things. "What did you say?"

"I said yes," he answered. "You see, I don't have time to dick around with the sheriff and all that crap. I want that sculpture and I want it soon and don't waste your breath asking why because it is my concern—"

"Why the hell would you want the butter head?" she cut in.

"I just said, 'Don't waste your breath asking,'" he said in exasperation. "Let's just say I'm an art lover and leave it at that."

"Let's not."

Shit, he hated aggressive women and she was looking very Muhammad Ali, standing over him with her jaw thrust out and her hands on her hips and those pale eyes flinty. He liked feminine women, not overtailored probable lesbos.

"What you should be concerned with here, Ms. Lind, is that I am going to get that sculpture and you are going to help me get it by bringing me the twenty-five hundred."

Now she really looked pissed. "And why would I do that, Mr. Dunkovich?"

"Because you are a big star about to become a bigger star who is working for Dwight Davies, the biggest self-righteous prick in the country, who will fire your ass in a second if he sees a certain photo of you sucking face with your girl-friend."

Jenn jerked back as if he'd slapped her. He'd literally rocked her back on her heels. Bingo. Mission accomplished.

"Where? Who told? Who were they?" Her voice was low and intense.

They? Jenn Lind automatically assumed a "they?" That was interesting. Had a little conspiracy paranoia going on, did she? Huh. Who'd have thought it? She looked so well-adjusted. But he could play that . . . nothing easier.

"Your fans here in Fawn Creek," he said smoothly, just a hint of goading pleasure in his voice. "You really aren't much of a people person, are you? I mean, I'm here for forty-eight hours, and bam, I get the down and dirty on Jenn Lind, the Honey of the Heartland."

She didn't say a word. She didn't have to. Her face had closed, grown cold and controlled. Her whole body vibrated with outrage.

"That's all beside the point," Dunk said. "I need you to pay these jerks. That's it. You do that and everyone's happy."

"Are they?" Her voice dripped ice. "What about all my fans here in town? What's to keep one of them from—"

"Ratting you out?" Dunk finished for her. "Come on. No one here wants you to be outed. They want you to be a star, honey, because they think it's gonna help them somehow."

"Then why'd they tell you?" Laser blue, those eyes.

He shrugged. "You know how it is when you got dirt on someone you think has gotten way above herself but you can't use it. You just gotta tell someone. They only told me because they figure I wouldn't care. But I do. I care twenty-five-hundred-dollars' worth."

"And you have that picture?"

"Probably one of the only *Fawn Creek Clarion*s still around."

"Shit. And what's to keep you from coming back again and again with it?"

"Tell you what. You hand me twenty-five hundred and I'll hand you that picture." Not that he had it. No one did, at least that Karin knew about. Who'd keep a twenty-one-year-old school newspaper? Lucky for him, Jenn didn't know that. She looked perfectly willing to believe that people kept their high school newspapers just on the off chance that some day something in it could be used to hurt her. Wow.

She really didn't think much of these people. For a second Dunk wondered why, but then what did he care? She had a weakness; he used it.

The bottom line was that when she handed him the twenty-five hundred and he told her he didn't have any picture, it would be too late. What was she going to do? Say the money he was holding was hers—and he had no doubt he could get her to hand him the cash—and that he'd blackmailed her for it? Just looking at the thread of panic hiding behind her enraged expression, he could tell that wasn't going to happen. No, sir, she wasn't going to risk it all for twenty-five hundred bucks. Which reminded him . . .

"I'll need that money in cash," he said, "by five o'clock this afternoon."

"I don't have that kind of money with me. I don't even have my checkbook with me. My ATM card is maxed out. Just how do you expect me to get this . . . this cash?"

"I don't know. I don't much care. Borrow it?" This brought another topic to mind. A very important one. If what the sheriff had said was right, Steve Jaax was staying at Jenn Lind's parents' place. "And, Ms. Lind? I want to make this next part crystal clear. You are not going to tell anyone that I've been in touch with the thieves. Especially Steve Jaax. Got that?"

She glared at him.

"Got that?" he insisted.

"I got it," she snapped.

A nurse—not Karin Ekkelstahl, Dunk realized with a stab of disappointment—appeared in the doorway. She took one look at Jenn's face and froze. She tried on a tentative smile.

"So, then, Jenny," she said, "what is it I can do fer you?" Jenn Lind's eyes had filled up with tears. Angry tears.

Her face twisted and she bit hard on her lips before pivoting on her heels and stalking toward the door.

"Get out of my way," she snarled as she pushed past the startled nurse.

The nurse's penciled brows almost banged into her hairline. "Now I wonder what bee's got in her bonnet."

Chapter Thirty-three

9:20 a.m.
Oxlip County Hospital parking lot

Jenn held it together all the way down the long corridor and into the elevator and to the first floor and through the lobby until she made it to the safety of her Subaru. There, behind the darkened window glass, she laid her forehead between her mittened hands on the steering wheel and cried.

This could not be happening again. They could not be doing this to her again.

Here she was again, on the very cusp of achieving a goal she'd worked her ass off for, and it *was* happening again. It was like that nightmare that had haunted her sleep for months after the state fair debacle, only in her dream the emcee had actually announced her name and she was actually standing on the podium, the crown inches from being placed on her head, and then, for God knew what reason, the people of Fawn Creek rose up en masse to slap it away. Only this was her waking life and they really had done it!

What was their deal? She pounded her fists against the steering wheel. She couldn't believe this. She couldn't believe she was crying about it! About *them*! But it had caught her so off-guard. One minute she'd been focused on the pleasant enigma of her relationship with Steve Jaax, feeling all sorts of agreeable anticipation and girlish expectancy and plain old enjoying the hell out of the unexpected . . . situation (she wouldn't call it anything more than that; she was by nature too cautious and by experience made doubly so) that had apparently caught them both by surprise. The next she'd been plunged back into the unpleasant sensations of her entire high school experience.

She was too old for this crap.

She took a deep breath. Why didn't matter. And it didn't matter that they'd betrayed her again. Just like it didn't matter why that whack job up there in the body cast wanted the butter sculpture. What was it about that stupid butter head anyway? Even Steve acknowledged it didn't have much real value. Not that it mattered. She still needed to find some money fast.

She banged her forehead forcefully against the top of the steering wheel, frustration finally outpacing despair. She had to think.

She supposed she should have insisted she saw Dunkovich's photo, but what difference did it make if he had it or not? All he'd need to do is drop a few comments into the right ear and soon some reporter would be interviewing some Fawn Creek native about it and no doubt whoever that native was would trip over himself spilling every detail about Jenn Lind: the fact that Fawn Creek wasn't her hometown, that she wasn't a native, that she had been disqualified from the Buttercup pageant for lying, and that she'd been gay in high school.

Why, why, why did Dwight Davies have to be such a dick? Why couldn't she work for a nice capitalist who didn't really care who his employees were once they stepped away from the camera? A man without a mandate to lead the country onto the heterosexual straight and narrow? Who would be content with his own sins and leave other people's alone?

Because that was who'd offered her a freaking fortune, was why. And she damn well better get used to it.

Success equaled security. The more success, the more security. She needed to keep her eye on the prize, not be distracted by Fawn Creek's seemingly limitless capacity to screw with her life. She needed to pull it together and work for what she wanted.

She scrubbed at her drippy nose and wet cheeks with her mittens. She was not going to let Fawn Creek mess this up for her. She had worked way too long and way too hard to just walk away without putting up one helluva fight.

She rolled her shoulders back, like a boxer preparing for the next bout and took stock of the situation.

She didn't have twenty-five hundred dollars and no one she knew up here had that sort of cash laying about, either. She briefly considered swearing Steve to secrecy and asking him for help but why should she trust him? She'd allowed herself to become a little too secure in Fawn Creek, and look what had happened? Rabbit punched when she wasn't looking. She should take heed of the lesson. Besides, Steve wanted the damn thing for himself. He wasn't likely to fork over the money so someone else could have it. No, she needed to come up with the money herself *and* keep her mouth shut. But how?

Unlike "real" cities, the banks up here were all closed on the weekends, and with all the snow last night's storm had dumped and more predicted, the five-hour trip down to the cities and back would be impossible. Added to which, she'd heard that another storm was blowing in from the Dakotas later this afternoon. Her folks might scrape together a couple hundred, and if they even had an ATM, which she doubted, that would put her close to a thousand. Heidi and Mercedes wouldn't have any money lying about. Not enough.

There was only one place she knew of where you could get thousands of dollars in bills. . . . Nah. She dismissed the idea. That was nuts.

She hadn't held a deck of cards in twenty years or more. Unless you counted the occasional gin rummy hands she played with Nat's eight-year-old niece. Sure, once she'd been right at home shuffling a deck of cards or bluffing her way to a pot of nickels and dimes. To say her parents and she were enthusiastic recreational poker players and had been since she could remember would have been an understatement. But all that had ended with her parents' trip to Vegas in 1982. Since then she'd sworn off gambling and trusted hard work, commitment, and focus to keep her life safe and predictable. She wasn't a gambler. Gambling was for suckers. Or desperate people.

She *was* a desperate person. . . .

All the rules she'd made for herself to keep her life on the straight path to success had been falling by the wayside over the last few days. What was happening to her? She couldn't really be considering this, could she? She'd probably only end up losing the few hundred bucks she did possess. On the other hand . . . if she didn't have twenty-five hundred dollars, it wouldn't make any difference if she had three.

Gambling. A short bitter laugh escaped her. Almost twenty-five years ago, a trip to a casino had cost her family everything and set her on the course her life currently followed. There was a delicious celestial irony embedded in there. No doubt about it, those damn Nordic gods really knew how to stick it to a girl. She just couldn't do it.

What choice did she have?

It was a long shot—a horrifically long shot, true—but right now horrifically long shots were her only shots at setting her life back on course. She couldn't let the AMS gig go without a battle royale. If her career fell apart now, what would she have? Okay. A decent retirement fund but not enough to weather the potential storms of the next four or five decades.

The twist of anxiety the thought provoked decided it for her: she'd hit the casino. She'd have to be careful, of course, and she'd need a disguise; no one must recognize her as Jenn Lind. Old Dwight wasn't a whole lot more forgiving of one sin over another and, in his book, gambling certainly constituted a sin.

She started the Subaru's engine and backed out of the parking lot, heading out of town.

Chapter Thirty-four

"—Krissie downloaded the photo to Kinkos Online and had them make a paper table cloth out of it. So the next time she was host for the Ladies' Five Hundred Club, they finish up their hands and go to the dining room and there's this beautiful spread and beneath that is the picture from the back of Vern's sock drawer of Lindsey, too, if you know what I mean," Cash said.

"Wow," Steve said, sincerely impressed. "Now that's retribution. It's like biblical."

"Yup," Cash agreed, pausing outside the barn door. "So then Lindsey goes squealing home and confesses all to her husband, not realizing their teenage son is listening in. The next day Junior shows up at school and proceeds to tell all the kids that Vern Nagel seduced his mom.

"Vern, who's understandably in a pissy mood anyway after being kicked out of his house and has set up camp at the Valu-Inn, gets a load of this, and after church that Sunday finds Dahlberg and tells him if his kid doesn't learn to shut his mouth, he'll shut it for him and, of course, Dahlberg gets all indignant about Vern threatening his kid and the two of them end up in this fistfight in the church parking lot, both their noses broke and Vern missing a tooth."

"Geez. So who ended up moving?" Steve asked.

"No one," Cash said, rolling open the door to the barn. "Dahlberg divorced Lindsey and married one of his nurses and Lindsey ended up marrying Vern. Krissie married one of Vern's business partners. The whole lot lives within three blocks of one another."

Steve was impressed. "Live and forgive?"

"Hell, no. They still hate each other's guts and have managed to drag half the town into taking sides. Not that it took much dragging. Needless to say, Lindsey quit the Five Hundred Club." Cash's brow wrinkled. "I think she plays bridge now."

This was unexpected. "But what about that small-town, one-big-happy-family thing?" Steve asked. "You know, the *Lake Woebegone* shtick?"

"Forget it," Cash said. "You know the thing I've learned about small towns? Everything gets magnified, both virtues and vices. Everything tends to be a little more black and white. At least, that's my perspective after a quarter of a century."

He waved Steve forward. "Here we go. Last stop on the tour."

He stepped aside, letting Steve enter first. Heidi had gone soon after Jenn, so left to their own devices, Steve had talked Cash into showing him around the place. The old guy had insisted on lending him appropriate outerwear, for which Steve was humbly grateful—down-filled baffles and felt liners really did make all the difference. The three of them, Cash, Steve, and Bruno, had tromped all over the Lodge's land: through the woods, along the overhang—pausing for a moment of reflective silence at the splotch on the frozen lake surface below that marked the landing pattern of "that guy who chased after the butter thieves"—across the field and up toward the back of the Lodge to a wooden outhouse that was revealed to be, in fact, not an outhouse at all but a sauna, and from there to the chicken coop, where Nina kept her Fancy Fowl.

Here Bruno, who had obviously held unpleasant memories of encounters with either Nina or her chickens or both, took off. That left Steve to express sympathy for Nina's fascination for her gorgeously patterned birds and regale Cash with their probable history as remnant dinosaurs—once more thanks to the Discovery Channel.

Now he preceded Cash into the dim interior of the barn. Beside him, Cash flipped on the lights.

It was a barn all right, but with unpainted, sheetrocked interior walls and a row of exposed floor joists overhead. Except for a workbench at the back, a dilapidated-looking tractor ("Hey, can I drive that?" "It's broke."), and a big, old-fashioned freezer chest, presumably the late resting place of his butter head, the barn was empty.

"It's warm in here," Steve said.

"Yup. We were thinking at one point that if the B and B really got going, we'd convert the barn into more rooms, so we had the walls put up and blown with insulation." He pointed at the joists overhead. "We were going to have a second level put in, too. But then we had a couple months there where we had people every single weekend and realized pretty quickly that innkeeping was not for us." He shook his head. "They wanted things. All the time, 'gimme, get me.' "

Steve wasn't paying much attention. He'd wandered over to the big, scarred worktable at the back and was running his hands over the rusty tools Cash had left scattered over its surface, a wave of nostalgia sweeping through him. Vises, hammers, saws and chisels and . . . a crowbar.

"You've got a crowbar!" He picked up the crowbar, relishing its weight in his hand.

"Yeah?" Cash said.

"I used a crowbar to make *Muse in the House,*" he said wistfully. "A crowbar, a hammer, and an acetylene torch. And some aluminum tubing."

"Muse in the House?"

Steve nodded. "My seminal piece. Someone stole it from my ex-wife's house just before our divorce."

"Sorry."

He shrugged. "It'll probably show up again someday. Great art cannot be hidden forever."

At this, Cash dug his hands into his back pockets and tilted his head, studying Steve. "That's what you do? Great art?"

"Yes. At least, I did once." His gaze fell to the crowbar, Jenny's words from the night before playing out in his thoughts. Her honesty and her obvious deep-seated and real concern for his art had been bracing. Biting, yes, but refreshing, too. And she'd been right; Verie should have been telling him that stuff. Not that he blamed Verie. He'd only been doing what Steve had been doing—enjoying the view without paying any attention to the fact that they were driving in circles.

It didn't matter to him that her comments hadn't been particularly, well, positive. He had file cabinets full of positive comments. What he didn't have was direction. He saw it now. He'd been on a celebrity treadmill. Just like she'd said. Or at least inferred. Really, when you thought of it, it was downright flattering that she'd cared enough to tell him the truth. He didn't know a woman like her—a woman who wasn't impressed with his celebrity, but just his art, a woman without pretenses who lived in the media world of pretense, a woman who didn't want fame for fame's sake but for safety's sake. A woman truly screwed up in some ways yet breathtakingly sane in so many others. A woman who made him feel eager to create. To explore. To seek inspiration. A woman with lips as soft as *semlors* and a body as pliant as . . .

"Steve?" Shit. Her father was studying him through narrowed eyes, as if he could read his mind.

"Yeah?"

"What do you mean, you did *once*?" Cash asked.

Whew. Steve looked the older man in the eye. "I'm a sellout, Cash."

"Huh?"

"I've been trading on my celebrity for years, satisfied to produce, forgetting how to create. I like celebrity. I like people knowing my name, recognizing me, knowing that they've seen things I've made. I'm a sellout for celebrity."

Cash cast a critical eye over him. "You seem sort of proud of it."

"I'm proud I've realized it. You can thank Jenny in part for that. You are witnessing an epiphany, Cash," he said gravely. "I have decided to eschew my present course. Ultimately, I want to be known because of what I do, not who I am."

"Oh."

Steve narrowed his eyes thoughtfully as he considered his decision. Where to begin? How to go about the Second Rebirth of Steven Jaax—the first rebirth being the butter head? How to begin and where? Like all great art, he supposed he ought to hark back to the past to discover the future. What better place to begin than with *Muse*? He would find it, liberate it, and set it up as his lodestar.

Plus, it would really piss Fabulousa off when she found out he had the thing in his possession.

Okay, maybe that wasn't exactly the most magnanimous motivation in the world. So what? He'd never claimed to be the poster child for altruism. Revenge would be sweet. Then, balance thus restored, he could be done with her once and for all.

His gaze fell on the acetylene torch again. Give him five seconds with the butter head and that torch and he'd have the key to his past, literally in the palm of his hand. And yet he intuitively knew he would need more to bring about the resurrection of his latent talents. Something fundamental. Something that would snap the commercial ties binding him to his celebrity. Something momentous and unambiguous.

"Damn," Cash said suddenly, drawing his attention. "It's almost nine o'clock. I promised Nina I'd wake her at eight thirty. Not that I'm supposed to tell you that. She'd like to maintain the illusion that as a healthy, hardworking Northerner, she rises early to greet each dawn."

"But I'm already up."

"She's made assumptions based on herself, and one of those assumptions is that anyone who lives in the city sleeps till noon given any opportunity. She'll be mortified you're up before her."

"Should I go back to my room and come down in a while?"

"Nah," Cash said and grinned. "It'll teach her not to make assumptions."

He exited the barn, waiting until Steve had followed before closing the door behind him. Bruno showed up to lead the way back into the Lodge, where Cash left Steve in the kitchen, after pouring a cup of coffee from the thermos Jenn had filled earlier to take to Nina. The silence after he left was amazing. No cars. No planes. No street noise. No voices. Nothing but Bruno's soft breathing.

As Steve had trailed behind Cash back to the house, he realized how he would go about stimulating his decaying talent.

He was going to buy the Lodge.

As soon as the idea came to him, he knew it was perfect. He also knew, within a few seconds more, that his idea might not exactly please Jenn. Oh, her words said clearly enough that she despised Fawn Creek, the Lodge, and everything and everyone in between, but her attitude wasn't quite so clear and sometimes her expression whispered of something quite different. He thought.

He didn't want Jenn to want what he wanted.

It was another one of those uncomfortable moral conundrums, and the fact that his feelings for her were quickly evolving beyond casual interest only made things more difficult.

He needed the Lodge. He needed the sanctuary it would provide, the quiet and unrelenting boredom that would jumpstart any imagination. The place was perfect for him. There was nothing to do here, no distractions, no public to impress, no media to court, no *parties.* Nothing but woods and quiet and a huge, empty barn just waiting to be filled.

He had to have it.

Chapter Thirty-five

11:20 a.m.
Blue Lake Casino

Ed White, the general manager of Blue Lake Casino, stood behind his office's one-way mirror overlooking the casino's vast interior and estimated the head count. Beside him his assistant, Paul Rodriguez, did glumly likewise. Tomorrow night the casino would host its first annual All-Amateur Dusk-to-Dawn Tournament, and so far not a quarter of the players they'd anticipated had signed up. It was that damn snow. Piles of it keeping the professional amateurs, tourists, and would-be poker sharks in the cities. And if the weather-man was right, another five to six inches would be dumped on them this evening. Nope, the only hope they had of this thing not becoming a complete bust was if they could some-how draw on the local population and at the same time siphon off some of the fishermen up early for Fawn Creek's Sesquicentennial Ice Spearing Tournament.

But how? They needed a hook, someone who would draw them up here from down there.

Rodriguez pointed at a woman in a cheap, plastic black wig and cheaper wraparound reflective sunglasses, sitting at the five-dollar blackjack table beneath the banner that read,

"DAWN TO DUSK AMATEUR TOURNAMENT—ONE HUNDRED THOUSAND DOLLARS TO THE WINNER!" Ed had noticed her earlier, Ed's job being to identify odd characters, and this little honey certainly fit that bill.

She was clearly as local as hell, because Ed recognized the short dress as being the same one he'd made his teenage daughter take back to Pamida last month. On his daughter, in the proper size, it had been naughty; two sizes too small, like the one this woman wore, it was plain wrong. It was so hoochie, in fact, that Ed, who had a long-standing familiarity with unsavory types, would have pinned her as a bank robber or con artist just on the basis of that dress alone. It was the sort of in-your-face dress women wore when they didn't want people looking at their faces. And it was doing its job. There was quite a little crowd around her.

"Look at that," Paul mumbled.

"Yeah," Ed said. "Nice. But we got other things to think about."

"No." Paul *tch*'ed. "I mean, look at how much she's winning."

Ed looked. Paul was right. The woman was sweeping quite a nice pile of chips into one of the casino's plastic buckets and looking around over the heads of a crowd that had gathered around her table. As they watched, she stood up and pushed her way through them, heading for the twenty-five-dollar stakes table.

And the group who had been clustered around her table followed her.

"Who is she?" Ed asked.

"Never seen her before," Paul answered. "But she's definitely from around here.

"It's not what she has, Ed. It's who she has. And she has a crowd. Locals. They like her."

She did, Ed allowed, but he had worked at casinos for more than a decade and he knew how fickle fans were. "As long as she's winning."

"Right," Rodriguez allowed. "So let's keep an eye on her and see if her luck holds."

Her luck did hold. In fact, it grew, as did the crowd around her table, yet the only emotion discernible on the visible portion of her face was grim satisfaction as the pile of chips beside her increased from a couple hundred to a couple thousand dollars. She won another hand and the people around her broke into spontaneous applause. She ignored them. Oddly, rather than offending them, they seemed to like her detachment, her impassivity, her inexcitability, her complete indifference not only to them but to her hand and especially her growing piles of poker chips.

But, of course! Ed thought with a mental snap of his fingers. Of course, they loved her. She was the quintessential Minnesotan but decked out like a well-maintained, well-stacked, older hooker. The dichotomy was irresistible. Minnesota Nice meets Nevada Naughty. At which point even Ed realized she might be worth having around. People liked a winner, people loved a local winner, and local people loved a local winner most of all. She *could* be a draw, and God knew with all this snow, they'd need every lure they could get.

He and Rodriguez worked their way through the crowd until they stood flanking their interesting gambler. She angled her head around, the dark lenses obliterating her eyes and brows. Her mouth, a bright slash of carmine, opened without a hint of a smile. "What?"

"I just wanted to congratulate you on a great run," Ed said, smiling.

"Gee, thanks," she said and turned back around. Nope,

the little lady was no gushing, trembling amateur—that was for sure. And she played smart but she had something else, too, something more important: that ineffable quality called luck.

Twenty minutes later, she suddenly stopped playing, counted out her chips, dumped them into the plastic pail on her lap, got up, and with a muttered, "Excuse me," started to work her way free of the ring surrounding the table. The people applauded.

"You have to get her back," Rodriguez whispered urgently. "I can make some calls. Maybe even get a reporter up here from the Poker Channel. Look at her. She's a bona fide flake. People will drive for miles to see a flake gamble."

"No shit," Ed muttered back and fell in behind the woman as she headed across the casino. They caught up with her as she fell into line at a cashier's window. "Miss, can we have a word with you, please?"

She looked around. "What?"

"You're one lucky woman," Rodriguez said by way of preface.

"Ya think?" Her cell phone suddenly rang and she jerked it out of the small pocketbook dangling from her wrist. "Yes? Paul? Paul, I can barely hear you. What? What? Listen, I'm driving by there in about a half hour anyway. Half hour! I'll stop then and you can tell me whatever the hell it is you're trying to tell me now!" she shouted into the phone before snapping it shut.

"You have quite a little fan club here, in case you didn't notice," Ed said, at his most genial.

With a sharply disgusted sound, she stepped up to the cashier's window as the lady in front of her finished and hefted her two containers to the ledge and dumped them into the waiting bin. Behind the partition, the cashier emptied this, in turn, into the counting machine.

"We'd like to extend an invitation to you, Miss . . ." Ed trailed off, inviting her to supply a name. She didn't. The cashier printed the electronic readout. Ed caught a glimpse of the number. Twenty-five hundred thirty dollars.

"A personal invitation," Rodriguez elaborated as the cashier counted out the bills and handed them to the woman, "to enter tomorrow's tournament. The buy-in is only a thousand dollars."

Their mystery woman turned around, stuffing the folded bills deep into some impressive cleavage. "No, thanks," she said, pushing between the men and heading for the exit. "I don't approve of gambling."

Chapter Thirty-six

12:30 p.m.
Town hall, Fawn Creek

"I hope those guys did a better job clearing the parking area on the Lake than they did in town here," Ken Holmberg told Paul.

Paul, who understood the statement to be Ken's way of holding him accountable, nodded as they drove the short distance to the town hall, where they were to meet the AMS people. The film crew had flown in between stormfronts this morning, arriving at the casino airstrip, which, being privately owned, had its own dependable plowing service. At Bob Reynolds's request, Paul had gotten hold of Jenny—Bob saying his cell coverage didn't extend up here—and he *thought* she'd promised to come straight over. The connection had been bad.

"I'm some worried about the fishing contest," Ken said.

The ice-spearing contest, the kickoff of the sesquicentennial, was slated for tomorrow. Last night's storm had kept the droves of anticipated entrants from arriving, though a number had made it to town ahead of the storm. Duddie Olson was already raking in a fair amount of cash by delivering pizzas out to little clusters of dark houses that had sprouted overnight across the Lake's surface, using the roads Paul had ordered Neddie Soderberg and Jimmy Turvold to plow across the ice.

"The turnout might not be what we'd hoped for," Paul allowed.

"If we get another storm this evening, you can kiss that seven thousand number good-bye. We'll be lucky to have a thousand," Ken said, shaking his head. "There were these guys from the cities thinking of coming up and taking a look at my plant while they were fishing. But I doubt they'll come now. Damn. I sure could use their—" He shot a glance at Paul, realizing what he'd almost admitted because Paul was pretty sure Ken had been about to say "money."

Ken cleared his throat. "I been thinking I could use partners. Getting to the age where I'd like to ease back some, you know?"

"Yup." Paul did, too. Rumor—again with his wife as conduit—had surfaced that last week Ken had filled out a loan application at the bank and the bank, in looking into it, had discovered the ninety thousand dollar underfunding of his company's pension account and were going to refuse the loan. The stress of being exposed as less rich, less powerful, and less honest than he presented himself to be was beginning to show on Ken's round red face; even his comb-over looked frayed. Paul knew Ken had pledged the cost of a new kitchen to Good Shepherd. He'd never live down the ignominy if he had to renege.

"I could just close the plant, I suppose."

Ken's expression darkened further as a knot of answering panic balled in Paul's belly. If Ken's business folded, it would be the beginning of the end of Fawn Creek. And Ken knew it. He might be a pompous small-town potentate, but at least it was a role he loved. He'd hate going from being a something to a nothing somewhere else. But he'd hate being publicly discredited as a crook in front of "his town" even more.

"I gotta get out of this bind, Paul," he muttered thickly. Which was as close to an admission that he was in trouble that Ken Holmberg was ever likely to make. "This sesquicentennial was going to be my shot at showing these guys from the cities what we got here. Or maybe find some other investors."

"Early days, Ken," Paul said, trying to sound confident. "And we got these AMS people here who're going to bring Fawn Creek national exposure."

Ken squared his shoulders as Paul pulled into the town hall parking lot and eased the truck into his reserved slot. "That's right," he said. Then, just to show that he wasn't worried, he reverted to his earlier harangue. "We gotta make sure those guys of yours don't plow the road they got out on the Lake any closer to the spring than they already have or we'll be fishing SUVs off the bottom all winter."

Their sortie the other night had confirmed Paul's suspicion that the ice right next to the road Ned Soderberg had plowed out to the dark houses on the Lake was punky where a spring fed into it.

"I'll be sure and tell 'em," Paul said, silently thinking he wouldn't tell Ned why because, hard as it was to admit, Paul just didn't think much of Ned Soderberg's character. He wouldn't put it past Ned to purposely steer out-of-towners onto thin ice just so he could charge them a pile of money to tow them out when they broke through. Truth was, he wouldn't have hired Ned at all if he didn't think so highly of his grandmother—particularly her *kransekake*.

"And tell 'em to keep the parking lots clear, too," Ken

added, getting out of the truck and slamming the door shut. "Just in case."

"You bet."

Ken practically trotted across the lot and into the town hall, Paul hard on his heels. He nodded to the receptionist, Dorie, on his way through the tiny lobby. Paul was pretty excited himself. As bad as the snow was for travel, it was good for pictures. Fawn Creek had never looked better. Heck, if AMS used shots of Fawn Creek all covered in this virgin blanket of snow, and of folks fishing, and snowmobilers partying, it could help revive their near comatose tourist industry.

Paul and the town council had done everything they could to make Fawn Creek look like an inviting, vital little community. All the local shopowners—even those whose businesses were no longer open—had promised to keep their neon signs lit and the display lights on twenty-four/seven so that the town looked thriving. Both the Kiwanis and the Rotary Club guys had made up schedules for all their members to drive and walk around town every few hours so the town center appeared lively, and Wendy Larson had agreed to harness up his old draft horses and drag a log across the north end of the Lake the moment the camera crew from AMS started shooting footage.

That oughta catch their eyes.

Paul and Ken hit the double doors to the council chamber at the same time, Paul pushing open the left and Ken the right, both of them wearing their Minnesota Nicest smiles on, full wattage. The five people waiting around inside, drinking coffee and perusing the aerial map of the county on the wall, exchanged looks. Minnesota Nice often caught people off guard like that.

A good-looking young blond guy in a black cashmere

turtleneck and a slate blue corduroy jacket sitting on the corner of Paul's desk lifted his head from the Blackberry he'd been studying and hopped to his feet. He came forward and took Paul's hand.

"Mayor?" he asked.

"You bet!"

"Great! At last we meet. I'm Bob Reynolds."

He threw a hand in the direction of a bored-looking older guy with a thin gray ponytail. "That's our director, Dieter Halnagel, and this is the rest of our crew: John, on camera"—a plump young fellow standing next to the map smiled at them—"Nick, lights"—a middle-aged Asian guy bobbed his head—"Benjamin is makeup"—a kid with lanky hair dyed black tipped two fingers over his eyes in a mock salute—"and Mandie is our gofer." The mousy-looking girl next to the Goth guy mumbled, "Hi."

Paul nodded to each in turn, then said, "This is Ken Holmberg, who's been instrumental in organizing our little celebration here. Ken owns Minnesota Hockey Stix."

"Is that a team? Never heard of 'em," the lighting guy said.

"No, no." Ken smiled and rocked back on his heels. "I make the sticks the hockey players use. We supply about eighty percent of the—"

"Cool." Bob angled his way around Ken and hooked his arm through Paul's, leading him to the window overlooking the parking lot. Ken, left behind, flushed, unused to being ignored. No doubt about it, if Ken did leave Fawn Creek, he'd find life in any other pond as a small fish real unpleasant.

Bob pointed out the window at the sky overhead. It was the color of sapphires with huge mounds of white clouds like whipped cream floating in it. The sun sparkled on the newly laid snow.

"How much are you going to charge me for all the special effects, Mayor?" Bob asked. "Just kidding. This is sensational, Paul. Better than I could have dared hope for. Isn't it, kids?" He looked over his shoulder.

"Lighting is going to be a bitch," the Asian guy said. "Too much white. It will bounce into everything. Show every little line in Lind's face."

"You let me worry about that, Gilly Flower." The kid, who on closer inspection might not have been that much of a kid after all, spoke confidently. "I'll make Jenn Lind look like she's still waiting for her first period."

Behind Paul, Ken choked.

"Where is our star?" Bob asked. "Or should I say stars? I heard Steve Jaax got here, too. And then there's the silent star of the show—Mr. Jaax's butter sculpture. I have to admit, I'm dying to see it."

"Me, too." The director spoke from where he slouched with his feet up on the council table. "I'm hoping there's something we can do with it, somehow integrate it into the credits. I suppose Jaax will have to sign off on our using its likeness for commercial purposes."

Paul wondered how to proceed, unhappy at having to disappoint the AMS people but not too worried about any repercussions. The butter head had never been anything more than a curiosity, a sideshow attraction to be gawked at and forget. The *real* attractions were Jenny and Jaax.

"I have some fabulous ideas of how we can juxtapose Jenn Lind's face over the butter sculpture image so that it will look like she's actually evolving from it," Dieter was saying. "It'll be VH1 all the way. Only without the music."

Then again, Paul thought, recognizing that Dieter had fallen in love with his own idea, maybe a guy didn't have to mention anything at all right now. Chances were still pretty good the dang thing would turn up, especially with that nut-case in the body cast over t'the hospital offering twenty-five hundred dollars for its return.

"Well, now, Mr. Reynolds, both Jenny and Steve"—Paul noted with satisfaction the slight widening of the director's eyes at his familiar use of Jaax's Christian name—"are up t'Jenny's folks' place. They have a little B and B north of town where they're staying."

"Can we stay there, too?" Bob asked at once.

"Nope." Ken found his voice. "Full up. But we reserved rooms for you and your staff." He put a subtle little sneer into the last word. Ken didn't like being looked down on. Especially by staff.

"Do they have cable?" the mousy gofer asked.

"I don't know," Ken answered tightly.

"Probably not," the pudgy cameraman sighed.

"Thank you, Ken." Bob shot his crew a warning glance: *Play nice or else.* "Mayor, I understand from the itinerary your office sent us that Ms. Lind is slated to start off the festivities this Sunday with an ice-fishing contest."

"That's right."

"Well, we were thinking we might shoot a cooking segment sometime during the contest right out on the lake."

"Great!" Paul enthused, making a mental note to call Wendy and have him oil up his harnesses.

"Brilliant! And we'd really like to have the butter sculpture there as part of it."

Paul's smile ratcheted down a notch. "Well, we'll sure see what we can do."

He was saved from making further promises by a knock on the council chamber door. "Come in!"

Dorie's peroxided head popped through the door. Behind her, Paul saw Jimmy Turvold hovering, his hunter's cap literally in hand. Good. He and Jimmy needed to have a little talk.

"Mayor? There's a guy here who says he's from *Ripley's Believe It or Not.*"

More news coverage! He'd heard rumors that *Ripley's* might be sending someone. Now they only needed to find that damn butter head. "Tell him we'll be out in a few minutes, Dorie."

"No need to have him cool his heels in the hall, Mayor," Bob said and then smiled. "AMS would love to hear what *Ripley's* is doing up here."

"Sure," Ken said before Paul could answer. "Show the guy in."

"And, ah"—Dorie glanced to her side—"Jim Turvold's here, too."

"I can see that. Hey, Jimmy. Can you just wait in the hall there a little bit and I'll be with you as soon as I can?"

Jimmy nodded and Dorie closed the door.

A minute later the door swung open again and Dorie ushered in a skinny, innocuous-looking man in a hooded sweatshirt emblazoned with the words BOSTON COLLEGE. He looked around the room at the eight pairs of eyes leveled at him.

"Hi. I'm Lou Wallbank from *Ripley's Believe It or Not?*" He seemed to be one of those people who issued any sentence as a question. "I'm here to tell you guys that that butter head you purportedly have? If authenticated? It's now been determined that it would in fact be the oldest intact butter sculpture in existence."

A record-breaking butter sculpture! Paul's thoughts spun out into the future. There was a guy down in the midsection of the state who'd built a special barn for the world's largest ball of twine. Paul wondered if he could get the city council to build a special revolving, see-through freezer for the butter head.

"It's a Jaax, too," Ken put in importantly.

"That's cool, I'm sure? But we're more interested in its age than its creator," Wallbank said apologetically.

"Thanks for coming all this way just to tell us that, Mr. Wallbank," Paul said. Ken, who was looking disgruntled, having once again been dismissed, clearly didn't understand the commercial potential here.

"Ah, thank you?" Wallbank said. "But, ah, I didn't come here just to tell you it was old."

"Oh?" Ken said.

"What are you here for then?" Bob abruptly asked, New Yorkers being impatient.

"I'm here to buy it? For the Ripley's Believe It or Not Museum?" Wallbank said.

"How much?" Paul asked, Canadians being practical.

"Ten thousand dollars."

Just outside the mayor's office, Turv, who'd been killing time by pressing his ear against the wall and eavesdropping, slid to the floor.

Chapter Thirty-seven

1:15 p.m.
Same place

Jenn pulled the Subaru into the town hall parking lot and turned off the engine, having dropped off yet more money at Sleeping Beauty's castle as per instructions given her by a jovial Dunkovich. When she'd asked where she was supposed to find the butter head—not bothering to mention that she'd already been this route once before in the last twenty-four hours—he'd told her the butter head was his problem and hung up. He hadn't bothered to ask how she'd come up with the cash, which was fine with her because she didn't intend to tell him. Or anyone else, ever.

In a way, it was too bad, because her run of luck at the blackjack table had been the stuff of gambling mythology: unprecedented, unanticipated, and unbelievable. Not that she'd been able to enjoy it. She'd been too furious at the fact of having been blackmailed, at the fact that the blackmail material had been handed to her tormentor by one of her Fawn Creek neighbors, and finally, at the fact that she'd had to dress up like a cheap whore in order to keep any of the reporters in town covering the sesquicentennial from looking too closely at her face and thus discovering who she was. A story about Jenn Lind, the Wholesome Honey of the Heartland, gambling would be a whole lot more interesting than how much lye it takes to process a pound of lutefisk.

Though she hadn't seen any familiar faces from the local news yet, she knew there were bound to be at least a few around, just like she knew where they'd be hanging out while they waited for the sesquicentennial to get under way, and it wasn't at Portia's Tavern. It would be the casino.

She slouched way down in the front seat of her Subaru and, after a quick look around to make sure the lot was empty, wiggled the cheap prom dress she'd found on Pamida's sales rack over her head. Just as quickly she slipped on her sweatshirt and jeans and exited her car, heading to Paul's office to see what he wanted. Probably to torture her with more sesquicentennial duties. As if going ice fishing tomorrow wasn't torture enough.

The only person up here she didn't currently despise— aside from Heidi and Mercedes . . . and her parents, of course . . . and that Holmberg kid at the gas station . . . and Mrs. Unger and, okay, maybe Mrs. Soderberg, but that was still up in the air—was Steve.

She felt bad about Steve. He'd been looking forward to seeing that butter head. It meant something to him—something decent, you could tell by the fervent look in his eye when he talked about it. And the poor schmuck hadn't played any part in her current predicament. Not that there was a predicament anymore.

The thieves had their "reward," Dunkovich presumably had his butter head, and once more she had a future at AMS. Thank God for that because she didn't have a whole lot else, like a social life, a home, a dog . . . a boyfriend. For a while there, she'd thought she saw something else ahead on that metaphorical road of her life but that had been a mirage. She had a career. A good career, she reminded herself. You didn't blow a good career because some guy you barely knew wanted to see a pile of butter he had whittled decades earlier.

A woman had to be practical.

Once inside the town hall, she slipped into the ladies' room just past the hall's front door and took off the wraparound sunglasses and the wig that had started their day in Pamida's Dollar Bargain Bin. She brushed her hair, studying herself in the bathroom mirror. She looked awful. Her eyes were swollen from her little crying jag—and there would be no repeats of that episode, thank you very much—her skin was pasty with the three-shades-too-light pancake makeup she'd troweled on, and her lipstick was so red it looked like she was wearing plastic clown lips.

Too bad. She was tired of always having to be "on" and Fawn Creek sure as hell didn't appreciate her efforts. No matter what she did or how she looked they weren't going to embrace her as their own. Nope. She was the perennial outsider here and always would be. There was no reason for her to extend even the smallest exertion. Besides, it wasn't like Fawn Creek was the real world, at least not her real world. In fact, after this second betrayal, she might suspect it to be some yet undisclosed circle of hell, one level up from the frozen lake. So, if Paul lifted up his skirts and ran screaming from the sight of her, so be it.

She left the bathroom and crossed the lobby, nodding to the receptionist, Dorie Mallikson (who really ought to bite the bullet and spring twenty-five dollars for a decent bleach job), on her way to the mayor's office. There she found that slacker friend of Eric Erickson's sitting on the floor next to the door.

"Hey," she said, looking down at him and rapping sharply on the door.

His mouth dropped open.

Ah! Come on! She didn't look that bad.

"Oh! Oh, Ms. Hallesby. I mean Ms. Lind . . . hey."

"Come in!"

Jenn opened the door and stepped through. "Okay, Paul, what's got your panties all in a twis—"

The day, already on track to be one of her life's least favorites, bottomed out. Bob Reynolds, dashing, decorative, and dapper, perched on the corner of Paul's desk, his hand wrapped around one of his knees in a pose straight out of *GQ*. Around him, in various attitudes of boredom, stood the film crew. They all looked very "coast"—east or west, take your pick—especially the guy with the straight black hair and waxed brows. She closed her eyes, cursing herself for forgetting they'd arrived.

"Jenn!" Bob hopped off the desk and hurried over, throwing his arms around her and kissing her on both cheeks. He draped an arm over her shoulders and spun her around to face the room. "Here's our star, kids! Jenn Lind!"

Everyone made appropriately excited noises except Dieter, the director, who remained slumped in his chair. She dipped her shoulder, squirming out of Bob's comradely embrace, and faced the crew.

"I'm sorry. The connection was bad. I couldn't hear Paul. I was out on . . . errands." She gave up trying to explain. "I look like crap."

"Dear One!" enthused the makeup artist—he couldn't be anyone else—approaching her and taking her hands in his, his assessing gaze scouring her face. "Do not worry! I live to be needed."

"I'm sorry, Jenn," Paul apologized. Behind him, Ken

Holmberg was staring at her in something approaching horror. "I thought you were at the Lodge. I didn't realize you were"—he searched around for some explanation of why she looked like she did—"doing stuff."

"It's okay." Best to get on with the work at hand. "So what's your time frame here?"

"Two days," the spoon-chested director stated. "So we have to start shooting like now, if we're going to get this spot Bob wants."

"What spot?"

"Remember when I said it would be cool if we could actually shoot a segment at the festival?" Bob asked.

"It's a sesquicentennial," Paul said.

"Whatever." Bob didn't even bother looking at him as he said it and Jenn found that really irritating. Paul was a good guy. "We want you doing your thing during the ses—celebration to appear on the very first show of *Checklist for Living*."

"What's *Checklist for Living*?"

"It's your show," Bob said serenely.

"No, it's not," she said. "My show is *Comforts of Home*. Did you smoke a little something on your way up here, Bob?"

He let out a phony, uncomfortable chuckle, watching her with the same expression he might have had if a dog had suddenly started speaking. She understood. The "Jenn Lind" he'd met had gone missing. She'd better find her fast if she wanted to preserve the persona.

"Go find some coffee in the lobby, why don't you, kids?" Bob said. The "kids" jumped up and scattered.

"Could I have the use of your office for a few minutes, Mayor?" Bob asked. He looked at Ken. "And you, too, mis—sir."

"Ah . . . sure." Paul left.

"Holmberg. Ken Holmberg," Ken snapped irritably, adding with a hard look at Jenn, "Don't do anything stupid to screw this up like you done at the state fair pageant, Jenn. This is important to more people than just you." He marched out.

She really despised him.

Bob slung his arm over Jenn's shoulders again. "Walk with me."

Walk with me? Oh fer— And he'd seemed like such a nice guy. Still, he was as close to a boss as she had here, so she walked.

He led her to the window. "We're all really excited about shooting up here. Deter is orgasmic. He loves this. He loves you." She doubted this. Orgasmic Deter had seemed much more interested in poking at a pimple on the back of his neck.

"We have some great ideas. Great ideas," he went on. "Marketing has been working overtime devising fresh ways of presenting you and the show and the first thing they did was to change the name."

"Fine," she said, trying to sound reasonable. "*Comforts of Home* may have been a bit hokey. But, Bob . . . *Checklist for Living*? It sounds like a catalog for medical screening: mammogram, colonoscopy, cholesterol."

"Yeah." He sighed, his expression commiserating. "But it turns out that the viewing public is getting sick of the idea of homes and hearths. They want things that help them facilitate and streamline their lives. You know: techno tips, downloads, charts, itineraries, tables." He lifted his hands, wiggling them on either side of his head.

She wondered if he was trying to be amusing. His hands dropped.

"Anyway, we're going to call your show *Checklist for*

Living. Which is frankly way hipper than *Comforts of Home*." He leaned his head closer to hers and whispered, "Between you and me, I always thought you were way too sexy for a show about making muffins."

From his suddenly sleepy expression, she concluded he was attempting to express a manly interest in her. She looked back, making no effort to hide her lack of womanly response. Unexpectedly, the memory of Steve's face closing fast toward hers, his expression unpremeditated and natural, filled her mental vision. It shook her. Not that she remembered Steve's kissing her—he was a really good kisser and well worth remembering—but that this young stud who embodied everything she generally found appealing—success, good grooming, financial security, sophistication, efficiency—should hold no appeal for her whatsoever.

He released her shoulders. "It's going to be cool, Jenn. At the beginning of each show, we're going to display a checklist geared specifically to that episode which people can download from our Web site. We'll have checklists for putting together the perfect party, for power parenting, for model pet owning, for the ideal romance. People love lists. It'll be fabulous."

Checklists? She was supposed to make checklists for people on how to live? This couldn't be happening to her.

"What about small-town values and back-to-basics lifestyles?" she asked.

"Yeah. Well. Marketing thinks that boat has sailed." He pressed her hand apologetically. "It's all about numbers now. People are freaking in love with numbers. How many, how often, how much . . . By the way, next month is National Immunization Month. So be prepared."

"What? You're going to make a checklist of the shots I

need and give them to me every ten minutes on air?" she spat sarcastically.

"Well . . ."

"What about Dwight Davies?" she asked, becoming frantic. They really meant it. They'd really entirely reformatted her show without consulting her! "What about his commitment to values-oriented programming?"

"Dwight's down with this," Bob assured her. "What could provide better values than to give people a way to make sure they haven't missed any steps in life? Dwight said—and let me quote—'People need help. We're going to help them.' Isn't that nice?"

She didn't want to help people. She wanted to cook. And maybe give people a few tips on taking care of their house plants. Not that she had any of those, either. Even house plants took more care than she could responsibly give.

"This checklist thing is going to work," Bob went on. "People love knowing they're making headway and what better way to do that than with a checklist?"

"But that's not what I do! I cook. Occasionally I bleach something. Once in a while I rub some candle wax on the bottom of a drawer to make it pull easier."

She couldn't make a checklist for the ideal romance; she couldn't even make a checklist for a failed romance!

"Oh," he scoffed gently, "don't worry about that. It doesn't matter what you do on the show. We'll take care of everything. You just do the magic you were hired to do, babe."

Babe? This was a nightmare. She had to call Nat. Now. Find out what the hell was happening to her big breakout.

"So"—Bob stepped back, rubbing his hands together—"what say we get Benjamin in here to do a little of his own magic on this poor face of yours. What have you been doing up here? Using a tanning bed? You are rough and red, babe."

She felt fuzzy, disoriented. A little kernel of panic sizzled in her chest. All the lovely control she'd thought she'd had over her career and life seemed to be slipping through her fingers like talcum powder, and there was nothing she could do to stop it. First Dunkovich, now AMS.

"You feeling ready to go out there and attack this show? We're going to call the first show 'Checklist for a Winter Wonderland Weekend.' It's gonna be money."

Chapter Thirty-eight

"It's like God looked down from heaven and suddenly woke up to the fact that we've been getting shafted all these years and has decided to make it right," Turv said, reverently fanning the wad of bills Jenn Hallesby had stuck in the castle.

Ned let him play with the cash. He deserved some fun.

Turv had hightailed it from city hall, making a beeline for Ned's garage after calling both Ned and Eric en route with the news that their little darlin' here—Ned paused to give the butter head under her burlap shroud a fond pat—was worth *ten thousand dollars.*

The true wonder of all this was that good news had just heaped itself atop good news, because earlier Eric, unemployed and bored, had decided to go check Sleeping Beauty's castle early and there found the twenty-five-hundred-dollar reward that guy in the hospital had promised them.

The Dunkovich dude had vetoed their idea of making a swap in the hospital parking lot, which had made Ned a little sorry since he'd planned to tell everyone they found the butter head while they were taking a walk and would then be hailed as heroes. Instead, Dunkovich had insisted on complete secrecy, telling 'em he'd leave the money and they could call and tell him where to find the butter head, adding to make sure it was well hid and keep quiet about their little "transaction."

Of course, they hadn't gotten around to stashing it and so they hadn't gotten around to calling him and now it looked like they weren't going to. Not with so many people interested in buying the butter head.

"I don't think it's God," Eric said, from where he sat on the Crestliner's battered prow, his legs dangling over the side as he puffed on a doobie. "I think it's Storybook Land, man."

Eric was high, having on his way back used a portion of the money he'd found in the castle to procure a little celebratory dope. Ned wasn't sure he liked Eric making executive decisions like that but in this case he couldn't complain. He was high, too.

"What're you talking about, Eric?" Ned asked, sticking the Ziploc bag full of dope back under the pilot's seat in the Crestliner. They couldn't afford to be too wasted. They had things to figure out.

"It's magic," Eric insisted. "You make a phone call and brownies come and leave money in Sleeping Beauty's Castle. I mean, that guy in the hospital is in a body cast—how else do you explain how that money came to be out there? Brownies." He giggled.

"Take the joint away from Eric, Turv," Ned said. "We got things to do and we don't wanta screw up a real nice deal here 'cause Eric can't hold his water."

Turv lurched up out of the broken-down sofa and plucked the joint from between Eric's lips, taking a drag himself before fastidiously pinching off the ember and sticking the rest into his shirt pocket.

"Okay, let's figure this out," Ned said. "Who all wants our little butter beauty here? We got an unofficial offer for ten thousand from *Ripley's*."

"*Ripley's* ain't gonna pay for stolen property," Eric said.

"No. But we can tell Jenn Hallesby that if her folks get it back they can sell it to *Ripley's* for ten and we'll sell it to her for seventy-five. They'll still make twenty-five for themselves. Then we got this guy at the hospital. He already paid twenty-five. We just tell him we been offered ten and he's gonna have to match that or forget about ever getting the butter head."

"He's never gonna go for that," Eric protested. Eric was proving to be something of a killjoy. "Why would he? He can't sell it to *Ripley's*, either. It's not his."

"Do you really think, Eric," Ned said, "that Dunkovich was going to hand this thing over to the Hallesbys? You don't get yourself busted up over a butter head, then pay twenty-five hundred dollars just to give it away, do ya? He's got something else in mind, and frankly, I don't give a crap *why* he wants it. I just care how *much* he wants it, and he's gonna have to want it pretty damn bad in order to get it."

"The mayor might be willing to do some back-door bartering for it, too," Turv suddenly announced. "I heard him tell the *Ripley's* guy that maybe Fawn Creek would just like to keep the butter head in Jenn Lind's hometown."

"You're kidding," Ned said, a little chagrined Turv had kept this piece of information back until now. "Well, that makes four."

"Four?" Turv asked.

Ned looked at his hand. He was holding up three fingers and he knew he should be holding up four. He thought a second . . . Oh, yeah!

"Four," he announced, his little finger popping up. "This

Jaax guy. I didn't think he'd want to buy it when I saw him on the television, but I didn't think anyone else would be willing to pay much for it. And I was wrong about that, and boy howdy, so maybe he'd be interested in getting in on the auction."

"Auction? That's slick, Ned," Turv said, impressed.

"Thanks," Ned replied modestly. "Now the way I figure it, we should get us at least ten thousand dollars easy. Maybe more."

Turv grinned. "So let's start making calls."

"This the mayor?"

Paul cradled the phone between his shoulder and his ear so he could open the bottom drawer of his desk and stick the insurance file folder back in place. "Yeah?"

"This is the butter head bandits." The guy giggled.

Higher than a kite, Paul thought with an inner sigh. Just like he'd suspected, the butter head had been stolen as a prank and now the "bandits" were trying to figure out some way to give it back without getting in too much trouble.

"Fine. Drop it off in the parking lot tonight when everyone's gone and stay out of trouble from now on."

"Whoa there, mayor. We're not dropping anything off. Not without getting paid."

Asshole kids. "Paid? What are you talking about?"

There was a long pause, a muffled conversation. "We're talking about seventy-five hundred dollars."

"What?" Paul exploded.

"Look, we hear that there's a guy in town who'll pay ten thousand dollars for this here thing but he might not feel like he has like legal ownership if he was to buy it from . . . well . . . from—"

"Thieves?" Paul said sharply.

"Yeah. So how about it? You buy it from us for seventy-five, then turn around and sell it to him for ten. That's a profit of twenty-five for you. Seems fair."

"No."

"Okay. How about seven thousand?"

Now Paul wanted that butter head. He wanted it to ride beside Jenn Lind during the parade. He wanted its image telecast all over the nation, raising curiosity about his town, and he wanted to make for it a little refrigerated shrine right in the town hall lobby. But there were moments that happened in a life that revealed to a man what he was—or had become. And in that instant, Paul finally knew himself to be a true Minnesotan, because no matter what anyone else in the country thought or was willing to pay, there was no way in hell he was going to pony up a thin dime to some blackmailing son of a bitch for a chunk of rancid butter.

"Are you insane?" He slammed down the phone.

Jenn was driving back from the first taped segment of *Checklist for Living*. She was frustrated, resentful, and angry, and that unnerved her because she shouldn't have been. She should have been happily complying with whatever Bob Reynolds and AMS asked her to do, especially since none of it was particularly unreasonable or excessive.

So what if they'd had to do three takes of "Winter Wonderland Weekend's Checklist" bullet number three: snow angels? It wasn't anyone's fault that she'd had to flop around in three separate unblemished patches of snow and wave her arms and legs like an idiot only to struggle to her feet and be told the crew had to reshoot because her ass had made too deep an impression in the snow. If it was anyone's fault, it was hers, because she'd allowed her ass to get that big.

Then why did everything in her rebel against it?

She'd always been a team player. Why was she reacting this way? Maybe she was the diva Nat had accused her of becoming. Maybe she was going through really early menopause. Maybe this was an early midlife crisis. Whatever it was, it was threatening to get out of hand.

Since she'd arrived in Fawn Creek, her family had been robbed, she'd been poked by her cooking mentor, forced to go out and ransom a butter head in a snowstorm, almost done the horizontal tango with Steve Jaax on a lunch counter, been blackmailed by a guy in a body cast, and donned a tacky disguise to play blackjack—and she'd arrived on Friday and it was only Sunday night. No wonder she felt like she might spin off into fifty directions at once.

She was a practical, deliberate, responsible woman who made measured and well-considered choices. She had to stomp on this madness fast before she did something stupid, something irredeemable. She just needed to get back on track, was all.

Her cell phone rang, and she flipped it open. "Jenn Hal— Jenn Lind here."

"This is the butter head bandits," the guy on the other end announced portentously, then ruined the effect by snorting.

"Are you high?" Jenn asked suspiciously.

"No."

She knew high when she heard it. "Yes, you are," she said, disgusted. "What do you want?"

"We know the butter head is worth ten thousand dollars. We want seven."

"Are you insane?" She wanted to shout at him that she knew they'd already sold the damn thing for twenty-five because she'd been the one who'd paid them. She didn't. She didn't want anyone to know about her involvement with Dunkovich.

"No," the guy answered seriously.

"You must be if you think I'm paying you anything more than the hundred bucks I already left you and for which you were supposed to leave me the butter head. Now you tell me where it is," she demanded, although she suspected that the butter head was already in Dunkovich's hospital room. "Now listen, you clowns," she went on, "if you don't stop calling me about this crap, I'm going to hunt you down and take that butter head and I'm going to—"

The phone went dead.

"What'd she say?" Eric asked eagerly.

"You know, for someone who is supposed to be the last word in nice, Jenn Hallesby can be a real bitch. She was about to tell me to put the butter head where the sun don't shine. And the mayor reamed me just as good," he added. "In fact, they used almost the same identical words."

"Maybe they're talking together. Maybe they think if they stick together we'll just give up and let 'em have it dirt cheap," Turv said. "Maybe they don't think we'll deliver it to 'em even if they do give us the money."

"Why would they think that?" Eric asked. "I don't want the damn thing."

"Because we already sold it to 'em twice and didn't?" Turv suggested.

Turv had a point.

"Jenn called us clowns," Ned told the pair, waiting for them to express the outrage he felt. They didn't disappoint.

"Where's she get off? She's the one who was playing patty-cake in the snow for the camera all afternoon. A woman her age . . ."

"Don't matter. What matters is that they're not taking us

serious," Ned said. "We gotta prove we mean business and that this is their last chance to get the butter head."

"How are we gonna do that?" Turv asked.

"Desperate circumstances, my friends," Ned said gravely, looking each of them in the eye, "call for desperate measures."

Chapter Thirty-nine

5:30 p.m.
The Lodge

Jenn parked the Subaru in the barn and was just coming out of it when she spied her dad and Steve tromping up the hill from the direction of the lake. Both men were dressed in ratty terry cloth bathrobes and Sorel boots, both men's calves—her dad's skinny, Steve's hairy—exposed in the area between. Steve was carrying a pail and her dad was holding a loofah. They spotted her at the same time.

"Hi!" Steve called out, lifting his hand in greeting. "We just took a sauna!"

"I see."

They continued smiling and tromping their way through the snow toward the back door, Jenn gazing after them longingly. She wanted to take a sauna. She wanted to be dressed in a ratty terry cloth robe heading back from the tumbled-down shack by the lake. She wanted to be walking next to her dad in companionable . . . companionableness. Or Steve. But she couldn't because she had other things she had to do. Like become phenomenally successful, she reminded herself, rolling the garage door shut and making her way to the Lodge.

Success meant security. She had to keep that thought foremost in mind.

"Is that you, Jenn?"

"Yes, Mom," Jenn answered, hanging her jacket up on one of the pegs in the back hall. Steve and her father were nowhere to be seen. They were probably doing more bonding somewhere.

Bruno evidently hadn't been asked to join the boys' club, either, because he lay in the mudroom atop her father's old snowmobile coveralls, snoring away. She squatted down next to him and stroked his big, smooth head. Poor Bruno. Left all alone—

"Bruno! Where are you, my prince?" From somewhere deep in the house, Steve's voice boomed. Then, lower: "It's just an endearment, Cash. Not a name."

Like he was on a switch, Bruno jumped to his feet, knocking Jenn over. He raced out of the room without a glance back, in such a hurry to get to his Beloved New Master's side that his back end fishtailed around the corner out from beneath him.

Jenn, on her butt on the floor, covered her face with her hands. *You're being stupid*, she told herself, *and overemotional.*

"I didn't realize when you left this morning that you'd be gone all day," her mother said from the kitchen. "I assume those AMS people got hold of you and that's what kept you?"

"Yeah."

"You know, Jenn, I've been meaning to ask you about— Oh, honey! What are you doing down there?"

Jenn looked up to find her mother standing over her, wiping her hands on a white kitchen towel. She looked so perfect. Straight out of *Verandah* magazine, with her triple-foiled auburn highlighted hair, dressed in charcoal gray slacks and a robin's egg blue twinset. She even wore resoled Pradas on her little feet.

Nina shouldn't have been here. She should have been lording it over some roulette wheel at a charity event at a Raleigh country club, not slinging Heart Healthy Hash in a ramshackle cabin in Minnesota. Jenn burst into tears.

Her mother sank down next to her, putting her arm around her. "Honey, what's wrong?"

Jenn said the first thing that came to mind. "Steve and Dad took a sauna!"

Instead of the confusion this statement should have engendered, her mother's expression melted. "Should we take a sauna?" she asked softly. "Come on, Jenny. Let's you and me take a sauna."

Jenn blinked up at her mother through grateful, watery eyes. "Okay."

Jenn squatted disconsolately in the low, windowless sauna, giving herself an occasional cursory swat with the cedar branch her mother had provided. Steam rose in waves from the hot stones piled in a pan atop the tiny wood-burning stove tucked in the corner, its flues angled up and out. Sweat poured off her body, soaking the too small bathing suit she'd found in the back of her bedroom closet.

The last time she'd been in this sauna had been ten years ago. She'd been here for a weekend, fighting a miserable head cold, and decided to take advantage of the head-clearing properties of a good steam. She had fired up the little stove, and had been wheezing and snuffling when the door had been thrown wide and a half dozen Fawn Creek women from her high school class had stumbled in, liquor bottles held high, laughs and burps erupting with equal velocity.

It was Missy Erickson celebrating the dissolution of her three-year marriage to Eric Erickson. No one had bothered to inform Jenn that the Lodge was renting out the sauna and main room for parties.

When they'd seen who was sitting naked in the sauna, the "girls" had insisted Jenn join them. Roosting on benches of various heights, her former classmates had entertained themselves by peering through the vapor, openly searching her body for some sign of artificial enhancement.

Jenn supposed she ought to have been flattered.

For her part, she'd been thankful for the obliterating steam. This was a northern Minnesota sauna, not a health club steam room, and the bodies the steam concealed were not the toned and tightened torsos of ladies who lunch but don't munch. Missy tipped the scales at two hundred pounds and Missy's friend Julie Wick, once the hottie of Fawn Creek who'd sent away for her bras from specialty stores . . . ? Well, Jenn hadn't been surprised by the effects of gravity on a quadruple-D boob.

"Pour some more water on the rocks, will you, Jenn?" Her mother broke through the memory.

Jenn reached over and scooped some snow from the bucketful they'd brought in and ladled it atop the big, smooth river stones. It vaporized with a soft hiss.

"Why don't you tell me about it?" her mother said. Her mom, a very modest lady, hadn't stripped to the buff, but still wore her terry cloth robe. A turban covered her hair.

"There's nothing to tell."

So much for trading mother-daughter confidences.

"Why are you doing this, Jenn?" Nina said unexpectedly. "This AMS show. I don't understand. And before you say anything, I'm not asking because of Dwight Davies's reputation. I'm asking because it's not making you happy."

Happy. Now there was an interesting choice of words.

"I'm happy enough," Jenn said, curling her lips up at the corner to prove it. "And I am going to be enormously successful when this thing finds its audience. You should see the fabulous amounts of money they're throwing at this show, Mom. And the production values are fantastic . . . and . . ." She blinked rapidly. Fabulous, fantastic, enormous. All the superlatives in the world wouldn't make this palatable.

She opened her eyes wide, willing the tears not to come. She tried to fake a laugh.

"Mom. They're calling it *Checklist for Living. Checklist for LIVING.*"

And she fell apart. Again.

She melted like the Wicked Witch of the West, right down onto her knees, burying her face in her mother's terry cloth–covered lap and wrapping her arms around her, crying like her mother could make it all better with a kiss.

"I hate this town, Mom."

"Jenny . . ." Her mother's hand, gently petting her head, checked.

"I do!" Jenny insisted. "Everything was going fine until I came here and now it's all falling apart. This town is like some evil place from a Stephen King novel sucking my life away."

"Jenny. Your employers would have changed the name of your show whether or not they'd come to Fawn Creek," her mother said calmly.

"I wouldn't be too sure about that. You don't know, Mom. You don't know what this town is capable of doing." Her parents never had understood what it had meant when the student council had given her name to the Buttercup judges.

"I know they can be small-minded and oversensitive but

I don't think of the people of Fawn Creek as being Destroyers of Worlds."

Jenn pushed herself upright, raking the damp tendrils of hair back from her face. "Mom, remember the year we moved here? The whole thing with the Fawn Creek student council and the Buttercup judges?"

"Jenny—"

"I know," Jenn broke in, embarrassed. "It's all in the past. I let it go. I really did. I thought I did. But then I arrived and Steve was here and he is so damned charmed by this place! He only sees the quaint and the quirky. It's infectious, even though I know better, Mom! Before I realized it, I started seeing things through his eyes and"—she lifted her hands— "damned if things didn't look not too bad. And Steve had me thinking that maybe over the years people had begun to . . . I dunno . . . feel I was part of the place. It's stupid. I feel so stupid."

"Why?" Nina asked.

"Because they're doing it again, Mom. They're fucking around with my future. I'm sorry!" she wailed. "I shouldn't have said fuck! But fuck, Mom! Someone's threatened to show the media that stupid picture of me and Heidi from the high school homecoming dance."

"Oh, Jenny. No one here would do that."

"They *have*! And I can't let that happen. I've worked too hard for this." She couldn't believe her mother was defending the town. It surprised and confused her. Her mom felt the same way she did about Fawn Creek, didn't she?

"For what?" her mother asked, sounding every bit as frustrated as Jenn felt. "Jenny, if your new employers are the sort of people who would fire you because of a picture . . . is it worth it?"

"Are you kidding?" Jenn asked, dumbfounded.

"No, I'm not. Why is it worth it?"

"To succeed? For security. Since when do you have something against security? I don't understand you and Dad. I go out and 'do' what you and Dad have spent twenty years 'planning' and then you act disappointed in me!"

"We're not disappointed," Nina murmured. Her eyes slid away from meeting Jenn's. "Jenn," she finally said. "I was forty-five, only five years older than you are now, when this business opportunity arose for Cash and I. It was an immense gamble. The initial investment would cost us literally all of our assets, but if it worked, we would not only be set for the rest of our lives but you, and your children, and possibly your children's children, would never want for any material thing. We thought we'd have a lock on the future for us *and* our descendants. So we took that gamble and we lost."

Such a short sentence with such long consequences.

"The next year was a nightmare, trying to figure out how to keep up appearances, declaring bankruptcy, trying to keep it from you, finding a buyer for the company. . . . Then some friends invited us on their annual trip to Las Vegas. We'd often gone with them before but this time we couldn't afford the trip. Of course, we didn't want them to know we couldn't afford high-stakes gambling anymore. We had an image to keep up, in spite of the fact that we only had a few hundred thousand dollars to our names. So we went. And once we got there, we started talking about . . . everything. We decided to play the long shot, to risk it all, and either win back our former lifestyle or change it."

She shook her head, smiling but without any bitterness. "You know what happened next."

"You lost."

"And moved here." Nina nodded. "I know you hated it.

But for us, moving from Raleigh was a relief, Jenn. I can't tell you how good it felt to stop worrying. About keeping up appearances. About how we were going to pay the bills. About what our friends would think. Moving here was like holding your breath for two years and finally being able to breathe."

Her mother stopped talking. It took Jenn a second to realize the implication.

"You like it here?"

Her mother lifted a shoulder, an apologetic movement. "Not at first. At first we were in shock and the adjustment took time but, gradually, we realized how much your father and I liked being together and not just at parties or to pass information to one another about the new landscaping or which season tickets to buy.

"I don't think we realized how much we'd grown to enjoy our lives here for a long time. But then, each trip we took to the city just seemed more and more unnecessary, more an inconvenience than a pleasure, and then we realized we've been happy here. And it was all because of something going wrong in our game plan."

"Why didn't you say something? Tell me?" Jenn asked, surprised but then not as surprised as she ought to have been. Perhaps she'd deduced as much on some level.

Her mother—her composed, regal mother—flushed, which was something of a trick in a sauna and indicative of the strength of her feelings. "We should have. But how do you say, 'All the terrible things we said about this town and this house? We were wrong.' We'd too much pride. And I think on some level we've always felt a little guilty for liking this town—especially knowing how poorly you were treated in high school. But that was high school, Jenny. And sometimes things that seem awful have a way of turning around."

"And you think that'll be my story, too?" Jenn asked in disbelief. "That after working my ass off for years I will just quit and my life will magically become fuller, richer, and more rewarding?"

"Isn't that what you want? Isn't that what everyone wants?"

"Yes," Jenn snapped back. "But with guarantees that no one will ever take them from me. And that's what I'm trying to get through AMS, Mom. Some guarantees. I want the sort of security we had before you and Dad blew it."

As soon as the words escaped, Jenn regretted them, but Nina, far from being offended, only shook her head sadly and laid her thin hand on Jenn's forearm. "Baby," she said softly, "haven't you been listening? We lost what we had by chasing after the same sort of goal you've set for yourself. There is no security. Not the kind you're talking about. There are no guarantees. They're illusions."

No, Jenn thought, her obstinacy tinged with panic, security was real. You just had to work for it. Be willing to pay the price. It was her mother who didn't get it. "I just don't want to end up . . ." Jenn trailed off, her eyes falling to the cedar branch in her lap, unable to bring herself to finish the condemning sentence.

So Nina said it for her. "To end up like your dad and I?" She sighed and her hand fell from Jenn's arm. "You know, Jenny, my darling girl, I am getting heartily sick of being a disappointment to you."

Startled, Jenn looked up. Her mother had that no-nonsense expression she'd worn so often when Jenn was a kid.

"It's our fault, I suspect. Because when we came here we really did intend to leave just as soon as we could find a way clear. We beat that drum for months and you"—she gave a short, derisive laugh—"well, you made it clear from the start that anyone worth his salt would not be content to languish in a backwater, nowhere place like Fawn Creek."

She had never heard her mom sound so coldly angry. "Mom?"

"No, let me finish." Her mother raised her hand to silence Jenn. "This has been too long unsaid. We didn't choose Fawn Creek, Jenny. We wouldn't have chosen it. But it's been good for us here. We don't feel like failures, Jenny, except"—Nina took a deep breath, then caught and held Jenn's gaze—"except when you tell us we are."

Jenn stared at her mother's face. Her jaw was set, her lips compressed, the angle of her head autocratic and vulnerable at the same time. She couldn't even refute the accusation. "I . . ."

"Listen, Jenny. Steve wants to buy the Lodge. He's offered two million dollars for the buildings and the land but he says he'll go up to three if necessary."

"What?" Jenn's breath left her chest in a whoosh. Her brain went into lockdown. *The Lodge gone? No.* That wasn't possible. Steve couldn't buy the Lodge. Steve didn't belong up here any more than she did. Less. A *lot* less. "Why would he want to do that?"

"He thinks it will be good for him. Good for his art, I mean. He says that you think so, too."

"I never said that!" The day, which had started so serenely, had gone to dreadful and was slipping into surreal. For the last eight hours, she'd seemed to exist in a perpetual state of unhappy surprise, barking the word "What?" every fifteen minutes.

"He thinks you did," Nina said. "He has a very high opinion of your opinion of his work."

"That's absurd."

Steve had actually been listening to her drunken rambling? Of course, he had. And now he planned to buy the Lodge, move all his equipment here, dive into his work, and enjoy a spiritual and creative renaissance. And he would, too. She had no doubt about it. It was just . . . such a Steve Jaax sort of thing to do.

How could he do this to her? And her parents? Because now . . . now it was all suddenly, hideously making sense to her. Her parents' stalwart refusal to accept her help hadn't been pride. They hadn't wanted to leave. They *still* didn't want to leave. But how could anyone in his right mind refuse an offer of that magnitude? Sure they could find another place but it wouldn't be here. It . . .

Jenn stood up, the cedar bough falling unnoticed to her feet. She was distracted and bemused and felt betrayed by Steve and unable to understand why. It was a generous offer. More than generous.

But then Steve would be here and she wouldn't. Not that it mattered. She didn't want to be here. She didn't care if the place burned to the ground. Did she? Her thoughts spun wildly.

"When is he going to take possession?" Her voice was barely audible.

"He's not," Nina said, both defiant and exasperated.

Jenn's head snapped around and she looked down at her frail, elegant mother, chin high as she stared her daughter down.

"Haven't you heard anything I've said, Jenny? This is our *home*. We're not selling it now or ever."

Chapter Forty

Steve lay spread flat on his back, balancing a glass of Barolo on his chest. Prince, né Bruno, was wedged between Steve and the couch, also on his back, his legs dangling limp in the air. Next to him, Nina sat at the end of the couch neatly snipping coupons out of *The Weekly Shopper* while beside her Cash read the newspaper and muttered about the latest candidate for the Green Party.

Across the room, Jenn shut the photo album she'd been looking at for the last half an hour. She hadn't asked Steve to join her, and something in her body language—the way she angled her back against him, a certain tension in the bow of her neck—informed him that it would not be a good idea to ask to be included. He really wanted to ask to see her pictures. He wanted to know what she considered important, or worth remembering. He wanted, in short, to be included in her life. Her past. Everything.

He suspected that in part had been the reason he'd been so enamored of the idea of buying the Lodge. Because even though Jenn discounted its importance, he knew better. He knew it was important to her, and he knew if he held it, he might have the means to keep her coming back. Not only to the Lodge. But to him.

In a way, the Lodge was Jenn's butter head. On the surface there was not much value, but important keys were buried within. He wondered if she knew. Or if Nina had told her that Cash had, instead of selling him the whole thing, agreed to sell him the barn and the quarter acre it sat on. He wondered if it pissed her off because she realized what he was doing or at least somehow intuited that part of it.

He sighed and lifted his head off the floor and poured a little more wine into his mouth and looked around at the others in the great room.

The phone rang in the kitchen.

"Get that, will you, Jenn?" Cash asked without looking up.

Without a word, Jenn got up and headed for the kitchen. Steve rolled over, pushed himself to his feet, and trotted after her, Nina's interested gaze following him.

He got to the kitchen door just in time to hear Jenn saying, "Whatever you're smoking, stop! I thought I warned you guys that I—"

She stopped abruptly, her expression revealing her disdain for whoever was on the other end. She glanced at Steve and said into the phone, "I don't want you to be in contact. I want you to leave me alone. And if you—" She stopped, held the receiver away from her ear, and stared at it crossly. "He hung up on me!"

"Who?" Steve asked, all sorts of hitherto ignored chivalrous impulses rushing to the fore.

"No one. Those guys with the butter head." She frowned at him. "You should let your hair grow longer. Not everyone is lucky enough to get curls, you know." She delivered these last sentences in an unwilling tone.

"You think?" he asked, pleased. "What did those guys want? Where's the butter head?"

"I don't know. They think I'm stupid enough to pay them twice for it. They called me on my cell earlier today and wanted more money. I told them no and now they're pissed off."

Jenn moved past him.

"Where are you going?" Steve asked, falling into step beside her.

"They told me to look on the front step. On the way, way small chance these guys have actually left the butter head out there, I am going, even though instinct tells me I have a better chance of finding a bag of burning cow poop."

She yanked open the sticky front door. A shoe box wrapped in twine lay on the ground before her, a trail of men's boots to and from a fresh set of tire tracks a short ways off.

"Your Prince is a crappy guard dog," she said, picking up the box. She held it up to her ear, giving an exploratory jiggle. Steve sniffed. It had an odd odor. A little off. Jenn must have smelled it, too.

"If those assholes have sent me a dead mouse," she said, unwrapping the package, "so help me, I will hunt them down and—" She stopped and frowned down at the open box. An oddly shaped, oddly scented . . . yellowish something lay on the bottom, slightly crescent-shaped and flattened. Steve recognized it immediately.

"What is this?" Jenn asked, frowning.

"It's an ear," he said. "The butter head's ear."

Jenn's nose wrinkled with repugnance, whether from the old freezer smell wafting up out of the box or the idea that someone would lop off the butter head's ear, he couldn't tell. He watched her closely thinking that under normal circumstances she'd have laughed. But circumstances were not normal.

Something was bothering her, something more than the delivery of the butter head's ear.

For himself, Steve wasn't laughing not only because the idiots who had his sculpture were violating a work of art—his art—but also because if they continued lopping off bits of her, they just might lop off the bit with his key in it. Or worse, lop off a piece and have the key fall out.

It wasn't like the key was suspended deep within the butter. Nah-uh. He'd quickly dug a hole, shoved it in, plastered it over with a plug of butter, and bang! The arrival of the bounty hunter had ended any further efforts.

"We have to get that butter head back," he said.

She looked at him. "Why? What's so important about the butter head, Steve? Why does everyone want it?"

"Everyone?" He tilted his head.

She flushed. "Yeah. You know, you, the mayor, the guy who offered the reward, and there's some other guy here from *Ripley's Believe It or Not* who'll pay ten thousand for it so they can stick it in the *Ripley's* Museum. The butter head is a suspiciously popular girl." Her eyes narrowed thoughtfully. "Is there something about this thing that I don't know about?"

"It's important. Really important," he began. "The fact is there's something in it that—"

"Steve," she cut in. He stopped, because she'd moved closer to him and was looking up at him all serious. He couldn't remember the last time a woman had looked at him with that expression—not of expectation, but of concern.

Thoughts of the butter head flew straight out of his mind, chased away by her obvious consternation. All on his behalf. She cared. About him.

"Steve," she continued soberly, "you know, maybe you're a little overinvested in this butter head."

"Really?" She was such a focused, objective, and competent woman—qualities he generally didn't particularly admire, except in Verie, and associated with desperate people who wasted their lives in a perpetual state of ambition. But if he wasn't like that . . . well, she was, but she was more than that. He'd seen another aspect of her, *felt* another aspect, a woman who had returned his kiss unabashedly, wholeheartedly, without restraint or self-consciousness. He found this combination of budding voluptuary and stoic entrancing.

"It doesn't belong to you, and I have to tell you, I don't think it's going to belong to you," she was saying, looking a little uncomfortable. "I'm trying to tell you not to get your hopes up about it."

She wanted the butter head, too, he realized. For whatever reason, it was important to her. Because . . . because he'd done it? Or maybe she wanted it for her parents. Because it meant something to them. That seemed even more probable.

"I could buy it?" he suggested. He angled his head. All she had to do was angle the other way . . . lean in an inch . . . give him some sign. Any sign. Because he was suddenly wary, for the first time in ages, afraid of taking the wrong step, of going too fast, of misreading her. She wasn't like any woman he'd ever known . . . and yet, conversely, she was in so many ways familiar to him. Gloriously so.

"I don't think so." She shook her head. The lights overhead stroked it platinum. "You know, not everything is for sale."

"I know." He nodded, watching her.

She hesitated and then suddenly poked him in the sternum

with her index finger. "This house. You tried to buy my home—I mean, my parents' home."

"Yeah," he agreed, not precisely certain why she sounded so accusing. "I can do great work here. I think this place could be really good for me."

"You should have told me you were planning to make them an offer."

"Why? I thought you'd approve," he said. "You were just telling me how much they wanted out of here but that they wouldn't accept your help, so I thought they might accept an offer from me. It was a win-win situation. They could get out of Fawn Creek and I could get a studio."

"Well, I was wrong. About them. For whatever reason, they don't want to leave here. I think they've got their ceme-tery plots paid for or something," she said gruffly.

She wouldn't own up to anything positive about her feel-ings for this place, this town. But if that was the way she wanted to play it, he could, too.

"Sorry you'll be stuck coming back here."

She shrugged. "I'll live."

"Maybe I'll see you."

"Well, I'll be in New York and—"

"I mean here."

"But my mom said they didn't sell you the place."

"Not the Lodge or the land, but they sold me the barn."

"What?" Jenn raked the back of her hair with her fingers. "Why doesn't anyone tell me anything?"

Steve had to say it, even though he was afraid of her re-sponse, and this was so unlike him, the hesitancy, this uncer-tainty, this caring so much about another's opinion of him. He hadn't even really cared whether his wives had liked him. *Him.* Not what he did or what he created.

"I can withdraw the offer, if you'd rather." He sounded stiff rather than nonchalant.

Jenn's gaze rose to his. She scowled, unhappy, confused, looking as uncertain as he felt, but he could count on her being direct and honest, with both him and herself. He knew that.

"No," she finally said, shaking her head. "No, don't do that."

He must have been getting old, he thought as he watched her go, distracted by her inner thoughts, because he found that simple sentence perfectly satisfying.

Dunk was having trouble sleeping.

He hurt. Karin, virtuous and voluptuous, had cut off his morphine. Twice today, once in the morning and the afternoon, she had insisted he get up and walk up and down the hallway, dragging his IV stand with him. She hadn't offered him anything for the resulting agony aside from a couple Tylenol with codeine.

But it wasn't the pain that kept him awake. It was the thought of those cheating assholes who were holding his butter head hostage. Early this evening the local network had run a piece about the popularity of Steve Jaax works and how every collector of modern art in the country worthy of the name had a Jaax.

Originally, Dunk had been thinking he could get maybe a hundred thousand dollars for an older piece like *Muse in the House* off the legit market. Now he was thinking four times that. He wanted that money. He needed it. And the key to it was literally here, in this pissant nowhere town, his for the taking. If he just knew where to look!

The thieving sons of bitches who were supposed to have called him and told him the butter head's whereabouts as soon as they got their money hadn't called. If he hadn't seen the panic in Jenn Lind's eye, he might have suspected her of ignoring his threats. But he had seen the panic, and if Dunk Dunkovich knew one thing, it was when he had a fish well and truly hooked; Jenn Lind had been gill-netted.

Which didn't solve his little problem, did it?

Beside him, the phone rang and Dunk snatched it up. It could only be one of two people: the assholes or Jenn Lind 'fessing up that she'd missed the drop.

"Who is this?" he spat into the phone.

"The butter head bandits."

"That's the stupidest thing I've ever heard. Where's my sculpture?"

"We got it." The guy was trying to sound nonchalant. Amateurs.

"Well, where is it?"

"I *said,* we got it. There's been a change of plans."

Dunk waited.

"We found out that we were undervaluing our stock, so's to speak. And now it appears there are other parties interested in acquiring the product."

The guy had been watching too many Quentin Tarantino movies. "Really? So you're trying to screw me?"

"Pretty much." The bastard sounded gleeful.

"How much do you want now?"

"We're not sure exactly."

"What?" What kind of deal was this? Ransomers calling just to chat? Or maybe they wanted his advice on how much to ask for? He didn't frickin' believe this!

"We still got feelers out, trying to determine exactly what our product is worth."

"Would you stop saying product? It's a butter head!" Dunk shouted into the phone.

"Okay, butter head, then," the guy came back sullenly. "We're calling to let you think on how much you're willing to bid for it, so think and"—his voice dropped dramatically—"hang close to the phone. We'll be in touch."

"Like I have a choice," Dunk sneered, but the line had gone dead.

Steve sat at the kitchen table two hours later, drinking a glass of milk and munching on a rice cake he'd smeared with Nina's homemade, unsalted peanut butter. At least it was recognizable, and besides, he was starving. He'd managed to get down most of Nina's FiberFabulous Tofu Loaf, but it wasn't exactly stick-to-your-ribs fare. No wonder Nina was so skinny.

The phone rang and Steve jumped. It was, he'd learned earlier today, the only phone in the house. It rang again.

He knew from experience that no one was going to race down here from wherever they were—and he wondered especially where Jenn was—to answer it. The Hallesbys did not center their lives around the ringing of phones or clocks or television programs, and neither did he, not since TiVo. Still, it was so high-minded, it made him grin. He wondered if he'd become as high-minded after living here a while. Probably. Jenny could be his mentor.

That Jenny figured prominently in his vision of his future he no longer questioned. The only real question now was how to get her to accept the same vision. As he pondered this, the message machine picked up, silently communicating its missive to whoever was on the other line. Then a man's voice came over the speaker.

"Look," the guy said in a grudging tone, "I know it's late. Sorry. But we forgot to tell you when we were gonna call you, so we're calling back to tell you now. Only we got more information for you to chew on, too. So that's another reason we're calling so late."

My God, Steve realized, it was the butter head thieves!

"So here's the thing," the voice continued. "That guy over t'the hospital? The guy who chased us on the snowmobiles and crashed? And that wasn't our faults, by the way. He went off the trail."

The thief sounded stoned out of his mind.

"Anyhow," the guy rambled on, "he's willing to pay big bucks for that sculpture. So if you want it, you can have it for—" he broke off.

"No!" Steve shouted, grabbing the phone. "Are you there?" he spoke frantically into the receiver. "Tell me you're there. Come on, man, *speak to me*."

A tinny voice came from the earpiece. "Who's this?"

Steve closed his eyes, breathing a sigh of relief. "This is Steve Jaax."

"Oh fer . . . where's Jenn?"

"She's not here. What do you want for the butter head?"

"Well, now that's just what me and my friends here were discussing when you went all postal."

"What do you want for it?"

The guy took a deep breath. "What'll you give?"

"I dunno. Twenty-five?"

"Come on, man," the guy sounded disgusted. "You gotta do better than that."

"Right. Thirty."

"Geesh," the guy sneered.

Steve had no idea where he was going to get the money but he would get it even if Verie had to charter a plane and fly here from New York. He had already planned to sell some of his collection to pay the Hallesbys. He might as well kiss good-bye to the Miró, too.

"Forty then," he said, adding as he heard the sniff on the other end, "Look, when do you want this? In what form? Forty thousand dollars is not going to be easy for me to come up with here."

"Forty thous—" It sounded like someone dropped the phone.

There was another long silence. Then the sound of a hand covering the mouthpiece and the mumble of excited, muffled conversation.

"Come on, man!" Steve said in exasperation. It was so close, he could almost see her, the sylph form, brilliant and graceful and irreverent and . . . Fabulousa's furious face when she heard the news. He'd carried the dream of retribution so long it was reflex. But now superseding it was the image of Jenn looking at him approvingly as he returned the butter head, sans key, to her parents' care. She might even tear up. Hell, he might.

"Just tell me where you want the money and where I can pick up the butter head."

The voice, when it finally spoke again, sounded strangled. "We gotta talk to another guy first. We'll be in touch."

"But I don't have a cell."

"Borrow Jenn Hallesby's," the voice clipped out. "Bye."

Chapter Forty-one

There was a picture in the family album taken the winter her father had forced them to spend an entire February week at the Lodge. He had rented an ice house, and every day he and her mother would get up, wrap themselves and Jenn in the layers of specialty store clothing he'd sent away for, and trudge across the lake to an outhouse-shaped, -scented, and -configured box. The ice beneath them would boom and groan as they went—which had scared the crap out of Jenn until one of the locals had assured her that such sounds were natural for frozen lakes.

Once to the fish house, her father would plunk her down on a bench between himself and her mom. Then they would wait in a state of breathless anticipation (though Jenn's state was nearer comatose) for some pathetic fish to drift beneath the open hole carved in the floor and through the ice so her father could throw a mini-trident at it.

He was not a successful spearer. Later Jenna would learn that the art of spearing came in the smooth release and directed fall of the spear and that throwing it only had the

effect of causing the spear to torque in the water and startle
the fish. Later, much to fishdom's sorrow, he would catch
on. But back then their days of attempting to catch their
own food were spent in uneventful torpor, lulled into a state
of semisomnambulism by the overheated fish house, the
dark and musty interior, the crackling of the woodburning
stove, their only light from the eerie fantastical glow of the
aquarium-like hole at their feet.

Occasionally, things livened up a bit, what with the excitement of a fish showing up and her dad jabbing, missing,
and swearing.

Anyway, the picture had been taken inside the fish
house. She couldn't imagine who the photographer had
been, probably the guy they'd rented the fish house from.
Her father's face was red with heat from the stove, the flash
from the camera's light flaring in his eyes, making them
manic with a red gleam. Her mother looked like she was
posing for *Ladies' Home Journal*, the consummate lady
being equally at home in the conservatory or fishing shack,
and Jenn was sitting stiff-legged on the bench behind him,
having edged as far away as possible from the proceedings,
her face transfixed with a familiar expression of horror and
resignation.

It was a good picture, perfectly summing up the whole
fish house experience and one she was not eager to relive
though that was precisely what she'd be doing in a few minutes when the Fawn Creek Sesquicentennial Fish Spearing
Tournament would officially begin. Jenn, decked out in the
latest lodge wear fashions, and cringing at the blast of arctic
cold that ripped at her parka hood, took the purring gasoline-
powered auger from Paul LeDuc's hands and shoved it into a
prebored hole.

"Let's go fishing!" she shouted into the microphone

above the sound of the wind and the engine noise, her voice booming out of the giant speakers flanking either side of the platform erected out on the ice for the festival. Later that day, if the weather allowed—and a quick glance at the lowering, scuttling bruised clouds above suggested otherwise—she'd do a cooking spot from the same platform for the AMS cameras.

At the sound of her voice, six hundred fisherpeople charged from the shore and ran for the dark houses set on the surface of the lake in strips and clusters. There would have been ten times that number but for the twenty mile an hour wind stampeding down from Canada that had driven away the meeker competition and closed all the roads to the west and most of those to the south.

"You get into your house before you get blown away!" Paul shouted at her, his hands clapped over his red ears. He pointed a short distance off at a small eight-by-ten structure with a huge sign painted on its side that read, DONATED FOR THE USE OF JENN LIND BY HANK'S HARDWARE, FAWN CREEK, MINNESOTA. She'd promised Paul she'd pretend to fish for at least an hour before escaping.

Paul was right, she thought. She should head right in there. But that meant heading in there with Steve Jaax, who'd asked her earlier if he could come fishing with her. She wasn't sure how she felt about that. Well . . . she acknowledged honestly, that wasn't exactly right; she knew precisely how she felt about it, and that was the trouble. This was crazy. She was starting to anticipate time with Steve and want more of it, and where the hell was that supposed to go? Oh, yeah. She was supposed to show up in Fawn Creek when he flew in from London or Paris to sequester himself in the great north woods and work on his art.

The trouble was, the way she felt right now, she suspected she would.

She didn't need that sort of complication. . . . Oh yes, she did. It was exactly what she needed. To feel alive and excited and a little nervous and completely involved in the moment.

She glanced out of the corner of her eye at her co–grand marshal. He was sitting on the top of the three steps leading down the platform, looking around with that fascinated expression, much, she suspected, like Jane Goodall had looked upon first spying the chimps of Gambia. Her father had found Steve a Norwegian fisherman's sweater to wear under the old army coat they'd found in the attic, a fur-lined bomber's hat, Sorel boots, and leather choppers. The fur-lined ear flaps were down, snapping in the wind. He looked goofier than hell and she wished she didn't find him so appealing. It was stupid. Maybe even dangerous.

He caught her looking at him and smiled. "What do we do now?" he yelled over the wind.

"Come on, Jack London," she said, holding out her hand. He reached up and took it, drawing her down to his side. He didn't let go of her hand as they lowered their heads against the wind and trotted to the ice house.

He pushed open the door and stepped back to let her enter. She ducked inside and looked around. It was a true Fawn Creek dark house, none of Mille Lac's notorious excesses of satellite television and water beds here, just a simple, wood-burning stove in the corner pouring out heat into the little room, a bench tacked to the wall, and on the opposite wall, cut into the floor and through fourteen inches of ice, a three-by-two rectangle of glowing aquamarine light.

A small trident, the prongs buried in balsam wood, rested against the wall while a spooled jig dangled motionless from a hook above the hole. It could stay there. The last time she'd been in a dark house her father had had the temerity to actually spear a fish. She could still hear his whooping laughter over her shrieks as the fish had flopped free and onto her feet and from there flopped back into the hole to be swallowed by the blue light.

Steve let out a low whistle, turning slowly in a circle. She watched him, wondering what he saw, if his eyes translated images in a manner different from hers, if he saw things clearer. Or maybe foggier. He certainly made her feel foggy. Just his presence clouded her thoughts, and for someone who had spent forty years congratulating herself on her clear thinking, this was distinctly uncomfortable.

"This is wonderful," he whispered as if he was afraid of talking too loud.

"It'll do."

"Do? Someone's already got the stove going and look!" He reached beneath the bench and pulled up a bucket filled with Sam Adams beer. "Fawn Creek has got to have the nicest people in the country."

As if she had been slapped in the face, she heard Dunk's voice. *Your fans here in Fawn Creek . . .* and *You know how it is when you got dirt on someone you think has gotten way above herself but you can't use it? You just gotta tell someone.*

The fog thinned. "Sure. They're regular saints."

"Why do you dislike this town so much, Jenn?" Steve asked, moving aside and stripping off his jacket. He pulled his choppers off and tossed them along with the bomber's cap to a shelf above the door. "Why do you dislike the people here so much? No one has been anything but nice since I've gotten here. I mean, even the name Fawn Creek couldn't be sweeter."

"Forget it," she said, shrugging out of her parka and hanging it on a hook. She looked over her shoulder at him. He was stripping off the Norwegian sweater. Under it he wore his usual white shirt, the tails hanging loose over his jeans.

The glow from the fishing hole swept up his body, rimming him with silvery blue, backlighting his white shirt and exposing the silhouette beneath. He was lean and well-toned. Too sexy by half. And the darkness was too intimate, too seductively warm. It had to be ninety in here.

"You want to know how Fawn Creek got its name?" she asked to distract herself. "I figured it out when I was doing a research project on the town for history class."

"Sure."

She sat down on the bench, leaning her head against the wall. The wind buffeting the house from outside gave the room a clandestine feel. "Tradition holds that the town was founded by some Swedish immigrants who were heading west to the Dakotas but came upon this little Eden by a bubbling creek and were so taken with it they couldn't bear to leave. So they set stakes, named their new town Fawn Creek, and the rest, as they say, is history."

"But you know different."

"I looked up the weather records. The winter this town was founded was one of the coldest on record." She unbuttoned the top two buttons of her blouse and began rolling up her sleeves. "That's the first clue. Here's the second and third. This is the sesquicentennial, right? The birthday of this town. And it's December." She looked at him askance.

"So?"

"Think about it. There are no fawns in December, and that creek? It would have been frozen."

Steve lifted one of his brows.

"However, there is a Swedish word pronounced 'fawn.' " She waited a beat. "It means shit."

He burst out laughing. "No!"

"Yes," she said, nodding. "You know how I think the town came to be? I think they got marooned here. I think they were trying to cross the creek, broke through the ice, and were soaked through. I think someone, probably the leader or even more likely the leader's wife, said, 'I'm not going any further than this shitty creek.' And thus, the name. Call it a premonition by the founding forefathers."

His laughter faded. He stepped closer, looking down at her. It was called chiaroscuro, she recalled, light and dark, and it made magic of the reflected light and shadows composing his face.

"What's it about, you and the town?" he asked, his voice probing. "Come on. Tell me. I'm going to be living here, you know. At least part of the year. So tell about My People."

He sounded all interested and earnest. Poor sucker. She remembered her own naive assumption that she'd be accepted in Fawn Creek.

"Please," he said.

Okay. "Why do you think people are so nice to you, Steve?"

"I know you think they're nice to me because of the celebrity thing, but really, I'm a celebrity everywhere and this is different. It feels different. It's not because of who I am."

"You're right," she agreed. "It's not because you're a famous artist, Steve. The people here are nice to you because they think you are going away."

He tipped his head inquiringly.

"Small-town people are always nice to those just passing through. Because you don't know anything and you'll only be here a short time. You won't be here long enough to . . . make waves."

"Waves? Come on." He laughed again, but this time not so easily.

She felt very old and very jaded watching her words sink in, dissolving his earlier pleasure. She didn't like herself very much in that moment.

"It doesn't take much to make a wave in a small pond, Steve. You live in a small town and you spend all your time looking for waves. You have to, because in a small pond, every ripple is going to eventually hit you. It's in your best interest to know where it's coming from and who generated it and when it's going to hit you and from what side.

"Whatever you do, however long you live here, you feel the repercussions of every act. They bounce back at you all your life. There's no getting away from mistakes. You make waves in a city and it gets absorbed. The same wave here can upend your little boat."

Steve sat down beside her. "At least here you do something and it has an effect. You have a chance of touching someone, of being noticed, of making a difference, good or bad. Like you said, Jenny, in the city, you can spend your life never connecting, never having your wave reach another person, let alone the shore."

"Thank God for it," she said gruffly. "I don't need that sort of connection."

"Everyone wants to connect to something." He glanced at her, looked away. "Someone."

Her breath jumped lightly in her throat. She almost moaned. He shouldn't say things like this to her. It was seduction pure and simple, using something far more alluring to her than good hair or a fab after-shave: understanding.

He bent forward, looking straight ahead, his forearms on his thighs, his hands dangling between his knees. "Why wouldn't you cuddle up with me out at Storybook Land? Why haven't you kissed me again?"

Whatever she'd expected him to say, it hadn't been that. *She* kiss *him*? She wasn't aware the prerogative had been only hers, but then, Steve Jaax wasn't the man she would have assumed from his press. He was a little awkward, a little vulnerable, though still incredibly self-assured.

"I don't know. I didn't want to be another notch on Steve Jaax's welding gun holster?"

"I wouldn't hit on you. Ever. Boy, it's hot in here." He'd started slipping his shirt's buttons out of their holes, starting at the top but not stopping at the second. Or the third. Or even the fourth.

This did nothing for her confidence. But he had kissed her, she reminded herself.

"Why won't you hit on me?" she blurted out.

"I only hit on young women," he said, as if this was a cause for congratulations.

She looked away from the chest muscles revealed by the open shirtfront. Not many guys in their late forties had chests like that. Not many guys in their thirties. Okay. It was a good chest at any age. "Why is this no surprise?"

He looked up at her, his head still bent to his task. He smiled ruefully. "It's easy with young women. They have no expectations."

"You mean for a second date?" she asked dryly.

"No. I mean *during* the date. A young woman, she's no more interested in a long-term relationship than she is in who the Bangles were. She's satisfied if a guy my age can get it up and keep it up long enough to fulfill the sexual contract. With the little blue pill, that's no problem." His gaze fell into the blue square of light. "Too bad they can't make little blue pills for conversation."

He looked straight into her eyes. His own seemed to have borrowed light from the fishing hole. He tipped his head in a subtle salute. "Older women like you demand wit and style and . . . art. I might not be up to the task. I might disappoint. I wouldn't want to disappoint a woman like you."

He reached up and slid the back of his hand across her cheek, sending a reactive shiver down her spine and curling her toes. "Damn, but you're an elegant creation, Jenny."

"Is this where you tell me you'd like to do me in marble?" She tried flippancy but the effect was wrecked by the slight tremble in her voice.

"No. I don't want to re-create you in any medium. I want to experience . . . us. Not you. Not me. *Us.* I want to make love to you."

She stared at him. It was too romantic. Too over-the-top romantic and she was not a romantic woman. She planned and analyzed and weighed cost/benefits. She had goals and schedules. She wasn't a romantic. Not her. Not Jenn Lind.

"Why aren't you with someone? You ought to be with someone. What are you holding out for, Jenny? Art?" he asked, studying her, looking solemn and oddly exposed.

No, not Jenn Lind. Jenny, however, didn't waste a second thinking about tomorrow. Jenny cried when she hurt. Jenny had dreams and fantasies. Jenny was a complete push-over.

"Who says I'm holding out?" Jenny whispered.

His breath caught. And then he was standing up, pulling her to her feet, and she was shedding her clothes while his

mouth fastened on hers in a hot, wet, long kiss, hungrily taking her breath away. She yanked his shirt off his shoulders—
and Lord, they were nice broad, heavy shoulders—and
down his arms, where one cuff caught around his wrist.

He released her just long enough to whip his arm frantically and shed the shirt all the way, his mouth still locked
against hers, making a frustrated, anguished, satisfied
moan. He unsnapped her bra and fumbled at the straps and
she brushed his hands away, ripping it off the rest of the
way, plastering herself urgently against him, belly to belly,
breast to chest, wrapping her arms around him like a vise.
Like she would never let go. He was warm and dense and
smooth and hairy and she sighed into kisses that went on
and on as his hands swept down her bare sides, gossamer
light with an artist's deftness, straight down over her hips
and around under her buttocks. He lifted her up, walking
her backward until she felt the rough planks of the fish
house wall against her back.

She wrapped her legs around his waist . . . and thank God!
Thank God, he worked with heavy metals because he made
her feel almost light, the way he pushed up into her against
the wall and found that ancient, maddening, sob-inducing
rhythm, carrying her, carrying them, right to places her
memory promised still existed and then—thank God, thank
God—straight into a whole new world of pleasure.

"I've got a terrific crush on you," she admitted half an
hour later.

"Is that bad?" he asked.

"I don't have crushes."

"You should," he said, capturing her face between his
hands and kissing her lightly. "You should have crushes

and infatuations. You should moon around and feel dazzled and rapturous and miserable."

"I should?"

"Yes. No. No." He shook his head, kissing the corners of her mouth. "I'm too selfish. You should only have a crush on me."

She turned so she could hide the smile his words had caused. This was so foolish. So romantic and ridiculous. And yes, she did feel a little dazzled. . . . Of course, it was hot in the fish house.

"I may be falling in love with you," he said.

She snapped back around and stared at him, startled, her fingers missing the buttonhole she was trying to push her shirt button into. He'd jammed his shoulder against the fish house door and was still gloriously shirtless, though he had, she noted, fastened his jeans back up.

"In fact, I'm pretty sure I am."

She felt her whole face bloom—there was no other word for it—filling with the delight of hearing him say those . . . The delight faded. Became suspicion.

"How many women have you said that to?" She dipped her head to the task of buttoning her shirt. She didn't want to see his expression. She got way too caught up in his eyes and the way he looked at her.

"Probably too many," he admitted.

"So I'm just another in a long line." She tried not to let it matter. She wasn't a kid. She didn't expect anything. She stepped into her slacks and wiggled them up over her hips.

"It's not that long," he protested. "And this is different. You're older."

She felt a burst of heat in her cheeks, thankful for the dim interior. "Wow. Color me wooed."

In answer, he reached out and cupped the back of her

head in his palm and pulled her face to his for a long, drawn-out kiss. When he finally pulled back, her head was spinning.

"I told you," he said soberly, "I like older women. I love your face. I love every grace note every year has imparted, every little bitterness-made line and every one made by laughter." His gaze swept her face with incredible tenderness and desire. He smiled. "Do you think you could have gotten pregnant?"

She came crashing back to reality. He was just like any other guy after all, worrying that their mutual lack of impulse control might have long-term effects. "Probably not. I'm not exactly in my peak reproductive years."

"Oh," he said. He sounded sad. *Disappointed*. And weirdly enough, she felt a faint echo of it.

"Still," she said, striving for the right balance of casualness, sophistication, and maturity, "I can't believe I could be this irresponsible."

"I'm not going to give you anything. I'm clean. Not virtuously clean. Physically clean. But I'm pretty virtuously clean, too. I haven't . . . You're the first in . . . a long time," he finished weakly.

Her sophistication crumbled at his awkwardness. She smiled. He was an original. She had to give him that. "How ever did you convince three women to marry you, let alone to go to bed with you?" she asked, shaking her head. "I would think with lines like yours women would run shrieking."

"They're not lines," he answered quietly, stepping closer.

She could smell him, a distinct scent, a warm male aroma. She'd read articles in *Psychology Today* about how when a woman became . . . romantically interested her sense of smell became heightened, accentuated, so when she realized that he smelled like a bottle of the world's most subtle and evocative and delicious *something,* she knew what it meant: she was in *such* trouble.

Her cell phone rang.

Chapter Forty-two

11:40 a.m.
Oxlip County Hospital, Room 323

"Where's my butter head?" Dunk spoke in a low voice into the receiver. He'd been waiting since seven o'clock this morning to make this call, shortly after his own little phone conversation with those assholes who'd stolen his butter head. He'd had to wait this long because Karin, concerned with his elevated blood pressure, had been hovering all morning. He'd finally gotten rid of her on some trumped-up errand but she could show up at any second. He didn't have much time to get his point across.

"I don't have it," Jenn Lind replied.

"I didn't think so," Dunk snarled. He was nervous and edgy. "Too bad. Because, unfortunately for you, Steve Jaax has just raised the ante on the sculpture."

There was silence on the other end. Immediately Dunk was suspicious. The knowledge that Steve Jaax had actively entered the equation pounded at his confidence. "He there? With you?"

There was another pause, then: "I'm in an ice fishing house. With Steve Jaax."

"You and him in cahoots, Ms. Lind? Because that would not be wise," Dunk bit out.

"No," she clipped back at once.

This deal had to go through and it had to go through now. If the idiots who held the butter head realized Jaax would go up even more for that damn sculpture, he'd be out of the running. Luckily, it hadn't occurred to them that anyone would pay more than what Dunk had already offered: fifty thousand. And he'd made damn sure they understood that if he even got a sniff that they'd been going back for rebids, he was pulling his offer off the table. That had seemed to do the trick. The plans were to make the exchange outside town. The thieves had informed him he would recognize them because they'd be wearing ski masks. He'd told them he had better recognize them because they'd have a fucking butter head with them.

He'd just have to talk Jenn Lind into doing him one more service, as a chauffeur, before he cut her loose.

"It would even be a career-killing move, if you understand my drift. In fact, if Jaax even *knows* about me, it could cause you all sorts of grief."

"We're not. He doesn't." Her voice was tight and small. She was scared. Good.

"He's offered the guys who have it forty thousand dollars."

She drew in a shuddery breath. "That's a lot."

"You bet," he agreed. "Now I'm going to tell you what we're going to do. I'm going to offer these jackasses fifty thousand. It's a preemptive bid. And they're going to take it unless you say something to Jaax and he comes back with a higher offer, which would be so stupid because that'll only mean you'll have to come up with even more money to beat whatever his next offer is."

"I can't . . . see how I can bring that off."

"I don't either, but you better figure out a way and you better do it quick. You better have that money by tomorrow evening, toots, or kiss bye-bye to your career."

"I'll see what I can do."

"You do that, Jenn Lind. You do that or you'll be staring at that picture of you in a lip lock with your girlfriend all over the Internet."

He smiled as he seated the phone in its cradle.

Karin Ekkelstahl, who'd volunteered to take a double shift in order to spend more time with a quickly healing, and thus imminently leaving, Walter Dunkovich, paused outside his hospital room. She took out her compact mirror and, after giving a quick glance around to make sure no one caught her primping, rolled up the lip gloss she'd purchased at the drugstore along with the magazines Mr. Dunkovich had requested. She suspected she was acting like a fool but a man hadn't looked at her with the sort of appreciative interest Dunk had expressed in years, not since she'd divorced Einer, retaken her maiden name, and gained all that weight. Dunk liked her weight; she could tell by the way his eyes roved over her chest whenever she bent over him to readjust his pillows. And he had the added recommendation of not giving a squirrel's patootie about Jenny Hallesby—*Oh, excuse me, Jenn Lind*—like every other celebrity-struck half-wit in town.

She frowned at her image in the little round mirror and inexpertly coated her chapped lips. As she did so, she heard Dunk talking to someone in tones that were so hard, nasty, and unfamiliar that she stopped midapplication and listened.

What she heard made her blanch.

Chapter Forty-three

11:50 a.m.
The Lake, Fawn Creek

"Who was that?" Steve asked curiously.

Jenn thanked God for the dark interior, and the fact that her back was turned, so he couldn't read her face. She had to think. "A guy from AMS asking about the cooking shoot."

"Oh." She felt his hands on her upper arms and then he was gently turning her around, his gaze searching her face. "Jenny, I got a confession to make."

She had a little confession of her own to make. But part of her resisted. The smart part—the part that shouted at her that she still had a chance of making this whole thing work, a small, small chance, but a chance and that to tell Steve now would only make things worse. Probably for her.

"I bought the butter head last night," he said in a rush. "The men with it called after everyone had gone to bed. I was hungry, so I was in the kitchen, and I answered the phone and it was them and I made an offer and they accepted it."

Yeah, until their next pigeon offered more. She tried to look surprised. "Why didn't you tell us this morning?"

"Because of what you said," he answered, "after we found the butter ear. You implied you wouldn't sell it to me or give it to me and I need it."

"Need? Why? And no bullshit about it being your epiphanal work. It's a twenty-two-year-old chunk of carved butter, which, people keep telling me, is freaking forever in butter sculpture years, missing at least one ear," she declared in exasperation. That damn butter head was going to ruin her life. *"Why do people want this thing?"*

He looked at her miserably. "Look, I don't know why anyone else wants this thing. I only know that your folks want it for sentimental reason because your dad told me so. And they're going to get it back, too," he said earnestly. "I'm not going to take off with it. It's your parents' and they can have it. I just need a few minutes alone with it."

"Okay," she said, "that's creepy."

"It has a key in it."

That stopped her cold. "A key to what?"

"A mausoleum crypt."

She sighed. "Okay, back to disturbing."

"No, it's not really," he said. "As part of the divorce settlement, my ex-wife Fabulousa demanded this very famous sculpture I had made and for which she'd modeled. I wasn't about to let her have it just so she could turn around and sell it to some drug lord just to spite me. Which is what she planned to do. She told me so.

"So I found this guy who, for a very reasonable price, broke into our town house and stole it. He then purchased a mausoleum crypt—see? See? Not so disturbing, huh?— and stuck the statue in it. He paid for the crypt in full, in cash, and paid like a zillion years' worth of—what would

they call it? Association fees?—in Fabulousa's name,
knowing that her private detectives would be looking into
anything with my name on it but never think of searching
under her name, her real name.

"Afterward, he sent me the key to the crypt. Unfortunately, I had the key on me while I was sculpting you in
butter and when the bounty hunter showed up I—"

"Stuck it in the butter head," she finished. It was all
starting to come together for her.

He nodded, delighted with her acumen. "Exactly."

"Who else knows about that key?" she asked.

He shook his head. "No one. Except the robber and
he's dead. Appendix burst a little while after I paid him
off, the poor bastard."

"Are you sure? I mean . . ."

He shook his head firmly. "I'm sure."

"You don't know a guy named Walter Dunkovich?"

"Nope."

Crap. She was willing to bet—no, she wasn't—but if
she did bet, she'd bet that Dunkovich knew about that key.

"I called Verie last night. He's supposed to be arriving
today with the money and I promise it will be worth every
penny of it."

"Is it worth a lot? This crypt statue?"

"I'm not going to sell it. It was my breakthrough piece.
I was able to capture the innocence, the drama and vulner-
ability, a sweetness in her . . ." His voice trailed off and he
shrugged. "Of course, it was all a lie. Man, did that mess
with my head for a while. But, no, it's not for sale."

"But if it was?" she insisted.

"Who knows? Six? Seven hundred thousand? It's a
moot point, though. Unless I either use that key or Fabulousa signs for a new key and opens that crypt herself, that

sculpture is as good as gone. And if I don't get it, I can guarantee Fabulousa's not."

"Aren't you a little much with your ex?" Jenn asked.

"She got everything in our divorce and dragged it out over years. I'm bitter, yes," he said. He didn't sound bitter. He sounded pleased. "Revenge is sweet, Jenn. And sometimes it's necessary. Sometimes you just have to put paid to a bill in order to move on. Come on, if you got the chance for a little redress against someone who'd made your life crappy for a long time, who'd made you doubt everything you thought you knew about yourself—your identity, your worth, everything—wouldn't you do the same?"

Of course she would: Ken Holmberg. Her thoughts flew back a couple decades to the state fair and how he'd given her hell for "cheating" and almost causing a "scandal" and then fast-forwarded to a few days ago to when he'd reminded her that her hometown status here was fraudulent and the cornerstone of her career was built on a deception. Hell, she wouldn't be surprised if he'd been the one who'd told Dunkovich about that stupid picture. Narrow-minded, complacent, self-satisfied, he represented everything about this town that she despised.

"Yeah," she allowed softly. She looked up to find him regarding her curiously. He'd trusted her. He deserved that key. Well, he sort of deserved it. More than Dunkovich at least. "Steve, I have to—"

Bang! Bang! Bang!

Someone was pounding on the fish house door.

"Hey, Jenn. Open up! It's me, your agent, Natalie! I'm freezing my ass off out here."

Jenn traded startled glances with Steve as she pulled

the door open to a figure straight out of Dante's Eighth
Circle of Hell, the one reserved for frozen fashionistas.
Nat looked even more Gorey-like than usual, completely
blanketed in head-to-toe black designer quilting, a silver
fox cap crammed down over her pale face. Even through
the layers, Jenn could see her shiver.

"Nat! What are you doing here?" she exclaimed,
swinging the door open wider and revealing a big, heavy-
shouldered, middle-aged man in a heavy cashmere coat,
impeccably groomed except that his weave was standing
up like a cockscomb in the wind. He had the implacable
mien of a Teutonic.

"This is Verie Meuwissen," Nat said, her teeth clattering. "He represents Mr. Jaax—"

"Verie! You came!" Though Steve had pulled a shirt on,
it was still undone, the edges flapping back in the breeze
exposing a nicely corrugated stomach and a well-planed
chest to the whole world. Which, thank God for the gale,
consisted only of Nat and Verie. Steve swooped out from
the interior of the fishing house and picked up the bear-
sized man and hugged him.

Nat's widened eyes rolled from Steve's bare chest to
Jenn.

"Thank you!" Steve was saying to his friend. "Did you
bring the money?"

"What are you doing here?" Jenn repeated to Nat.

"Can we come in?" Nat said, looking longingly at the
fish house.

"I'm afraid it will be a little too close," Jenn said,
shooting a glance at Verie.

"Then come with me," Nat said. "I have a room at
someplace called the Valu-Inn and we have to talk."

"As do we, dear boy," Verie intoned to the still fondly smiling Steve.

Nat was right. Jenn and she did have to talk. And unless Nat had fifty thousand dollars, she wasn't going to like what Jenn had to say.

Chapter Forty-four

"Okay, you did your fish thing, we've had lunch, you made nice with the locals, but now we're here and now I want to know: who are you and what have you done with Jenn Lind?" Nat demanded, tossing her coat on the double bed that took up most of her room at the Valu-Inn.

Jenn swept her hair back with her hand, trying to figure out where to begin, how much to reveal.

"What are you doing with your hair?" Nat asked in patent exasperation. "It's all . . . down and . . . messy. You look like a Sharon Stone wannabe. No," she amended, "you look like you just got lucky in a *fishing shack* with Steve Jaax! *Steve Jaax!* Are you nuts? If you wanted to have monkey sex with someone, why didn't you pick someone no one knows so if he goes public no one will believe him?"

"Steve's not going to say anything," Jenn mumbled, adding defensively, "And I *prefer* to think that he's the one who got lucky."

Nat threw up her hands. "Have you been drinking antifreeze? Steve Jaax will tell anyone anything at anytime. He's *disastrously* honest. Watch." Before Jenn could react she'd stabbed a series of numbers into her cell and held it up to her ear. "Verie? Nat. Is Steve with you? Put him on."

"What are you doing, Nat?" Jenn asked uncomfortably.

"Steve, this is Nat. Did you have sex in the fishing house with Jenn Lind?"

She held the phone up, sliding the speaker phone volume to max.

"Yes," Steve's voice boomed with perfect composure. "We did. I'm pretty sure I'm in love with her."

Jenn couldn't help it. She felt the corners of her mouth lifting.

Pinning Jenn with a cold gaze, Nat snapped her phone shut. "Point taken? Aw, come on! Stop with the goopy smile. . . . Oh. My. God. You're falling for him."

"No," Jenn said. "No! He's a romantic. I'm a pragmatist. He's a serial monogamist. I'm a loner. We came together for a few nice moments and that's it."

"How nice?"

"Fantastic." She shook herself. She was telling Nat the truth. At least what she knew to be the truth. What she felt wasn't necessarily the truth. Objectively, their . . . tryst in the fish house had been a very nice, an obviously much-needed escapade, one she would always look back upon fondly. But it was time to start moving forward again. To deal with the obstacles in the road ahead, not to spend time mooning over the view in the . . . rearview . . .

Her eyes widened. My God. She'd had a detour. Her jaw went a little slack with the wonder of it.

"Jenn? Jenn!"

She'd had a detour. She hadn't planned on it, made allowances for it, or anticipated it. For the first time in years, she'd thrown away the road map, closed her eyes, and followed some internal device. And for a short time, she'd been a tourist enjoying the trip rather than a long-haul driver carrying a load. She'd taken a detour. Who knew what she might do next?

"Jenn. Have you heard anything I've said?" Nat demanded angrily.

"No," Jenn shook her head. "Now how is it you're here, Nat?"

"I begged a ride on Verie's charter plane, and let me tell you, that was not a fun ride. I think they closed the airport as soon as we left—"

"That's not what I meant," Jenn broke in. "I mean *why* are you here?"

"I'm here because Bob Reynolds called and informed me that my client and AMS might have a problem."

"Well, he's got that right," Jenn announced, feeling strangely empowered. "We do have a problem. A big problem. In fact, I was going to call you today."

Nat turned around and tried to sit on the table only, because she was so short, she had to hop up to do so. She crossed her spindly little arms over her narrow little chest. Her face was flat and expressionless. "Speak."

"Gladly," Jenn said, striding up and down in front of Nat, her irritation mounting with each step. "Do you know what they've done? They've changed the entire format of the show, the whole concept, without consulting me! And do you know what they are going to call this newly revamped show they expect me to host? *Checklist for Living!*"

Nat's mouth twisted a little but she only said, "Continue."

Jenn stopped pacing to face her and stare. "*Checklist for Living*, Nat. They are going to make cheat sheets for life and I am going to present them on each show and go through them, point by point. Do you know what our checklist for the first episode is?"

Nat shook her head.

" 'Checklist for a Winter Wonderland Weekend.' Check point one was 'Traveling Smartly and Safely.' I had to put tire chains on a Mercedes GL class SUV."

Nat didn't blink.

"Number two, Nat, was 'Be Fashionable and Fun in Designer Chic Lodge Wear.' They made me wear flowered pink stretch slacks, Nat. On national television." Her voice trembled. "Do you know what my ass looks like covered in pink flowers? Your grandmother's sofa."

"Jenn, I'm sure—"

Jenn held up her hand and Nat subsided into silence. "Not content to display my upholstered ass upright, they then made me do check point number three, 'Whimsy and the Winter Wonderland.'

"The 'whimsy' entailed me flailing around in the snow like a dying sea lion in order to make a snow angel. A process I was forced to repeat three times because each time I did, my flower-covered ass dug so deeply into the snow that the resultant angel looked like it had a butt tumor."

Nat's eyes were round and her lips had tightened into a little, pleated circle.

"If you laugh, Nat, I will have to feed you to the huskies."

Nat cleared her throat. "I'm not laughing."

She wasn't, either. Her face had that grim, determined look she got when she was going to do battle with network heads and publishing moguls. She popped off the table, her little stick arms akimbo. Jenn stood aside, prepared to watch as she sicced her mini-mongoose on that snake Bob Reynolds.

Rather than marching out the door, Nat stopped in front of Jenn and glared up into her face. "What the hell is wrong with you?"

Jenn couldn't have been more surprised if Nat had bitten her. "What do you mean?"

"My God, Jenn, so you had to put some chains on a tire. Don't tell me you actually did the work because I won't believe it. And then they asked you to put on some clothes you felt made your ass look big. So what? If your ass looks that bad, they'll block it out. Believe me, their sponsors don't want you to look bad in their clothes."

"It's not just that," Jenn said, a little surprised she was having to explain this. "It's this checklist thing. *Checklist for Living?* Come on, Nat. It's obscene."

Nat ignored the comment. "What have you been doing up here, Jenn? Listening to your own press? Well, let me give you a little reality checklist. One, you're not a national star yet. Two, if you want to be a star you'll play the game. Three, no one has asked you to do anything anyone could possibly kvetch about. Yet you've managed."

Jenn backed away, confused, her earlier feeling of empowerment seeping away as worry took its place. She'd counted on Nat to be in her corner, to fight the good fight for her. But Nat didn't think this was the good fight. And Nat wasn't in her corner. She was in Bob's and Dwight Davies's and AMS's. In ten years of working together, Nat had never sold Jenn out. She couldn't believe her agent was doing it now. Maybe she wasn't. Maybe Nat was right.

"Look, Jenn," Nat said, her expression relaxing. "I've talked to Bob and I told him it wasn't well done, him springing all these changes on you the way he did up here. And he agrees and he's sorry. But the bottom line is, we've got work to do and he has footage to shoot tomorrow afternoon before they take off and he wants some sort of assurance that you're on track with all this. I said you could give him that."

Jenn caught herself about to rake her hair back from her

face. Instead, she moved away from Natalie, toward the window, her thoughts a tempest.

"Jenn, you have worked harder than any person I know in order to get to where you are at this moment." Nat's voice followed her, vibrating with the need to convince Jenn. "I have to ask myself why someone who has worked that hard would be willing to throw it away because she didn't like the new title of her show. And the only answer I can come up with is that you're afraid. Afraid, ultimately, of making it big. You don't dare believe it and you're afraid it's going to be taken away from you like . . . like Raleigh was. You're so afraid that you think it would be better to throw it away before it can be ripped away."

Jenn's brow furrowed with consternation. Fear of success? Was she a candidate for some Dr. Phil special? Was she being that goofy? Maybe she was. Nat was right. She had worked twenty years to get to where she was right now. It even made a bizarre sort of sense.

"Jenn"—Nat's voice was quiet, reassuring—"no one's going to take this away. Only you can screw this up. The sky, my dear, dear friend, is literally the limit. But"—her voice hardened—"if you sign off on this now, no one will touch you. Oh, shit, yeah, maybe a second-rate station or a fourth-rate cable company, but this opportunity will have passed you by. Is that what you want?"

No. Of course not. "No." Jenn looked over her shoulder. Her agent stood where she'd left her, her hands folded in front of her. "I don't know what I want."

"I do. You want success. You have always been driven by the 'Need to Succeed.' " Nat cracked an ironic smile. "Now I don't know what bucolic haze you've been wandering around in up here over the last few days, and I admit Steve

Jaax is cute. But this town and Steve Jaax—they're not the real world. They're not *your* real world."

Nat was right. It had all gotten screwed up, all twisted. Jenn's navigation system had momentarily faltered.

"Don't you want to know that your future is secure, rock-solid, guaranteed? You stick to the AMS script, and I promise you, it is."

Yes. That was what she'd always wanted. "Yes."

"Then for God's sake, Jenn, shake the snow off your boots. Focus on the future. Be that guided missile I know and love."

Jenn wasn't a fool, no matter how foolish she'd been acting. She wasn't. She wouldn't be. "Okay."

"That's more like it." Nat's small body relaxed.

"But, Nat?" Jenn said, slowly turning. "There's another problem."

"I knew it! I knew there was something more behind this bizarre Jenn Lind thing." Nat slammed the heel of her hand into her forehead. "What now?"

"There's a certain little tiny piece of my past that Dwight Davies might take exception to."

"Crap. I knew you were too good to be true! Okay. We'll deal. Abortion, drug abuse, child out of wedlock?" Nat ticked off a list, watching Jenn closely.

"No, no, no."

"Felony conviction, jail time, gambling habits?"

"No."

"You don't smoke, don't have any DWI. I know you're not gay, so what is it?"

Hearing it like that, the list of infractions that in Dwight Davies's mind were grounds for expulsion, twisted Jenn's stomach into a knot. How could she work for someone so sanctimonious and self-important? He was just Ken Holmberg on a bigger scale. On the other hand, she'd known that when she signed the contracts. "Any of those things could get me written off the show?"

"Some more than others, but on a day when Dwight was in a bad mood, yeah. Why? Which one is it, Jenn?"

"I—"

"No. Don't tell me," Nat broke in. "I don't want to know. The less anyone knows, the better. The question is, can you fix it? Shut it down for good?"

"It depends. Some people might . . . There could be talk."

"Talk?" Nat scoffed. "Talk we can probably control. Concrete proof is a different matter. Bills of sale, hospital records, photos? Not so easy to discount. Can you get rid of the proof?"

"I could if I had the money."

"*Someone here is blackmailing you?* Shit, hon. No wonder you hate this town. Okay. Can you get the money? Friends? Family? Jaax?"

Steve? No. Aside from wanting the sculpture for himself, he despised Dwight and thought that working for him made a person morally suspect. Still, he'd said he "probably" loved her. You had to admire that sort of honesty, didn't you? He might give her the money if she asked. But it wouldn't be enough. She needed the entire fifty thousand.

There was only one place to get that sort of cash that fast. But to risk everything on the turn of card and some all but forgotten expertise she'd had as a kid? She took a deep breath, amazed she was even considering going back to the casino for a second time. It was contrary to everything she believed in. She wasn't a risk taker, she wasn't a gambler, and she wasn't someone who played outside the rules. Was this how her father had felt when he'd arrived in Vegas? Okay. That had failed. But . . . had it?

She shook her head; the answer to that question wasn't the issue right now. What was at issue was her life.

The winner of the All-Amateur Dusk-to-Dawn Tournament took home a cash prize of one hundred thousand dollars in addition to whatever winnings they took from the table. It was crazy and the odds were against her, but it had already worked once and maybe lightning would strike twice. Besides which, it was an amateur tournament, and what with the snowstorms keeping people from driving in from outside the area, most of those playing in the tournament would be local.

"Jenn. Is there any chance you can fix this?" Nat asked.

"A small one," she answered. "But I'll need to come up with a thousand dollars first. How much do you have?"

Nat opened her purse. It was her future, too.

Chapter Forty-five

Hilda Soderberg was in the kitchen putting the finishing touches on the various dishes she'd prepared for old Johanna Nygaard's funeral tomorrow. She stood in the middle of the tiny, square kitchen and eyed the ranks of glass and ceramic casserole dishes like a field marshal surveying her troops. Two chocolate sheet cakes took over the linoleum-topped kitchen table, and Esther had promised to make two yellow— not that anyone would eat them, with her chocolate being offered, but Johanna had been a popular woman at the retirement home, so maybe—and that took care of dessert. On the counters, Hilda had a tuna hotdish, a tater tot hotdish, a scalloped salmon hotdish, and a casserole overflowing with meatballs. So that would be enough hotdishes then. Nels Youngstrom was bringing the ham and rolls, and the church kitchen was well supplied with coffee and Hawaiian Punch. Which only left the salads.

Which meant Jell-O, and while Hilda's second drawer on the left side of the sink never held less than twenty packages in various flavors, what she didn't have was miniature marsh-

mallows, and you can't make a decent pineapple-lime Jell-
O salad without marshmallows and Johanna certainly deserved a decent salad for her sendoff. Which meant Hilda
would have to go to the grocery store.

Now normally, Hilda would have walked the eight blocks
to the store but snow completely choked the sidewalks and
covered the street. It occurred to her that Neddie wasn't too
slick at his plowing job, but just the fact that he'd been gain-
fully employed by the city for over a year now kept her biting her tongue. Besides, Neddie seemed to be straightening
up some lately. And she knew the snowstorms, one hard on
the heel of another, were keeping him up and on the highways to all hours of the night. Fact was, he was still in bed,
and for once she wasn't going to yell at him to get out of it.
Besides, once he woke up, he'd be in the kitchen stealing the
food for Johanna's funeral and that just wasn't right. So, instead, Hilda resigned herself to taking his noisy, stinkin'
snowmobile out again.

She headed for the back door, pausing to poke her head
into Neddie's bedroom. She didn't worry that he might have
guests. He wasn't really a bad boy. Just lazy. Neddie had been
acting different the last few days, too, spending a lot less time
in front of the television and more time outdoors. Maybe he
was finally starting to wake up and smell the coffee.

It was with this optimistic thought in mind that Hilda decided to make Neddie a special lunch when she got back
from Food Faire: *julbrodsigrid*, potatoes with dill and homemade sausage. She smiled, feeling fonder of Neddie than
she had in a long time. Dear Neddie loved to eat.

Chapter Forty-six

3:35 p.m.
The Food Faire parking lot

"Explain to me why we are in this grocery store again, dear boy," Verie intoned as they waited for the stocky female cashier to bag his purchase.

"You'll just have to trust me on this," Steve said. "The Lodge is unique and wonderful, and you are lucky you are being allowed to stay there. They don't accept guests."

"What a novel marketing strategy," Verie said. "A B and B that doesn't take guests."

"Exactly," Steve agreed, then suddenly snapped his fingers. "I need Doritos," he said to the cashier. "Where are they?"

The young cashier pointed to the far corner of the store. "Take your time. It's not like we're overrun with customers."

That was an understatement, Steve thought as he trotted down the center aisle, passing an old lady jabbing some poor teenage stock clerk in the breastbone and demanding to know where he'd shelved the multicolored miniature marshmallows. Steve nabbed a box of Pop-Tarts on his way to the snack section, which was, he noted, in weird proximity to the pharmacy aisle. He stopped to peruse the choices—cool ranch or classic?—when he heard a male voice on the other side of the aisle, where the aspirin would have been. He was clearly talking on his cell phone.

"Look, Stan, thanks for calling me back. I know you've heard it before and I hate like heck to call you at home on a Sunday, but can't you put off the bank on that audit a while longer? I've got the money. I've just got to make it liquid, you know?"

Steve could practically see the sweat pouring off this poor shmuck's forehead, he sounded so miserable. He shouldn't be listening. He plucked the classic Doritos giant bag from the top shelf and heard the guy on the other side say, "Okay, then. If you gotta on Monday, you gotta on Monday. It'll be funded. Fully funded, yeah. Ninety thousand. I know"—his voice had gone from wheedling to spiteful—"and then you can apologize when you sign that loan over to me. Bye then."

Quickly, before the poor guy came around the corner and was embarrassed, Steve took off down the aisle. At the cashier, he tossed his bag down and grabbed a pack of gum.

Verie eyed the food. "B and Bs generally offer some form of sustenance at some point during one's stay. Typically breakfast. Thus the name bed and *breakfast.*"

"You will fall in love with Nina Hallesby. But not her cooking. In fact, before we head back there, we should go to Smelka's." Steve fished some crumpled bills out of his pocket and handed them to the cashier just as a man, the same man he'd met the day he arrived, came up to the counter with a bottle of double-strength aspirin.

"Smelka's," Verie said. "You have gone native, Steven. Have you ordered your mukluks, yet?"

"Wait until you have had a *semlor* and then sneer," Steve

said, nodding at the guy—Holmes? Hamburg?—who flushed and nodded back.

"Hey, Mr. Holmberg," the cashier said as she loaded the bags into Steve's waiting arms.

Steve accepted them and headed out of the store, his thoughts moving along unfamiliarly un-Stevecentric paths. This guy needed to fund something or other at the bank before he got a loan approved. Apparently, he really wanted that loan. And apparently, he was embarrassed about whatever straits he'd gotten himself into. The guy was some industry leader here in town. . . . That was it. He made hockey sticks and he was the biggest single employer in Fawn Creek. Poor bastard.

Steve pushed the store's glass door open using his shoulder and headed toward Cash's truck, which Cash had lent him this morning so Steve wouldn't be "stuck on that lake all day if you don't have to." Jenn had gone off to the motel with her agent in her Subaru. He wondered how long she would be and hoped it wouldn't be long.

Steve liked being with Jenn. He wanted to hear her take on this Holmberg guy and maybe explain to her again why it was okay to seek vengeance against his ex-wife, because he had the unpleasant suspicion he hadn't done a very good job. At least, he wouldn't have been convinced and he really didn't want Jenn to think poorly of him. For the first time in God knew how long, another person's opinion of him as a human being, not as an artist, really, excruciatingly mattered. Love, he decided with delicious melancholy, could be painful.

He opened the truck door and was shoving the bags in while Verie went around to the passenger side when his eye was caught by a fluttering brown sheet. Steve backed the truck out of the parking space and looked. Between the truck and a big, shiny new gas-guzzling SUV, there was a snowmobile, something large and covered with burlap strapped to its rear end. A gust of wind snickered across the lot and plastered the material against the form beneath.

Steve stopped the truck. He knew that form. He'd given birth to it.

"What are you doing, Steven?" Verie called from within the truck cab.

"I'll be just a minute." He moved toward it, his eyes never straying from the snowmobile, as though afraid if he blinked it would disappear. He reached out, his heart jackhammering in his chest, and unhooked the bungee holding the burlap in place and pulled it up.

It was the butter head. But the butter head so changed, so hideously transformed she was barely recognizable. Little patches of freezer burn splotched the weirdly flaky surface of her "skin," and her brow, once a lovely, flawless expanse, had sunk in, now creating a simian shelf of brow above her drooping eyes. Someone had cut off her rooster's comb bang and turned it into a pair of balloon tire lips. Her left ear was missing.

"Poor butter head," Steve murmured, running his hands lightly over the disfigured face. It was like the Butter Head of Dorian Gray, only that would be Jenny Lind. It was a good thing Jenny wasn't here; she'd likely be dousing it with lighter fluid by now. This reminded Steve that he was in a public area, hovering over stolen property. There was no question of him calling the cops. Now that he'd actually seen his poor baby, he decided she'd be better put out of her misery or at least, for the sake of Jenny's vanity, kept out of the public eye, and really, he only wanted one thing from her. The key.

He closed his eyes briefly, imagining Fabulousa's shriek of defeat when he called to tell her what he had. Oddly, the imagined rage didn't evoke nearly the satisfaction that he'd have expected. But then, the reality was sure not to disappoint.

Quickly, he skirted around to her back side. It was still there: the big curl behind her right ear. He looked around for something to dig with and spotted a snow scraper lying on the dash of the SUV next to him.

God bless Fawn Creek, he thought fondly. No one locked their cars.

Five minutes later he held a small metal key in his hand. He flicked it once in the air, catching it deftly as he headed back toward the truck.

"This sounds extremely shady, Steve," Verie said, from where he sat next to Steve. They'd turned up a sloping drive and were creeping toward the top.

"It is," Steve said. "But, Verie . . . *Muse in the House!*" On the ride to the Lodge, he'd told Verie everything as his friend's placid countenance grew more amazed with each passing minute. "It was never included as part of the divorce settlement because you can't award something neither party has. So I show up with it twenty some years after the fact, and as they say, possession is nine-tenths of the law. I'll say it was a gift from an admirer who bought it on the black market."

"They'll never believe that."

"I don't care!" Steve said gleefully. "What's she going to do? You can't steal something you own, can you? And when *Muse* went missing, we were still married."

They pulled up in front of the Lodge and Steve turned the engine off. He climbed out of the cab, collected the grocery bags, and started up the slope toward the front door. Verie pulled his antique alligator-trimmed suitcase from the floor and began trudging after him.

"I'm going to love it here," Steve said, the image of the barn doors flung wide and steel and sparks and fire flaring within filled his head, marching right alongside the image of Jenny and him eating hotdish on the bench under the pine trees.

"Hm," Verie said, pausing at the top of the slight incline to catch his breath and let his gaze travel over the Lodge. "Is it safe?"

"Where you'll be staying it is. It's dangerous where me and Prince sleep."

"Prince?" Verie's face lit with delight. "Dear boy! I've been waiting forever for you to come out—"

"Prince is my dog."

The delight faded. "I knew it was too good to be true. And since when have you had a dog?"

"Since here," Steve said, turning the knob and ramming his shoulder into the door.

It took three tries before it finally flew open. Steve stepped aside and Verie entered on tentative steps, like someone expecting an ambush. He took one look at the haphazard interior with its seventies-style living room suite and swung his hooded gaze toward Steve. "Charming."

"Is that you, Steve?" a man called.

"That's Cash," Steve informed Verie.

Cash arrived a second later followed by Prince, who took one look at Steve and went into paroxysms of joy. Gingerly, Verie sidestepped the happy reunion taking place mostly on the floor and extended his hand to Cash. "Thank you, sir," he intoned, "for allowing me to stay in your home. I understand I am a rare exception to an understandable rule."

"Nina is going to love you," Cash said, shaking his hand.

On cue, Nina appeared in the doorway. Today she was wearing Audrey Hepburn ski pants and a Tyrol patterned sweater.

Verie played his part to perfection, gliding across the floor and taking Nina's hand. Brushing his lips across her knuckles, he declared himself "enchanted." Not to be outdone, Nina tipped her head to a regal degree and pronounced her pleasure at meeting so celebrated an art authority. Any observer would have sworn her hand was kissed on a daily basis by diplomats and ambassadors, and just as Steve knew he would, Verie reacted with amazed delight. In short, they fell for each other like a ton of bricks, Nina offering to take Verie on a tour and Verie insisting only if she allowed him to offer her his arm.

They strolled off in total harmony, leaving Steve and Cash behind, and finally Steve could ask the question uppermost in his mind.

"Where's Jenny?" Light of my life, goddess of my hearth, he might have added had he not intuited this might be a bit much for her father.

"She called a little while ago. She's still at the Valu-Inn with Natalie, her agent, and said she would probably stay with her the night. She said there's some stuff they have to hammer out concerning AMS," Cash finished, looking disgruntled.

"The whole night?" Steve echoed unhappily. It wasn't just that he wanted to see her—he just wasn't as eager to make the call to Fabulousa as he thought he should be and he wanted to know why and Jenny—clear-sighted, practical Jenny—would have some insights. He also just wanted to be with her. He liked *being* with her.

"She also said she'd call you later." Cash shrugged. "Sorry."

"Not as much as I am," Steve said.

Having delivered his message, Cash picked up the newspaper Steve had bought for him and wandered off toward the great room. Alone, Steve stuck his hand in his pocket and withdrew the crypt key. He'd spent twenty years anticipating this moment. What the hell was he thinking? No, he hadn't. *When* he thought about it, which wasn't all that often, he'd certainly anticipated the next few moments with relish. Unholy relish.

Yup. There was nothing wrong with unholy relish.

He headed for the kitchen. He had a call to make.

Chapter Forty-seven

12:15 a.m.
Monday, December 11
Blue Lake Casino

The snow and wind that had kept the poker players in the city were also keeping the fishermen who'd come up for the sesquicentennial off Fawn Creek's lakes, streets, and snowmobile trails. As Fawn Creek had a dearth of nightlife, the fishermen had headed north, bringing with them a full complement of Fawn Creekians. The town's movers and shakers followed their guests, nipping at their heels like nervous sheepdogs, afraid their charges would get lost. Among them was Paul LeDuc, who had grabbed a stool at a slot machine by the poker tables, where he had a pretty good view of the entire casino floor.

He was at the casino for one reason alone: duty. Duty to the sesquicentennial, to their town, and to many of the families in that town. Someone definitely needed to keep an eye on things. As mayor, it seemed natural that the duty should fall to him.

Hopefully, by tomorrow things would have righted themselves. "Things" being the huge percentage of people here from Fawn Creek, not only the tourists and fishermen but townspeople, his townspeople. Worse, the fools were betting on this fool tournament and betting heavily, too. Including Ken Holmberg, who seemed to have lost his mind. Ken had entered the casino with the fevered look of an addict, marched right up to the registration table, and slapped down a thousand dollars to enter the tournament.

Paul was worried about Ken. He really was. A sheen of oily sweat covered Ken's round, troll-like face, and his comb-over kept sliding off his balding dome. He had a feverish quality to him that went beyond the physical. When Paul had questioned Ken about the wisdom of gambling, he'd grabbed hold of Paul's wrist with shaking fingers and declared he intended to let "Providence make the call"— whatever the hell that meant.

Paul, who'd gotten more intelligence from his wife earlier today, had a feeling Ken's luck and his drive had less to do with the divine than with desperation. Ken was trying to fund that damn pension before he was publicly exposed as a crook, which would force him to leave the town in shame.

But so far, Ken was doing okay, too. He'd made it through the first round of play and was cleaning up at the second table. Paul wished he could feel good about it since Ken sure as hell did. With each hand he won, he seemed to gain more confidence. He wasn't sweating quite as freely as he had earlier, and the uncharacteristic tentativeness and humility with which he'd earlier addressed Paul had disappeared. His usual smug, overbearing manner was quickly returning.

He must have felt Paul watching him because he tossed his two pair faceup on the table with an arrogant flourish, caught Paul's eye, and gave a complacent shrug, lifting his thumb heavenward as if to say, *The Big Guy's with me*.

Paul managed not to shake his head and turned around on

his stool, noting that the guy from *Ripley's Believe It or Not* was chowing down on a burger at the bar while the entire crew from AMS was dolefully plugging nickels into the slot machines and sipping the free beers Ed White, the casino's manager, had ordered up in the hopes of loosening up some inhibitions. Not local inhibitions, Paul knew because Ed—who was at heart a good guy—had confided that he didn't encourage the Fawn Creekians to gamble because he didn't want to have to pay for a lot of community goodwill Gamblers Anonymous stays.

The Poker Network's cameraman was wandering around shooting random footage. Earlier Ed had also confided that the cameraman was here returning a favor to the assistant manager but so far hadn't found anything interesting enough to hang a story on. That had abruptly changed when she showed up.

Paul had been talking to his wife on his cell phone, seated in the booth next to the registration table, and had bent double under his own table in order to hear his wife over the din in the casino when he'd heard a woman ask, "If I played in your tournament, would you have to know my name?"

"Yes," Ed had said. He sounded surprised and excited. "You know, we have to report it for tax purposes and that sort of thing."

Paul, interested, had quickly finished the call. Cautiously, he'd unfolded from his crouch and lifted himself up to peek over the top of the banquette.

"Crap," she said. "Would anyone else?"

She wore a black wig and wraparound sunglasses, her face covered in a thick layer of beige makeup with bloodred lipstick extending way beyond the edge of her natural lip line. Not a hint of emotion showed on her smooth countenance. She might have been wearing one of those semitranslucent Halloween masks. She also wore what had to be, in Ed's admittedly limited experience, the ugliest evening gown he'd ever seen. It was far too small for her figure and her bosom overflowed its neckline like a half-set custard.

"No. I can keep that quiet. Just you and me and Uncle Sam."

"Okay," she said and snapped open her purse, withdrawing a thick wad of bills, mostly tens and twenties. "Where do I sign up?"

She was incredible. Heads had started turning the minute she'd entered, most notable among them that of the Poker Network cameraman, who'd taken one look, stubbed out the cigarette he'd been puffing, and picked up his camera.

He'd been following her ever since.

As had what was quickly becoming an impromptu "mystery woman" fan club. They crowded around the table she was playing at now, jostling one another for a better view. She was pretty impressive, Paul had to admit. She played like a professional, her face utterly impassive as she slowly but surely worked her way through first one group of competition and then another.

At this rate, she and Ken would end up playing against each other.

Wearily, Paul rubbed his hand over his face, feeling the first rasp of morning stubble sprouting on his chin. His eyes stung from the smoke, and his mouth felt cottony and probably smelled foul. He was already bone-tired and—he glanced down at his wrist watch—there were still at least another six hours to go before the tournament ended and the visitors went back to town and he could go home to bed for a few hours' rest before the next day's festivities began.

Which reminded him: he'd better call Ned and Jimmy and make sure they were out plowing.

*   *   *

"Yeah, yeah, I understand, mayor!" Ned slammed down the phone and turned to Eric and Turv. "The mayor wants us out plowing an hour before sunrise."

Turv got up and stretched, a flurry of cheese doodle crumbs raining from his lap. The munchies hit Turv harder than most. "We better get to bed then," he said.

"I suppose. Just think, you guys, by nine o'clock tomorrow morning, I'll be telling Paul LeDuc where he can drive his plow." The thought made Ned smile. "I know we coulda seen if Jaax would be willing to up the ante, but fact is, I'm getting a little sick of this." He flapped his hand toward the butter head.

In point of fact, Dunkovich had unnerved Ned that morning when he'd threatened to do unspeakable things to him if he did go to Jaax. Not that he'd told Turv and Eric about that part of the conversation. Nor did he intend to.

"And we're not greedy bastards, you know," he added, peeking from the corner of his eyes to see if this bit of bullshit would be accepted. It was. "Yup," he went on expansively, "our luck has changed! We're golden, guys. Twenty-four carat. Nothing can stop us now."

"Then why didn't you tell Paul LeDuc to screw himself now?" Eric asked.

Ned looked at him in pity. Sometimes Eric could be a real moron. "Because, Eric, a guy can't be too careful."

Chapter Forty-eight

Heidi Olmsted, worried that Bruno might not be adjusting to his new role as Celebrity Companion, decided to take advantage of one of the few mornings she didn't feel like heaving her guts out and drive to the Lodge. Blizzards didn't bother Heidi, who had raced the Iditarod five times, and she knew Jenny liked to get up before dawn to begin the busy business of being Jenn Lind, so she wasn't worried about waking her when she arrived before dawn.

She went to the kitchen door and peered through the window, fully expecting to see Cash sitting at the table, furtively packing away his day's portion of forbidden calories. Instead she saw a big, solid-looking, middle-aged man in a ruby red dressing robe, his silver hair neatly combed, his cheeks so closely shaved they gleamed, gracefully buttering the piece of toast he held in a beautifully manicured hand.

Heidi had no idea who he was.

Her gaze fell to the floor. A pair of jean-clad legs lay protruding out from the other side of the table. The rest of the body was lost to view. The thought had just occurred to

Heidi that the man at the table might have killed the man on
the floor when the man at the table looked up and saw her.
He smiled and, using the butter knife, waved for her to come
in.

She hesitated. On the one hand, she had another life to
consider these days. On the other, she owed it to the Hallesbys, all of whom she was very fond of, to confront their potential murderer. Or what if he had them tied up somewhere?
Stranger things had happened in Fawn Creek. But then the
man lumbered to his feet and Heidi realized how easily she
could outmaneuver him, so she pushed the door open and
stepped inside, eyeing him uncertainly.

"Hello." He had an elegant, cultured voice shaded with an
accent Heidi recognized as German. "I am Verie Meuwissen, sole proprietor of the works of Steve Jaax."

"Where is Steve?"

Verie pursed his lips and inclined his head in the direction of the legs. Heidi inched sideways until she had a view
of the man lying on the floor. It was Steve Jaax and he was
most definitely alive. His forearm, flung over his face, ob-
scured most of his features but his chest rose and fell easily,
or at least as easily as possible with a giant malamute head
on it.

"Hi, Heidi," Steve said. He sounded melancholy. Bruno
opened his eyes and gave her a thump of his tail in recognition but otherwise didn't make any effort to get up. So
then, Bruno was easing into his new role without too much
trouble.

"Hi."

"Please," Verie said, "won't you have a seat, Miss . . ."

"Heidi Olmsted but Heidi is fine."

"Excellent." Verie beamed and pulled out a seat for her.
Feeling a little like she'd just arrived in Oz, Heidi sat. Verie

waited patiently for her to settle herself and returned to his side of the table, where he snapped open his cloth napkin and let it float to his lap.

"I have been informed, sub rosa, of course," he said, "that in order to survive the culinary experience here, it is imperative to fuel the engine early, before the cook arises." He held held up a plate of toast. "Toast?"

She took a slice.

"Coffee?"

She nodded gratefully.

"What's wrong with him?" she asked, nodding at Steve.

Verie poured her cup of coffee and handed it to her. "Last night he had a revelation of some personal magnitude, which he is all in a dither to share with Ms. Lind but the drat woman has gone missing, in spite of pledges to call him, so he's in a peeve. He has been awake or rather, I should say, he *tells* me he has been awake all night, waiting here by the phone for her call. I suspect he slept on the floor. Either way, I am embarrassed for him, though I have tried to be supportive by rising at this ungodly hour to breakfast with him."

"Why would he do that?" Heidi asked curiously.

"He fancies himself in love with her. Sugar?"

"What?" Heidi said. Oh, sure, she'd noticed the sparks yesterday. But this had to be a one-sided infatuation. She couldn't imagine Jenny doing anything impulsive or unplanned or unwise. Like a relationship with Steve Jaax. "Does he overreact every time he has a crush?"

"I don't have crushes," Steve announced from the floor.

Verie leaned over the table, motioning her to do likewise. "It has progressed beyond infatuation," he said in a stage whisper. "No gifts were exchanged but apparently bodily fluids were."

Heidi drew back.

"Um." Verie nodded confidingly. "It was all very Coen brothers. Very 'If This Fish House Is Rockin', Don't Come Knockin.' "

"No! They did it in the fish house?" She couldn't believe it. Jenny Hallesby doing the horizontal tango with a relative stranger was stretching credibility but Jenny Hallesby having sex in a fish house during a fishing tournament? Amazing.

Maybe there was hope for her yet. And if Steve actually did love her . . . Jenn Hallesby had made Heidi's last two years in high school, which could have been pretty miserable, not only bearable but enjoyable. In Heidi's opinion, no one deserved a love affair more than Jenny.

"Does Steve think he's in love often?" she asked and waited breathlessly for Verie's answer, amused by herself. Pregnancy had made a romantic of her.

Verie paused to consider her question, dabbing at his mouth with his napkin. "No," he finally said. "Now that you mention it, not since . . ." He leaned sideways. "What was your third wife's name, dear boy?"

"Margot."

"Ah, yes. Thank you." He straightened. "Not since Margot. That was nine years ago."

"Maybe he really does love Jenny," Heidi suggested.

"It's possible," Verie allowed, picking up his toast and spreading jam on it.

"I wish you wouldn't talk about me as if I'm not here," Steve said reproachfully from the floor.

Heidi put aside her natural shyness, made bold by her loyalty to Jenn. "All right," she said, "why do you love Jenny, Steve?"

Steve didn't answer. His arm remained covering his eyes and he stayed motionless for so long that Heidi had begun to suspect that he'd fallen asleep when he finally spoke. "I . . . complete her."

Heidi set her coffee mug on the table with a bang. "Oh fer God's sake . . ." she muttered in disgust.

Steve dropped his arm and rolled over, Bruno's head dropping to the floor with a *thunk*.

"No," he said, climbing to his feet. "I'm good for her. I've never been good for someone before. I've always been probably not such a good idea. But I'm a good idea for Jenn. Do you know where she is?"

"Nah-uh. I just came to see how Bruno was."

"I thought his name was Prince," Verie said.

"That's just an endearment, Verie," Steve said, his guilty gaze flickering to Heidi.

"If you renamed Bruno—" The phone rang.

With an expression of intense relief, Steve reached over and snapped it up. "Good morning. This is the Lodge, the Hallesby family's bed and breakfast and future studio of sculptor— What? Jenny? Is that you? Where are you?"

His basset hound–homely-handsome face creased with frustration, he looked over at Verie. "I can barely hear her. The connection keeps drop— Jenny? Yeah. I hear you now." He squeezed the phone to his ear. "No. You don't owe me any explanation."

He was quiet a minute, but from the exasperation on his face, Heidi could tell he wasn't getting too much of whatever it was Jenny was saying. Then he said, "It's a moot point. I already have it. You don't need to— I said I ALREADY HAVE IT! Jenny? Jenny!"

With a quick, annoyed movement, he slapped the receiver back on the base.

"Where is she?" Heidi asked.

"At the casino, making the finals in some poker tournament."

"What? Jenny doesn't gamble. Why would she enter a poker tournament?"

"She told me this guy who's put out the ransom for the butter head is threatening to tell the AMS people, and by extension Dwight Davies, about your homecoming kiss if she doesn't come up with enough money to outbid me for it. The prize for the tournament is a hundred thousand."

"Holy crap."

"Yup."

"A kiss? That's ridiculous," Verie said.

"Yup," Steve said, raking back his hair with one hand. "If I hadn't been so . . . Damn it."

"But why did she call you?" Heidi asked.

Steve cast her a glance as guilty as it was pleased. "She knew I wanted it and she is beginning to suspect that she might just win this tournament. She wanted to tell me why I wasn't going to get the butter head and that she was really sorry."

"But you said you had it," Heidi said slowly, not feeling particularly enlightened.

"Not the butter head. The thing that was hid in the butter head but I don't think she heard me." His face darkened. "She also told me who she was playing against in the last round, and one of them is Ken Holmberg."

Heidi sat back in her chair and slapped her palm against the table. "Good. If she's got to gamble, I hope she whips his pompous ass."

"I don't think you do," said Steve seriously, wiping away Heidi's smile. "I overheard that guy in the grocery store today. He's being audited by the bank tomorrow, and from what he said, I don't think the results are going to make anyone happy. I think," Steve said, choosing his words carefully, "I think this guy is up at that tournament trying to win the wherewithal to make up the difference in some pension he's underfunded."

"Shit," Heidi said. "Shit. If Minnesota Hockey Stix folds that means about fifty people out of work. That means fifty families with no income, no insurance, and no pensions. Most of them will have no choice but to leave." She shook her head. "Do you know what the loss of fifty families means in a town this size?"

Steve headed for the back hall. A second later he emerged with Cash's parka, the keys to the truck jangling in his hand.

"What do you think you are doing, Steven?" Verie asked. "This isn't your problem. This isn't your hometown. It isn't like you to interfere."

"Maybe it is this time," Steve said soberly. "Tell Cash I borrowed the truck again but I'll bring it back full." And with that, he was gone, leaving Heidi looking at Verie askance.

"But where is he going?" she asked.

Verie expelled an extravagant sigh. "I think he's gone to save the town."

Chapter Forty-nine

6:10 a.m.
Hilda Soderberg's kitchen
Fawn Creek, Minnesota

Hilda Soderberg was cursing as she hit the garage opener. Seventy years she'd been making *aebleskiver* and never once an accident, but today, getting the cast-iron pan out of the overhead cupboard, it had slipped from her hand and fallen on her foot. It hurt like a *helvete* and it was getting worse. She thought maybe she'd broken something, and as she had to put on a funeral supper, which she had no intention of missing, she supposed she'd best go to the hospital so if they wanted to put a cast on it or something, they could get it done with quick.

She expected Neddie back anytime now, but Neddie wasn't always the most dependable person in the world, and he might stop off to visit one of his no-account friends. So Hilda, being that breed of northern Minnesotan who wouldn't trouble the devil for a light, bundled herself in layers of warm clothing and hobbled to the detached garage, knowing she would find Neddie's snowmobile parked inside since Neddie would have driven the Chevy to the city garage.

Sure enough, there it was just where he'd left it. She hit

the garage opener and pocketed the remote she kept on the table by the door. The hospital was only half a mile away, so she didn't think twice about straddling the seat and starting the motor.

She did wonder a bit about whatever it was that Neddie still had bungee-corded to the back loosely wrapped with a sheet of burlap, but only a bit. Her foot hurt her like the devil.

She gunned the motor.

Dunk was bored and anxious all at the same time. He kept looking at the clock, counting down the minutes until Jenn Lind brought him his money and he could get his butter head. The exchange, to take place at Storybook Land, was scheduled for nine o'clock, so he'd given Jenny until eight thirty to get him the cash. It was only ten after six now.

He picked up the remote and flipped through the channels. Nothing, nothing, and weather. The hospital didn't subscribe to cable. He turned off the set, wiggling in his bed.

His skin beneath the heavy body cast was beginning to itch. He thought about hitting the nurse's button and hoping Karin would come and stick that little bamboo whatchamacallit down his neck but Karin was off today.

He wished she wasn't.

Maybe after this was all done, he'd mosey on back to town and take her out to dinner somewhere. And afterward they'd mosey on back to her place and he'd see if he could get her to put on the ducky scrubs so he could take them off.

The thought brought to mind her many and repeated urgings for him to get up and move around as much as possible so he'd be "back in top form soon." He wondered if she'd meant anything by that.

He swung his legs over the side of the bed and carefully

lifted himself into an upright position. Not bad. Not bad at all. He walked around the bed, feeling more optimistic about the speed of his recovery with each step, and headed for the window.

It was still snowing, by God. Was it ever clear up here? They must have about five feet of snow on the ground. . . .

He stared, unable to believe his eyes. The butter head, perched jauntily on the back of a snowmobile, coyly draped in fluttering brown burlap, sat right under his window in full view. He rubbed a hand across his eyes. Still there.

His eyes widened as he realized the potential here. He could have the key to that mausoleum crypt without paying these suckers a penny. And when Jenn Lind showed up, he could just pocket that cash for himself. If he could get down to that snowmobile before whoever drove it here did, he could drive the butter head somewhere out in the woods and stash it under some brush somewhere until such time as he could return, melt it down, and retrieve that key. Then he could hitchhike back to the hospital.

If.

He hobbled to the narrow closet and opened it. His boots lay neatly on the floor, the snowmobile suit he'd been wearing at the time of the accident hanging above it. Excellent.

As time was a definite factor here, Dunk didn't have the luxury of easing into the snowmobile suit; instead, he yanked it on and *that* hurt like hell. He balanced awkwardly beside the bed and shoved his bare feet into the boots as the idea of trying to bend over to pull on socks was enough to make him break into a cold sweat. Then he cautiously stuck his head out the door of his room and, seeing no one nearby, hobbled as quickly as possible to the emergency stairwell.

The trip down was not pleasant, but finally, ten minutes later, he stood outside in the hospital parking lot right next to the butter head. Miracle of miracles, the key was still in the ignition. He wouldn't even have to hot wire it.

He grunted as he pulled the burlap back over the butter head and resecured the loose bungee cords that held it in place, then eased himself on to the seat, the body cast digging into his thighs as he sat down and turned over the engine. It purred to life. Turning the throttle and looking around to make certain no one was watching, he drove slowly out of the parking lot and onto the road, still covered with a half foot of snow.

God must love him, he decided, smiling as he drove sedately down the road, the butter head jouncing companionably against his back. No one else was out trying to navigate through the glistening white snow blanketing every road and side street. So when Dunk heard the powerful drone of heavy equipment behind him, at first he didn't think much of it. Until the drone revved up and the sound started to close, fast.

He looked over his shoulder to see a two-ton snow plow barreling down on him and knew he was in trouble. He couldn't see much of the guy's face but he saw enough to realize the guy was pissed and coming for him, and something inside told him he was coming for the butter head, too. Panicked but purposeful, Dunk twisted the throttle hard. The snowmobile flew forward, and in answer, the sound of the engine behind him roared higher. Damn it! Couldn't anything be simple?

It was just not fair! He was going to some pretty fucking heroic lengths here, what with getting out of his hospital bed and all. Why couldn't this guy just let him have the damn thing?

Well, he would soon enough. He opened up the throttle and in a few minutes hit the edge of town and headed straight for the lake. He'd like to see that snowplow try to catch him there.

As soon as he was in sight of the lake, Dunk saw just how he was going to lose the plow. A Ford Bronco was parked right in the center of the access road the city had plowed onto the lake. All Dunk had to do was whoosh by its left side, and so long, plow. He grinned, easing up on the throttle as he approached the lake. Some guy stood beside the SUV flapping his arms and yelling at him, even going so far as to step right out into the path Dunk had been planning to take. Asshole. Dunk veered more sharply to the left and onto the ice. Behind him he heard the snowplow's brakes squeal. Good-bye, sucker. He was home free.

And then the ice cracked open.

The nose of the snowmobile plunged into the ice. All around Dunk the lake splintered apart in slow motion, the hole around the snowmobile's front bubbling and widening as more and more of the machine was swallowed by it. He looked up, stunned. All around people were running toward him, screaming and shouting. The water was up over his ankles, freezing cold, boiling like it was hot. He tried to stand up, but only managed to thrust his legs deeper into the frigid water.

He was going to die, he realized in bewilderment. There was no possible way he could survive. He was going to die. For a butter head.

He didn't want to die. It was a waste. His life had been a waste—he saw that now. He wanted to live, to be a good person. To date Karin Ekkelstahl. He didn't give a fuck about an IRA!

A second sharp crack announced the end. The hole yawned and the snowmobile dove toward the bottom of the lake, taking Dunk, encased in thirty pounds of Fiberglas and plaster, along with it.

"Oh, no, you don't, you stupid son of a bitch!" Ned flung himself out of the snowplow's cab and raced toward the quickly sinking snowmobile. The asshole had driven straight over the spring, right where they'd set flags. Why even the jerk in the Bronco had tried to warn him off, but no, he'd had to go and break through.

Well, he was not taking Ned's butter head with him. Butter floats. All Ned had to do was make it to the butter head and undo the bungee cords holding it. But he had to get there fast. The lake was real deep in that spot. If the butter head sank along with the snowmobile, they'd never find it.

Ned was almost there. Just a few more yards. A few more . . .

With a giant crack, the lake swallowed the guy, the snowmobile, and the butter head.

"NO!" Ned shrieked, ripping off his hat and coat and tossing them aside as he dove headfirst into the water. The shock of the icy blast drove the air from his lungs. He opened his eyes and saw a pale, waxy face staring up at him through the darkening water, slowly growing smaller and smaller. He kicked feverishly, frantically, reaching . . . reaching . . . Almost. Almost!

A hand grabbed his arm. He spun around, gurgling, and saw a guy's face a few feet from his, his eyes wide and staring. Beneath him the butter head was shrinking fast. This asshole was going to make him lose the butter head. Furiously, Ned tried unwrapping the guy's hand but he had a death grip on him.

"Gi ob me!" Ned screamed under water. The guy just kept right on staring at him and clinging to him.

Ned looked down. The butter head had disappeared.

With a few savage and highly graphic mental curses, Ned began kicking for the surface, towing his unwanted passenger along with him. He broke the surface to find the hole surrounded by people. Next to him, the asshole popped up, choking and sputtering.

A cheer went up from those around them, confusing Ned. He looked around to see what they were cheering for. Some others flung them ropes; one guy found a lifebuoy. Other people ran to get blankets. The guy in the hole next to him still clung to him like a tick on a dog, leaning his forehead against his shoulder.

"God bless you, mister. You saved my life!"

Chapter Fifty

6:40 a.m.
Monday, December 11
Blue Lake Casino

"Can we call a break? I need to pee," the math major from St. Cloud State, one of the five remaining contestants in the all-night poker tournament, asked. He'd been visiting his grandparents in Fawn Creek over the weekend and had been trapped by the snowstorm blocking the roads south. He'd entered the tournament more out of boredom than anything else, and no one could have been more surprised than himself at his still being in the running.

"Come on," he whined. "We haven't had a break in a couple hours, and man, there's a hundred thousand on the line here and I don't want to be distracted by my bladder, 'kay?"

"Let the kid pee, fer chrissakes," said one of the other five, an Asian guy who'd come up from the cities for the fishing tournament.

"Let the boy go," Jenn drawled, letting loose with the Southern accent she'd spent the last twenty years replacing with round Minnesota vowels.

Next to her, the other female finalist, a barrel-shaped old

lady who'd arrived early in the week driving an RV packed with grandchildren and covered with casino stickers from around the country, nodded. Ken Holmberg, rounding out the quintet of finalists, shrugged.

The dealer shot a questioning glance at the casino manager, a big, good-looking Indian named Ed White, who nodded from his vantage on the edge of the roped off area.

"Ladies and gentlemen, we'll be taking a fifteen-minute break," the dealer announced as a pair of guards moved in to stand post beside the table. The kid shot up and ran for the bathroom, while Jenn got up slowly.

As far as she was concerned, the break was just postponing the inevitable because there was no way the kid was going to win. Every time he picked up a pair, his forehead beaded up. You couldn't win a poker tournament with a "tell" like that. Jenn, groomed by beauty pageants and accustomed to being under the hot glare of studio lights, had no "tells." She just plastered on a pleasant pageant expression—okay, maybe it wasn't so pleasant, but she'd had a lot to think about lately, so make that a neutral expression—and emulated a mannequin.

The old lady and the Asian guy weren't going to go home with that hundred thousand plus, either. The old lady was running out of luck and the Asian guy played too cautiously. If fate had its way, Jenn would end up going head-to-head in the final hands with Ken Holmberg. Which she had to admit, she was looking forward to. Ken represented Fawn Creek at its worst: puffed-up, boorish, and condescending.

He was beginning to really piss her off.

For one thing, he insisted on calling her sugar puss, and every time she took a pot, he rolled back in his chair, lacing his pudgy little fingers over the shirt straining over his little potbelly, grinned, and said, "Oh, wow, now. The little lady's managed to take one. Good fer you, sugar puss."

When he won, he'd lean back, tuck his pudgy thumbs in the belt straining around his padded belly, and announce loudly, "Yup. I'm gonna win this thing. You guys might as well quit now. Can't mess with Providence's plan." Like God had personally fingered him to be Saint Ken of the Green Baize Table. Well, Ken was about to have an unpleasant revelation, because he was not going to win. She was.

She was going to win this tournament, tape the next six points on the "Winter Wonderland Weekend Checklist," judge the Fawn Creek sesquicentennial lutefisk contest, ride at the head of their parade—sans butter head—and return to New York, where she would then embark on a career that would make her the Katie Couric of the Kitchen. Or whatever Bob Reynolds wanted to make her.

And she was going to be happy. Very happy. And two years from now, she would have a dog. And name it something like Alfred. Or Neil. Or Prince.

And Steve? The thought of him brought a wave of confusion and guilt. She probably shouldn't have called him during the last break, but the feeling that she was going behind his back wouldn't leave her alone, eating at her concentration until she'd had to call and confess, which was such a Minnesotan trait—stalwartly owning up to your actions—that under normal circumstances she might have laughed. These were not normal circumstances. The connection had been bad and she couldn't tell his reaction from the choppy phrases that had been transmitted. She hoped, fervently, that he understood.

She guessed their future—if you can even have a future on the basis of a few days, which she knew objectively was unlikely, but unobjectively completely bought into—all hung on how much he'd wanted to screw over his ex-wife. If he couldn't see that a career was more important than revenge . . . Ah, hell. She didn't know what she was thinking anymore. Why couldn't Nat have come with her to the casino? She was Jenn's Cold Voice of Reason, and things were getting murky again. Oh, yeah. Jenn was supposed to be incognito. Nothing must hint at any connection between "Ms. Uri" and Jenn Lind.

Her stomach, never reliable under stress, was twisting up in knots. She started from the cordoned-off area, heading for the bar, where they kept a supply of Pepto-Bismol on hand. The spectators on the other side of the velvet ropes cheered and clapped her on the back like she was their champion as she edged her way through them. It tweaked the kernel of disquiet in her stomach further. She wasn't their champion; she was *her* champion.

Jenn could safely swear that she would never wear a polyester wig again for the rest of her life after today. The thing was hot and it itched like crazy and she suspected it smelled, too, but that might have been her old Buttercup pageant dress, dragged out of mothballs to be added to her visual arsenal of diversionary tactics. No one in the world would ever guess that the overpainted, undergirdled, middle-aged woman in the black wig and falling out of her dress was that model of homemaking virtue, Jenn Lind.

Inside, the bar was crowded but she found a narrow place to shove in and waved to get the bartender's attention. He gave her a quick smile and held up two fingers, mouthing, *Just a couple minutes* before hurrying off to fill another order.

"—I don't know why we needed some aging bucolic beauty anyway."

She froze. She knew that voice. It was Bob Reynolds. And he was sitting immediately to her right, his back to her as he spoke in a low, terse voice to—she glanced sideways—Dieter the Director.

"It's Davies," Dieter said, stirring his drink. "He's in love with all her virtue. He rhapsodizes about how she embodies American female decency."

"Crap," Bob said tiredly. "Give me a week and I'll find a half dozen younger, prettier women who've been certified by the Vatican as saints, are willing to work for half what Davies is paying Lind, and don't take themselves so damn seriously. Man, this is a glorified cooking show, and she better wake up and realize it."

Her heart pounded.

"Ja," Dieter sympathized. "Diva."

"Okay, ma'am, what can I do ya?" The bartender's voice startled Jenn, and she backed away, bumping into Dieter. He turned around and looked straight up into her face.

Her breath jolted to a stop in her throat, as Jenn waited for the recognition to dawn in his eyes. Yeah, her disguise was good at a distance with strangers, but he was right here and he'd just spent an entire day staring at her face through a camera lens.

"Hey!"

Here it comes, she thought. She swallowed hard.

"You're the lady from the poker tournament, aren't you?"

Behind the dark glasses, she blinked in surprise. He didn't recognize her. Not as Jenn Lind. There wasn't a flicker of familiarity in his face.

"Yeah."

"Let me buy you a drink," he said. "I've been cheering for you."

"Thanks, but I . . . I got to get back," she said, thickening her Southern accent. Then she turned tail and raced from the room.

She had just broken free of the door and was feeling the rush of relief when someone took hold of her arm and spun her around. She looked up into Steve's face. She broke into a huge smile, surprised by the surge of pleasure the sight of him brought her until she realized he wasn't returning her smile. His face was somber, his resemblance to a soulful bloodhound even more pronounced than usual.

She'd known he would be upset with her for going over his bid to secure the butter head. She'd thought he would understand. But then, she hadn't given him much of a chance to do that. She'd just . . . done what she needed to do.

"We've got to talk," he said.

"I'm sorry, Steve. But I can't trash my future so you can thumb your nose at your ex-wife. Please don't ask me. Please understand."

He shook his head. "We have to talk."

"I can't. Steve, I can't even be talking to you. Too many people know that you and Jenn Lind are both staying out at the Lodge. They see us together and they might put two and two together."

He didn't argue, and for that, at least, she was grateful. "Okay. Come on." He steered her through the casino toward the restrooms at the back. As soon as they reached the ladies' room, he pushed the door open, took her arm and pulled her in after him. A trio of older women in polyester stood in front of the sinks comparing the weight of their bandit cups. Otherwise it was empty.

"Ladies, could we have the room for a moment?" Steve asked politely. "That color pants, by the way, is wonderful on you," he told the lady nearest him. "You should always wear tangerine."

The woman blushed and stammered, as pleased as she was affronted. "Oh fer— Well, I never. Come on, girls."

"Thank you," he said to their departing backs. As soon as they'd left, he stuck the wedge the cleaning company used under the door.

"What are you doing here, Steve?" Jenn asked.

Steve leaned against the sink. "I have two important things to tell you."

"Yes?"

"First, I have the key to the crypt. The thieves left their snowmobile in the grocery store parking lot while I was there. The butter head was strapped to the back. So I just dug the key out."

Jenn's eyes widened. That meant . . . nothing. She might have guessed that Dunkovich wanted the butter head for that key but Steve claimed no one else knew about it and she had to assume that Dunkovich still wanted the butter head.

"I called Fabulousa."

Jenn's attention snapped back to Steve. "I'm sure it was a defining moment."

"No." He shook his head. "That's what I had to tell you. It wasn't a moment. It wasn't anything. In fact, it was sort of anticlimactic. I called and I said, 'Fabulousa, I am looking at the key to the vault that holds *Muse in the House*. What do you think about that?' And she said, 'Oh, you mean the sculpture that is sitting upon my living room table and upon which I am right now looking?' "

He did a really good Boris Badenov impersonation.

"I don't understand."

"Turns out my thief friend, Timmy, sold Fabulousa the

whereabouts of the statue about three weeks after he stole it. He's not even dead. He just got worried I'd find out and come after him, so he wrote a note saying he was dead and mailed it to me."

"Oh, Steve, I'm sorry," she said, touching his arm. His face was all creased with unhappiness and filled with sweetness.

"It's all right," he said, taking her hand and raising it to his lips. He kissed her knuckles. "I was actually sort of impressed she'd never sold it. I mean, she's had it for years and she's never sold it, so it must mean something to her and that means she must have some sort of a soul, right? I told her so, too, and she said she was never as much of a bitch as I thought she was, and I said I was never as big of a prick as she thought I was."

Steve's brow furrowed pensively. "I thought having that statue would somehow make up for that part of my life, the divorce. I thought if I had it, I'd be done with Fabulousa. But, Jenny, I'll never be done with her. She's there. In the past. And she always will be. For all the shit she put me through, and it was a lot, it was shit that made me who I am and *I like who I am.* Most of the time."

"Great. But I don't understand what this has to do with me."

"Because of the second thing I have to tell you: Ken Holmberg needs to win this tournament."

At this, Jenn snorted. "He can stand in line."

"No, Jenny. I heard him talking and he's in trouble unless he can come up with ninety thousand dollars by tomorrow. He's in real trouble, Jenn. Like legal trouble."

"Gee, I'm looking down the track but I don't see the pity train coming."

"Look, I have forty thousand dollars—"

"And I need fifty," she finished in exasperation, "in less than two hours. This is the only way. Besides, you told me that revenge was sweet. How much sweeter could this be? Ken Holmberg is a pompous ass. He deserves what he gets."

"I just told you, Jenny, the whole revenge thing . . . it's a waste of time. And besides, it's not like Ken is the only person who'll suffer if you do this. What about his employees? What about the town? Heidi told me that if his hockey stick plant folds, the town will follow."

The domino effect. She knew all about it. She hadn't lived in Minnesota, listening to the virtues of small-town life for twenty years, without understanding the economic realities that faced most small towns. On the surface, fifty families might not seem like a lot, but in the delicate ecobalance of a small town, it was immense.

But she wasn't going to feel sorry for them. No way. Her gaze shifted away from his. "I don't see how this is my problem. What do I care if Ken Holmberg goes belly up and chooses to close shop? What do I owe these people?"

He reached up, balancing her chin on his fingertips and tenderly turning her face toward his. He gave her a lopsided grin. "Everything. Think, Jenny. I know you try to ignore it or discount it or whatever else you want to call your denial of this town and what it means to you, what it's done for you, but stop trying to look past Fawn Creek and look *at* it."

His hands fell lightly to her shoulders and he dipped a little at the knees so he could look her squarely in the eye. "They made you. If Jenny Hallesby hadn't come to Fawn Creek, there wouldn't be a Jenn Lind. Just like if Fabulousa hadn't screwed me over there wouldn't be a Steven Jaax. You learned how to cook here, how to appreciate good food, right? You learned how to appear calm and confident by copying these people here, right? You got on television the first time because of this town, right? And now the fate of Fawn Creek is in your hands."

She didn't want to hear this. She didn't want the fate of Fawn Creek in her hands. And it wasn't! If Fawn Creek was on the verge of imploding, it was Fawn Creek's fault. She bent down to pull the wedge from under the door. He straight-armed the door shut. She looked up at him, her face taut.

"Jenny, what are you doing here?"

"Trying to make sure my life is on track. Trying to guarantee myself a little security."

"*What* life, Jenn?"

His words hit her like a slap. Her head even tilted back as though she'd received a blow. "Ouch."

"And you want security? Commit a crime and get a prison cell. But if you want a life, walk away from this, from AMS, and start working toward a dream, not a goal." He flung out the words she'd thought the night of the blizzard like he'd read her mind. Oh, man. He didn't play fair. But then, she wouldn't expect him to.

"I *have* plans. I don't *have* a dream," she said, trying to sneer the word but only managing to sound lost.

"Then it's time to find one."

"*Tournament players, please return to the table,*" a male voice piped in through the loudspeaker system said. "*Tournament players, please return to the table.*"

"Life isn't secure, Jenny," Steve said. "You can't control it and there are no guarantees. People are born, people die, and in between, they take chances. Sometimes there's a big payoff and sometimes they go bust. But one constant holds true: the unexpected happens. Like you happening to me and me happening to you. Whatever you decide to do, that'll stay true." He gave her his crooked smile.

"Last call. Last call. Will the tournament players please return to the table now? Play will begin in five minutes."

"I have to go," Jenn said.

"I'll be in the bar."

She made it back to the table just as the other contestants were taking their seats. She was waiting at the velvet rope for the guard, who was occupied with doing something for Ken, to let her in when a female voice whispered in her ear, "You beat the pants off him, Jenn."

Caught off guard, she swung around. Missy Erickson was standing next to her, smiling encouragingly. The last time she'd spoken to Missy had been in the sauna ten years ago.

"Excuse me?" Jenn asked.

Missy leaned forward and pitched her voice so only Jenn could hear. "Don't know why you're in disguise but we figure you must have a good reason so that's okay by us. But we want you to know we're behind you. It's about time someone took old Holmberg down a peg."

Jenny, caught between amazement and despair, felt her mouth opening and shutting like a guppy's. "We? Us?" she finally managed.

"Sure," Missy whispered back, looking amused. "Most everyone from Fawn Creek knows who you are. How couldn't we? We've known for years. You'd have to be a blind, self-centered idiot not to realize who you were—like Ken. You don't got to say nuthin'. Just wanted to wish you good luck, is all." And with that, Missy melted back into the crowd.

The guard finally saw Jenn and hurried over to unsnap the rope and let her through. Would Missy feel that way if she knew what Ken's loss would mean to her father, who Jenn knew worked at Stixs, or the rest of the town?

Jenn took her seat. Her thoughts scattered in disarray, she glanced around. It was weird seeing so many faces she knew in that crowd: Greta Smelka, Einer Hahn, Missy Erickson, Leona Unger and the Jorgenson twins, the guy who owned Hank's Hardware, and at least a dozen others, and she saw it now: they did know her, unlike the AMS guys sitting at raised tables toward the back, watching with bored detachment. They kept smiling at her and nodding encouragingly, turning the prick of conscience into a stab.

"What's wrong, sugar puss?" Ken said, drawing her attention. "Getting cold feet? You don't want to quit, do you?"

"No," she said, steeling her resolve.

Half an hour later, the Asian guy, the old lady, and the kid from St. Cloud were out of the game, and true to her predictions, Jenn found herself sitting across the table from Ken Holmberg. He kept taking off his stupid MOSQUITO: THE MINNESOTA STATE BIRD cap, swatting his thigh and putting it back on. And smirking at her. Once he'd even said, "Don't worry, sugar puss. I'll buy you a real dress once I've won."

In front of him were twenty thousand dollars in chips. In front of Jenn were twenty-five. The game was Texas Hold 'Em. Seven cards in all, each player first receiving two facedown, then "the flop," where the dealer laid three cards faceup on the table, and finally two cards dealt faceup by the dealer, one at a time, called the river. Each player would make the best hand possible out of the cards available.

"Shall we begin?" The dealer slid out the preflop cards. Jenn tipped the corners of her cards up. Two kings. Ken opened with a thousand-dollar bet. She called.

The dealer turned over the three flop cards. A king of spades, an eight, and a ten of clubs.

For the first time since she'd begun playing last night, Jenn's body reacted to her hand. Her heart thundered in her chest. She could win this whole thing. Right now. All she would have to do was go "all in." Ken would call, because Ken would never let a woman bluff him, and she would win. She could walk out of here, pay off Dunkovich, and return to the life she'd known.

And Fawn Creek could die.

She looked up, a little light-headed.

"Your bid, Ms. Uri," the announcer prompted.

"Yeah, I know," she said, taking another peek at her cards. She sighed and the Poker Network's camera swung toward her like an accusatory eye.

She looked up and saw Paul LeDuc rubbing his hand over his face, looking careworn and nervous. Leona Unger and the guy from the hardware store stood nearby and— Good Lord, Heidi was here, too, right behind Missy Erickson. Heidi blew her a forlorn little air kiss for luck, and Jenn smiled until she realized that it was a kiss that had landed her here.

She'd never been embarrassed by the fact that she'd kissed Heidi. She'd felt a little guilty because Heidi had been so obviously mortified by all the attention, but she'd never been embarrassed. Just like she wasn't embarrassed by her friendship with Heidi and never had been. That friendship would have to be carefully monitored from now on, though. AMS and Dwight Davies would be watching her from here on out. She'd have to be careful not to do anything suspect or open to speculation. She guessed that included sex in fish houses, too.

Jenn frowned, troubled by the thought of living life

according to Dwight Davies's rules. Why hadn't this seemed like such a big deal last week? She'd made compromises before and managed to live with them in order to achieve that Holy Grail called security. But in the few days since she'd been here, she'd been more relaxed, more irritated, more surprised, more comfortable, more engaged, and more *herself* than she had in years. Wasn't . . . wasn't that security of a sort?

What had Heidi said? *It's not a matter of choosing a home as much as accepting where it is.*

Was Heidi right? Could Fawn Creek really be Jenn's home? This crappy little place filled with back-stabbing, gossiping, holier-than-thou small-town elitists?

In all the years I've known you, the only place you are relaxed, the only place you're not worried about making an impression, the only place you wear comfortable clothes and no makeup, the only place you swear is here. Why?

Because no one here cares.

No, Heidi had said. *Because they know you.*

Damn it. They *did* know her. Far better than Dwight Davies and Bob Reynolds and even Nat. They knew her. No, that was not what Heidi had really meant; she'd meant that warts and all here they *accepted her.*

"Can't make up your mind, sugar puss?" Ken asked, his voice dripping with confidence. "If you can't stand the heat, stay of out the kitchen."

Like he could afford to . . . Behind the dark glasses, her eyes widened. Dear Lord, she realized, Ken was reenacting her father's path twenty-four years ago. It was like she'd been plunged into some bizarre world where someone was doomed to repeat the same bad decisions over and over again, and she was doomed to be a spectator. She wondered faintly if Ken had a teenage daughter, and if she'd hate wherever they ended up as much as she hated . . . No, she didn't hate Fawn Creek. She'd used it as a scapegoat, an excuse to be afraid of taking chances or exploring options.

She'd told herself she'd lost her best friend because of this town, but the truth was, she'd found her best friend. And her parents, who'd been nothing but vague, benign presences in Raleigh had become full-fleshed people here. And then there was Steve. . . .

"Ms. Uri."

"I'm thinking!"

Fawn Creek wasn't a great place. It was provincial and patriarchal, and it had a huge small-town chip on its shoulder, but it was . . . her town. Her hometown, she guessed. And she couldn't be part of its extinction. She just couldn't.

Abruptly, she reached down and swept a quarter of her chips out onto the table. "I'll bid five thousand."

Ken's brows nearly climbed up to his cap, and she knew he had a good hand. He was a lousy bluffer. He made a show of vacillating, finally raising her bid by five thousand. She practically threw her chips into the center. She had nine thousand left. Ken had fourteen.

The dealer flipped over a jack of diamonds. Ken bet seven thousand. Jenn called. The crowd buzzed. The commentators hummed. Ken called.

The final card turned over. It was a king.

She had four kings. She bit her lip. She tapped her nails on the table.

He went all in. She called with the last of her money. He turned over a straight, king high.

With a magnificent show of feigned disgust, she surged to her feet and threw her cards facedown on the table. "Congratulations," she said.

The crowd went nuts. Ken surged up out of his seat,

pumping his stubby arms in the air, making a weird "Whoop! Whoop!" sound and looking like he might stroke out at any minute. His round face had flushed the color of federal bricks, and his comb-over flopped limply against the back of his neck. Missy Erickson stared at her, disappointed but sympathetic. Paul looked relieved. Heidi nodded.

Ken, grinning like an idiot, started to reach for her cards but she slapped his hand away. "Nah-uh," she all but spat. "You won. I concede it, but you are not going to see my cards. I called your bid and the person who calls *never* has to show their cards. Right, dealer?"

The dealer must have felt the laser-like lash of her glare because he nodded nervously. "That's correct."

"Ah. Come on, suga—"

She swept the cards from the box and shoved her kings deep inside. "Bite me, sugar puss," she said succinctly.

Her insides were trembling, and she felt light-headed, almost giddy. Maybe regret would set in later but right now she felt amazing. Relieved. Free.

She'd done it. There was no way she could buy the butter head now. Dunkovich would in all likelihood sell the photo to some tabloid rag, Dwight Davies would fire her as well as try to blacklist her, and she was fairly certain she'd be replaced by a younger woman on *Good Neighbors*. On the other hand, the view in her rearview mirror had never looked better, and though she couldn't quite make out every turn and curve in the road ahead, she had no doubt it was going to be an interesting route.

With a luxurious sigh of relief, she casually took the wig off her head and tossed it on to the poker table, followed close behind by her dark glasses. The Poker Channel cameraman swung toward her. She reached the rope separating her from Heidi and leaned over it, capturing her friend's face between her palms and giving her a big, fat kiss on the mouth.

"Thanks, Heidi," she said and, hiking up her pink satin skirt, stepped over the rope.

She was halfway to the bar when she heard someone hail her. "Jenny Hallesby."

She stopped and turned to find Karin Ekkelstahl of all people bearing down on her, a grim, determined look on a face made for grim, determined looks. She was wearing a nurse's uniform.

"Yeah?" Jenn said, still walking as Karin fell into step beside her.

"I had to come by and tell you something."

"So tell me."

"I'm Mr. Dunkovich's nurse. And I told him about you and Heidi kissing at homecoming. I swear I didn't think it would do any harm but he was watching you on the television and he was all gaga over you and he'd been sort of flirting with me and"—her lips pressed together so tightly they almost disappeared—"well, you took the Fawn Creek crown from me."

"And you didn't want me taking him," Jenn said.

"Yup. But turns out he's not worth having," Karin said roughly. "I heard him blackmailing you. That's . . . *wrong*."

And as they all knew, Karin Ekkelstahl was not one to tolerate "wrong."

"And the picture?"

"He lied. There is no picture."

Jenn waited for the outrage to hit, the realization that all this had been for nothing and that she'd jettisoned a career for no reason at all. But there had been a reason, and it didn't have anything to do with that stupid butter head.

She patted a miserable, defiant, and guilty Karin on the arm. "Ah, hon. Don't knock yourself out over it," she said and left her behind.

Steve wasn't in the bar. He was in her dad's truck waiting right outside the front of the casino, listening to the radio.

She scooted in and he grinned at her. Prince, aka Bruno, lumbered up off the floor and popped onto the bench seat between them. Jenny draped an arm over his huge neck and gave him a hug.

"Are you a hero?" Steve asked casually.

"Yup."

"No one will ever know."

"Nope."

His grin got wider. "Seems like you're not the only hero in Fawn Creek. I just heard on the local radio station that some snowplow driver risked his life to dive in after some idiot snowmobiler whose machine broke through the Lake. Saved the guy's life."

"Screw it up or save it. That's the Fawn Creek way," Jenn said as Steve turned out onto the road, the end of the truck nearly slipping into the ditch as they fishtailed. She would probably need to make him pull over and take over the driving duties in a short while, but he was so obviously having fun and no one else was on the road.

"So," she said, trying to find the right tone, "when are you going to be moving here? Because I think I ought to notify the state patrol, since I've become so civic minded and all."

"Moving here *part-time*," he said. "Not full-time. I couldn't live in a place like this full-time. Neither could you. I mean, we'd go nuts." He glanced over at her, a little too casually, to see how she reacted to his use of the plural pronoun.

We. She leaned her head against the seat. She liked it. She might even love it. "You're probably right. Where are we going now?"

"Anywhere you want."

"What do you say we just head off for a while and see where the road takes us?"

"Good idea." Steve smiled at the road ahead.

"And later," she said, feeling the contentment spreading through her, "later, we'll go home."

Dear Reader,

Yes, there are busts made out of butter at the Minnesota State Fair, but not of the fictional "Buttercup finalists" put on by the equally fictitious Minnesota Dairy Federation. Instead, the butter sculptures are of the young women vying for the title "Princess Kay of the Milky Way," a competition with a long tradition sponsored by the Midwest Dairy Association. No little girl who's ever visited the "Great Minnesota Get-Together" ever passes up the opportunity to see one of the princesses sitting in her refrigerated kiosk being sculpted.

Likewise, the northern part of my state has many small towns struggling to find their place in the modern economic climate. Many, unhappily, have already faded into history, while others have reinvented themselves and flourished. There is no Fawn Creek and no Oxlip County, but they have their progenitors in the small towns where I spent long, lazy summer months "up at the cabin" and later those where I lived as an adult. Like my heroine, Jenn Hallesby, my fondness for small towns is based on late-blooming appreciation, respect, a jaundiced eye, and a wry smile.

My best,

Connie Brockway

CHRISTINA DODD

GREAT READ
GUARANTEED
OFFER ENDS OCTOBER 1, 2006
SEE INSIDE FOR DETAILS

Trouble in High Heels

"A MASTER."
—KRISTIN HANNAH

SIGNET

GIVE HIM THE SLIP

by Geralyn Dawson

Gorgeous, smart and determined to make it on her
own, Maddie Kincaid thought she finally found the
simple life in Brazos Bend—and the perfect bad
boy in Luke "Sin" Callahan. That is until the
killers got on her trail. Now Maddie's mastered the
art of giving them the slip...

0-451-21963-5

"Read Geralyn Dawson and fall in love!"
—*New York Times* bestselling author
Christina Dodd